Ayrshire Murders

AYRSHIRE MURDERS

E. R. DILLON

FIVE STAR
A part of Gale, Cengage Learning

GALE
CENGAGE Learning·

Farmington Hills, Mich • San Francisco • New York • Waterville, Maine
Meriden, Conn • Mason, Ohio • Chicago

GALE
CENGAGE Learning·

LIBRARY OF CONGRESS CATALOGING-IN-PUBLICATION DATA

Dillon, E. R.
  Ayrshire murders / E. R. Dillon. First edition.
    pages cm
    ISBN 978-1-4328-2878-3 (hardcover) — ISBN 1-4328-2878-9 (hardcover)
    1. Murder—Investigation—Fiction. 2. Scotland—History—1057–1603—Fiction. I. Title.
  PS3604.I462A97 2014
  813'.6—dc23   2014011932

First Edition. First Printing: August 2014
Find us on Facebook– https://www.facebook.com/FiveStarCengage
Visit our website– http://www.gale.cengage.com/fivestar/
Contact Five Star™ Publishing at FiveStar@cengage.com

Printed in the United States of America
1 2 3 4 5 6 7 18 17 16 15 14

To my son, Paul J. Tuger, whose knowledge of the Middle Ages proved to be a valuable resource to me in writing this story.

ACKNOWLEDGMENTS

My thanks and appreciation go to the following: Gary Green, DVM (Covington, Louisiana), who suggested opiate alkaloid (powdered poppy) to incapacitate a horse without killing it (two grains is sufficient to put a large animal into a stupor for three to four hours); and to James Mackay, whose biography *William Wallace: Brave Heart* served as a source of historical reference.

HISTORICAL NOTES

Sheriff Reginald de Crawford (Crauford) of Loudoun, Sheriff of Ayrshire (died 1297). Uncle of William Wallace (Scottish patriot). During the reign of Scottish King William the Lion, the hereditary title of Sheriff of Ayr was bestowed upon the Crawfords.

Sir Fenwick, English knight (died 1297). In 1291, Sir Fenwick ambushed Scottish rebels in the pass at Loudoun Hill, located at the head of the Irvine Valley. Among the rebels killed was Malcolm Wallace (William Wallace's father). Sir Fenwick died at that same location in 1297 in an ambush led by Scottish rebel William Wallace.

Edward I, King of England (1239–1307) a/k/a Edward Longshanks (meaning "long legs") and Hammer of the Scots. Edward spent much of his reign reforming royal administration and common law. After brutally subjugating Wales, Edward turned his attention to the north to claim feudal suzerainty over Scotland. He met with both lay and ecclesiastical opposition during his military campaigns there. His deliberate destruction of Berwick, which was meant to terrorize the Scottish people into subjection, was the worst atrocity ever to stain the pages of English history. Shortly after the Berwick incident, Edward confiscated the Stone of Destiny, which was the Scottish coronation stone, and brought it to Westminster. Edward died in 1307, before the issue of overlordship of Scotland was settled.

Sir Andrew de Moray (died 1297). Sir Moray raised his standard in 1297 in northeastern Scotland against Edward I, who considered him a menace. While his father languished in an English prison and his uncle was held hostage on English lands, Sir Moray harried English garrisons in the vicinity of Perth and Banff, causing many to fall into his hands. Sir Moray fought at the battle of Stirling Bridge in 1297 and died of his wounds several weeks later.

Sir Henry de Percy, 8th Baron Percy (1273–1314). Sir Percy fought under King Edward I of England in Wales and Scotland and was granted extensive estates in Scotland, which were later retaken by the Scots under Robert Bruce. Edward I appointed Sir Percy as Castellan of Ayr and Warden of Galloway, circa 1296. Sir Percy died at the age of 41, of unknown causes.

Philip IV, King of France (1268–1314) a/k/a Philip the Fair. Philip's policies during his reign strengthened the French monarchy. On occasion, Philip exercised his right as overlord to exact punitive damages from his vassal Edward I by confiscating the English king's fiefdoms in France. Philip's alliance with the Scots rarely amounted to actual support in men and material for them, especially during Edward's military campaigns against Scotland.

Sir Nicholas de Segrave of Leicestershire (1238–1295). Sir Segrave was appointed Castellan of Ayr while in the service of Edward I of England. Sir Segrave championed Edward's cause in Scotland until his death in 1295 at the age of 57.

Robert Wishart, Bishop of Glasgow from 1271 to 1316. One of the six Guardians of Scotland and a leading supporter of William Wallace and Robert Bruce during the Wars of Scottish Independence. Bishop Wishart was foremost among those who opposed the English occupation of Scotland, and he was closely involved in all of the diplomatic negotiations with Edward I. After years of opposing the English, Bishop Wishart was captured in 1306 and incarcerated in an English dungeon. He remained in captivity for the next eight years, during which time he went blind. He was released after Robert Bruce's triumph at the Battle of Bannockburn and lived out the rest of his life in relative peace in Scotland. He died in 1316, at which time his body was entombed in a crypt in Glasgow Cathedral.

ALL OTHER CHARACTERS in this novel are fictitious, as is the village of Harefoot Law. Any similarity to actual persons or locations is entirely coincidental.

SCOTTISH WORDS, TERMS, AND CUSTOMS

bloodwite: penalty or fine under law for committing bloodshed

breach of arrestment: disregard by a debtor to an order to pay a debt or deliver promised goods

burn: river

byre: barn

deforcement: resisting arrest or obstruction of justice

kirk: church

law [in conjunction with a location]: hill

lawburrows: a fine to anyone who threatens the safety of another

It was customary for a married woman in medieval Scotland to retain her maiden name after marriage.

woolfell: the skin of a wool bearing animal with the fleece still on it

CHAPTER 1

April, 1297
Ayrshire, Scotland

Crimson tongues of fire licked at the dry thatch on the roof of the stone cottage. The blaze flared up into the night sky with the brilliance of a bonfire. A flock of white-faced sheep, bawling in fright, milled about the fenced enclosure adjacent to the fiery dwelling.

Seven men inside the sheep pen only added to the confusion. One stood alone with his back to the gate. The other six rode horses in the shrouded anonymity of dark cloaks and hoods.

Kyle Shaw advanced on the scene just as the horsemen began to close in on the lone man on foot. From what he could see by the light of the flames, steel glinted in every man's hand. The drawn hoods marked the horsemen as raiders who preyed on helpless folk and left them bereft of their stock and sometimes their lives.

The man guarding the gate looked anything but helpless. He brandished a long weapon over his head to keep the raiders from driving the sheep from the pen. His comportment was more like that of a warrior than a cottar, and he seemed well able to defend himself. He was nearly as tall standing on the ground as the raiders were seated on their dark horses.

Kyle rode toward the sheep pen at a full gallop, intent on foiling the raid in progress. He leaned forward to urge his sorrel gelding to leap the low stone fence. The horse landed in the churned mud among the sheep, sending the wooly creatures scurrying in all directions.

On approaching the raiders, Kyle drew his battle axe from the leather loop on his saddle. Although a sword hung from the belt at his waist, the axe was his weapon of choice. With a tapered blade on one side of the metal head and a spike on the other, it was deadly at close range.

"Stand down in the name of the law!" Kyle bellowed. His voice cut through the cacophony of bleating sheep, shouting men, and roaring fire. His deputation was as yet unofficial, but no one there would know that.

The nearest raider, who appeared to be the leader, swung around to face the intruder. He beckoned with his sword for one of his companions to come with him. The other raiders remained in position to continue their harassment of the man on foot.

The two raiders started toward Kyle, taking care to maintain a six-foot span between their horses.

Kyle spurred the gelding forward to meet the raiders head on. He recognized the formation in which they rode, for he and his comrades-in-arms used that same tactic many times in battle to strike Flemish horsemen from both sides at once.

When the raiders were nearly upon him, Kyle veered his mount to the left to force a confrontation with the leader.

While the other raider thundered by on the far side, the leader swung his sword in passing at Kyle, who raised his battle axe to block the forceful stroke. He brought the gelding around and rode back to where the leader was wheeling his mount to take him on again.

The leader charged, striking out with his sword.

Kyle presented the shaft of his axe to deflect the blow. The edge of the sword blade stuttered along the protective strip of metal riveted along the length of the hardwood handle.

The leader swung back his arm for another stroke. Kyle urged the gelding to crowd his horse, forcing him into the lethal strike zone of the short-handled axe. The clang of metal rang out as Kyle thwarted the downward stroke of the sword with a backhanded swing leveled at the man's neck.

The leader flinched to the left at the last second, suffering only a glancing blow to the back of his right shoulder, rather than the loss of his life. He reeled in the saddle as he swung his mount's head around and set spurs to its flanks. The horse thundered across the enclosure toward the low stone fence, scattering sheep in its path.

The other raider, who by then had circled back, was now bearing down on Kyle, who pivoted the gelding to face him.

Moonlight glimmered on the steel head of the battle axe in Kyle's hand. The sight of the weapon poised and ready to strike appeared to intimidate the raider, for at the last instant, the man stood up in the stirrups and hauled back on the reins.

The raider's mount made a valiant attempt to stop, but its muscular shoulder slammed into the gelding's chest. Both horses scrabbled in the soft mud to keep their footing, snorting and rolling their eyes.

Kyle grabbed at the saddle bow to keep his seat.

The raider took advantage of his foe's momentary inattention to thrust the sword at him at point-blank range.

The churning movement of the horses spoiled the raider's aim, causing the tip of the blade to skid along the leather scale armor under Kyle's dark red cloak, bruising the flesh beneath instead of piercing it.

The raider cursed his luck, more concerned it seemed with missing an easy target than with moving out of range. Before the raider could rectify his fatal error in judgment, Kyle leaned toward him and delivered a hacking blow to his skull. The axe struck the man's head with a metallic clunk, to Kyle's surprise.

A savage oath died on the raider's lips as he tumbled from the saddle. The frightened horse bolted, dragging the dead man through the muck for several yards before his booted foot slipped from the stirrup.

Kyle turned the gelding and rode over to where the man on foot still held the other raiders at bay.

None of the raiders appeared eager to test the lone man's prowess with the weapon he wielded. At the sight of their leader departing in haste, all four readily abandoned their post. They wheeled their horses and took flight, plowing through a sea of sheep that parted to let them pass.

As Kyle drew closer, he recognized the long-handled weapon in the hands of the lone man on foot. It was a Lochaber axe, favored by Scottish folk for its versatility. With an eighteen-inch blade on one side of the head and a sharpened hook on the other, it served as a tool to reap grain and to pull fruited branches within reach.

Its other use was far more formidable.

In half a dozen bounding strides, the man on foot overtook the retreating raiders. He thrust out the Lochaber axe to drag the slowest horseman from his mount with the metal hook. A single chop with the wicked blade silenced the scream that came from the crumpled figure of the raider writhing on the ground.

The two riderless horses followed the other raiders over the low stone fence and loped after them into the night.

The lone man turned his bearded face toward Kyle, his hands on the long handle of the Lochaber axe, his booted feet braced in the mud. The glow from the flames on the roof gilded his scowling countenance. A leather belt bound the waist of his homespun tunic, the frayed hem of which reached only to his bare knees.

Since pursuit of the raiders in the darkness was futile, Kyle halted the gelding ten feet from the man. He returned the battle axe to the loop on his saddle and held up his open hands to show they were empty. He remained mounted in case the man mistook him for a raider.

"Kyle Shaw, Deputy Sheriff of Ayrshire," he said. "Do you want help dousing that fire?"

The man cast a fleeting glance at the smoke rising from the smoldering thatch. Most of the straw-like material was reduced to ashes, leaving the charred rafters to jut skyward, reminiscent of enormous ribs. The four stone walls of the cottage remained intact, blackened with soot, but undamaged by the blaze.

The man's gaze returned to Kyle's face. "Too late for that now," he said with the soft burr of a Scotsman. He rested the butt end of the axe handle on the toe of his boot. "How came ye to be here, friend?" His manner was amiable, but he kept both hands on his weapon and never relaxed his stance.

"I saw a light from the road," Kyle said. "I hoped to find a place to rest for the night before continuing on my way."

"And ye just happened to pass along that lonely stretch of road," the Scotsman said, a dark eyebrow cocked in disbelief. "At this hour?"

"Aye," Kyle said, returning the man's steady gaze.

"It is unwise to meddle," the Scotsman said, "even if ye are a man of law, as ye claim."

"Reginald de Crawford, Sheriff of Ayrshire, will vouch for my deputation," Kyle said.

After a moment of thought, the scowl faded from the Scotsman's face. "The name's Macalister," he said. He slung the axe across his brawny shoulders like a yoke, draping a hand over either side of the long handle as he started toward the wooden gate.

Kyle wondered at the abrupt change in Macalister's attitude

at the mention of Sheriff Crawford's name, but he made no comment about it. As he nudged the gelding forward with his heels to keep pace with the man's stride, he reflected on the letter that he received six weeks earlier from Sheriff Crawford. In that brief communiqué, the sheriff wrote of his concern over growing civil unrest in the shire and the increase of rebel activity. He implored Kyle to come back to Ayr at the earliest opportunity to resume his former office of deputy.

In Kyle's opinion, one man of law more or less in the entire country would make little difference. King Balliol of Scotland still languished in the Tower of London for leading an unsuccessful revolt against Edward of England. To discourage further rebellion, King Edward stationed English troops at every Scottish castle large enough to pose a threat. The aggressive tactic only served to inflame a Scottish populace already chafing under the harsh yoke of English domination.

In spite of the uncertain state of affairs, Kyle complied with Sheriff Crawford's urgent plea. If the old sheriff asked for help, he must truly need it. Reginald de Crawford was a proud Scotsman, like Kyle's own father, James Shaw. Those two men held each other in high regard and shared a lifelong friendship because of it.

The real reason Kyle decided to return home, however, was far more personal. Bitter words exchanged with his father in their last letters resulted in an abrupt end to their communication. Although that was over five years ago, Kyle's presence in Ayrshire would afford him the opportunity to seek out his father and try to smooth over the breach.

On reaching the gate, Kyle dismounted to stand beside Macalister.

Kyle was taller than most men of his acquaintance, owing his height to his Viking ancestors, who also endowed him blue eyes as pale as ice, and tawny hair that fell in waves to his broad shoulders. Macalister, though, loomed over him by half a head and carried twice his weight on a solid frame built like the trunk of a tree. From what he could see of the man's features in the vague light of the moon, he appeared to be close to his own age of thirty-three years.

Macalister laid the axe along the top of the low stone fence, but he stayed within easy reach of it. He cupped his hands around his mouth and yelled: "All clear!"

His shout brought a couple of shadowy figures out from behind a wooden barn huddled in the darkness a short distance away. Silhouetted against the skyline, they took the shape of a boy and a stub of a man bent with age.

As the old man approached the gate of the sheep pen, his pace slowed. His lined face was closed and wary. His homespun tunic bore the stains of long use, and his cloak flapped around a wiry body spare of flesh. The smell of sheep clung to his clothing.

The boy trailed several yards behind the old man, his eyes wide in his ashen face. From what Kyle could see in the dim light, he appeared to be around eight years of age. He wore only a thin shirt under a homespun tunic gathered at the waist with a short piece of hemp rope. When he reached the gate, he crossed his arms over his scrawny chest to keep from shivering in the cold night air.

"How many dead?" the old man said.

"Two," Macalister said.

The news elicited a grunt of approval from the old man. "Not near enough for the trouble they caused, though," he said, spitting through the gap where his two front teeth were missing. His gaze shifted to Kyle. "Who's that?" he said, squinting in suspicion.

"The deputy that Crawford sent for," Macalister said.

Shrewd old eyes raked Kyle from head to toe, taking in the

leather scale vest over the finery under his cloak. "He don't look like much," the old man said with a snort of disdain.

"Ye lost nary a sheep because of him," Macalister said.

"I know that," the old man said, annoyed. He waved a veined hand in the direction of the barn. "I watched from yonder."

The old man hardly seemed grateful, as if he assumed it was Kyle's duty as a man of law to apprehend malefactors like those raiders, no matter the danger or how paltry the wage. Unfortunately, the assumption was correct, despite the fact that his appointment as deputy sheriff was still pending.

He gave in to an urge to glance back at the old man's cottage. When he did, the sight of the burned-out roof struck a discordant note in his orderly mind. The reaving of stock was practically a national pastime in this country, given the number of impoverished souls forced to eke out a living in it. Pinching a stray lamb now and then to feed hungry children was one thing, but the willful destruction of a man's home was something else entirely. It smacked of a sinister motivation behind it.

"Those raiders tonight came for more than sheep," Kyle said to Macalister. "They meant to do some damage. And I happen to know one of them wore a helmet."

"Of course," Macalister said. "They're Southrons." His tone suggested no further explanation was necessary.

"English soldiers?" Kyle said. "But why did they come here?"

"Southrons don't need a reason," Macalister said.

"Do you know where they came from?" Kyle said.

"I might," Macalister said, "but I'd need to take a look at them to tell for sure."

"I'd like to see them for myself," Kyle said.

Wisps of smoke drifted in the air as they all walked across the sheep pen to where the dead men lay sprawled in the muck twenty feet apart. The raw gaping wounds looked black in the darkness, as did the widening pools of blood beneath the bodies.

Macalister bent over the nearest corpse and drew aside the dark cloak.

Light from the moon was sufficient for Kyle to see the dull sheen on the chain metal links of a hauberk. Bull hide armor covered the dead man's upper body, and part of a metal helmet showed through a gap in the fabric of his hood.

"Only Southrons wear such fine gear," Macalister said. He walked over to the other corpse and used the toe of his boot to turn the body face up. Smears of mud obscured most of the dead man's features.

"Do you recognize either of them?" Kyle said.

"I cannot tell," Macalister said, peering down at the upturned face.

Kyle stood aside while Macalister and the old man swooped down on the dead men like vultures. He watched in silence, his face impassive, as they stripped the bodies of everything of value. Even the boy joined in to pull off the boots.

He recognized the need for thrift, for this was a poor country and a prudent man let nothing go to waste. Had he been sworn in as deputy at that time, though, he would have been bound by law to confiscate the spoils as evidence. As it was, he could in good conscience allow them to keep it for themselves.

When they finished, Macalister dragged the bodies, one at a time, to the edge of the pen, where he heaved them over the low stone fence. The restless sheep seemed calmer after that.

The old man held up a small leather purse taken from one of the bodies and shook it next to his ear. The clink of coins within brought a gap-tooth smile to his lined face, making him look years younger. "This will buy a lot more than a new roof," he said. He loosened the binding tie and peered inside the purse. After selecting one of the coins, he handed it to the boy. "Take this to yer mam, Hob."

Hob ogled the coin in his hand with reverent awe. "But I

want to stay," he said, tearing his gaze from the money to look up at the old man.

"Ye'll be safer at home in case those devils return later this night," the old man said. "Away with ye, lad." He gave the boy a gentle shove. "Tell yer Uncle Guthrie all is well here."

Before the boy could take a step, Kyle laid a hand on his thin shoulder. "Just a moment, Hob," he said. His tone was kindly, which made the boy hold still, instead of twisting free to run away in alarm. To Macalister, he said, "Do you plan to sell that plunder?"

Macalister's powerful body froze into wary stillness. Only his eyes moved to exchange an uneasy glance with the old man before his gaze returned to Kyle. "Why do ye ask?" he said in a neutral voice.

"I want that mantle," Kyle said, pointing to the cloak draped across the pile at Macalister's feet. "How much will you take for it?"

The old man blew out a pent-up breath in palpable relief.

Macalister's taut muscles relaxed. "Ogilvy can tell ye that better than me," he said, tilting his head at the old man.

A sly expression crossed Ogilvy's lined face at the chance to turn a quick profit. "Two groats," he declared with authority, "and that's giving it away."

"For two groats," Kyle said, "I could buy a good milk cow." He shook his head. "Nay, I'll give you one penny in the King's silver." The offer was low, but he reasoned that the old man still came out ahead no matter what he got for it.

Ogilvy scrubbed at the stubble on his chin with his knuckles. "Since it was ye who helped to secure the plunder," he said, "I'll settle for one groat."

"There's a hole in the hood that needs mending," Kyle said. "I put it there myself. I'll go as high as two pennies, but no more."

"Four pennies, then," Ogilvy said, his expression hopeful. "It surely must be worth that."

"That's the same as a groat," Kyle said.

"I know that," Ogilvy said, indignant. "I didn't know if ye knew it." He heaved a sigh, watching Kyle from the corner of his eye. "I suppose I could part with such a fine article for three pennies."

"My offer stands at two pennies, or no deal," Kyle said.

"Done," Ogilvy said. He spat on his hand and held it out to Kyle, who did the same.

After they shook hands to seal the bargain, Ogilvy peered up at Kyle with new respect in his eyes. "Ye drive a hard bargain for a foreigner," he said.

Macalister laughed, his white teeth gleaming in the darkness. "He's no foreigner," he said "He's kin to James Shaw."

Ogilvy snorted in disgust. "How was I to know?" he said. "He don't talk like us, and he don't look like us."

Kyle ignored the jibe. Many a lowlander chose to adopt the English mode of dress, preferring fitted leggings under a long-sleeved, high-necked, coat-like garment to a plain cloak over a shapeless tunic. As for his speech, the past six years that he spent among the French improved his accent, along with his manners.

He fished a couple of silver pennies from his coin purse and dropped them into the old man's waiting hand. He took the cloak Macalister handed to him, shook the mud from it, and folded it in half. "Tell your ma to wash and mend this before she cuts it down for you," he said, wrapping the garment around the boy's thin shoulders. "I want to see you wearing it the next time I come out this way."

Hob clasped the edges of the wool cloak with one hand and clutched the coin in the other. He tipped back his head to get a good look at his benefactor. His smudged face reflected doubt, as though he was unsure of what he did to merit such a prize. "Thank ye, sir," he said in a small voice.

"Where do you live, Hob?" Kyle said.

"Just beyond the next field," Hob said, indicating the direction with his chin.

Kyle ruffled the mop of hair on Hob's head. "Go on home, then," he said.

Hob ducked through the bottom slat of the timber gate and scampered away.

Kyle watched the departing boy glance back at him three times before vanishing into the darkness. When he turned to Macalister and Ogilvy, he caught them staring at him, their faces inscrutable.

Macalister was the first to look away. "Let's get this plunder out of sight," he said to the old man. He gathered an armful of the booty and picked up his long-handled axe. After opening the gate wide enough to squeeze through, he started toward the shadowed hulk of the barn.

The old man picked up the leather boots with tender care, a pair in each hand, and passed through the gap between the gate and the stone fence. "Be sure to drop the latch," he said, "or ye'll be rounding up sheep till dawn." He turned and hastened after Macalister.

The two men left the armor behind for Kyle to carry. He tied the unwieldy pieces in pairs and slung them over the saddle. One of the helmets he picked up bore a split in the crown that he had put there with the blade of his axe. Dried blood stained the jagged edges. The damage was extensive, but in skilled hands, it could be repaired. He hung it, along with the other helmet, from the saddle bow. He led the gelding through the gate and shut it behind him.

He hurried to catch up with the two men as they trudged along the beaten path. "I take it the cottage isn't yours," he said, falling in step beside Macalister.

"Never claimed it was," Macalister said.

"I guess you don't live here, either," Kyle said.

Macalister shook his head and kept walking.

"You never told me where you thought those raiders came from," Kyle said.

"It was just a guess," Macalister said.

"I'd like to hear it."

"The closest garrison."

"Why?"

"So they don't need to travel so far."

"I meant, why take the chance?" Kyle said. "If English soldiers are exposed as raiders, they'll face the noose." The skeptical look Macalister shot at him prompted him to add, "You don't think so?"

Macalister took a deep breath and let it out before he spoke. "King Edward needs to fill his coffers," he said, staring straight ahead as he walked, "and he's none too particular how he does it. This is sheep country, so the Southrons lay a heavy tax upon wool, whether shorn or on the hoof. Edward approves, as long as most of the collected moneys end up in the royal treasury. What the Southrons don't tax, they take, like they tried to do tonight. If folks fail to pay the tax, unjust though it is, they're turned off their land, with nothing to barter once the crops are seized and the stock taken away."

"What's the justiciar doing about it?"

"Ye have been away too long," Macalister said. "Edward replaced our own justiciars with Southron nobles. As if that's not bad enough, the clerks make it worse. I'm ashamed to own them as fellow Scots, drawn as they are into crooked ways by the lure of easy money. The clerks collect the tax, as they always did, but now they double the amount due and keep the extra for themselves. The new justiciars allow it because they get a cut of the takings."

"So, you're saying that what the English can't confiscate," Kyle said, "they simply take in the raids?"

"There's nothing simple about it," Macalister said. "The raiders know exactly where and when to strike, as though the raids were planned."

"After I settle in at the garrison," Kyle said, "I'll poke around to see what I can find out."

"The Southrons won't take kindly to a sharp nose in their affairs," Macalister said. "If ye aren't careful, ye'll stir up a hornets' nest for yerself."

By that time, they reached the barn, and a dog inside began to bark, a fierce throaty sound barely muffled through the upright planks on the timber walls.

Kyle and Macalister stood to the side to let the old man open the rough wooden door.

The interior smelled of cow manure and fresh hay. A rectangle of moonlight intruded far enough into the gloom for Kyle to see a tan dog straining at the end of a chain attached to its spiked collar. The beast growled deep in its throat, its lips drawn back in a snarl. He was relieved to see that the chain was attached to an iron ring bolted to the side wall.

The dog was an Alaunt, a short-haired breed notorious for its uncertain temperament. Its chest was broad, and the jaws in its bull terrier–like head were massive. Such a beast could track a full-grown stag and pull it down with ease. It was also capable of making short work of any man foolish enough to stray within reach of those bared teeth.

"Down, Fergus," Macalister said, his voice sharp and commanding.

The dog skulked away to flop down against the side wall. It rested its square head between its paws on the earthen floor, its ears pricked and its eyes watchful.

Ogilvy placed the leather boots on the bed of a wagon that stood against the wall across from the dog. He hovered over them, as though reluctant to let them out of his sight. "Put that stuff over there," he said, indicating a shadowed corner with a careless sweep of his hand.

Kyle lifted the armor from the saddle and stacked the pieces where Macalister had deposited his load. Between them, they created a substantial pile of goods.

"Have a care where ye peddle these things," Macalister said, leaning on the handle of his axe, "lest ye rouse suspicion as to how they came into yer possession."

"Do ye think I'm a dim-wit?" Ogilvy said, taking umbrage at the suggestion. "I'm twice yer age, lad, and that makes me twice as smart." He lifted an oil lamp down from a wooden peg and set it on the dirt floor. After digging in the sheepskin pouch at his waist for a moment, he produced a pair of flints. He struck them together several times, and once the wick flared to life, he hung the lamp back on the peg.

The yellow light from the flickering flame barely illuminated the aisle that ran between the four wooden stalls, two on either side. A ladder at the back led up to a hayloft under the peak of the timber roof. A single horse stuck its head over one of the low stall doors and nickered at Macalister, who walked over to pat its gray neck.

In the stall beside the horse, a black-faced cow placidly chewed its cud as it looked out at them.

The subdued lighting cast Macalister's blunt features into high relief. His was the open and honest face of a man who said what he meant and meant what he said. His hair was brown, cropped short, and his eyes were dark, peering out over a bushy brown beard.

Kyle felt those dark eyes upon him, gazing with curiosity at the white seam of a scar that ran from temple to jaw on his clean-shaven face. The wound, sustained on a battlefield, came from a Flemish halberd, the wielder of which died shortly thereafter. Although long healed, the scar stood out against his tanned complexion. It was the only blemish on his lean and finely chiseled features.

He fingered his bruised ribs through the leather scale armor. He was tired and hungry, and the last thing he felt like doing was riding in the dark for another hour or so to reach his destination, which was the port town of Ayr on the western coast. "Where will you sleep tonight?" he said to the old man.

"In the loft," Ogilvy said, jerking his thumb over his shoulder.

"I'd appreciate it if you put me up for the rest of the night," Kyle said. The old man's hesitation prompted him to add, "I'll pay you for it."

"Ye mistake me, lad," Ogilvy said. "I don't want yer money. That was a kindly thing ye did for my grandson. The least I can do is what little ye ask. Hob don't lack for warm things to wear. He just forgets to put them on. He'll treasure that mantle, though, and he'll wear it, because ye gave it to him special." He started to walk away, but he turned back. "What made ye do it?"

"He reminded me of . . ." Kyle said. He let the sentence die away, the words tight in his throat. Ogilvy's innocent query, like a well-aimed arrow, pierced an old wound that never really healed. He finished by saying, "someone I used to know."

Ogilvy nodded his gray head. "There's not a soul alive who never lost somebody or something," he said with uncharacteristic empathy. "A few years back, my son died of the fever. It grieved me sore, but I wasn't the only one to suffer from his passing. Hob lost a father. Hob's mother lost a husband. Guthrie lost a brother-in-law who was closer to him than a real brother." His eyes took on a faraway look. "I still think on him from time to time." He shook himself to recover from his momentary lapse.

"Ah, well, it does no good to dwell on it, does it?" He turned away to rummage through the jumble on a low shelf. When he located a small stool and a wooden pail, he ducked into the cow's stall.

The old man's words gave Kyle a measure of comfort as he led the gelding into an empty stall. He stripped off the saddle and bridle, and slung them across the wooden partition. He removed his cloak and the scale armor, and hung them up beside the tack. After filling the manger with sweet hay, he picked up his cloak and draped it over his arm, ready to turn in for the night.

In a short while, Ogilvy came out of the cow's stall holding a pail half full of frothy milk. "I usually get more than this from her," he said. "With all that going on earlier, I forgot her milking. I hope it don't throw off her yield for too long."

Ogilvy upended the pail and slurped at its contents. He passed the container to Kyle, who downed several mouthfuls.

The milk was warm and rich with butter cream, the best Kyle had ever tasted, or so it seemed in his present state of hunger. He handed the pail over to Macalister, who drank some of the milk and gave the rest to the dog, who lapped it up and licked the sides of the container.

When they were ready to settle down for the night, Macalister took the dog outside to chain it near the sheep pen in case the raiders returned. He came back a few minutes later and helped the old man bar the door of the barn.

They all climbed the ladder to the loft, with the old man in the lead holding the oil lamp. When they each found a suitable place to sleep, the old man blew out the flame.

Kyle removed his boots and stretched out on the fragrant hay under his cloak, his dirk near at hand. Nights spent in open fields beside companions of dubious character made him wary of trusting too readily.

He hardly noticed the acrid smell of the smoking wick that lingered in the air. His last thought before falling asleep was of taking the two dead men with him when he went to the garrison in the morning, since their bodies were his only proof that English soldiers might also be raiders.

Sometime later in the night, a distant but unrelenting sound penetrated the cobwebs in his head. He strained to hear over the sonorous snoring that came from Ogilvy's corner of the loft.

Recognition of the source of the sound jerked him to full wakefulness.

The dog outside was barking.

CHAPTER 2

Kyle sat up and pulled on his boots. The hay to his left rustled as Macalister stirred. Ogilvy rolled onto his side, and his snoring ceased. The dog's barking seemed louder in the ensuing silence.

The darkness inside the barn was absolute. Kyle crawled over to the edge of the loft, mindful of the abrupt eight-foot drop just ahead. He felt his way to the ladder, with Macalister right behind him.

The scrape of his boots against the wooden rungs echoed in the hollow barn. When he reached the earthen floor, he felt along the wooden stalls to the front door as quickly as he dared, collecting the battle axe from his saddle on the way.

Macalister was more familiar with the configuration of the barn and reached the entranceway first. He removed the bar and opened the wooden door. The first light of dawn flooded the interior, bright after the stygian darkness inside. He retrieved his long-handled axe from where he had propped it against the wall beside the door and stepped outside.

Kyle hastened after Macalister, following him along the dirt path to the sheep pen. The taint of smoke still hung in the chilly air. A thin mist swirled around their feet, boiling up in their wake. Except for the barking of the dog and the intermittent bleating of sheep, he saw nothing to cause alarm.

The dog fell silent at its master's approach, wagging its tail and whining softly.

"Good boy," Macalister said, patting its furry head.

After a moment, the sheep settled down and ceased milling about the enclosure.

"Do you see anything amiss?" Kyle said, walking up to the wooden gate. His gaze swept the outer perimeter of the sheep pen.

Macalister looked around him. "Not a thing," he said. "But Fergus did. He's not one to sound off without cause."

Belatedly, Kyle realized the serious error he had made. He swore under his breath as he ducked through the top slat of the gate. Once inside the pen, he strode along the stone fence, searching for black smears of blood on the cap stones, which marked where Macalister had disposed of the bodies. When he found the place, he leaned forward to peer at the ground below. A cursory glance confirmed his fear. Even if wolves or other predators had come during the night, the bodies were too heavy for them to drag away. As he headed back to where Macalister stood by the gate, a cock crowed in the distance.

The whole expanse of the eastern sky grew brighter. The dark hulk of the barn began to take on shape and color. The surrounding trees loomed against the skyline, each branch a vivid green with spring budding.

"The raiders came back," Kyle said.

"How do ye know?"

"The bodies are gone," Kyle said. He gnashed his teeth at his own lack of foresight, knowing he should have taken steps to prevent the loss of his only real evidence.

"Too bad about that," Macalister said.

Kyle glanced over at the roofless cottage. "Do you need me to stay to help clean up?" he said.

"That won't be necessary," Macalister said, following his gaze. "I'll give the old man a hand."

"I'll be on my way, then," Kyle said.

He returned to the barn to gather his belongings and saddle up. Ogilvy was still snoring in the hayloft when, a few minutes later, he mounted the gelding and rode outside.

With a parting wave to Macalister, he set out along the dirt lane that took him through a stand of trees beyond the open yard. He failed to notice the small woodland the night before, although its presence explained where the raiders went and how they disappeared so completely in the darkness.

When he drew nearer to the main road, he saw the grassy field through which he had ridden in the moonlight to get to Ogilvy's cottage. It was a wonder he made it through there at all, riddled as it was with marshy places glazed with standing water. Any one of those shallow pools might conceal a bog that could swallow both horse and rider in under a minute. His mount would no doubt sink more quickly, for unlike the hardy but smaller pony common to Scotland, the gelding was a tall muscular warhorse that he had brought with him from across the sea. As a reward for such sureness of foot, he promised the horse an extra measure of oats when he reached the garrison.

The morning was clear and radiant under the burnished blue vault of the sky. The air was crisp and fresh after the recent rain, and the road stretched out before him like a thin ribbon. The open country all around was well suited for grazing sheep, being a rolling tableland of grassy hills and dales. To the east, a distant wall of trees marched along the horizon, and to the west, an occasional stone cottage broke the monotony of the landscape stippled with green spring growth.

He took his time covering the last few miles of his journey to Ayr. All was quiet around him, except for the jingle of harness and the snuffle of the horse's breath. At that moment, the strife and dissention that threatened to tear apart his homeland seemed far removed, as though such troubles were the lot of those who lived on distant shores. Yet, there was no reason to doubt the reports that reached him in Flanders, while he served as a mercenary in the army of King Philip IV of France. With no king on the Scottish throne and Edward of England camped on their doorstep, all of Scotland stood on the brink of revolt.

All too soon, the red sandstone bell tower of St. John's Church came into view over the tops of the trees ahead. Beyond that, the crimson and gold pennant of England fluttered above Ayr Castle within the garrison walls. The emblem was as yet indistinguishable, but he saw it for what it was, a symbol of English domination.

Ayr Castle sat on the south bank of the River Ayr overlooking the Firth of Clyde, guarding the mouth of the river to keep seafaring marauders from sailing upstream to raid inland towns and villages.

The townsfolk of Ayr lived and worked in the shadow of the garrison walls. Their harbors were never at rest, open to trade from both the river and the firth. A hundred years earlier, King William the Lion recognized the value of the port town's location on the western seacoast and raised Ayr's status from a fishing village to a royal burgh. As a result of the imperial boon, commerce flourished and the burghers prospered. Eventually, they built a bridge over the River Ayr, which enabled the burgeoning population to spill onto the north bank.

Kyle approached the outskirts of Newton, which the new town that sprang up on the north side of the River Ayr came to be called. He shared the road with folks from nearby villages headed into town with their dog carts and pony-drawn wagons filled with goods to trade and sell at the marketplace in Ayr.

The wind carried to him the nauseating smell of the tannery mingled with the stench from the slaughterhouse further down the river. Malodorous though they were, those industries were vital to the town's economy. That was where farmers and herdsmen took their sheep and cattle for slaughter. That was where butchers and fleshers, skinners and tanners prepared the wool-fells, hides, and meat for export.

It occurred to him that exportation was a good way for the raiders, whom he now knew to be English, to dispose of their spoils for profit. Though the attempt at Ogilvy's was unsuccessful, others in the shire had lost their stock to night raids, according to Macalister. The stolen animals could be loaded onto a merchant vessel bound for market across the sea, with the ship's master paid well to ensure his cooperation. The raiders would hardly use the port of Ayr, though, because of the risk of owners recognizing their own stock. They likely funneled their booty through some other quay along the coast, but the question was: which one?

The bells of St. John's rang in the morning hour of terce, calling the faithful to Sunday Mass. He crossed the stone bridge leading to the south bank of the River Ayr. The sun glimmered on the surface of the water below rushing toward the Firth of Clyde a short distance away. Beyond the garrison walls to the right, the masts of merchant ships in the harbor jutted skyward like skinned saplings. Seagulls screeched and circled overhead, fighting for scraps of rotted entrails from the slaughterhouse and squabbling over refuse from the castle midden.

The old town of Ayr lay before him, a maze of cobbled lanes with gutters down the center that reeked of slops from chamber pots. Cramped wooden houses and shops lined the streets. Women in oatmeal-colored bonnets ambled toward the market-place, their empty baskets on their arms. Men sat on their front steps, gossiping with their neighbors. Street urchins and their mongrel dogs disrupted traffic, frightening ponies and provoking shouts of anger.

Kyle turned west onto Harbour Street and followed it to St. John's Church, with its square bell tower reaching for the heavens. He tied the gelding's reins to the rail out front and ascended the stone steps. He opened the huge doors to enter the vestibule, letting the doors close gently behind him.

Inside, Mass was already underway. The priest droned on in Latin, and his words echoed from the vaulted ceiling. The interior was cold and heavily scented with beeswax candles and old wood. Mullioned windows set high in the stone walls on either side cast a muted illumination over a small crowd of people standing together, facing the altar.

Kyle remained behind those in attendance and glanced around him. There were some who made an ostentatious display of their wealth, dressing in rich velvet robes and mantles trimmed with fur. Others wore mended but clean homespun as their Sunday best.

As his eyes grew used to the dim lighting, he noticed a thin woman in a shadowed corner with a veil on her head. She knelt on the hard flagstone floor, her hands folded in prayer, her thumbs pressed against her heart, as though to hold it in place. She looked more like the Madonna in the niche above her than a flesh and blood woman, until she lifted her bowed head. Though her face was unlined, she was well past the bloom of youth. Her eyes were squeezed shut, crinkled at the corners, and her lips quivered in silent prayer. Her anguished expression made him wonder what mortal sin she committed in the past for which she must atone with such fervor.

Before long, the priest uttered the final benediction. Kyle stood aside as the crowd began to shuffle out through the double doors and into the sunlight. The church was almost empty when the thin woman in the corner climbed to her feet and smoothed the wrinkles from her skirt. As she turned to leave, a stout woman with the face of a gargoyle latched onto her elbow. The gargoyle woman steered her through the entranceway and down the steps with such haste, the veil slipped from the thin woman's head, revealing a thick braid of light brown hair trailing down her back.

Kyle left the church and went over to where the gelding stood dozing at the rail. He untied the reins and led the horse to the marketplace, which was situated in the open stretch of sandy ground between St. John's and the garrison wall. The sun was warm there in the protected lee, so he removed his cloak and tucked it into his saddle roll.

The marketplace bustled with activity. Merchants presented their goods under striped canopies. Vendors showed off their products in colorful stalls. Peddlers hawked their wares in singsong cadence. Customers haggled for bargains, their voices excited and shrill. Chickens in wicker coops squawked. Dogs fought over scraps of food. A goose escaped from its cage, and a handful of children chased after it trying to catch it. Their laughter and shouts added to the din. On the far side of the grounds, a spitted sheep's carcass hung over an open fire, with a small boy beside it slowly turning the handle. The smell of animal droppings blended with the aroma of roasted mutton.

Kyle ambled through the stalls, threading a path toward the roasting meat. Along the way, his idle gaze wandered over the people around him. As he passed a cloth merchant's cart, he noticed a woman looking at a stack of green woven fabric. From the profile she presented to him, he guessed her age to be around twenty-five years. She appeared to be in mourning, for her garment was black, a harsh contrast to her fair skin. A strip of black linen served as a belt around her slender waist. The black bonnet on her head covered all but a single strand of light auburn hair, which blazed in the sun with the vivid color of life.

His pace slowed to watch her reach out a slim hand to touch the ribbons on display. She fingered the silky streamers, caressing first a forest green one, then a bright gold one, as though unable to make up her mind between them.

Then, for no reason that Kyle could discern, she turned her head and looked directly at him. Her delicate features were lovely, with a sprinkle of reddish freckles across her nose and hazel eyes that changed to green in the sunlight.

He stopped to stare openly at her, his hunger forgotten. Although her beauty drew him, it was the air of sadness about her that held him. The generous mouth made for laughter curved down at the corners, and the straight line of her shoulders bowed slightly, as though weighed down with a heavy burden. No stranger to the pain of loss himself, he recognized the signs when he saw them. While unaware of the cause of hers, he knew it was heart-deep and very bitter.

After an awkward moment, she lowered her gaze and stepped around him. The soft fabric of her skirt fluttered in the breeze as she made her way through the crowd. By the time he gathered his wits about him, she was more than twenty feet away.

"Who was she?" he said, turning to the cloth merchant.

The cloth merchant merely shrugged his shoulders.

Kyle watched the departing woman for a moment longer, her head up and her step firm, as though she knew what she wanted and how to get it. He was about to turn away when he saw a helmeted English man-at-arms in light armor sidle up beside her.

The man-at-arms said something to her that caused her to increase her pace. He thrust out his arm to block her way, forcing her to acknowledge his presence. She turned away from him and started in another direction. He grabbed her wrist to stop her. She pulled back and twisted her arm to break free of his grip.

Kyle strode toward them with the gelding in tow, unmindful of those he bumped into along the way. When he arrived on the scene, he laid his hand on the man-at-arms' shoulder and spun him around. "Leave her be," he said.

The astonished man-at-arms released the woman's wrist. He shrugged off Kyle's hand, his upper lip curled in a sneer. "Who do you think you are?" he said. His face, or what could be seen of it behind the nosepiece of his Norman helmet, might have been comely but for the stamp of dissipation upon it. His jowls were fleshy from overindulgence in food, and his eyes were bloodshot from too much ale and too little sleep.

"As deputy sheriff," Kyle said, "it's my duty to keep civil order in the shire." He took a step closer, forcing the shorter man to look up at him. "You don't look civil to me."

People began to gather around them, craning their necks to see what was going on.

"There's no harm in talking to the woman," the man-at-arms said, blustering. Kyle's towering nearness forced him back a pace. A flush of humiliation darkened his countenance, for that single backward step caused him to lose face before the onlookers, and he knew it.

"Do you want to talk to him?" Kyle said, turning to the woman.

"I do not," she said, her tone emphatic.

"You heard the lady," Kyle said to the man-at-arms. "Now, move along."

The man-at-arms' visible features under his helmet turned from brick-red to purple. "What I do with her is none of your business," he said between his teeth. "Captain Sweeney will hear about this." He gathered his bruised dignity about him and stalked off, pushing his way through the crowd. Every few steps, he threw a venomous glance over his shoulder in Kyle's direction.

The woman's eyes flashed green fire in the morning sun. "He's a pig," she said under her breath.

Kyle heard her comment and suppressed a smile. "Allow me to escort you to where you wish to go, mistress," he said.

"I would like that," she said.

As they set out together, his protective male instincts emerged, a natural reaction to a woman in distress. It was the intensity of his feelings that took him by surprise, for only one other woman ever moved him so. He walked beside her through the marketplace, scarcely aware of the people around him or the vendors hawking their wares.

"Ye have the advantage of me, Master Deputy," she said, "for I don't know yer name."

"Kyle Shaw, at your service," he said. "By the way, who's the pig?"

"That's Archer from the garrison," she said with a shudder. "Thank ye for making him go away."

"My pleasure," he said, his pale blue eyes on her attractive profile.

She stopped at the baker's pushcart, where a pretty young woman in a frilly white cap held a newborn infant in her arms.

"Good morrow to ye, Kyle Shaw," she said, with a curtsey. She avoided the other woman's questioning gaze as she waited for Kyle to take his leave.

Kyle liked the sound of his name on her lips. After a slight bow to her, he started once again toward the roasting meat with the gelding in tow. After a couple of steps, he realized he had forgotten something important.

"Mistress," he said, turning back to her. "I didn't get your name."

"It's Joneta," she said, flashing a row of small, even white teeth in a smile.

After breaking his fast on a chunk of roasted mutton and a mug of watered ale, Kyle rode under the iron portcullis of Ayr Garrison. Sunlight glinted on the metal helmet of the guard looking down from the watchtower above a pair of massive timber gates.

A thick curtain wall of stone surrounded the garrison. The barracks, the stable, and the other outbuildings within its bounds were built of wood, situated along the inner wall so as to face the open courtyard, at the center of which was a raised platform and a gibbet. The three-story castle keep, also made of wood, was constructed against the seaward wall, where keen-eyed sentries could scan the Firth of Clyde for invaders prowling the sea.

There was much activity in the courtyard when Kyle arrived. A person of importance had just ridden into the garrison with an escort of armed soldiers and a string of mules laden with supplies. The castellan stood on the top step in front of the main hall of the castle, as though waiting to formally greet the visiting dignitary.

Kyle slowed the gelding to a walk, his head turned to gaze at the visitor who stood out like a peacock among the drably clothed English soldiers around him.

A foreigner of noble rank and bearing, the man sat tall and erect in the saddle. He was about forty-five years of age, with a long face and arched brows. His hair was black with silver at the temples. The dark moustache under his high-bridged, arrogant nose was pencil thin, and his dark goatee came to a point on his chin, giving his features a devilish appearance. His mantle of green velvet was trimmed with ermine, fastened at the neck with a large ruby brooch. His linen tunic was the same green hue, threaded with gold, which glinted richly in the sunlight with every movement. He rode a sleek bay horse, with fringes on its soft leather bridle and tooled with tiny gold studs along the brow and cheek bands. He dismounted with lithe grace, and his manner was courteous to the waiting groom, who took the reins from his gloved hand.

The foreign nobleman seemed oblivious to the commotion

around him of braying mules, officers shouting orders, and men scurrying to unload supplies.

Kyle headed toward the stable, drawing curious glances along the way. On the far side of the courtyard, a dozen or so archers shot practice arrows at targets of straw. Several soldiers sat on the wooden benches in front of the barracks, cleaning their gear or sharpening their weapons. Others walked about or stood in small groups, talking and laughing among themselves.

Only one man among the soldiery took an inordinate interest in Kyle's arrival. He was the kind of fellow nobody seemed to notice, whose weathered features and nondescript garments blended with his surroundings, like a chameleon. He paused at honing the edge of his dagger to give Kyle a long thoughtful look. His farsighted blue eyes under bristling gray brows followed the passage of both horse and rider until the walls of the stable hid them from view.

Kyle entered an elongated low-roofed building that, typical of most stables, was open at both ends, with a wide aisle between box stalls on either side. The gaps under the eaves where the timber rafters met the walls let in light and air, although the ventilation did little to dispel the rank smell of horse urine.

He rode down the aisle without haste in search of the groom. Along the way, horses extended their heads over the half-doors, velvety nostrils dilated and ears pricked toward him. Unlike King Philip IV's royal stable, which housed hundreds of horses, this one had no more than fifty stalls and even fewer horses.

Several yards ahead, a man was backing out of a stall that held a huge black warhorse. The magnificent creature showed no fear at the man's presence. It only tossed its noble head and pawed the dirt floor.

From what Kyle could see, the man was no groom. His short leather tunic fitted him like it was made for him, and the precious jewel in the hilt of his sword winked and glittered as he

moved. He was too engrossed in closing the half-door and slid-
ing the bolt into place to heed the gelding's approach. When the
man turned, he drew in a sharp breath at finding a horse and its
rider the length of an arm away.

"God's wounds!" the man cried, his eyes wide in surprise.
"That steed treads like a wraith." He was perhaps in his early
twenties, of middle height, with flaxen hair and candid blue
eyes. His features were pleasant, and his manner too refined for
that of a common man-at-arms.

Kyle reined in and patted the gelding's reddish-brown neck.
"He does walk softly," he said. His gaze shifted to the horse in
the stall. "That's a handsome black."

"He is that," the man said.

"Is he yours?" Kyle said.

The man's Adam's apple bobbed in his throat before he
spoke. "Nay," he said. "I was just looking in on him."

Kyle's interest sharpened. The reflexive swallow and the need
to explain indicated the man was clearly nervous about
something, but about what was not as clear. He let the silence
stretch between them, waiting to see what the man did next.

Early on, his father had taught him the significance of certain
facial expressions and mannerisms. The ability to read people
proved useful to him later when he served as liaison between
the provost marshal of the French king's army and mercenaries
accused of criminal offenses. In his experience, suspects under
interrogation rarely told the truth, whether from fear or guilt or
shame. Those with something to hide often gave themselves
away with subtle body movements indicative of lying, like the
slight lift of a shoulder or touching the face or neck. Proficient
liars were harder to spot, but even those skilled at deception
slipped up if allowed to talk long enough. Listening, in his
opinion, was just as important as observing.

The man licked his lips, another sign of nervousness. His

blue eyes took in Kyle's bulging saddle roll and the stains of travel on both horse and rider. "Are you billeted here?" he said.

"In a manner of speaking," Kyle said. He introduced himself as the deputy sheriff.

The man seemed relieved. "I'm Upton," he said. "Will you be staying in the barracks?"

"Not if I can help it," Kyle said.

"That's good," Upton said.

"Why is that?" Kyle said, watching him without appearing to do so.

Upton blinked once before he replied. "No reason," he said in a voice an octave higher than before.

Hesitation, however slight, often preceded a falsehood, and a rise in tone implied deception. The man was lying, but Kyle let it go for the moment. "Are all of the stalls taken?" he said, changing the subject.

"You might check the ones halfway down the row," Upton said. "Nobody wants those in the middle."

"Thanks for your help," Kyle said with a disarming smile. He nudged the gelding forward and continued down the aisle.

After a moment, he glanced over his shoulder and saw what he expected to see: Upton hurrying from the stable as fast as his legs could carry him. It occurred to him that the man might have hidden something in the stall, or worse, injured the horse.

He turned the gelding around and rode back to where the sleek black head stuck out over the half-door. He dismounted to make a cursory inspection of the horse and its quarters, but he saw nothing amiss. There was no place in the plain square stall to conceal anything. The animal appeared to be sound, despite the mud caked under its belly and down its long legs. The water in the bucket looked clean, and the hay smelled fresh, with no visible poisonous weeds mixed in it. He would check on the horse again later, so he took note of the stall's location along the row. It was the only one with a pigeon's nest in the opening under the roof.

He led the gelding down the aisle. Somewhere near the middle, he found fourteen empty stalls, all of which showed signs of long disuse. Old hay moldered in the feed bins, and the earthen floor stank of rancid droppings. He tied the reins to the nearest post and stepped into the first vacant stall. After a thorough inspection of each one, he chose the least offensive of the lot.

Unsure when the groom would return, he rolled up his sleeves, exposing the scars from long-healed burns on his forearms. He set about mucking out the stall himself with a shovel he found in the tack room.

Nearly an hour later, he settled the gelding into freshened quarters and gave its sorrel coat a good brushing. As promised, he poured an extra measure of oats into the newly cleaned feed bin.

He carried a couple of empty wooden pails out into the courtyard to fetch water from the well. On his return, he hung one pail inside the stall for the gelding. The other he used to wash off the mud and grime of his two-week journey from Flanders, after which he shaved to make himself presentable to the sheriff. He dried himself with his soiled shirt, changed into fresh clothing, and buckled his sword belt over the leather scale vest. He stored the saddle and the bridle in the tack room and left the stable carrying his saddle roll with him.

He crossed the courtyard to the sheriff's office, which was a small two-room outbuilding set against the east wall. The door stood open to let in the sunlight, so he went inside without knocking. The front room was furnished with a pair of stools, a table with a tallow candle on it, and a wooden bench under a window in the side wall. A curtain hung over the entryway to the rear chamber.

He dropped his saddle roll onto the bench and started toward the chamber in the rear. The only sound in the room was the heavy clump of his boots on the timber planking. Before he reached the curtain, a gnarled hand swept it aside from within, and Sheriff Reginald de Crawford stepped through the doorway.

The sheriff looked nothing like the robust man Kyle remembered. The decline in his appearance went far beyond that expected of someone well past sixty years of age. A wasting disease had ravaged his body, leaving him sickly and frail. His linen shirt and woolen leggings hung from his emaciated frame. The blue eyes in his bony face were dull with opiates, and his sallow skin was wrinkled and dry, like old parchment. Even his gray moustache seemed to droop with fatigue.

Shocked disbelief flashed across Kyle's face for only an instant before he regained command of his countenance. The sheriff's condition appalled him, and his natural inclination was to conceal it to spare the old man's dignity. Involuntary reactions like his own just then were similar to what he observed in others during his interrogations. Probing questions often provoked a strong emotional response in a suspect. Those intense feelings, although fleeting, reflected what was really going on inside a person. The body always told the truth, despite the contradictory words coming out of the mouth.

Sheriff Crawford caught the fleeting expression on Kyle's face and smiled. "Now ye see why I sent for ye," he said. His rich baritone was at odds with his skeletal appearance.

"If you needed me sooner," Kyle said in earnest, "I would have come."

"Ye are here now," Sheriff Crawford said. "That's all that matters." He walked over to the bench and lowered himself onto it with a weary sigh. "I plan to stay with my daughter in Kilmarnock for a while. She says I must rest or I'll never get well."

"When are you leaving?"

"On the morrow."

"So soon?"

Sheriff Crawford peered at him with the eyes of a man who knew his days were numbered. "I cannot do very much anymore," he said. "Ye must stand in my place for a time. I'll get Sir Percy's clerk to enter yer name into the official records. Then, as deputy, ye will be the one who keeps peace in the shire. If Reginald comes back before I do, he will execute the duties of this office, with yer able assistance, of course." He was apparently well satisfied that his eldest son and namesake would carry on in his place as Sheriff of Ayrshire, a hereditary title held by the Crawfords for generations.

Kyle leaned against the wooden table. "When is Reginald expected?" he said.

"Not for some months," Sheriff Crawford said. "There's trouble brewing in the north. Moray raised his standard against the English, and from what I hear, he convinced Inverness and Elgin and some of the other castles to stand with him." He shook his head, his countenance grave. "I'm sorry to call ye back while things are so unsettled, but I don't trust anyone else to hold this post for my son, even for a short time."

"What about my father?" Kyle said.

Sheriff Crawford lowered his eyes and shifted his weight on the wooden bench, as though the question made him more uncomfortable than the hard surface on which he sat. "James Shaw," he said in a flat voice, "was killed five years ago."

Kyle's stomach lurched, as if the floor had dropped out from under him. "Killed?" he cried in disbelief. "How?"

Sadness etched every crevice of Sheriff Crawford's gaunt features. "It happened at Loudoun Hill," he said, lifting his gaze to Kyle's face. "I know little more than that."

Kyle's fingers curled around the edge of the table, his grip so hard his knuckles turned white. "Why not?" he demanded, his tone harsh. "He was your friend, wasn't he?" He knew better than to rail at a feeble old man, but at that moment, anger and frustration overrode any compassion he might have felt.

"I looked into the matter right away," Sheriff Crawford said, "but it came to naught. My inquiries to mutual acquaintances met with closed mouths, or else they chattered loud and long, but imparted nothing of use. Some said James was a hero. Others called him a traitor to the Scottish cause. When I think back on it, I believe my being sheriff hindered more than helped at the time."

"Why is that?"

"Although this high office was bestowed upon my family by Scottish kings of old, I only retain my post now by the grace of Edward of England. It goes without saying that I am bound, as ye will be as deputy, by all strictures imposed under English law. Those I questioned about yer father's death knew that and likely mistrusted me because of it."

The bells of St. John's rang in the noon hour of sext. Kyle gazed out the open doorway, staring inwardly at his own thoughts, oblivious to the sunlight flooding the courtyard or the wind churning up dust from a passing horse.

The news of his father's death upset him more than he was willing to admit aloud. Five years earlier, he received a letter from his father insisting that he come home because of worsening conditions from English occupation throughout Scotland. For reasons of his own, he wasn't ready to go back, and he wrote his father telling him so. He never received a reply to that or any subsequent letter he sent to his father. Grief at the loss of his father far outweighed any relief he experienced on learning that death, not anger or disappointment, kept his father from corresponding with him all those years. He had let his father down, and he knew it. It was too late to make amends.

The only thing left to do now was to find out what really occurred that day at Loudoun Hill. If treachery was involved, he would bring the murderer, or murderers, to justice. It was what he did as a man of law.

"Where is he buried?" he said, rupturing the uneasy silence that fell between them.

"I don't know," Sheriff Crawford said. The sincerity on his face was genuine, but he pressed his thin lips together in a way that suggested if there was more to tell, he was unwilling to do so.

"All right, then," Kyle said, folding his arms across his chest. "If I am to carry on in your stead, you must catch me up with what is yet to be done in the shire. Are all taxes collected, counted, and delivered to the royal coffers?"

"Sir Percy handles that now," Sheriff Crawford said, "by order of the English king."

Kyle chewed on his lower lip. "Very well," he said after a moment. "Has the Kirk yet paid its dues to the Crown?"

"Sir Percy himself deals with the Kirk, by order of the English king."

"I see," Kyle said. "Am I authorized to convene an assize to sit in judgment, as a sheriff is wont to do?"

"Sir Percy presides over all cases brought to court, both civil and criminal, by order of the English king."

"And should Sir Percy render an unfavorable verdict, am I to arrange for execution of the felon and confiscation of his chattels, as required for payment of bloodwite?"

"Actually, Sir Percy turned all punitive duties over to the English marshal here in the garrison."

"By order of the English king, no doubt," Kyle said dryly. He took a deep breath and let it out slowly. "The length of my absence from the shire puts me at a disadvantage, so perhaps you can tell me exactly what there is left for me to do as deputy."

"To pursue brigands," Sheriff Crawford said, "and to arrest all who disrupt civil order. Those who live in the shire are powerless to defend themselves, so ye must see to their protection. The force of law must be strong enough to contain the predators who seek to devour innocent folk." He spoke with a fervor that lit his tired old eyes with a feverish zeal.

"Ah, well," Kyle said. "A noble undertaking, indeed. That is why I was summoned here, and that is what I shall do."

"Despite the reassignment of certain duties to Sir Percy," Sheriff Crawford said, "there is still much required of this office. As sheriff, I am required to witness royal documents. Ye are not authorized to do that, even as deputy. Should the occasion arise, either I or my son will handle that. In the event of an invasion from sea-roving bandits, ye will be required, in my absence, to provide stores for the garrison and make sure the burghers are prepared for battle. That has not happened in many years, but I thought I should mention it, just in case."

Sheriff Crawford made a move to rise from the bench when a sudden frown puckered his brow. His breath came in ragged gasps. His hand trembled as he fumbled in the leather pouch attached to his belt. He took out a small phial, which he shook near his ear to ascertain the measure of its contents. After removing the cork stopper, he took a swig of the fluid inside. He replaced the stopper, wiped his mouth with the back of his hand, and closed his eyes.

Kyle pushed away from the table to stand upright, ready to help but unsure what to do for the old man.

After a moment, the sheriff's breathing returned to normal and his drawn brows relaxed. He opened his eyes and got to his feet, wincing as he straightened his stiff joints. He was a tall man, and his extreme thinness made him look even taller.

"Ye can put yer gear in there," Sheriff Crawford said, indicating the rear chamber with a tilt of his head. He started for the doorway with the phial clutched in his claw-like fingers. "There are things I must do before I leave on the morrow." He paused after a couple of steps and turned his head toward Kyle. "I'm glad ye are here, lad. Yer father would be pleased that ye came back."

Gray light seeped through cracks in the shuttered window, waking Kyle from a sound sleep. He rubbed his eyes and looked around. For a moment, he wondered where he was, until he recognized the rear chamber of the sheriff's office and the man who slept on the pallet against the far wall, as still as death except for the soft rasp of his shallow breathing.

Kyle rose to his feet, taking his cloak, which had served as a blanket, with him. The air was so cold, his breath came out in a white plume. He set to work on the brazier, dropping oak chips onto the banked coals and blowing on them until a tiny blaze flickered to life. The sparse furnishings in the chamber took on shape and form in the meager light. He poured icy water into a pottery bowl to wash his face and shave the stubble on his chin. By the time he finished dressing, the bells of St. John's sounded the hour of prime, the signal for the start of a new day.

He fastened his cloak at the neck and went outside into the early morning chill. He closed the door behind him before heading for the kitchen, the only outbuilding in the garrison made of stone because of the constant risk of fire. At the sight of smoke pouring from the chimney flues, he quickened his pace in the hope the baking was already underway. There were others moving about in the courtyard, and some were walking in the same direction as he was.

When he reached the low stone building, he stepped through the open doorway into stifling heat that smelled of old grease and raw bread dough.

The kitchen was large, with a huge oven built into the side

wall and a fire pit in the center of the floor filled with glowing charcoal. Barrels of salted foodstuff stood against the back wall, along with jars of oil, crocks of grain, and other dried goods. A large pottery crock hung over the fire pit, suspended from a sturdy iron arm designed to swing the pot away from the flames to add ingredients or to cool it down for cleaning. The bottom of the crock was blackened with soot, and the number of chips around the lip suggested the pot was old, which was a silent tribute to the skill of the cook, since pottery cracked and broke if exposed to high temperatures or if cooled too quickly.

Half a dozen townsfolk hired to prepare meals for the garrison glanced up from their chores. Their faces were flushed from the heat, and their sleeveless tunics were streaked with stains. Five of them stood at a wooden table with flour to the elbow, kneading coarsely milled barley and water into a brownish dough and shaping it into small flat cakes. After baking, the chewy flatbreads would serve as a filling meal.

The sixth man tended the crock, stirring its contents with a long wooden ladle and feeding logs into the fire as needed to keep the temperature even.

Kyle walked over to the crock to peer inside. A thick porridge of hulled oats bubbled within. Its surface was studded with yellow lumps that looked like pieces of cooked apple. It smelled fresh enough, but there was no telling how old it really was. Once the liquids in a crock came to a boil, it was common for cooks to continue adding ingredients to it for days.

He looked over at the men kneading the barley dough. It might be an hour or more before the flatbreads were ready, so he settled for the porridge. He picked up a glazed clay bowl and held it out to the crock tender, who barely spared him a glance as he ladled a generous portion into the shallow receptacle.

When Kyle returned to the office, Sheriff Crawford was already dressed, with a packed leather bag on the bench by the door. The lighted brazier in the corner tempered the chill in the front room. They sat at the table and split the porridge between them. While they ate, they polished up old memories, during which neither of them made any mention of James Shaw.

When they finished eating, Kyle went to the stable to make arrangements for the groom to hitch up a wagon and bring it around to the sheriff's office. He walked down the aisle to the gelding's stall to check the water level in the bucket and to add fresh hay to the feed bin. He left the stable to go to the kitchen, where he took a couple of flatbreads, which were now ready and hot from the oven. He returned to the office and gave the flatbreads to the sheriff, who wrapped them in a scrap of cloth and put them in his bag to take on his journey.

Kyle sat at the table to wait with the old man until it was time to go, listening to him talk about his grandchildren and the things he would do whenever he recovered from his illness.

A knock on the door brought Kyle to his feet on the assumption that it was the groom with the wagon. He picked up the sheriff's bag and opened the door.

A leathery man of middle years stood just outside the office. He looked more like a farmer than a groom in his ragged-edged homespun tunic and coarse cloak. He appeared to be unarmed, except for the bulge in one of his home-tanned leather boots, where a sgian-dubh was concealed.

"I come to see Sheriff Crawford," the man said, his weathered face somber and intent.

Kyle stepped aside to let him enter and closed the door behind him. He dropped the sheriff's bag onto the bench and leaned a shoulder against the doorjamb, his arms folded across his chest.

The man tramped into the front room, bringing with him cold air and the scent of horseflesh. He doffed his gray felt cap, ruffling his shaggy brown hair in the process.

"Brodie's the name," he said to Sheriff Crawford. "There's a matter I must speak to ye about." His brown eyes shifted to Kyle before returning to the sheriff. "In private."

"I'm leaving for Kilmarnock within the hour," Sheriff Crawford said. "I don't know when I'll be back, so while I'm away, Master Shaw will stand in my place as deputy sheriff. Ye must address yer complaint to him."

Brodie twisted his felt cap with his large chapped hands. "But he be a Southron," he said, his disapproval evident in the downward turn of his mouth.

"He's no more English than ye are," Sheriff Crawford said. "Now, take yer ease there on the bench, and state yer business."

Brodie took a seat as bidden, his back ramrod stiff. "It's my Megan," he said, looking from the sheriff to Kyle and back again. "She were defiled and murdered, and it were a Southron what done it."

CHAPTER 3

Kyle moved away from the door to sit at the table where he could see Brodie's face. He searched for any sign of deceit to indicate that the man's accusation against the English might be in retaliation for some past offense. All he saw was sorrow in the crumpled forehead and the deep vertical lines between the heavy eyebrows. "Is there a witness to the deed?" he said.

"Not exactly," Brodie said. "He were seen creeping about the wood."

"Was he alone?"

"Maybe a couple of other Southrons was with him."

"Is Megan your wife?" Kyle said.

"My daughter," Brodie said, his voice strained, as though from a constricted throat.

"How old was she?" Kyle said.

"Just turned sixteen," Brodie said. "She never gave me a bit of trouble in all that time. Well, not much, anyhow. She were pretty, and the lads liked to hang around her."

"Who found her body?" Kyle said.

"A couple of youngsters out hunting," Brodie said. "They were tracking rabbit when the dog started worrying at a pile of logs. They hoped to find a warren under it, so they pulled it down to take a look." He swallowed hard to gain control of his emotions. "The dog dug at the mud, and that's when they found my Megan. One stayed put while the other came to fetch me."

"Where did he take you?"

"To a glen off the track," Brodie said. "It were deep in the wood near a burn. I'll never forget the place as long as I live. Neither will the two lads."

"Is your daughter's body still out there?"

"Nay," Brodie said. "We carried her to the chapel. The priest there sent me get the sheriff before they laid her out proper. He said he'd want to see her as we found her."

"He's right about that," Kyle said. He drummed his fingers on the table, contemplating whether to mention how it would have been more helpful if they had left the body where they found it at the actual scene of the crime, before they trampled all over the murderer's footprints or befouled other vital evidence. Recrimination was useless, since the harm was already done. He heaved a sigh of exasperation and continued with his questioning.

"When did you last see your daughter alive?" he said.

"Early on Friday," Brodie said. He made the sign of the cross on himself. "Unluckiest day of the week."

"I don't hold with such nonsense," Kyle said. "Friday is a day like any other."

"It were unlucky for my Megan," Brodie said, a haunted look on his bearded face.

Kyle lowered his brows in thought. "That was three days ago," he said. "Didn't you notice she was missing?"

Brodie bowed his head to look down and away, a sign of shame.

"Was she ever gone that long before?" Kyle said.

Brodie lifted his head, his chin thrust out in anger. "Of course not," he said. "She were a good girl."

"Then why didn't you go looking for her?" Kyle said.

Brodie's head sank again, his shoulders slumped. "I thought she run away with that Southron. She spoke of him when she thought I weren't about."

"Did she ever mention his name?"

"Nay," Brodie said. He raised his head to meet Kyle's pale blue gaze, his brown eyes cold and hard. "But I know him to look at."

Kyle turned to Sheriff Crawford. "I will need to see the girl's body as soon as possible," he said. "I'll stay here until you leave, if you wish it."

"No need for that," Sheriff Crawford said. "I'll be fine. Why don't ye take Master John along? He's good at that sort of thing."

"John Logan?" Kyle said in surprise.

"Aye," Sheriff Crawford said.

"I didn't think he was still around," Kyle said.

"He is," Sheriff Crawford said, "and still dodging lonely widows who chase after him."

Kyle smiled at the image the sheriff's words conjured in his head. "Is his shop on the same street?" he said.

The sheriff nodded. "Ye can gather him up on the way out of town," he said.

"Master Brodie," Kyle said. "I want the apothecary to examine your daughter's body. He may find something that will lead to her killer."

Brodie rose to his feet, his large fists clenched. "I already told ye who done it," he said.

"You did," Kyle said, rising from the table. "And I will keep that in mind. In the meantime, I want you to take us to where your daughter's body lies. If you need a mount, I can secure one for you."

Brodie shook his head. "I come here on Reggie," he said.

Kyle laid a gentle hand on Sheriff Crawford's forearm. The withered limb under his fingers felt as slender as a child's arm. "God speed on the road," he said. "Mend well under your daughter's care."

"Thanks," Sheriff Crawford said. "If ye need me before I come back on my own, send for me. Kilmarnock is not that distant."

"I will," Kyle said. The knowledge lay heavy on his heart that such a thing would never come to pass, for the old man would soon be gone far beyond anyone's reach.

He drew in a deep breath and released it slowly, turning his mind to the business at hand. He put on his cloak and opened the door. When he stepped outside, he came face to face with Reggie, the homeliest creature he ever laid eyes on.

Reggie was a shaggy brown hill pony with a swayed back and a Roman nose. The white blaze between its beady eyes only accentuated the convex curve of its long face. The pony greeted Kyle with laidback ears and rolling eyes. When he tried to pass, the surly beast lunged at him with its neck stretched to the limit and its mouth open to bite. He leaped aside, though he needn't have bothered, for the lead rope brought the pony's head up short.

Brodie stood in the doorway with a wide grin that transformed his sober face into one beaming with good humor. "Reggie means ye no harm," he said.

"Is that what you're riding?" Kyle said, appalled.

Brodie nodded, still grinning.

Kyle ran a skeptical eye over the shaggy brown pony before he hurried across the courtyard in search of the officer of the watch.

He found the man in the barracks with several other English soldiers. He introduced himself to the officer, and as he related the news to him about Brodie's murdered daughter, a couple of the soldiers present exchanged a furtive glance.

"If Upton is free," Kyle said, "I'd like to take him with me in case there's trouble."

The officer of the watch was a stout Englishman with gray

hair thinning at the crown and a ruddy complexion. "Upton's not on duty this morning," he said. "Shall I send him over to the sheriff's office?"

"Aye," Kyle said. "If you find him in the next few minutes, I'll be in the stable."

He went there to saddle the gelding. He was cinching the girth strap when Upton walked up to the stall.

"You summoned me?" Upton said, spreading his elbows on the half door. He appeared relaxed and at ease, unlike the last time they met.

"A couple of villagers found a girl's body at dawn this morning," Kyle said. "I want you to go out there with me." He dropped the stirrup in place and patted the gelding's sleek neck. "I could use one more man besides you."

"I'll find somebody and meet you at the sheriff's office shortly," Upton said before hastening away.

Kyle led the gelding through the half-door and climbed into the saddle. On the way up the aisle, he passed the stall with the pigeon's nest in the opening under the roof. He looked inside, but the black horse was gone. He left the stable and rode over to the office as Sheriff Crawford was coming out the door.

"With all this going on, I almost forgot to take my leave of Sir Percy," the sheriff said. "It's only a courtesy, but it's the kind of thing he expects." He started across the courtyard. After half a dozen steps, he began to wheeze.

Kyle thought Sir Percy should be the one to seek out the sheriff in deference to the old man's ill health and many years of faithful service. He kept his opinion to himself because, at that moment, Brodie walked out of the sheriff's office.

Reggie the pony stood still while Brodie clambered onto its back. The shaggy beast was short and stocky, while the man was tall and lanky. His long legs hung down on either side of the rounded belly, nearly touching the ground. He seemed completely oblivious to the absurdity of his appearance.

A moment later, Upton rode up on a rawboned bay horse. "This is Turnbull," he said, indicating the English soldier who came with him on a roan gelding. "He's all I could find on such short notice."

Turnbull was an older man with craggy features, thin lips, and dark eyes that missed nothing. "You only found me because I didn't see you coming," he said dryly.

Kyle smiled at the easy banter between the two men, who were apparently familiar enough with each other for such verbal sparring.

It was close to midmorning when Kyle led Brodie and the two English soldiers across the courtyard and out the garrison gates. They rode through town to Tradesmen's Row, turning down the crooked street to pass the cramped shops where the silversmith, the baker, the tailor, and other craftsmen plied their skills. Women carrying wicker baskets strolled from shop to shop, some buying, some merely browsing.

Kyle halted before a small stone building that glared in the sunlight from a recent coat of whitewash. An alleyway wide enough for a wagon to pass separated it from the shop next door. He dismounted and handed the reins to Upton.

He entered the front room of the apothecary shop, inhaling the fragrance of the aromatic spices inside. The heavy scent came from bunches of dried herbs dangling from the low rafters. Pots and jars of every size lined the shelves along the side walls. A brazier stood in the corner with an iron grill across the top.

A handsome man in his early fifties stood at the table, mixing a greenish paste in a stone mortar with a stone pestle. He was of average height and build, with a full head of steel gray hair. When he looked up, his clean-shaven face broke into a grin. "Well, if it isn't Kyle Shaw," he said. He wiped his hands on a scrap of cloth and came around the table to greet him.

At the back of the shop, a matronly woman in a long gray garment was rummaging through the jars and phials on the shelf in front of her. She glanced up as Kyle walked toward John. Her pleasant features exhibited only mild curiosity at their reunion before she turned away.

"John Logan," Kyle said. "You haven't changed a bit since I saw you last."

A dimple flashed in John's left cheek as he laughed. "I wish that were so," he said. "What are ye doing in town? Are ye passing through?"

"Nay," Kyle said. "Sheriff Crawford left the shire in my care as deputy until he feels up to coming back. He's probably on the way to his daughter's house in Kilmarnock as we speak."

"He told me he was leaving when he came by yesterday," John said. "Yer name never came up, though." The smile faded from his handsome face. "He should have gone away to rest long before now."

"How long has he been ill?" Kyle said.

"He started getting low the summer past," John said. "He's been going down ever since. I tried various medicaments on him, but none of them seemed to work. He says the poppy juice helps him, but all it really does is put him to sleep." He peered at Kyle intently for a moment. "Ye seem different somehow. Ye don't look so"—he groped for the right word—"so angry as ye did before."

"Nothing has changed," Kyle said, his expression grim. "Did you know my father was dead?"

"I heard," John said.

"Nobody wrote to tell me," Kyle said, with a note of reproach in his tone.

"We were afraid ye would come back," John said. "The Southrons were causing much strife in the shire at the time. It was better ye stayed put where ye were across the sea."

"Better for whom?" Kyle said, with a harsh edge to his voice.

"Better for those who suffer the most when there's trouble," John said. "Like women, children, and poor folk who stood to lose everything if the Southrons came down any harder on them. Besides, there was nothing ye or anybody else could do to bring yer father back from the dead."

"Do you know who did it?" Kyle said.

"I do not," John said. "And before ye ask, neither do I know where he was laid to rest." His green eyes narrowed in speculation. "But ye came here for a purpose, for there's news in yer face. Spit it out, lad."

Kyle told him about the dead girl. "Brodie's taking us out there now," he said.

"Can he prove the Southron did it?" John said.

"Not really," Kyle said. "He says English soldiers were seen nearby about the time the girl disappeared."

"That isn't even enough to bring a charge," John said, "much less hope it sticks."

"That's why I want you to check over the body," Kyle said. "You might find something that will tell us who did the deed."

"Give me a minute to close up shop," John said.

"Can't your apprentice take over for you?" Kyle said, tilting his head toward the woman in the rear of the shop.

"I have no apprentice," John said. He picked up a small empty jar and began to put the greenish paste from the mortar into it. When it was full, he wiped the lip with a cloth and inserted a cork stopper. "Yer compound is ready, Mistress Campbell," he said to the woman.

Mistress Campbell put the phial in her hand back on the shelf and approached the table where John was waiting for her. Her pace was unhurried, and her brown eyes never left his handsome face. She took the jar from him, brushing his fingers with her own as she did so. "Thank ye, Master John," she said. She dug half a penny from her purse and pressed it into his palm.

John walked with her to the front of the shop. After she stepped outside, he closed the door behind her and turned the key in the latch.

"Is she your lady-friend?" Kyle said.

"She's a paying customer," John said, walking back to the table.

"She fancies you," Kyle said.

"I've no time for that sort of thing," John said. He dampened the cloth and covered the remainder of the greenish paste in the mortar with it. He led Kyle through the curtained doorway to his sleeping chamber, where he buckled a leather belt around the waist of his woolen tunic and slipped the long strap of a rawhide pouch over his head. He settled the bag against his hip, picked up his dark wool cloak, and headed for the back door.

Kyle followed John outside into a lush garden rife with herbs and other flora. Pruned bushes stood in neat rows beside budding perennials. A dirt path through the center led to an open-sided shed with an old wagon on one side and a brown mule dozing on the other.

The mule perked up at their approach. John threw a faded blanket across its back, heaved a battered saddle into position, and buckled the sweat-stained girth strap. He fastened the bridle in place, after which he led the mule around the garden and up the wide alleyway with Kyle keeping pace beside him.

When they reached the street, Brodie, Upton, and Turnbull greeted John by name. Practically everyone in the shire knew John or knew of him, as no one possessed a greater knowledge of simples and ointments than John Logan.

"How's the gout?" John said to Turnbull.

"Tolerable now," Turnbull said, "thanks to those compresses you gave me."

Upton turned on Turnbull, his brow furrowed in concern.

"You never told me you were ailing," he said. "I would not have insisted you go along today."

"Don't cluck over me like a broody hen, boy," Turnbull said, his voice gruff. "I wouldn't have come if I didn't want to."

Upton seemed satisfied with the response, but he kept a close eye on Turnbull after that.

Kyle and John mounted up, and they all continued on their way. In a short while, they entered a sprawl of houses that were newer and larger than the ones in the older part of town. These dwellings, although built of wood, were nicer and set farther apart, each with a garden plot beside it. Trees were more plentiful there, and the roads were broader.

"Master Brodie," Kyle said. "Take the lead from here, if you please."

They all fell in behind Brodie, who led them down a shady lane, where women worked in their gardens, children played in the streets, and dogs barked at passing horses.

Farther along the lane, they approached a blacksmith's shop. Three saddled horses, sleek and long-limbed, stood out front tied to the rail. There was nothing unusual about horses at a blacksmith's shop, except these were stamping their hooves and shifting at the end of their reins. As Kyle drew closer, he saw the cause of their restlessness.

There was a large dog in the side yard, chained to a stout post, around which the grass had been worn down to bare dirt. The brute paced back and forth, ears pricked, muscles rippling under its tan coat. Saliva drooled from the massive jaws in its square head. Its dark eyes were fixed on the open front of the shop where the horses fidgeted at the rail. The chain rattled with each step the dog took.

Kyle recognized Macalister's dog, Fergus. It took no great stretch of memory to do so, for once seen, the great beast was hard to forget. "Hold up, Master Brodie," he said. He turned aside into the blacksmith's yard, and the others filed in behind him.

At the sight of new intruders, Fergus launched into a frenzy of barking, straining toward them at the end of the chain, choking itself on the spiked collar around its neck.

Kyle rode up to the wooden rail and halted. The barking increased the agitation of the other horses tied there. Soon, his own mount began to fret. He dismounted to lay a soothing hand on the gelding's long nose. At that moment, the low voices coming from within the shop grew sharp with anger.

He tied the reins to the rail and walked under the porch roof to listen to the heated conversation already underway. He was not surprised to see Macalister at the back of the shop beside the forge.

Macalister wore a leather apron over his homespun tunic. He held a hammer in one hand and a length of flattened steel in the other. Three armed and helmeted English soldiers stood several paces away from him, their profiles illuminated by firelight from the forge.

One of the soldiers appeared to be an officer. He pulled off his helmet and pushed back his chain mail coif to expose cropped black hair. His face was comely, shaven clean in the Norman fashion. His bearing was imperious, like that of a lordling who expected obedience without question. His body was muscular and well-built, although he was not as tall or as broad as Macalister. He did the talking, while the men-at-arms stood behind him with their hands resting purposefully on the hilts of their swords.

"Any trouble from you," the officer said, "and you'll find this shack burned to the ground and that mongrel of yours charred black in the rubble."

Macalister glared at him from under lowered brows. "If anybody harms that dog," he said, "they shall pay dearly for it."

He slammed the hammer onto the anvil in front of him to emphasize his point.

The officer blinked at the loud noise, but he stood his ground. "Do you dare threaten an officer about the king's business?" he said. "I'll drag you into court for lawburrows."

"It's not a threat," Macalister said, barely mastering his evident contempt. "Consider it a promise to any fool who does it."

The officer and Macalister glowered at each other for a full minute, their eyes locked in an unblinking stare, their booted feet braced.

One of the men-at-arms leaned toward his companion, as though to speak to him. Whatever he was about to say went unsaid, for he caught sight of Kyle barely a yard behind him. "You!" he cried, his dark brows drawn together. "What do you want?"

Kyle recognized Archer from the confrontation with him at the marketplace, and the man obviously remembered him. "Don't mind me," he said. "Continue with what you were doing."

The sound of their voices caused the officer to swing around. A flush of anger mottled his fair complexion as his cold gray eyes fastened onto Kyle, who returned his gaze. The officer's body stiffened, as though in recognition. He turned back to Macalister. "I'll be watching you," he said, jabbing the air with a blunt finger. He turned on his heel and strode from the shop with his men a step behind him.

The sight of the English soldiers emerging from under the porch roof set off another round of barking. Fergus lunged toward them, only to be jerked to a wheezing halt at the end of the chain.

The officer hung his helmet from the saddle bow. While he untied the reins from the rail, he glanced over at Brodie, who was scowling fiercely at him. His gaze slid to Upton and Turnbull as he mounted his horse. "What are the pair of you up to?" he said to them.

"Escort for the sheriff's deputy," Upton said.

"Carry on, then," the officer said. His gray eyes shifted to Kyle, who at that moment was walking out from under the porch roof. "See that the deputy minds his own business from now on." With a snort of disdain at Fergus, he wheeled his horse and started down the lane. The men-at-arms mounted up and followed along behind him.

Macalister came out from his shop and whistled at Fergus. With a downward motion of his hand, he signaled for the dog to cease barking, which it did.

Brodie stared after the departing English soldiers, his fists clenched and the rim of each nostril white and pinched over the angry set of his thin lips. The tenseness of his body caused the shaggy pony under him to shift uneasily. "That were him," he said, his voice hoarse with emotion.

"Which one?" Kyle said.

"The bareheaded one," Brodie said. "He's getting away. Ye must go after him."

"Before I accuse him or anybody else," Kyle said, "I need proof to link him to the murder. I can't arrest him just because he's English."

Brodie turned to Kyle, exasperation on his bearded face. "He and those with him were in the wood that day," he said. "Who else could have done it?"

"I'm afraid Sir Percy won't see it that way," Kyle said.

"He certainly won't," Macalister said, joining the conversation. "That's Lucky Jack Sweeney, Captain of Horse at Ayr Garrison. The two with him are Weems and Archer, his henchmen." He rested his calloused hands on the wooden rail. "In case ye don't know it, Captain Sweeney is Sir Percy's eyes and ears. It'll take a lot to induce him to convict his favorite."

"Lucky Jack appeared none too pleased with you," Kyle said.

"I think he recognized me at Ogilvy's the other night," Macalister said. "He's vexed because he cannot outright accuse me of interfering with his criminal activities without giving himself away. How could he know I was there during the raid, unless he was, too?"

Brodie sat on the shaggy pony, aloof and silent as he listened to every word of their conversation.

"Do you know for a fact Sweeney was there?" Kyle said.

"If he wasn't," Macalister said, "then somebody else rode a horse like his, with a white patch on its near front leg."

"He is about the size of the one who got away," Kyle said, recalling the blows exchanged with the leader of the raiders. "I left a bruise on him that will hurt for days. It was only by sheer luck he escaped. I guess that's why they call him Lucky Jack." He turned a puzzled frown on Macalister. "If he cannot arrest you for thwarting his unlawful pursuits, what did he want?"

"He tried to chivy me into striking him," Macalister said.

"That's a hanging offense," Kyle said.

"I know it," Macalister said. "He's a persistent fellow, so I must be on my guard around him. If he cannot get me one way, he'll try another."

Sweeney reined in as soon as the blacksmith shop was out of sight. He looked back the way he came, a thoughtful expression on his face. "They know too much," he said to Archer beside him.

"Who does?" Archer said.

"The blacksmith and that meddling deputy," Sweeney said. His gray eyes grew as hard and flat as steel. "Get rid of them."

★　★　★　★　★

Kyle and Macalister each reflected on their own thoughts after Sweeney's departure. It was Brodie who broke the silence that had fallen between them.

"That's a right fine beastie tied there in the yard," Brodie said to Macalister. "I don't think he cares much for Southrons."

"Nay," Macalister said with a laugh. "He doesn't." The amusement on his face ebbed as his gaze shifted to Upton and Turnbull.

"Does he hunt?" Brodie said.

"Better than most," Macalister said, his dark eyes on Brodie.

Kyle pulled the reins loose from the rail. "We'd best be on our way," he said, mounting the gelding. "We've much to do."

"Where are ye bound?" Macalister said.

"To Harefoot Law," Brodie said.

The mention of that particular village caused vertical lines to appear between Kyle's tawny eyebrows. He glanced over at John in time to catch the delicate sympathy on the older man's face. Of all places in the whole country, he reflected with an inward groan, it had to be Harefoot Law.

Chapter 4

Kyle drew in a deep breath and let it out in a long, soundless sigh. He knew well the way to Harefoot Law. That was where, fifteen years ago, he found happiness and the promise of a bright future. That was where, six years ago, he plumbed the depths of despair. The passage of time dulled the ache in his heart, but the last thing he wanted now was to resurrect painful memories buried so carefully and so deliberately. In the intervening years, experience had taught him that what was done, was done, and no amount of brooding or gnashing his teeth could ever change it.

He reminded himself that this undertaking was not about him. It was about a dead girl whose blood cried out for justice. Her murderer must be caught and hanged, and the matter laid to rest, as his own would never be. It seemed fitting to him that the newly bereaved father should be the one to lead them to that place of sorrow. "Master Brodie, if you please," he said, with a sweep of his hand toward the lane.

They left the town of Ayr behind them, riding southward toward Alloway across undulating sand dunes. When they came to the River Doon, they turned inland to follow its meandering course upriver. Sandy hillocks gave way to rolling grassland. After several miles, the forest closed in around them. The river became narrower and darker, winding its way through the trees.

Before long, they reached a ford in the river and crossed over to the village on the other side. The five-mile journey took less time than Kyle remembered, perhaps owing in part to his reluctance to get there.

Harefoot Law was more of a settlement than a village. A scant dozen weather-beaten timber houses lined either side of a dirt lane. Light from the morning sun showed the decay and neglect that had gnawed at the humble dwellings over the years.

An ivy-covered chapel with a peaked slate roof stood on a rise at the end of the lane. A rectangular stained-glass window beside the arched front door looked out over the village. A graveyard lay to the right, with ancient headstones jutting at odd angles from hallowed ground.

Kyle slowed the gelding to a walk, falling in behind the others as they rode up the dirt lane. His gaze swept the faces of the villagers around him, none of whom looked even vaguely familiar. Women paused at their chores, and small children stopped playing to stare openly with wary eyes. A couple of old men sitting on a fallen log ignored the intrusion and continued their game of knucklebones.

Kyle halted in front of the chapel and slid to the ground. "Wait here," he said to Upton and Turnbull. He signaled for Brodie and John to dismount and follow him through the arched front door.

Upton gathered up the reins, and with a quiet word to Turnbull, he led their mounts over to the graveyard to graze.

The interior of the chapel was cold after the warmth of the sun outside. Light poured in through the single window, illuminating four stone walls bereft of furnishings. The polished granite altar at the far end was bare, with a solitary candle burning beside it. Smoke from cheap tallow hung in the air, trapped against the wood-beamed ceiling.

An old priest with a kindly face and tonsured gray hair came out from behind the altar. The brown robe on his wiry frame flapped about his ankles as he shambled toward them on sandaled feet. He greeted John and Brodie by name. When he drew near to them, he gave Kyle a long, hard look.

"Is that ye, Master Kyle, in the flesh?" the old priest said, as though doubting his own eyes.

"The prodigal returns at last, Father Ian," Kyle said. His smile faded when he noticed the purple and yellow blotch over the old priest's right eyebrow. "How came you by your injury?"

Father Ian raised a gnarled hand to the bruise on his forehead. "This is nothing compared to what is lost," he said. "Night before last, I heard a noise in the chapel. I went to see what it was and stumbled upon a pair of thieves. Before I could cry out for help, they overcame me. By the time my wits came back, the holy monstrance was gone. The gold chalice was missing from the altar and so was the ivory crucifix over it. I know those were taken for their value, but they also took the altar cloth. I admit it was fine, with some kind of ivy design embroidered in gold thread along the border, but it would hardly fetch half a penny at market." He turned to Kyle, perplexity on his lined face. "What could they possibly want with the altar cloth?"

"Perhaps they used it to carry off the items they stole," Kyle said.

"Of course," Father Ian said. "That makes sense."

Kyle looked at the old priest with concern. "Are you now recovered?" he said.

"Aye," Father Ian said. "Except for the occasional ache in my head."

"Perhaps Master John can give you something for that," Kyle said, turning to John, who nodded his concurrence with the suggestion.

Father Ian waved aside the offer with his hand. "Not necessary," he said. "It only bothers me when I bend down, so I don't bend if I can help it."

"Did you get a look at the thieves?" Kyle said.

Father Ian shook his head. "It was dark, and their hoods were drawn," he said. "I only recall that one was bigger than the other." His gaze shifted from Kyle to Brodie and back again. "But ye didn't ride all this way to hear me prattle on about my woes. Come, the girl lies on a bier through there." He indicated the dark curtain that covered an opening in the wall behind the altar.

Brodie took a step toward the curtain, but Father Ian laid a hand on his arm.

"It's best if ye stay here for now," the old priest said gently. "Let these men do what must be done."

Brodie hesitated for the space of a heartbeat before turning away without a word. He went over to kneel before the altar on the cold flagstone floor. He bowed his head, his felt cap crushed between his clasped hands.

Father Ian led the others behind the altar. He thrust the curtain aside to enter the passageway, beyond which lay his sleeping chamber at the rear.

The trestle table that served as a bier stood against the stone wall on one side of the passageway. The illumination there was poor, yet Kyle clearly saw the delineation of a body under the black pall draped over it. The figure beneath the cloth was slight, larger than a child, but smaller than a full-grown woman.

Father Ian approached the makeshift bier and removed the black cloth from over the body, exposing the gray wool homespun shift soiled with patches of dried mud and torn at the neck. Her long, wavy red hair was matted with twigs and dried leaves. A soft leather shoe clung to one foot, while the other foot was bare and smudged with dirt. "She is exactly as she was found," he said.

Kyle gazed down at the dead girl's face. She was so young, so still, like a white marble statue. Only the stippling of purple bruises around her mouth marred the beauty of her features.

"I'll need more light to do a proper job of this," John said.

While Father Ian went to fetch a lantern, John drew the dagger from the sheath at his waist and slit the dead girl's shift from neck to knees.

Kyle averted his eyes out of respect for the girl's dignity. The blade was sharp, and the preparatory work took less than a minute.

"She's ready now," John said.

Kyle looked up to see the girl's garment hanging down on either side of the bier. For propriety within the chapel walls, long narrow strips of linen covered her breasts and pubes.

John removed the single shoe from her foot and let it drop to the flagstone floor.

Kyle bent down to retrieve the shoe. "I shall hang onto this," he said, tucking it into the pouch at his side. "My guess is that its mate will be found where she was buried."

Father Ian returned with a lighted lantern and placed it at the head of the bier.

Kyle and the old priest watched in silence as John picked up the lantern and began his examination.

He passed the light slowly over the entire length of the girl's body, scrutinizing every visible part of it. He pulled back her lips to peer into her mouth. He inspected the fingernails on each of her hands. He turned her body to the side to examine the back of her head, her spine, her buttocks, and the back of her thighs. He noted the slight swelling below her navel. When he finished, he straightened up and set the lantern on the bier.

He cleared his throat, his brow furrowed in concentration. "The recent cold weather contributed greatly to her preservation," he said, "but from what I can tell, she's been dead no more than three days. The purple staining on her back, her buttocks, and under her thighs shows where the blood has settled.

That means she lay on her back for some time after she died. There is no discoloration of the tongue, so she wasn't poisoned."

He turned the girl's body to expose the dried blood in the tangle of hair at the back of her head. "These cuts on her scalp suggest she was pushed or thrown backwards hard onto stony ground," he said. "The impact was forceful enough to stun her, but not sufficient to kill her."

He gently returned her body to supine position. He leaned forward to cup his left hand over her mouth, clamping his thumb under her lower jaw. In doing so, the fleshy part of his outer palm pressed against her nose. "Her assailant put his hand, like so, to keep her from crying out," he said. "See how my fingers line up with the bruises here. The bluish tinge around her lips indicates she died from suffocation."

He then lifted the girl's left hand to display her fingers. "I found scrapings under three of her nails that look like skin. Since there are no marks on her own body, it appears she scratched someone shortly before she died, likely the person who attacked her."

He restored her hand to its place alongside her thigh. "I cannot say for certain that she was violated, as Brodie claims," he said, "but her assailant may well have done so, while she lay helpless in his grasp. The fact that he tried to keep her quiet suggests what he was doing was shameful and that he feared discovery." For a long moment, he gazed down in silence at her ashen face, as though trying to make up his mind about something.

Kyle mulled over John's findings thus far without the slightest doubt as to the truth of every word. He was well acquainted with the depths of depravity to which a man could sink, although not from personal experience, thank God. He hired out his sword in a foreign land in order to leave behind him reminders of his past life. It was no surprise to learn that others did the same, although many for darker reasons than his own. The mercenary service seemed to attract the unsavory element of society: footpads, debtors, murderers, thieves, and others fleeing from the law. The worst of the lot, in his opinion, were the rapists, who preyed on women and who bragged about their exploits round the campfires at night.

"There's more," John said with gravity.

The simple statement brought Kyle back to the present. He watched with keen interest as John held his open hand over the girl's belly without touching her skin. The distension there, although negligible, looked out of place on her slender form.

"She appears to be with child," John said.

Father Ian's face registered his surprise, but he quickly recovered his composure.

"Are you sure?" Kyle said.

"As sure as I can be without cutting her open," John said. He glanced from Kyle to Father Ian and back again. "I will do so, if I must."

Kyle pondered whether the girl's pregnancy was integral to her murder. "I don't think that will be necessary," he said after a moment.

John looked relieved to hear it, and so did Father Ian.

"How far along was she?" Kyle said.

"I would guess about four months," John said.

"And you are certain she was smothered?" Kyle said.

"I am," John said. "It might have happened by mistake, but it could have been done on purpose."

"So," Kyle said, "we're looking for a man with scratches somewhere on his body."

"My guess would be the upper body," John said, "like the face or neck, or even the chest or forearms."

"Is there anything further?" Kyle said.

"Not that I can see," John said. "My examination is complete, with both ye and Father Ian to bear witness. The women may now prepare the body for burial."

"When the village women see that girl's belly," Kyle said, "they will know her condition. There is no need to add shame to the Brodie family's sadness and loss. I would suggest that only the girl's mother be allowed to wash and dress her body."

"Her mother died some years ago," Father Ian said. "There is an elder sister who can render that service, though."

"Will you see to it that no one but she tends to those final duties, then?" Kyle said to Father Ian.

"I will," Father Ian said. He stepped up to the bier to cover the girl's body with the black cloth, after which he led them back into the chapel.

Brodie was still on his knees before the altar. There was a woman kneeling beside him, with a thin shawl on her head. The two of them climbed to their feet when they saw Kyle, John, and Father Ian approaching.

The woman looked about seventeen years of age. Her brown hair was bound in a single braid pulled forward over her shoulder and tied at the end with a black ribbon. The raw edge of her homespun woolen tunic reached only to her calves, which made her look taller than she was. Grief clouded her plain features, which bore a remarkable resemblance to Brodie's. She was lanky and big-boned like him, but in a softer, more feminine way.

"I am Esa," she said in response to Kyle's questioning gaze. "Megan is, or rather was, my sister."

"What did ye find out?" Brodie said, looking from John to Kyle and back again, anticipation on his bearded face.

Esa laced her fingers together in the classic pose of waiting. She hardly seemed the patient type, though, with her bold stare and the hint of challenge in her lively brown eyes.

Esa's hands, like her father's, were large and capable, well suited to hard work as a farmer's daughter, and, Kyle noticed, of a size to fit the pattern of bruises on Megan's face. Then again, so were her father's and possibly that of every other man in the shire. He ceased his idle ruminations to relate to them an abbreviated version of John's findings. "I'm sorry," he said when he finished.

The news of his daughter's pregnancy brought a look of stunned disbelief to Brodie's face. Except for clenching his fists, he stood motionless, frozen with shock, as though unable to take it in. "It cannot be so," he said in a hoarse whisper. "Ye must be mistaken."

"Father Ian can bear witness to the truth of it," John said.

After a moment, Brodie's countenance began to darken. Anger and frustration became evident in his frowning brow and the tightening around his eyes.

Throughout Kyle's narrative, Esa's expression remained unchanged. Her plain features showed neither dismay nor surprise, only sadness.

Kyle fixed his eyes on her for several heartbeats, peering closely at her. She gave no outward sign of distress under his scrutiny other than the tightening of her laced fingers, noticeable only because of the sudden whitening of her knuckles. It was enough to persuade him that she knew something about her sister's demise, and he was determined to find out what it was. In his experience, the direct approach was the most effective, if not always the most well received.

"How long have you known about Megan's condition?" he said. He spoke to her quietly, as he would to a wild creature ready to bolt at any instant.

A fleeting shadow of anguish and despair passed over Esa's face. "What makes ye think I were privy to her secrets?" she said, her manner defensive.

"Tell me about her," Kyle said, changing his approach. "What was she like?"

"There's not much to say, really," Esa said. "She were pretty, and all of the lads around here were keen on her."

"Did she favor one above the other?" Kyle said.

"Not really," Esa said. "She liked them all."

"Can you think of anyone who wished to do her an injury?"

"Nay, I cannot," she said, averting her eyes.

"What about the English soldier who came to see her?"

Esa shot an uneasy glance at her father before she answered. "She thought he were handsome," she said. "She liked his attentions."

"A little too much, it seems," Brodie said with suppressed anger.

"If you think of anything that might be helpful," Kyle said to Esa, "send word to me at Ayr Garrison. You should know that Father Ian will see to it that only you are to wash and dress your sister for burial."

"Thank ye for that, at least," Esa said.

Kyle was about to turn away when he thought of something else. "Who are those lads you say were keen on her?"

"Tullick and the two louts who hang about with him," Esa said, her disapproval obvious in the tightness around her mouth. "Ye can find them working in the field, unless they found a way to get out of it."

"Where is the field?" Kyle said.

"I can take ye there," Brodie said before Esa could respond.

"I'd like that," Kyle said, "but first, it is important that I see where your daughter's body was found. Can you fetch the lad who brought you out there?"

"I know the way," Brodie said.

"I want to talk to him about it," Kyle said.

"I'll see if I can find him, then," Brodie said. He turned on his heel and hurried toward the arched front door, as though eager to be gone from the chapel and the sorrow it held for him.

Kyle followed Brodie outside, leaving John and Father Ian in the chapel with Esa. He walked around to the graveyard and picked his way through the maze of tombstones.

He went over to a neglected corner on the far side of the burial grounds. The late morning sun behind him cast his shadow across a pair of graves set close together, one of average size and the other smaller, both overgrown with weeds. The stone marker at the head of each plot was made of brown granite streaked with beige and red, with the occupant's name and date of death chiseled into it.

He stood there in silence, letting the years slide backwards over his head. Forgotten memories rushed at him from the recesses of his mind. With a sigh of resignation, he lowered himself to one knee and began to pull out the weeds. No matter how far he went or how long he stayed away, the guilt and shame of past sins always seemed to find him. When he finished clearing both plots, he bowed his head, his eyes on the larger grave.

"I still miss ye, Ada Munro," he said, unaware of lapsing into the accent of his youth. His gaze shifted to the smaller grave. "Rest in peace, Jamie boy. Forgive me, the both of ye."

He climbed to his feet and was swatting the dirt from his leggings when Father Ian walked up to stand beside him.

"It's a sad business," Father Ian said, shaking his head. "Very sad, indeed."

"What is?" Kyle said, giving him a sharp glance.

"Brodie's daughter," Father Ian said. "Do ye think the Southrons did it, like Brodie claims?"

"It's early days yet," Kyle said, resting his hand on the hilt of his sword.

The old priest fingered the frayed end of the hemp rope binding his spare waist, his eyes on the newly weeded gravesites.

"Why did ye come back now, of all times?" he said.

"Sheriff Crawford asked me to come," Kyle said. "I didn't know he was ailing until after I got here."

"The shire is ailing worse than Sheriff Crawford. Things go on that folks can only whisper about in private and with care as to who they whisper them."

The piercing gaze the old priest leveled at him brought a smile to Kyle's lips. "I'm no spy for the English," he said, "if that's what you think."

"The thought never crossed my mind for an instant," Father Ian said with a snort of derision. "Otherwise, I would not speak to ye of such things."

They started walking back to the chapel to await Brodie's return.

"Whatever happened to old man Mackenzie?" Kyle said, adjusting his stride to match the old priest's shorter step. "I didn't see him or his sister in the village. Come to think of it, I didn't see anybody I knew from when I used to live around here."

"Mackenzie quit the shire years ago, like so many others," Father Ian said. "Between the raids and the taxes, he lost everything. When his sister died, he gave her a decent burial before he moved on alone to look for a safer place to start over. He won't find it in this country, not as long as Edward of England keeps his boot on our neck." He shook his head, his thin lips pressed together in disgust. "I hoped things would improve when Sir Percy came to Ayr Garrison last year. It turns out he's no better than the others."

"Why so?" Kyle said, glancing over at the old priest.

"Not a month ago, young Gib from this village saw four soldiers from the garrison hang a shepherd without cause. It was done under the cover of darkness, so I took it to be an act of spite. I brought the matter to Sir Percy's attention, even naming the Southrons who did the deed. When Sir Percy learned that the eyewitness was an underage boy of Scots descent, he dropped the charges and dismissed the case. He refused, so he said, to dignify such blatant prejudice against the English with a hearing."

"Did you complain to the justiciar?"

"Of course not," Father Ian said, bristling with righteous indignation. "He's a Southron, just like Sir Percy. Rather than wasting good parchment, I took up a collection for the shepherd's widow. She needed that more than the empty promise of a fair hearing she would never get."

"I still would have informed the justiciar about it," Kyle said. "He has the ear of the English king, as you know."

"And the heart of a snake," Father Ian said. He spat on the ground, taking care to miss the burial plot beside him. "William de Ormesby may be Justiciar of Scotland, but that devil's spawn has no interest in justice. Scotsmen of rank and position have already been made to swear the oath of fealty to Edward of England. Ormesby wants men of lesser status to do the same, to bring them to heel since there are a greater number of them. God help the wretch who shows the slightest bit of reluctance to comply with his demands. The shire is crawling with bands of Southrons with leave to coerce and bully as they please. If that fails to work, then there are fines and sequestering. Some have even been outlawed and hanged." He laced his fingers together in a semblance of prayer as he walked. "Our plight may sound hopeless, but rest assured we do have friends in high places."

"Amen to that," Kyle said, assuming the old priest was referring to God and the saints in heaven. "For one so isolated, you are well informed as to the goings-on in the shire."

"That I am," Father Ian said, "thanks to the holy brothers who bring news whenever they pass this way. They call themselves black friars for the color of their robes."

Kyle thought no more about it, since it was not unusual for members of the clergy to make the rounds of out-of-the-way chapels to atone for serious sins in their past before taking the cowl.

Kyle and Father Ian rounded the front corner of the chapel to find Brodie standing by the arched door talking with two boys. On the ground beside them lay a brown and white dog, a mongrel with the long nose and floppy ears of a kennet hound and the square shape and wiry hair of a terrier.

The boys appeared to be related, for they shared the same ruddy complexion and wide blue eyes. Their bodies were thin but sturdy under their woolen tunics. The dark smudge of peach fuzz on the shorter youth's upper lip put him at twelve or thirteen years of age, whereas the other boy, though slightly taller, looked no older than ten.

"This here is Ewan," Brodie said, indicating the shorter, older boy. "He's the one who fetched me after he found my girl in the wood." He pointed at the other boy. "That is his brother, Gib."

"I want to find out who hurt Megan," Kyle said to the boys. "I need your help to do that. Can I count on you?"

The boys exchanged a glance before nodding their heads in agreement.

"Let us away, then," Kyle said. He took the reins from Upton and mounted the gelding.

Upton and Turnbull climbed into their saddles.

"You carry Ewan," Kyle said to Upton. "Turnbull can take Gib. That way, we'll make better time getting there and back."

Upton leaned down to offer a hand to Ewan, who grasped his wrist and scrambled up behind him. Turnbull helped Gib onto the back of his mount.

Both boys clung to the soldiers like burrs, and the grins on their youthful faces suggested that their dislike of the English took second place to their first chance to ride a full-sized horse, as opposed to the smaller ponies indigenous to Scotland. A valid excuse for shirking a day's work only added to their joy.

At a word from Ewan, Upton started for the trees on the eastward side of the village. Turnbull followed after him, with the mongrel dog trotting close behind the horses.

Kyle waited for Brodie and John to mount up before the three of them set out after the others.

About half a mile along the trail, Brodie urged his pony to overtake Upton, who rode at the head of the group. "Be sure to keep to the deer track up ahead," he said. "I'd hate to tell Ewan's mam her son's not coming back." He waved a hand at the rotted grass and muck on either side of them. "We call that a quagmire. Hungry for flesh, it is. Watch yer step, or it'll suck ye down."

Upton slowed his horse to let Brodie pass him on the cramped path, apparently now content to follow at a more cautious pace. He kept his face forward to avoid Turnbull's grinning countenance.

They rode through the heavily wooded forest, keeping to threadlike paths in tangled underbrush that barely stood aside to let them pass. The footing was slippery from moss and decayed forest detritus. They skirted standing pools of murky water in search of more solid footing on higher ground.

After a while, they left the cool shadows of the dense woodland behind to enter a secluded glen near the river. Sunlight filtered through the sparse branches overhead. Patches of clover grew up through the dried brown grass on open ground that sloped gently down to the water's edge. It was a peaceful haven, serene and bright, except for the dark oblong of raw earth that scarred the verdant spring growth.

"Stay back while I look for sign," Kyle said as they all reined in.

He dismounted and walked forward to examine the ground around the shallow grave. The mud was still soft from the recent rain, crisscrossed with hoof and paw marks from deer, rabbit, and other creatures that watered there. He frowned down at the large boot prints, which he identified as Brodie's, and the smaller imprints belonging to the two boys.

"If the murderer left any tracks," he said, "they're gone now." He walked over to where Ewan sat perched on the rump of Upton's horse. "Tell me exactly what you did when you first got here this morning."

"Gib and me, we watched for a while," Ewan said. "We hoped some critter would come along for water, but nothing did. We were fixing to go deeper into the wood when the dog took to nosing about them logs by the burn." He pointed at the jumble of half-rotted limbs along the bank of the creek, left there during the rainy season when the water ran high.

As though on cue, the mongrel dog trotted forward to sniff at the deadwood, cocking a leg at each piece to leave its mark on it.

"I thought there might be a clutch of rabbit under there," Ewan said. "Gib and me, we broke down the pile to take a look. The dog got to digging in the mud, and that's when we found her." He fell silent, as though at the end of his tale.

"What did you do next?" Kyle said.

"I went to fetch Master Brodie," Ewan said.

"How did you know it was Megan?" Kyle said.

"I recognized her," Ewan said.

"Even with all that mud on her?"

"She were under a mantle."

"What mantle?"

"The mantle she were wrapped in."

"Did you remove the mantle?"

"Only enough to see what was under it."

"That's when you saw her face?"

"Her hair," Ewan said. "I just saw her hair."

"You recognized her by her hair?"

Ewan nodded. "It were long and silky," he said, "and of a color that flamed in the sunlight."

Kyle caught the wistful expression on Ewan's face. Despite the boy's tender age, he was evidently old enough to appreciate the things that enhance a woman's beauty, even a child-woman like Megan. "Then what did you do?" he said.

"I told Gib to stay put," Ewan said, "while I went for Master Brodie."

"You weren't afraid," Kyle said, turning to Gib, "that the murderer might come back and find you here?"

The expression on Gib's face indicated that the possibility never even entered his mind.

"It would not trouble Gib if he did," Ewan said, speaking up in his brother's defense. "He once seen the Southrons hang a man from a tree in the dead of night, and they never knew he were there watching."

Kyle nodded absently at Ewan, his mind already moving to another matter. He picked up a stick and poked around the soft dirt within the shallow grave. After a moment, he tossed the stick aside. He lifted up each piece of deadwood to look under it. Not finding what he was looking for, he trod the perimeter of the glen, sweeping the underbrush aside here and there to peer at the exposed ground beneath. He walked to the open center, his tawny eyebrows drawn.

"It's not here," he said.

"What's not here?" Brodie said.

Kyle removed the girl's shoe from his pouch. "The mate to this," he said. "As your daughter lay on the bier, she wore but one shoe. Did you perhaps lose the other while carrying her body to the chapel?"

"Ewan and Gib walked behind me the whole time," Brodie said. "They would have seen the shoe fall and surely would have picked it up."

Kyle paced the length of glen, frowning over something Ewan had told him a moment before. "How came you to see only Megan's hair?" he said to Ewan. "Was not her face visible when you laid back the mantle?"

"Nay," Ewan said. "Just her hair."

Kyle's gaze settled upon Brodie perched upon the shaggy pony. "When you removed your daughter from the grave," he said, "what position was she in?"

"What do ye mean?" Brodie said dubiously.

"Was she lying on her back?" Kyle said. "Or was she on her side, or maybe even on her face?"

Brodie's brown eyes strayed to Ewan and Gib, who were watching him. "I think she were on her face," he said, his manner hesitant. Encouraged by nods from both boys, who had borne witness to the disinterment, he added with more confidence, "Aye, she were face down, with her cloak wrapped about her."

Kyle then addressed John. "During your examination of the girl's body," he said, "did you only find blood settled along her back?"

"I did find it so," John said. "Blood drains to the body's lowest point after death. From the amount of discoloration I found along her lower body, she must have lain on her back for at least a full day after her death."

"So," Kyle said, "she was put in the ground face downward, with one shoe on and the other nowhere in the vicinity. That suggests to me she was buried in haste, with little care as to her placement in the grave. However, more importantly, it suggests she was killed elsewhere, and her body later moved here for burial."

"That Southron tried to hide his foul deed," Brodie said sullenly.

"I wonder," Kyle said, gnawing on his lower lip. "I doubt he would take the time to wrap her in her mantle and dig a grave to lay her in. He would likely dispose of her body as quickly as possible, perhaps dumping it deep in the woods for wolves to consume, or else sinking it in a bog, of which there are many around here."

He held up the girl's shoe for Ewan and Gib to see. "I need to find Megan's other shoe," he said. "You boys are familiar with these woods, so I want you to keep a sharp eye out for it on your hunting forays. If you find the shoe, mark the location and get word to me right away. I want to see the place with my own eyes, for that might be the very spot where she was killed, and there might be something there to lead to her killer. Will you do that?"

"Aye," the boys said in unison.

With the business at hand finished, Kyle mounted the gelding, and they all started back to Harefoot Law. Brodie led the way at a brisk pace, as though anxious to put the glen far behind him.

When they reached the village, Ewan and Gib slid from the backs of the horses to the ground. Their faces were wreathed in smiles as they scurried away together.

"Do ye still want to go to the field?" Brodie said.

"I do," Kyle said.

Brodie turned the shaggy pony's head northward, and Kyle, John, and the two English soldiers followed him through the woods. After wending their way through the trees for a short while, they came out into an open stretch of land. Thorny brambles and briars dominated the landscape. Several large parcels of ground that had been cleared were already striped from the plow in preparation for spring planting.

Kyle and the others advanced into the field behind Brodie, who rode over to where able-bodied men from the village were chopping at shrubs and digging up roots to clear more usable ground. Several children were busy dragging the uprooted fronds over to a huge pile for later burning.

Brodie exchanged a greeting with the nearest villager, who doffed his cap and expressed a word of sympathy on the loss of his daughter. He acknowledged the man with a nod before he called out to Tullick and two other young men who answered to the names of Alex and Will. "Come hither," he said, his voice raised. "I'm wanting a word with ye."

Tullick was a well-built young man with dark hair and dark eyes. His bearded features were regular, neither handsome nor plain. Alex was short and heavyset, with limp red hair and a straggly reddish beard. Will was tall and thin, with a pallid complexion and a pronounced overbite. All three wore belted tunics that reached their knees, with their sleeves rolled back to the elbow. None of them looked older than twenty.

"I'm sorry about Megan, Master Brodie," Tullick said, his booted foot on the wing of his spade, ready to shove the blade into the earth. "As ye can see, I've work to do here and cannot stop to chat just now."

A man with a salt-and-pepper beard and gray hair at his temples laughed aloud. "That never bothered ye before," he said. His comment elicited a round of guffaws from the men around him.

Tullick ignored the jibe. "Another day, perhaps," he said. He leaned his weight on the spade and pushed down on the wooden handle to pry a tough rootstock from the dirt.

"I'm not here for a chin-wag," Brodie said. "Deputy Sheriff come out this way on business. He wants to question ye some."

Every man in the field paused at his labors, his eyes on Tullick, Alex, and Will, as though to see what they would do.

CHAPTER 5

Tullick exchanged a glance with Will and Alex before he propped the handle of the spade on his shoulder. Alex and Will did the same, and all three headed over to where Kyle sat on the sorrel gelding beside Brodie. Their pace was slow, and the concern on their faces at being called to account by a man of law was understandable. None of the three seemed unduly alarmed, though, as they shuffled to a halt a couple of yards away.

Kyle noted that each of the three young men bore superficial grazes on his forearms, likely from briar thorns. He saw nothing, though, that resembled the distinctive pattern of fingernails raked across bare skin. He fixed his gaze on the most likely of the trio to hold a female's interest.

"How well did you know Megan?" he said to Tullick.

"Well enough to bid her the time of day," Tullick said. "Master Brodie called me now and then to help him with the heavy work on the farm. She were there most times I went." His dark eyes shifted to Brodie and back to Kyle. "I cannot believe she's really gone." The sadness on his face turned to hatred in a single heartbeat. "It were that Southron's fault."

"Did you see him kill her?" Kyle said.

"Nay," Tullick said, "but he come out this way three days past, him and his fine dark horse. I saw that well enough."

"Do you know him by name?" Kyle said.

"Lucky Jack, they call him," Tullick said, his upper lip curled in contempt.

Kyle next questioned Alex and Will. He learned that they, too, worked for Brodie on occasion. They also claimed a passing acquaintance with Megan, and they saw Jack Sweeney in the vicinity around the time she disappeared.

During Kyle's interrogation of Tullick, Alex, and Will, the village men in the field had drawn close to listen. For them, it was a welcome diversion in their mundane existence. Kyle took advantage of their proximity to make an announcement.

"I shall call Lucky Jack Sweeney to account for his movements on Friday," he said to the lot of them. "In the meantime, be on the watch for any amongst you who takes flight, for he may be the murderer seeking to escape the noose. Send word immediately to me at the garrison so I may bring the hounds to hunt him down."

The village men glanced at one another, nodding their accord with Kyle's request. They might spurn English law, but Megan was one of their own, which made it unlikely any of them would shield the man who killed her.

By that time, the sun was high overhead. The village men abandoned the field, carrying their tools with them as they headed to their houses for their midday meal. Brodie went along with them to join Esa at the chapel, while Kyle, John, Upton, and Turnbull started back to town.

About halfway to Alloway, Kyle gave in to a compulsion to turn off the beaten track. The others followed as he rode up the northward path through a belt of trees.

John gave Kyle a sidelong glance. "It's still there," he said, "if that's what ye might be wondering."

"How do you know?" Kyle said, his eyes on the trail ahead.

"I've seen it," John said.

Kyle glanced at the older man riding beside him. "Why?" he said, intrigued.

"It was on my way to the village beyond it," John said.

They left the trees behind to enter open country. The land stretched out before them on an almost level course, bathed in sunlight, rich with spring clover. Off in the distance, a boy with a black and white dog tended a sizeable flock of sheep.

Two hundred yards ahead of them in the middle of a ploughed field stood a small cottage, which looked like a rectangular blot of gray stone and thatch on the pristine landscape. A fat sow and half a dozen goats roamed within a wood-rail fenced enclosure next to the dwelling. The thread of white smoke rising from the chimney stood out against the expanse of blue sky.

"Who lives there now?" Kyle said, reining in.

John eased the mule up beside him. "A young couple in need of a home," he said.

"I see they fixed the roof," Kyle said.

"It needed fixing," John said.

Kyle drew in a deep breath, filling his lungs with fresh air. "I always liked it out here," he said, looking around him. "It's so peaceful."

"It reminds me of home," Upton said with a heavy sigh.

Kyle turned to look at the young English soldier. "Where are you from?"

"Cumbria," Upton said.

"Which part?" Kyle said.

"West of Carlisle." Upton tilted his head at the other English soldier. "Turnbull was a family retainer at the manor there. Father insisted I take him along for protection." He snorted affably. "If anybody needs protecting, it's Turnbull. The old relic's getting on a bit now, and he's far too ancient to be chasing round after me."

Turnbull rolled his eyes to the heavens, as though in mute appeal for patience.

"You hail from border country, then," Kyle said.

"I do, indeed," Upton said.

Kyle smiled. "That explains your tolerance of us Scots," he said.

"Border folk try not to get involved in disputes between kingdoms," Upton said. "Too many of us have kith and kin on both sides."

"Ayr is quite a distance from Carlisle," Kyle said. "How came you to be posted at that garrison?"

"The luck of the draw, I suppose," Upton said. "I've been there for nearly a year now."

"Then you know more of what goes on than I," Kyle said. "Has anyone in the barracks ever missed curfew?"

"Quite a few," Upton said with a laugh, "and often, too. Sometimes they come back in the morning. Sometimes they don't. Sometimes only their horse shows up at the gate." He shrugged his shoulders. "It does no good to ask what happened to the rider, because nobody seems to know. I've learned the hard way that sniffing up the wrong tree can earn a man a bruise or two."

"It sounds like discipline is lax there," Kyle said. Such an environment, in his opinion, was ideal for English soldiers to raid the countryside at night, only to return in the wee hours without ever being missed and no questions asked. "I counted forty-odd horses in the stable, but there must be more men than that billeted in the barracks. How many would you say?"

"About ninety or so," Upton said. "It's hard to get an exact count with all the comings and goings from other garrisons. It seems men are always transferring in or out."

Kyle mulled over Upton's words, his eyes on the pastoral scene spread out before him. As he looked on, four mounted English soldiers burst from the trees along the far side of the open field, driving ahead of them a skittish cow and a couple of ewes.

The shepherd boy in the field spotted the soldiers coming toward him. Their westward course, as they headed toward Ayr, would take them straight through the middle of his flock, which would scatter the sheep and make it difficult to separate out the interloping ewes.

The boy whistled to the dog and made a sweeping motion with his arm. The dog circled around behind the sheep and began nipping at the backs of their legs, racing back and forth until the entire flock was on the move. The dog harried the sheep until the whole lot shifted closer to the cottage, thus taking them out of the path of the oncoming soldiers.

"That's a well-trained dog," Kyle said with appreciation.

"The boy didn't do so badly, either," Turnbull said, interjecting one of his infrequent comments.

"It looks like somebody just paid their rent," Upton said.

"I doubt it was collected gently," John said with a sigh.

Upton shaded his eyes from the glare of the sun with his hand. "The fellow in the lead sits his horse like Sweeney from the garrison," he said. His upper lip twitched in disgust. "He and those bullies with him enjoy their work a little too much to suit me."

"Do you recognize the others?" Kyle said.

"That's Inchcape on the black horse," Upton said. "The two others must be Weems and Archer. Sweeney hardly goes anywhere without them."

"That's a magnificent black," Kyle said, his eyes on Inchcape's horse in the distance. "It looks a lot like the one in that stall when I first met you."

"It is the same horse," Upton said.

Kyle turned the full brunt of his stare on Upton. "If you don't mind my asking," he said, "exactly what were you doing in the black's stall that day?" He posed the question without really expecting an answer.

"I was checking for mud," Upton said, his gaze steady and clear.

Kyle could tell Upton was speaking the truth, but the response he received was nonetheless baffling. "Why?" he said.

"To see if Inchcape had ridden the black the night before," Upton said. "It rained earlier, you see, and the road was muddy."

"And did he?"

"He must have done," Upton said. "Its legs and belly were crusted with dirt, as I suspected."

Kyle peered more closely at Upton, wondering at the young man's interest in the nocturnal activities of a fellow soldier. "Men will often venture forth in inclement weather for a woman's favors," he said.

"I doubt Inchcape did that," Upton said with a grin, "seeing as how she would likely charge him twice the usual fee. He's no prize, even on a good day."

John shifted in the saddle, as though anxious to be away. "Why don't ye go on to town," he said to Kyle. "I'll be along later. I cannot rest until I see what harm those Southrons might have wrought on those folks yonder."

"It isn't that far out of our way," Kyle said. "We'll tag along with you."

John led the way across the grassy field, lifting a hand to wave at the shepherd boy, who reciprocated in kind.

They rode into the woods and followed a well-used track through the trees. When they came to a shallow creek, they splashed through ankle-deep water to enter the small village ahead of them.

The villagers there were gathered around an old woman who sat on the ground in front of one of the houses. Wiry gray hair stuck out from beneath her off-white cap, and her homespun tunic was bunched up around her chubby knees. She was rocking back and forth, clutching to her ample bosom the head of a dead white dog. She seemed quite unaware of the blood dripping from the gaping wound in the dog's chest.

No one noticed Kyle and the others drawing near, for the hooves of their mounts made no sound in the soft dirt. He doubted the villagers would have heard them in any event, for a middle-aged woman in a long brown tunic knelt beside the old woman, hurling invectives in a shrill voice at the recently departed English soldiers and volubly cursing Sir Percy and every other English nobleman, including Edward of England.

The woman in the long brown tunic abruptly ceased her denunciations the instant she looked up to see Kyle, John, and two English soldiers watching her from only four yards away. Stark terror flickered across her sharp features, and her face paled markedly. She rose slowly to her feet, as if unsure whether to run for her life, or stand her ground and beg for mercy.

The other villagers looked on in grim silence. Every one of them, including the woman in brown, knew the penalty for maligning the English king. Offenders were either flogged or mutilated, or both, which punishment was meted out in public as an example to others.

Since the English were notorious for dealing harshly with Scottish folk, the villagers expected no less from Kyle and the soldiers with him. When such treatment was not immediately forthcoming, they took heart that they might somehow escape retribution, which would have been swift, as well as painful.

John dismounted and walked over to the old woman seated on the ground. The villagers parted ranks to let him through. They were acquainted with him, both as a skilled apothecary and as a fellow countryman. Yet, their greetings were cool and reserved, as though they welcomed him, but disapproved of the company he kept.

"Mistress Fenella," John said to the woman in the long brown tunic. "What happened to yer mother?"

The old woman spoke for herself. "The Southrons come for the rent," she said. "I've not a penny in my purse, so they took my good milk cow and the ewes I planned to bring to market."

She laid her plump cheek against the soft fur on the dead dog's head. "There were no need to kill Bawsie," she said, sniffling loudly. "She were old and crippled. She would not hurt a soul." Her dark eyes narrowed and glittered brightly for a brief moment. "He did it for meanness, the haughty one did."

"Mam owes more than she can pay," Fenella said to John. "The Southrons put her out of the house." She wrung her hands together. "With so many mouths to feed, I've not a coin to spare to help her." She waved a hand toward the mangled plants in the tiny garden plot adjacent to the dwelling. "They trampled the crop, too. Now, there will be no cabbage or turnips for the children to eat."

John bent down to grasp the old woman's elbow to help her rise. "Mistress Hamilton," he said. "What will ye do? Where will ye go?"

Fenella slipped her hand under the old woman's other elbow. "She will stay with me," she said. "It's the least I can do for my own mother."

Mistress Hamilton released her hold on the dead dog with great reluctance. She lumbered to her feet with John and Fenella's assistance and tugged her shapeless tunic into place. "I won't miss that old house," she said as she reached up to straighten the off-white cap on her gray head. "The roof leaks every time it rains."

For a long moment, the old woman stood without moving, her hands held out before her, frowning down at the smears of bright red blood on her palms. At last, she lifted her eyes to look directly at Kyle. Her stark gaze seemed to sear through him without seeing him. "Three a violent end shall meet," she said. "The fourth shall cause his own defeat."

Fenella made a strangled sound deep in her throat. She seized the old woman by the shoulders. "Mam!" she cried, shaking her soundly.

Mistress Hamilton stared at her daughter as if she had just sprouted horns. "Unhand me, girl," she said, bristling with indignation as she pushed the younger woman away.

Upton and Turnbull shifted uneasily in their saddles at the old woman's pronouncement against them. The horses stamped and blew in response to the sudden nervous tension of their riders.

Kyle soothed the gelding by stroking its reddish-brown neck. He was not a superstitious man. Neither did he give credence to signs or portents. He only believed in what he could see and feel. Yet, he wasn't surprised to hear his demise would be untimely. If truth be told, wasn't all death untimely? In any case, he lived by the sword, or more accurately, by the short-handled battle axe, so he held no illusions about eventually dying at the hand of a foe who used his own weapon of choice. Experience and skill got him this far, but there was always the risk that one day he would face someone who was either a split-second faster than he was, or just plain luckier, and that would be the end of him.

The villagers exchanged fearful glances. The last thing they wanted was for Kyle or the soldiers with him to charge Mistress Hamilton with witchcraft. She would be burned alive at the stake, and they might well suffer a similar fate for harboring a witch in their midst.

"She's not herself today," Fenella said to John in an effort to forestall such an indictment.

The villagers joined in, murmuring their concurrence that Mistress Hamilton was, indeed, talking out of her head. They urged Fenella to take her mother inside to rest.

Fenella cast an anxious glance at Kyle, as though expecting him at any moment to point an accusatory finger at her and her mother to have them arrested. The benign expression on his face encouraged her to hustle the old woman, protesting with every step, into her house.

With the two women out of sight and hopefully out of mind, the remaining villagers bade John farewell and proceeded to disperse. One of them even brought his mule over to him to hasten his departure. Not a soul stepped forward to consult him about this malady or that injury, as they were wont to do on his infrequent visits there.

Kyle caught the eye of an able-bodied young man. "You, there," he said, pointing at him. "Stand your ground."

The young man froze. "Aye?" he said, quaking in his boots at being singled out from among the others.

"Get a spade," Kyle said, "and bury that dog."

The young man sagged with relief. "Aye," he said. He touched his forehead with the knuckle of his forefinger before hurrying away to do as he was bidden.

On the way back to Ayr, Kyle sent Upton and Turnbull on ahead in order to have a private word with John. He told the older man what Father Ian had mentioned concerning Ormesby's deplorable treatment of the Scottish gentry and of Sir Percy's dismissal of the charges against the English soldiers who had hanged a local shepherd without even a hearing.

John took the news in stride. "Ormesby's every deed has Edward of England's approval and support," he said. "Sir Percy does, too, for that matter. Any decision either of them makes carries the weight and might of their king behind it. Sir Percy may be young, but he's the real power in Ayrshire, as was Sir Nicholas de Segrave, Sir Percy's predecessor. It was Segrave who initiated the curtailment of Sheriff Crawford's authority and limited his duties until he became naught but a baillie with a fancy title." He looked over at Kyle, his expression grave. "The same goes for yer post as deputy. If ye don't yet know it, ye soon will."

"Sheriff Crawford informed me of that before he left," Kyle said. "There's a certain satisfaction in running felons to ground, but I never liked collecting taxes anyway. That's just another way to take money from folks who can barely afford to keep food on the table."

John rode in silence for a while, scowling at the road ahead. "What do ye think she meant?" he said at length.

"She was riled," Kyle said, picking up John's line of thought with ease, for he too wondered about Mistress Hamilton's pronouncement. "Rightly so for what Sweeney and his cronies did to her."

"But it was against us she spoke, not them," John said.

Kyle shrugged his broad shoulders. "If it bothers you that much," he said, "why don't you ask her about it?"

"That's not a bad idea," John said. He seemed well satisfied with the suggestion. He then gave Kyle a sidelong glance. "What about the Brodie girl's murderer? Do ye think one of the villagers did it?"

"I do," Kyle said.

"Which one?" John said

"It's hard to tell just yet," Kyle said.

"It's one of those lads ye spoke to in the field, is it not?"

"More than likely," Kyle said.

"How do ye know?"

"All three of them lied to me."

"What did they say?"

"It was what they didn't say," Kyle said. "None of them admitted to being keen on Megan, like her sister told me they were."

"Perhaps they didn't want to give ye cause to think them guilty."

"That may be so," Kyle said, "but one of them is culpable. I just need to think of a way to flush him out."

It was early afternoon when Kyle and John reached the outskirts of town. They rode through the streets to Tradesmen's Row, where John took his leave and turned aside to go home.

Kyle continued on to the garrison. As he rode under the portcullis, he saw a somber gathering of townsfolk beginning to collect around the raised wooden platform in the center of the courtyard.

A grim-faced man of considerable girth, whom Kyle recognized as the English marshal, stood with smug self-assurance at the bottom step leading up to the platform.

Kyle reined in to hail an English soldier walking across the courtyard with a halberd slung over his shoulder. "What's going on over there?" he said.

The soldier paused to squint up at Kyle in the sunlight. "The marshal sets the floggings for Mondays," he said. He gave Kyle a look that suggested he should already know that. "And today be Monday."

Kyle nodded his thanks to the soldier, who went over to join the other men-at-arms stationed around the platform with their halberds grounded. The town's burghers endorsed corporal punishment for thieves, drunkards, and other petty offenders, but few of them approved of an English marshal carrying out the sentence, which explained the grave expressions of those assembled there to watch.

Kyle made his way over to the stable. After tending to the gelding, he hurried across the courtyard to the main hall, which was situated on the ground floor of the castle, in the hope that he was not too late to get something to eat.

He was.

The cavernous hall was empty of soldiers, and the long tables in it were littered with crusts of bread, gnawed bones, and other remnants of the noon meal more than an hour past. A handful of adolescent boys from the streets of Ayr, pressed into willing service with the promise of a free meal, worked under the watchful eye of a rotund townsman with a willow switch in his hand. They collected clay mugs into a basket and tossed food scraps to a pack of dogs rooting through the straw on the timber-plank floor. Every now and then, when their willow-switch-wielding overseer wasn't looking, one of the boys would sneak a choice morsel from the table and slip it into his mouth.

The administrative offices were located above the main hall on the second floor of the castle, as were the sleeping quarters for those in command of the garrison and the occasional guest of the castellan. Since Sir Percy's office was in such close proximity, Kyle decided it was time to call upon him to introduce himself. His appetite could wait until later.

He strode toward the stairway built against the back wall and mounted the wooden steps two at a time. He walked down the long hallway running between the chambers on either side. The door at the far end was open, so he went there first. His wide-shouldered frame filled the doorway as he paused to knock lightly on the doorjamb.

A lean Scotsman of middle years was seated at a desk in the receiving room. He raised his eyes from writing in a neat hand with a quill pen on a rectangular piece of vellum. The shelves behind him were filled with rolls of parchment, and the anteroom he occupied led to a larger chamber beyond.

"May I help ye?" he said.

"Where is Sir Percy's office?" Kyle said.

"This is it," the man said. "I am Neyll, Sir Percy's clerk." His voice lacked any semblance of welcome or warmth, though it was carefully civil, in keeping with his station. His forehead was wide, rendered tall by his receding hairline. His hair was as black as his eyes, which peered out from deep sockets with a shrewd intelligence. His features were ordinary and unremarkable, unlike the burgundy tunic he wore, which was made of the finest linen, like that imported from Flanders, embroidered on the sleeves and cut in the latest fashion. The belt about his trim waist was studded with semiprecious stones, and his dark moustache and beard were neatly clipped.

Kyle detected the scent of roses coming from the man's clothing. He sniffed again to make sure. "Will you let Sir Percy know Kyle Shaw, Deputy Sheriff, is here to see him?" he said.

Neyll placed the quill in the upright holder in front of him and laced his fingers together. "Do ye have an appointment?" he said.

"I do not," Kyle said, "but he will want to see me."

"Sir Percy sees no one without an appointment," Neyll said. Although he was seated, he somehow managed to look down his long nose at Kyle looming over him. His disdainful gaze took in the dusty clothing and the tawny hair in disarray about the broad shoulders. "He is a very busy man."

"So am I," Kyle said. He strode past Neyll's desk to enter the chamber beyond.

Neyll jumped to his feet, knocking over his low stool in his haste to get around the corner of his desk. "Halt!" he cried as he ran after Kyle. "Ye cannot go in there without an appointment."

Sir Henry de Percy sat at a marble-topped oak desk with his back to the window. He looked up as Kyle bore down on him with the clerk nipping at his heels like an ill-tempered dog. "That will do, Neyll," he said.

Neyll hesitated, his face flushed and his lips set in an implacable line. He opened his mouth to protest, but apparently thought better of it, for he closed it again without saying a word. He cast a scathing glance at Kyle before he gave Sir Percy a bow barely decent enough to satisfy protocol. He turned on his heel and marched back to his desk in the anteroom.

Sir Percy was younger than Kyle expected, being no more than twenty-four years of age, with soft brown eyes and cherubic features. The cut of his velvet clothing was simple, yet the garment was well made, and the midnight blue color flattered his tanned complexion. His only adornment was a signet ring on the middle finger of his right hand and a gold ring set with a lustrous stone on the third finger of his left hand. His bearing was that of a man aware of his importance, but such was expected of an English nobleman who bore the heavy responsibilities of his office. Kyle got the impression, though, that Sir Percy would be happier out in the open air hawking and hunting, rather than confined to a desk.

The other furnishings in the office consisted of a side table, a wash stand near the window overlooking the courtyard, and a huge storage trunk in the corner. In front of the desk were two high-backed carved chairs, one of which was occupied by the foreign nobleman who arrived at the garrison on the same day as Kyle and who now wore a light blue velvet garment trimmed with silver cording.

"I beg your pardon for the intrusion," Kyle said. "I'm—"

"I know who you are," Sir Percy said, interrupting him without being rude. "I heard you when you came in."

"I failed to notice you were in conference," Kyle said. "I can come back when you are not otherwise engaged." He inclined his head in a slight bow to the foreign nobleman, who acknowledged him with the vapid wave of a hand.

"That won't be necessary," Sir Percy said with a bland smile. "Besides, you look like a man with something on his mind." He leaned back in his cushioned chair, his elbows on the padded arms, his fingers forming a tent while he waited for Kyle to speak.

"You're right about that," Kyle said. "What I have to say concerns the rape and murder of a village girl three days ago. The dead girl's father claims an English soldier did it. The man was seen in the vicinity about the time his daughter disappeared."

"The girl's death is a tragedy, of course," Sir Percy said, flicking an imaginary speck of dust from his velvet sleeve, "but those folks are always blaming us for everything that goes wrong in their pitiful lives."

"Perhaps their lives would not be so pitiful," Kyle said, "if you English treated them better."

Sir Percy got slowly to his feet, sweeping aside a parchment roll to place his hands flat on the polished marble surface of his desk. He leaned forward, his soft brown eyes suddenly fierce as they held Kyle's gaze. "I suggest you tread with care, Master Deputy," he said. "You are speaking to the Castellan of Ayrshire, appointed by the King of England himself."

"Then perhaps as castellan," Kyle said, returning Sir Percy's piercing gaze, "you can put a stop to English soldiers from this very garrison raiding homesteads in the shire."

"You are mistaken," Sir Percy said, his manner cold. "That is the handiwork of Scottish rebels."

"Those were English soldiers who raided Ogilvy's homestead the other night," Kyle said, his tone emphatic. "They did it under the cover of darkness, hooded like bandits."

"How do you know this?"

"There were four witnesses to the deed."

"Where are these so-called witnesses?" Sir Percy said.

"You are looking at one of them," Kyle said. "I saw the raiders with my own eyes."

"How could you see them if it was dark?"

"They set the roof ablaze, and I got a good look at the two who were killed."

"That is a serious accusation," Sir Percy said. "I will need to see the bodies for identification."

"The bodies are gone," Kyle said. "The raiders came back later in the night and carried them off."

Sir Percy turned away, but not before Kyle caught the twitch of the man's lips. He was unsure whether relief or concern prompted the barely perceptible contraction.

"How inconvenient for you," Sir Percy said as he walked over to the unshuttered window. He looked down into the courtyard, his hands clasped behind his back. "These are desperate times, Master Shaw. There is rebellion lurking in every dark corner. Even as we speak, Sir Andrew de Moray is sowing the seeds of dissension and unrest in the northern shires against English occupation, and that despite his father and his uncle held prisoner on English lands." He swung around to face Kyle, his compact figure silhouetted against the bright light outside. "Bring me proof of English involvement in those raids, and I will take it from there."

"There is one other matter which I must call to your attention," Kyle said. He related how English soldiers not an hour past turned Mistress Hamilton out of her home, killed her dog, and trampled her garden.

Sir Percy walked over to his desk and stood behind his chair. "If tenants don't like being turned out into the street," he said, placing his hands on the cushioned back, "then they should keep their rents current. I've given Captain Sweeney leave to handle collections as he sees fit." He raised his hand to forestall Kyle's objection. "Tenants must either pay what is due or face eviction. That's my final word on the subject."

Sir Percy then gestured toward the foreign nobleman who sat quietly throughout their conversation. "I wish to introduce

Count Aymar de Jardine," he said. "He is Royal Envoy to King Philip the Fourth of France."

"Your humble servant," Kyle said with a courtly bow.

From the corner of his eye, he caught the glance Count Jardine exchanged with Sir Percy. The count's raised eyebrow gave him the impression that neither nobleman expected such gracious manners from the rough-looking deputy sheriff standing before them.

"This is Kyle Shaw, as you heard upon his entrance," Sir Percy said to Count Jardine. "He is the son of James Shaw, a Scotsman loyal to Edward, King of England."

Kyle felt his jaw drop in astonishment. Sir Percy was surely mistaken. His father long ago pledged his fealty to the Scottish throne, and as a man of integrity, he would never repudiate such an oath.

He admitted to himself that much had happened during his six-year absence from Scotland. Men were known to change sides during a conflict in less time than that, but James Shaw was the least likely to do so. Allegiance was a serious matter to him. Renouncing his king would impugn not only his character, but his honor, too, and he would have found that insupportable.

He thought he knew his father well, yet Sir Percy's next words cast a shadow of doubt on his perceptions and made him wonder what had occurred to make his father turn his back on his long-held principles.

"Before I agreed to let Sheriff Crawford send for you," Sir Percy said to Kyle, "I took the liberty of going through my predecessor's correspondence. It was in those communications that I discovered your father's loyalties lay with the English cause. I shall, of course, expect no less from you in the execution of your duties as deputy." He sat down at his desk and laced his fingers on the marble surface before him. "Count Jardine has urgent business with King Edward's parliament in Berwick. Your first official undertaking as deputy will be to escort him to Leith." He turned to Count Jardine by way of explanation. "Hiring a boat from Leith around to Berwick will shorten your journey by several days."

Kyle frowned in bewilderment. "Berwick no longer exists," he said. "I heard King Edward sacked the castle and set the town afire."

"That did occur," Sir Percy said with a frosty demeanor. "However, since then, my lord the King has ordered Berwick to be rebuilt and resettled. It is under English control now, and court is still held there."

"I see," Kyle said. "So, when does *m'sire le comte* wish to depart?"

"Within the hour," Sir Percy said.

"Within the hour?" Kyle said, incredulous. "While it would be an honor to attend to such a distinguished nobleman as Count Jardine, I cannot in good conscience absent myself from the shire at the present time. I am in the midst of investigating the village girl's murder."

"You can do that when you get back," Sir Percy said. "The safety of the French envoy takes precedence over all else. Thus, I place him in your capable hands."

Kyle fought to keep his temper in check. "As you wish," he said between his teeth. By the time he returned from Leith, the girl's murderer, if the fellow had any sense at all, would be long gone. To Count Jardine, he said, "The roads are quite decent to Edinburgh. The port of Leith is just beyond it. Will you and your servant require a carriage?"

"Alas," Count Jardine said, "my manservant came down with the ague shortly before leaving France. He is in good hands, but I am now on my own. I am an excellent horseman, and I much prefer riding a spirited steed to the confines of a carriage." He spoke with a pronounced French accent.

"Our journey will be through open country," Kyle said. "With respect, *m'sire,* your garb marks you as a man of wealth to anyone inclined to mischief."

"I do not run from danger," Count Jardine said, "but neither do I seek it out. I applaud your perspicacity and will dress appropriately for our journey. I shall now retire to my chamber to await your summons."

Sir Percy got up from his chair to bow to the count, who took his leave and withdrew through the anteroom. He collapsed into the chair with a heartfelt sigh of relief as the French envoy's footsteps faded down the hallway. "I'm glad he's only passing through this time," he said. "I'll never forget his last visit here, although I'd like to." He began shuffling through the pile of documents in front of him. He looked up after a moment, and his face registered mild surprise at seeing Kyle still standing before his desk. "Do you require something further?"

"Count Jardine arrived the other day with an escort of English troops," Kyle said. "Surely, they can escort him on to Berwick."

"Those troops were bringing supplies from Carlisle," Sir Percy said. "Count Jardine happened to be traveling along the same route and apparently attached himself to them. As for my providing an escort for him, what if something dire befalls Philip's precious envoy under English protection? God forbid I should risk my neck in such a manner. You, on the other hand, are a Scotsman, and it is well known that France bears you Scots no ill will."

"So, if anything happens to the count in my care," Kyle said dryly, "it is only my neck at risk."

Sir Percy had the grace to blush. "You mistake me," he said, trying to gloss over his verbal blunder. "I cannot risk France declaring war on England over such an incident. Pray, be so kind as to see Count Jardine safely to Berwick. And I don't care how you get him there. Just get him out of here, and as quickly as possible."

"Very well, then," Kyle said with a stiff bow. From that moment on, Count Jardine was his responsibility. Though the epitome of courtesy and graciousness, the man was still only a diplomat, whose sword, which looked more decorative than serviceable, would be useless if they ran into trouble. He strode from Sir Percy's office, marveling at how quickly he went from lawman to nursemaid.

CHAPTER 6

As Kyle passed through the anteroom on his way out, he noticed the smirk on Neyll's face. It was apparent the man had heard every word he spoke in Sir Percy's office. No confidences had been compromised, so there was little cause for alarm. It did occur to him, though, to be more careful in the future.

As clerk, Neyll was privy to all communications, whether sensitive or otherwise, to and from the Castellan of Ayrshire who, at the English king's command, kept his finger on the pulse of his corner of Scotland. A man in Neyll's position might prove either useful or dangerous, depending on how he handled the information entrusted to him.

Kyle decided to walk to the marketplace, both to cool his temper over the delay in his investigation of the village girl's murder and to get something to eat.

He arrived to find the activity there winding down. Some of the merchants had already packed up and gone home, leaving empty stalls behind them. Others stayed to peddle the last of their goods. Decent food would be hard to find, for by that time of day the milk would be sour, the bread stale, and the meat dry and stringy. That did not deter him from purchasing a couple of mutton pasties to silence the insistent growling in his stomach. He devoured the crusty morsels and washed them down with tepid buttermilk from a tarred leather cup. It wasn't enough to fill him up, but it would hold him over for a while.

He started back for the garrison, contemplating the quickest route to take to Leith, when he spied Joneta, still dressed in black, crossing through a row of stalls ahead of him.

She was some yards distant and in the company of a young man and three women, one of whom was hunched and shriveled with age. The other two were young and pretty, dressed in long homespun tunics that flattered their shapely figures. The young man, dark haired and lean, carried a wicker basket and walked beside one of the women, who wore a frilly white cap and who held in her arms an infant swathed in soft wool. He remembered seeing that young woman when he first met Joneta.

The other young woman wore no cap on her head, as was common for an unwed female. Her neatly plaited hair was the color of honey, and she was almost as tall as Joneta. Her comely features looked familiar, but he could not recall from where he knew her. He dismissed the notion that he knew her at all, since she would have been only a child when he last lived in the shire.

Joneta walked beside the elderly woman, a hand under her elbow to steady her faltering steps on the sandy ground. Their pace was slow, and they made frequent stops to look at this item or that article on display.

They were headed in his direction, so he made no move to intercept them. As they worked their way toward him, his gaze lingered on Joneta's face. She was as lovely as he remembered her. Ever since he met her two days ago, he had wondered about her. He wasn't ready to take another wife just yet, but when he did, it would be someone like her.

It crossed his mind that she might not necessarily be a widow, that she might be mourning the loss of a child or some other member of her family. The thought that she might be married disturbed him more than he expected it would. He was about to turn away when he saw Captain Sweeney with a couple of men-at-arms approaching Joneta and those with her. He recognized

Archer's stout figure, and he assumed the skinny one was Weems, both of whom seemed to be Sweeney's constant companions.

Sweeney walked up to the young woman in the frilly white cap and leaned down to whisper something in her ear.

Kyle could not hear Sweeney's words, but whatever he said provoked an immediate angry reaction from the young woman.

Joneta, her hazel eyes wide and wary, stepped forward to take the infant from the young woman's arms.

Kyle started toward them, rapidly closing the short distance between them.

The lean young man dropped the wicker basket, heedless of the onions and sea bream that spilled out as he interposed himself between Sweeney and the young woman with the frilly white cap. "I'll thank ye to leave Meg be," he said, his fists clenched, his chin thrust out.

Vendors in nearby stalls looked up to see what was going on. People walking by stopped to stare openly, drawn by the raised voices.

Sweeney apparently took exception to the young man's interference, for he shoved him backwards into Archer and Weems, who grabbed his arms to hold him fast.

The elderly woman shook her veined fist at Sweeney. "Pick on somebody yer own size, ye bully!" she cried.

The elderly woman's remonstration brought a smile to Sweeney's lips. He reached out to playfully tug at one of the ties dangling from Meg's frilly white cap.

The cap slid from her head, loosing a cloud of auburn hair. The glaring sun ignited the reddish tresses to a fiery crimson. Her blue eyes, no longer shaded by the frilly brim, gleamed like polished sapphires in the bright light.

Sweeney froze with his arm extended, his gray eyes riveted to Meg's face. The color drained from his ruddy features, leaving him ashen and gaping, as if he'd just seen a ghost.

Kyle arrived on the scene in time to catch the stricken expression on Sweeney's face. Joneta and the elderly woman noticed it, too, after which they exchanged a quick nervous glance.

Clearly upset at Sweeney's boorish treatment of her in public, Meg snatched the frilly cap from his hand and thrust it back on her head.

The abrupt movement broke the spell.

Sweeney dropped his arm, suddenly reanimated. "I was only having a bit of fun," he said with a shaky laugh. To his men, he said: "Let's away. Turn him loose." He looked pointedly at Meg. "For now."

Archer and Weems released their grip on the struggling young man and followed after Sweeney, who had already disappeared behind the next row of stalls.

The young man put his arm around Meg's shoulders. She responded to the tender concern on his angular face by leaning into him, evidently taking comfort from his closeness, which somewhat lessened the trembling of her hands.

"Good morrow," Kyle said in greeting, drawing their notice for the first time. He bent down to put the onions and sea bream back into the wicker basket. He stood erect and handed the basket to the young man, who took it with a curt nod of thanks.

"Are ye one of them Southrons?" the elderly woman said, giving Kyle a guarded look.

"Of course not, Gram," Joneta said with a note of reproach in her voice. "That is the new deputy sheriff, Kyle Shaw."

Kyle felt inordinately pleased that she remembered his name. "I'll be happy to escort you home," he said. "Only to discourage Sweeney from bothering you again, of course."

"Drew can do it," Joneta said, indicating the young man. She lifted the whimpering infant to her shoulder and gently patted its back. "I thank ye for the offer, though. It was very kind."

"Is that the bold one's name?" Gram said. "Sweeney?"

"Lucky Jack Sweeney, Captain of Horse at Ayr Garrison," Kyle said.

The elderly woman narrowed her eyes at Kyle for a moment before looking over at Joneta. "We should go," she said. "I'm feeling rather poorly."

"Good morrow," Joneta said to Kyle with a dazzling smile that made his heart skip a beat.

With the excitement now over and no likelihood of any further diversion, the onlookers lost interest and began to move on.

Kyle watched Joneta and the others walk away, wondering at Sweeney's odd reaction to Meg—or did he react to Meg's appearance?

Only when the stalls blocked Joneta from view did he depart from the marketplace. He made his way to the garrison stable where he found Upton helping the groom water the horses.

He approached Upton, who was gathering up the empty pails. "I need you to secure a week's provisions for four men," he said, absently rubbing the velvet muzzle of a gray horse that stuck its head out over the half-door of its stall. "Count Aymar de Jardine, Royal Envoy to King Philip of France, has pressing business with King Edward's parliament in Berwick. We are to serve as escort and must leave within the hour."

"We?" Upton said, setting down the pails.

"You, me, and Turnbull," Kyle said. "After you saddle the horses, kindly fetch the count from his chamber. I'll be waiting in my office."

"Even if the weather holds," Upton said, "it will take at least ten days to get to Berwick."

"We're only going as far as Leith," Kyle said. "How long that takes will depend upon the count, not the weather. He might be a fine horseman, but he's no young buck." He started to leave, only to turn back. "Wear full armor and tell Turnbull to do the same."

"Are you expecting trouble?" Upton said.

"I always expect trouble," Kyle said, "and I'm rarely disappointed."

Upton hurried away to prepare for the journey.

Kyle saddled the gelding and led it over to the sheriff's office, where he packed a few things to take with him.

The bells of St. John's rang in the midafternoon hour of none as Kyle, Count Jardine, Upton, and Turnbull rode across the courtyard toward the garrison gates.

A soldier in nondescript garb, with blue eyes and a weathered face as brown as old leather, sat on one of the benches in front of the barracks. He appeared quite interested in the small group of horsemen leaving the garrison, for his candid gaze followed them until they clattered across the wooden bridge beyond the gates and disappeared from sight.

Kyle led the way up the cobblestone streets of Ayr with the gelding prancing sideways and champing at the bit in high spirits, eager to be away.

Count Jardine rode beside him on a lively bay. He wore a light brown tunic with a wide leather belt, a tooled leather jerkin laced to the neck to protect his chest, and a jaunty brown cap with a long white feather in the band. His only ornamentation was a large ruby brooch, which held his dark brown cloak closed at the throat. He sat on his horse with the ease of a man used to the saddle.

Upton and Turnbull wore black bull hide armor on their upper bodies and conical metal helmets with nose guards of the Norman style. They brought up the rear, leading a pony carrying their provisions and the count's small travel trunk.

"Do you wish to take the main road?" Kyle said to Count Jardine.

"Is there another way?" the count said.

"There are lesser roads we can take," Kyle said. "They will cut off nearly a day's ride, but there are no inns that way. We'll be sleeping on hard ground under the stars."

A ghost of a smile tugged at Count Jardine's lips. "It may astonish you to learn," he said, "that it won't be the first time I have done so."

"As you wish, *m'sire*," Kyle said. He touched his heels to the gelding's flanks and sent it into a canter. The others stayed close behind him. For the next couple of hours, the only sound they heard was the drumming of hooves on packed earth. Whenever the horses tired or if the terrain grew too difficult to negotiate with ease, they slowed their pace. Otherwise, they held to a steady lope. They followed the track across the open fields, over the rolling hills, and through the woods.

From the time he left the garrison, Kyle could not shake the feeling of being watched. Though subsequent glances over his shoulder revealed no one behind them, the skin at the back of his neck still prickled after two hours into the journey. He began to wonder whether he was imagining danger where there was none, and he chided himself for being overly concerned with Count Jardine's safety.

Before long, the sun dipped behind the tops of the trees to the west, and the chill of early evening began to descend upon them. They were approaching a bend in the road when Kyle called for a break. The horses dropped their heads to graze on the sparse grass beside the road.

"We should be halfway to Strathaven by now," he said to the count. "There's a village down that track to the east. I'm sure we can find a byre there in which to pass the night."

"I intend no slight to those good people," Count Jardine said, "but I would rather suffer a rock for a pillow than bed down with lice and fleas in moldy straw. Perhaps we can camp elsewhere." He eased his position on the saddle with an involuntary wince. "Not too far from here, if at all possible."

Kyle noted that the count was as bone weary as he was. Though he would never admit it aloud, he was more than ready to lay his head on a pillow of stone. "There's a burn further up the road," he said. "That's as good a place as any to set up camp."

They pressed on at a pace considerably slower than when they first set out. As they plodded up the road, the count caught one of the fleeting glances Kyle cast behind him.

"I assume you're on the lookout for Scottish rebels," he said. "Sir Percy warned me of their presence in this region."

"As Royal Envoy of France," said Kyle, "you have more to fear from the English than from us. Scotland has long counted France as a friend. Our King Balliol even appealed to your sovereign Philip for troops when he led the rebellion against Edward of England. By the time French support arrived, Balliol had already given himself up to Edward to stop the bloodshed. No one faults Philip of France for tardy messengers and treacherous seas." He reached down to pat the gelding's sweaty neck. "Most folk around here don't mind living alongside the English. It is the English who go out of their way to make life difficult for them."

Count Jardine rode in silence for a long moment. "Several years past," he said at length, "English seamen went on a rampage in the French port of La Rochelle. You might have heard of the incident. It was I who negotiated with Edward of England to compensate my lord King Philip for damage to the harbor and for the loss of seafaring vessels, which the English seamen had burned. At the time, Edward impressed me as a ruthless man, driven by ambition and excessive greed. Subsequent dealings with him have done nothing to change my opinion of him."

"You'll get no argument from me about that," Kyle said.

Behind him, Upton and Turnbull exchanged the sort of glance that indicated they, too, were of the same opinion.

"Long before I met you this morning," Count Jardine said, "I knew you by reputation. King Philip made fond mention of you some once or twice at Court."

"How very kind of him," Kyle said. "I must admit that our first meeting was rather informal. We slogged through a muddy field together on the outskirts of Ypres during a minor skirmish with Flemish troops. I understand the English are still squabbling with Philip over trading rights there."

"With good cause, it seems," Count Jardine said. "English sheep produce the long-fibered wool highly prized by weavers. Flemish weavers and fullers are renowned for turning such wool into woven garments of the best quality. Those same skilled weavers can turn flax into the finest linen, which is far superior to that from any loom in either England or France." He patted his saddle roll purposefully. "France, on the other hand, makes the most excellent wine from sun-ripened grapes. With such marketable products at hand, it is no wonder there is conflict over which country has the right to trade with whom."

"That explains the demand for long-haired sheep, no matter the source," Kyle said, his mind on Ogilvy and the other homesteaders who were still at risk of losing their stock to raiders. There was nothing he could do about it at the moment, but upon his return, he would ascertain Sweeney's movements on the night of Ogilvy's raid.

Dusk slowly closed in around them. A cold wind blew in from the north, causing the branches of the trees around them to bob and sway. The track ahead seemed to end abruptly at a river. The gelding splashed into the knee-deep water and drank deeply before ambling across to the far bank, where the track continued on through the woods.

Kyle forded the river with the others. "We shall pass the night here," he said. "Upton, take Turnbull with you to find a decent place to camp upstream."

The English soldiers dismounted, abandoning their horses on the side of the track to crash away into the thick undergrowth.

Count Jardine climbed gingerly down from the bay. Kyle threw his leg over the gelding's bowed head as it grazed and slid to the ground. Before either man could work the kinks from his cramped muscles, Upton erupted from the underbrush in a shower of twigs and leaves, with Turnbull at his heels.

"This way, if you please," Upton said. He and Turnbull gathered the reins of their horses and led them away through the dense brush.

Kyle and Count Jardine followed with their own mounts in tow. Briars tore at their clothing and brambles scratched their bare skin. They shortly emerged in a small clearing under a huge pine tree. A thick carpet of dead pine needles around the base of the broad trunk would provide ample insulation from the cold ground. The whisper of purling water marked the river's location just beyond the thicket of alder and beech.

Upton and Turnbull removed the load from the pack-pony before stripping the saddles and bridles from the horses and hobbling their forelegs. Turnbull went to the river to fill a skin bottle with fresh water to drink, while Upton carried the sack of provisions over to the huge pine tree.

Count Jardine made himself comfortable on a protruding pine root. He kept his saddle roll close beside him, as though afraid to let it out of his sight.

In the middle of the open area, Upton scraped dead pine needles aside with his booted foot. When he had exposed a sizeable circle of bare earth, he gathered an assortment of dead limbs and piled them in the center.

"No fire tonight," Kyle said. "A cold supper will have to do."

"If Scottish rebels offer no threat," Count Jardine said, "from whom do you expect danger?"

"These are perilous times, *m'sire*," Kyle said. "For your safety, I prefer to err on the side of caution."

The count seemed satisfied with Kyle's response.

They shared a simple meal of coarse brown bread and hard cheese in the deepening twilight. They passed around the skin bottle of water to wash down their supper.

Count Jardine, with the tact of a true diplomat, politely declined to drink the water. It was obvious he preferred the contents of the stoppered flask he took from his saddle roll. "Water is for washing," he said. "There is nothing like good wine from Gascony." He produced a carved horn cup into which he poured a measure of the dark red liquid from the flask. "You may taste it, if you so desire, but I warn you, you'll spurn your English ale ever after."

Since Upton sat beside the count, he was the first to partake. "It's sweet, like a clary," he said with appreciation. "A wine fit for a king, or in this case, a king's envoy."

Count Jardine gazed upon Upton with interest. "Know you aught of wines?" he said.

"A little," Upton said, "and only because a wine merchant tried to cheat Sir Percy by passing off a batch of new wine as that aged on the dregs." He grinned into the fading dusk. "From then on, Sir Percy insisted that I sample every keg before he laid out a single penny for it."

"Have you a favorite?" Count Jardine said.

"I prefer the sweet ones," Upton said, passing the horn cup on to Kyle.

"This is good," Kyle said, after taking a sip. "The best I've had in a while."

"High praise, indeed," Count Jardine said, "from someone who can boast of dining with the King of France."

Kyle chuckled as he handed the horn cup to Turnbull. "I wouldn't exactly call it dining," he said. "We just set up camp near Ghent, when one of my men presented me with a hot pie. Apple, I think it was. What he failed to tell me was that he had pinched it from a Flemish baker. I found that out for myself when the baker showed up moments later demanding the return of his pies. It seems several went missing from the rear window of his shop where he put them to cool. His Majesty King Philip and I ducked out the back of the royal tent with the apple pie in hand. The baker saw us making our escape and chased after us brandishing a stick. Philip and I consumed the evidence on the run. As I recall, it was the tastiest pie I ever ate."

Count Jardine threw his head back and laughed aloud. "You are too modest, Master Kyle," he said, still smiling. "Tell me about your Scottish rebels. Will we see any, do you think?"

"In this tangle of woods," Kyle said, "fifty rebels could be lurking on the other side of that thicket, and we wouldn't see a single one." He pulled his cloak around him against the cold evening air. "But with respect, *m'sire le comte,* they're not my rebels. More than likely, they're poor folk who don't take kindly to watching their children starve because of heavy taxes levied upon them to fill Edward of England's coffers."

Count Jardine took the carved horn cup Turnbull returned to him. "Ah, yes, Edward of England," he said, his expression grim. "A damnable thorn in Philip's side."

"A damnable thorn in everyone's side," Kyle said. "Folks around here want to raise their children in peace and tend their herds without interference. They've had precious little chance to do either with the English harrying them."

"You approve their rebellion, then?" Count Jardine said. The troubled expression on his face was barely visible in the failing light.

"Men who take the law into their own hands," Kyle said, "even if their cause is just, place themselves outside the law, not above it. As sheriff's deputy, I am sworn to uphold the law, no matter that the law is English."

Count Jardine nodded in approval. "So," he said, changing the subject, "Sir Percy couldn't wait to see the back of me." He laughed without humor. "I cannot blame him. A year past, I carried a mandate to him from Philip of France, ordering the closure of the port of Ayr."

"Perhaps he feared you brought ill tidings this time, too," Kyle said. "Ayr's harbors are the busiest of any along the western coast of the lowlands. If those harbors close, trade will cease, and as every merchant knows, without trade there is no profit."

He lifted his eyes to the silvery rim of the moon beginning to show over the tops of the trees. "Get some sleep," he said to Upton. "I'll stand first watch and wake Turnbull for the next."

The English soldiers settled down on the ground, huddled in their cloaks on either side of the count, who wrapped himself in his wool mantle and rested his head on his saddle roll.

At the edge of the clearing, Kyle found a shadowy place to stand under an ancient oak where he could keep watch over the others. He leaned against the gnarled trunk, relaxing his weary muscles as much as he dared. He let the soothing sounds of the night wash over him, though the friendly chirp of crickets failed to dispel the feeling of being watched. He placed a ready hand on the hilt of his sword, his weapon of choice on this particular occasion. Should a foe beset them in the darkness, he did not want to risk accidentally bludgeoning a member of his own party to death with his battle axe.

Across the clearing, pale radiance from the moon gave the

white pony substance and form as it grazed. The darker horses beside it blended into the gloom of the trees behind them.

As the night wore on, the moon crept higher in the starlit sky. Except for the forlorn howl of a lone wolf in the distance and the bark of a fox somewhere nearby, the forest was at peace. Kyle was beginning to sag with fatigue when the sudden hoot of an owl on the limb above him startled him to full wakefulness. He detached himself from the shadows and trod soundlessly over to where Turnbull slept beside Count Jardine.

"It's time," Kyle said, tapping Turnbull on the shoulder.

Turnbull clambered to his feet with a grunt. He clapped his metal helmet on his head and trudged over to the ancient oak to stand watch in the shadow of its branches.

Kyle stretched out on Turnbull's pine needle bed, his sword within easy reach. He drew his cloak around him, and despite the discomfort of the bulky leather scale armor, he sank into a dreamless sleep.

Something woke Kyle an hour later. He lay on his back, listening for whatever might have disturbed his slumber. The forest around him was quiet.

Too quiet.

No crickets chirped.

No nocturnal creatures shuffled through fallen leaves rooting for food.

He sat up to peer at the horses, whose acute senses he trusted more than his own. The white pony stood on the far side of the small clearing like a silver statue, its head raised and its ears pricked toward the ancient oak.

Instantly alert, he looked over at Turnbull, whose face was a whitish blur under the oak tree's spreading limbs. A light breeze stirred the branches, transmuting shadows on the moonlit ground into fearsome shapes. He stared long and hard into the darkness, unsure whether one of the shadows actually moved with the deadly stealth of a hunter stalking unsuspecting prey, or whether it was merely a trick of the light. He kept his eyes trained in that direction, and after a long moment, he decided it was only his imagination. He was about to lie back down when he caught the unmistakable glint of naked steel in the moonlight.

"Turnbull!" he shouted. He leaped to his feet, sword in hand. "To arms!"

The undergrowth beyond the pine tree suddenly thrashed to life. Dark figures swarmed over Upton and Count Jardine as they tried to rise.

Kyle heard someone cry out in anguish. Before he could engage the shadowy form of the nearest intruder, a savage blow from behind sent him sprawling. A heavy weight pinned him to the ground. Gauntleted hands on the back of his head shoved his face down into the soft earth to smother him. A booted foot on his right wrist rendered the sword in his hand useless. He bucked and writhed, but try as he might, he could not dislodge his assailant. In desperation, he clawed for the dirk at his waist with his left hand. His fingers closed about the hilt. He drew the blade and stabbed repeatedly behind him until the sharp point sank into yielding flesh. With a howl of rage, the weight on his back lifted abruptly.

Kyle scrambled to his feet, spitting out pine needles and cursing roundly. Unable to distinguish friend from foe among the dark forms scuffling in front of him, he struck out with the flat of his blade. The blow connected solidly with flesh and bone, eliciting a gratifying grunt of pain.

The dark form of an intruder, faceless under a drawn hood, detached itself from the shadows to advance on Kyle. The intruder circled to look for an opening, and then suddenly lashed out with the sword in his left hand.

Steel rang against steel as Kyle blocked the stroke with his blade. The shocking impact of the powerful blow traveled up his arm to his shoulder. The finer aspects of swordplay never appealed to him, unlike his former comrades-in-arms who augmented their income on occasion by betting on the outcome of their practice matches. His own skill was sufficient to defend himself, and he was satisfied with that. The intruder standing before him in the moonlight, however, possessed no finesse at all, for he wielded his weapon more like a club than a sword.

The intruder lunged, attempting to come up under Kyle's guard.

Kyle parried the thrust with a metallic clang.

The intruder recovered, only to back away, gripping the hilt with both hands, poised to deliver another mighty wallop.

Kyle braced his feet, his sword ready, but the blow never came.

A shrill whistle rent the air, coming from the shadows beyond the pine tree. Kyle's adversary lowered his sword before sinking into the darkness behind him.

The intruders vanished as quickly as they came, crashing away into the brush until the forest was quiet once again.

Kyle heard nothing further in the ensuing silence, except the rasp of his own breath. It was useless to give chase in the darkness, for it would be like seeking a shadow among shadows. At that moment, he was more concerned about the fate of his companions.

He lifted his arm to sheath his sword, wincing at the sharp twinge that shot across his shoulder. A low groan from under the pine tree brought his head around. The blade of his dirk glinted at his feet where he had dropped it. He bent down to pick it up, hefting the finely honed weapon in the hope that the sound came from a wounded intruder.

"Mon Dieu!" said a weak voice from the shadows.

Kyle's anxiety level went up a notch. He sheathed his dirk

before dropping to his knees to feel along the ground. Almost at once, his hand met with the downed man's shoulder. The fabric of the man's woolen cloak felt wet and sticky to the touch. His questing fingers continued along the man's upper body until they come into contact with the smooth hilt of a knife and the cold metal of the brooch beside it.

"M'sire le comte!" he cried, fearing the worst.

Count Jardine clutched at Kyle's cloak, pulling him close with remarkable strength for an injured man. "It is vital that Philip of France gains possession of my belt," he said, his thick accent nearly unintelligible. "It must not fall into English hands, do you hear?"

"Rest easy," Kyle said, gently disengaging the count's fingers. He assumed the man was raving, as did some who were severely wounded in battle.

"Promise you will take it to Philip," the count said with a note of desperation in his voice. "Place it only in his hands."

"You have my word on it," Kyle said. His own alarm grew as the circle of warm wetness expanded around the protruding hilt. "I must stop the bleeding, *m'sire,* but I can't see a blessed thing in this gloom. I must move you into the clearing." He turned his head to bellow for help. "Upton! Turnbull! To me!"

When no response was forthcoming, he grasped the count under the arms and dragged him, moaning softly, out from the shadows.

Moonlight shone down on the knife sticking out high on the count's chest. The hilt jutted at an odd angle, tilting toward his neck. Although misdirected, the blow was meant to kill, delivered with sufficient force to cleave through the count's stiff leather jerkin. A deep groove on the brooch showed where the tip of the assailant's blade had struck the gold facing, only to skid off to lodge in the count's upper shoulder, rather than in his throat.

Kyle could not stem the flow of blood without first removing the knife. He grasped the hilt and gave it a sharp tug. The blade slid free of gristle and sinew, causing the count to draw in a sharp breath before losing consciousness. Copious amounts of blood gushed through the slit in the woolen cloak.

Kyle pressed down on the wound with the heel of his hand to staunch the flow. "Upton! Turnbull!" he shouted. The others might also be hurt or worse, but his primary duty was to the count, who, if left unattended, would bleed to death in minutes. He increased pressure on the wound. Only when the bleeding stopped would he dare leave his charge to search for his men.

A groan came from somewhere behind the huge pine tree.

"Upton," Kyle said. "Is that you? Are you hurt?"

"It's me," Upton said. "Or rather, what's left of me." A rustle of pine needles announced his arrival from the shadowy depths. He stepped into the moonlight with his hand to his head. When he saw the count lying on the ground, he stopped in his tracks, letting his hand fall to his side. "Is he dead?"

"Not yet," Kyle said.

Count Jardine's eyelids fluttered open. "Is it that bad?" he said, a note of panic in his voice.

"A flesh wound, *m'sire,*" Kyle said. "Lie still or you'll bleed afresh." To Upton, he said, "Light a fire, then see to Turnbull. He doesn't answer my call."

Upton knelt at the bare place that he had earlier prepared for a campfire and bent to the task of striking the flints taken from the pouch at his side. Once the tinder caught, he blew on it, adding dry pine straw and rotted limbs until the blaze lit up the clearing. He then hurried over to the oak tree to look for Turnbull.

Count Jardine tried to take in a deep breath, but ended with an indrawn hiss through clenched teeth. "Forget what I said concerning my belt," he murmured to Kyle. "It is of little import."

Kyle unfastened the ruby brooch binding the cloak at the neck and tossed it aside. "I am neither blind nor stupid, *m'sire le comte*," he said in a low voice. "The intrigues between France and England hold no interest for me. I would have done as you requested, however, because I gave you my word on it."

He laid back the edges of the count's cloak and set to work untying the laces down the front of the leather jerkin.

A grimace barely resembling a smile touched the count's lips. "I never considered you a fool, Master Kyle," he said. "I thought they killed me, which is why I spoke thus earlier. I shall live, I think, to carry out my own commission." His eyes gleamed in the firelight. "I pray you will tell Sir Percy nothing of what passed between us."

"You have my word on that, too," Kyle said, loosening the last tie. He opened the jerkin and peeled the soggy linen shirt from the wound. He frowned down at the blood oozing forth. From what he could see, the cut looked clean, but even the tiniest bit of lint or thread embedded deep in the flesh could cause it to fester. At that moment, though, the unchecked seepage presented a more serious problem.

There was only one sure way to stop the flow. In preparation, he picked up the knife used to inflict the wound and buried the blade in the glowing embers.

Upton's cry of dismay impelled Kyle and the count to look toward the oak tree.

"I found him," Upton shouted. "He's hurt." With the strength of youth, he hefted Turnbull's body like a baby, one arm under his knees and the other under his shoulders. He staggered into the clearing toward them.

"Lay him there by the fire," Kyle said.

Upton deposited Turnbull on the ground with a grunt, only

to hover like an anxious mother over a feverish child. The only damage he found was under the chain mail coif after pushing it back. "I think his head is broken," he said, peering down at the dark patch in the gray hair.

Kyle observed the shallow rise and fall of Turnbull's chest. He liked the older man who hardly ever spoke a word. Reticence to him was an endearing quality, since he could not abide chatterers. "Do what you can for him," he said.

While Upton tended to Turnbull, Kyle ministered to the count. With difficulty, he removed the sleeveless jerkin and the stained linen shirt. The movement, minimal though it was, reopened the wound and started it bleeding again. He ripped the sleeve from the shirt and used it to sop up the blood. He slipped the sheath from his own belt and removed his dirk from it.

"Bite on this," he said, touching the edge of the leather sheath to the count's lips.

The count showed strong white teeth as he complied.

Kyle took the knife from the embers and laid the red-hot tip against the wound.

A brief sizzle brought forth a throaty groan from Count Jardine.

The smell of scorched flesh prickled Kyle's nose. "It's done," he said, setting the knife aside.

He ripped the other sleeve from the count's shirt, and after folding it several times, he saturated the fabric with wine from the count's flask. He squeezed out the excess liquid and placed the wad of linen over the seared flesh, directing the count to hold it in place. He then tore four long strips from around the bottom of the shirt to use as bandages, one of which he gave to Upton to bind Turnbull's head.

He tied the linen strips end to end and wrapped them around the count's chest and shoulder as tightly as he could to keep the wad of cloth pressed against the wound. By the time he finished, the count's teeth were chattering, both from shock and from the cold night air. With permission, he dug through the count's trunk to find a clean shirt and another mantle to replace the one soaked with blood.

Turnbull lay unmoving by the fire, his face drained of color, completely oblivious to Upton's handling of him to clean the gash on his scalp, to bandage his head, and to wrap him in his own cloak.

The count, although still in pain, seemed more comfortable now that he was warmly dressed and his injury bound. He leaned back with a grateful sigh, resting his head on the cloak, which Kyle had folded in such a way as to turn the bloodied portion to the inside.

Kyle picked up the knife to examine it by the light of the flames. The blade was about five inches long, single-edged with a sharp point. The four-inch hilt was fashioned from the antler of a deer.

"This is no weapon," he said, "although your assailant used it like one. The blade is too short, you see, to do any real damage in combat, and the blunt side limits the direction of a man's stroke." He turned it over in his hands. "This is a butcher knife, the kind folks around here use to cut an animal's throat before gutting and bleeding it out."

"Scottish rebels did attack us, then," the count said, more as a statement than a question.

"I wonder," Kyle said.

"The proof is there in your hand, *mon ami,*" the count said. He attempted to sit up, but failed. He fell back, his face contorted with pain. "What more do you need to convince you?"

"It's too neat and tidy to suit me," Kyle said. "We Scots are a frugal breed, and no self-respecting Scotsman, rebel or otherwise, would ever purposely abandon such a fine knife, whatever his cause or conviction." He rubbed a thoughtful hand over the stubble on his chin. "It seems more likely someone wants the rebels blamed for this. If news reached King Philip that Scottish rebels foully murdered his envoy, the good relations between France and Scotland would end. Such news would go a long way to support Edward of England's claim that he does not desire war with France, and that his hands are full subduing rabble in both Scotland and Wales."

"Do you think King Edward is behind this attack?" the count said, incredulous.

"It's possible," Kyle said. "But one of Edward's appointees here in the shire might have ordered it done to curry royal favor."

"If you mean Sir Percy, forget it. That buffoon couldn't find his way to a stinking privy without someone to point the way."

"Well, somebody knew when we were leaving," Kyle said. "They also knew how many of us were going and where we were headed." He sat in silence for a moment, pondering whether they should continue on to Strathaven in the morning or turn back for the garrison. The count's condition was stable for now, but there was always the danger of fever setting in. The next few hours were crucial.

The campfire was burning low, and Upton left Turnbull's side to gather more wood. He soon returned with an armful of broken limbs. He took a flaming stick from the fire to light his way as he went to bring their belongings out from the shadows under the huge pine tree. He was about to toss his makeshift torch onto the fire when a gleaming red object on the ground caught his eye. He stooped to pick it up. "You dropped this," he said, handing the ruby brooch to the count.

"Merci beaucoup," Count Jardine said. His fingers found the rough scratch left by the knife's tip in the gold face. "Ironic, is it not," he said, "that Edward of England, who apparently wants

me dead, gifted me with the very bauble that saved my life." He turned his head to glance around him. Not finding what he sought, he tried to sit up again, and this time he succeeded. "I don't see my saddle roll," he said to Upton.

"This was all that was there," Upton said, indicating the pile of gear in the clearing.

"My saddle roll is gone," the count said to Kyle. "They must have taken it with them."

"No harm done," Kyle said. "I'll wrap your things in your brown cloak. It will do for now."

"You don't understand," the count said, his expression grim. "When they discover that what they seek is not in my saddle roll, they will come back to get it."

The count's words brought Kyle to his feet. The darkness around him took on a menacing aspect, and every shadow became suspect. Though unaware of why the attackers wanted it or even what it was, he knew where it was. He also knew his present position, with two out of four men down, was indefensible. His only hope was to set out in haste, taking an alternate route back to the garrison, before the attackers realized the failure of their undertaking and doubled back to rectify it.

"Upton," he said. "Make ready to leave at once."

"What about Turnbull?" Upton said. "He cannot be slung over the saddle like a sack of grain. It might kill him."

"You pack the gear," Kyle said. "I'll see to Turnbull."

While Upton went to catch the pony, Kyle patted cold water from the skin bottle on the unconscious man's face. He called out his name, shaking him gently at first, then with more vigor, but to no avail. Nothing seemed to rouse Turnbull from his deathlike sleep.

Kyle sat back on his heels, wondering what to do next. He'd seen John bring suchlike ones around using the juice of a common plant to do so. He racked his brain to recall what kind of plant it was, until a single word flashed into his mind.

"Onions!"

Upton looked up from testing the strap that held the count's trunk in place on the pony's back. "Pardon?" he said.

"There should be some onions growing wild around here," Kyle said. "Go take a look while I saddle the horses."

Upton took a firebrand along on the hunt, and by the time he returned with a fistful of wild onions, the horses were saddled and bridled, and Kyle was helping the count to his feet.

Upton knelt beside Turnbull's inert body and twisted the long green stems to release the pungent juices. "Come back to me, old friend," he said, holding the bruised fronds close to the unconscious man's nose.

His efforts produced no reaction whatsoever, not even the tic of an eyelid.

"Turnbull! Wake up!" he cried. Fretting over the lack of response, he practically shoved the malodorous greens up into the prone man's nostrils. "Don't you die on me, you old rascal."

Turnbull's nose twitched in his craggy face. Suddenly, his arm came up to bat away Upton's hand. "God's eyes!" he growled. "Are you trying to kill me, boy?" He scrubbed at the burning skin around his nostrils with the back of his hand.

"Prickly as a hedgehog, as usual," Upton said. His soft laugh ended with a loud sniffle. He wiped his eyes with his wrist. "Bloody onions." He turned away to kick dirt over the campfire to put it out.

Turnbull sat up with a groan. He picked up the skin bottle lying on the ground near him and used the water to wash the onion residue from his face. He was still muttering to himself about the stinging in his nose as Upton hauled him to his feet.

"No more lazing about for you," Upton said. He slung the older man's arm over his own shoulders and set out for where

Kyle was helping Count Jardine climb onto his bay horse in the moonlit clearing. "We have a hard ride ahead of us, so let's get you mounted."

CHAPTER 7

The thunder of hooves in Kyle's dream grew louder and more annoying, until the sound changed into an insistent pounding on his door. He opened his eyes to a murky dawn filtering through the shuttered window in the rear chamber of the sheriff's office.

His first thought was for Count Jardine. The ride back to the garrison had been taxing, both for the count and for Turnbull. The latter made no complaint, stoic that he was, though his pallid complexion and white-knuckled grip on the saddle bow showed he was neither hale nor hearty, despite the pretense that he was.

The count, on the other hand, fared rather badly, nearly toppling from his horse on two occasions, thus forcing them to a snail's pace for the last half of their journey. They arrived shortly after midnight, and with Upton's help, Kyle practically carried the count, white-faced and unsteady on his feet from the loss of blood, up to his chamber over the main hall of the castle. He ordered Upton to take Turnbull to the barracks to see to his welfare, while he stayed only long enough to help the count into bed.

Before withdrawing, he took the count's belt, leaving his own in its place, so the count would know who took it. Though it was unlikely any further harm would befall the envoy under Sir Percy's care, he thought it prudent to move the belt with the much-sought-after item in it to a safer location, since whoever was looking for it was willing to kill for it. When he left the chamber, the count was snoring fitfully, undoubtedly from pain and exhaustion, but still very much alive.

Kyle rolled from his pallet, stiff and weary from a long day in the saddle followed by a short night's sleep. He threw his cloak around his shoulders and made his way to the front room. On opening the door, he saw Upton's anxious face before him in the half-light outside.

"It's Captain Sweeney," Upton said without ceremony or greeting.

Kyle raked his fingers through his ruffled hair. "Can't it wait until morning?" he said.

"It is morning," Upton said.

"What about him, then?" Kyle said without enthusiasm.

"He's dead."

"So, Lucky Jack's luck finally ran out," Kyle said. "I'm not surprised. What happened to him?"

"He was murdered," Upton said. "Inchcape found his body at the Bull and Bear not half an hour ago. He says somebody cut him up pretty badly last night. He says it's rather a mess."

"That means trouble for the rebels," Kyle said, scowling at the implications. "Sir Percy will see to it that the violent death of an English officer translates into a rebel plot. He will no doubt order a thorough investigation in the hope of exposing the ringleaders, even if it means stretching the facts a bit to make himself look good before his king."

He beckoned for Upton to come inside. "Have you seen the body yet?" he said, closing the door behind him.

"No," Upton said. "Inchcape sought me out in the barracks, and I came to see you straightaway. I sent him back to the tavern to make sure nobody goes into Sweeney's room."

"Good man," Kyle said. "I want you to go to Brodie's house right away to ascertain his whereabouts last night. If no one can vouch for him, bring him in. Turnbull is in no shape to ride, so take another man or two with you. Stop by Master John's shop on the way out and ask him to meet me at the Bull and Bear as soon as he can get there."

"Do you really think Brodie did it?" Upton said.

"If I thought Sweeney raped and murdered my daughter," Kyle said, "I'd be tempted to kill him. It's the old way in this country. Blood kin's right, that sort of thing."

Upton shifted from one booted foot to the other, as though reluctant to contradict him. "Brodie has, or rather had, the right to challenge Sweeney to fair combat, but only in accord with English law."

"Brodie isn't English," Kyle said. "Now, off you go."

After Upton left, Kyle put on his clothes and his boots. As he was washing his face, he got a good look at himself in the polished metal mirror above the washstand. His eyes were red-rimmed, his tawny hair disheveled, and the two-day stubble on his chin only accentuated the white scar running down the side of his face. He took the time to shave and comb his hair. After all, Sweeney wasn't going anywhere.

When he was ready, he rolled up the count's belt and stuffed it into the pouch at his side. He crossed the courtyard to the castle and went up to the count's chamber. He found the count sleeping soundly and left him undisturbed, since rest was the best remedy for illness or injury.

He then sought out the officer of the watch to assign three soldiers to him. He sent the first soldier to guard the count's door, with orders to let no one into the chamber except John Logan or himself. If anyone else tried to gain entry, the soldier was to notify Kyle immediately.

The second soldier was dispatched with a message to Sir Percy advising of the count's return, his condition, and that a guard had been posted at his door.

Kyle took the third soldier with him to the stable to saddle their horses. Together, they rode from the garrison, passing through near-empty streets on their way to where Inchcape stood watch over his captain's body.

The Bull and Bear Tavern was a two-story, wood-framed structure situated among the fine stone houses built along Harbour Street facing the River Ayr. An alley on either side separated the public establishment from its well-do-do neighbors.

The beasts depicting the tavern's namesake had been carved into a weathered board, which hung from a signpost out front. Inside the wide gates, a stable on one side and sleeping quarters on the other formed a small courtyard, where travelers could debark from either horse or carriage safely on the tavern's doorstep.

Unlike other taverns in the vicinity, which offered a quiet respite to townsfolk at the end of a long workday, the Bull and Bear catered to English soldiers from the garrison who indulged in gaming and drinking, and whose rowdy conduct often led to drunken brawls. The sleeping quarters weren't all that clean, but they were handy, and the tavern keeper turned quite a profit renting them out by the hour for purposes other than sleeping.

Kyle and the English soldier with him rode into the Bull and Bear's courtyard and dismounted. He noticed two men and two women standing together outside the tavern door. From their haggard appearance, he surmised their slumber had been interrupted.

One of the men, a short, heavyset fellow in a rumpled black velvet tunic and pointed red slippers, broke from the group and hurried over to greet Kyle.

"It's not my fault that Southron got himself killed," the man said, wringing his pudgy hands. "This is a respectable tavern. Always has been."

"Are you the keeper?" Kyle said.

"Aye," the tavern keeper said. His small dark eyes darted from Kyle to the English soldier, then back to Kyle. "Are ye the marshal from the garrison?"

"I am deputy to the Sheriff of Ayrshire," Kyle said. "Who are those people?" He indicated the man and the two women who were watching his every move.

The tavern keeper drew himself to full height, which barely reached Kyle's shoulder. "They work for me," he said.

"I'll need to speak to each of them," Kyle said. To the English soldier beside him, he said: "Close the gates and bar them. Let no one in or out, except for John Logan." His eyes rested on the tavern keeper. "That applies to him as well."

"Are ye shutting me down?" the tavern keep said, incredulous.

"For the time being," Kyle said. His gaze swept the buildings hemming the courtyard. "Is there another way out of here?"

"There's a door to the kitchen out back," the tavern keeper said. "It leads to the alley."

"What about the windows overlooking the alley?" Kyle said, tilting his head toward the sleeping quarters on the second floor.

"They are quite narrow," the tavern keep said. He puffed out his chest with proprietorial pride. "I built them that way to keep folks honest." The mild curiosity on Kyle's face prompted him to add, by way of explanation, "Patrons cannot climb out the windows, ye see, so they must come down to pay their bill."

Kyle acknowledged the tavern keeper's ingenuity with a nod of approval before escorting him over to where the other man stood beside the two women. That man was middle aged, with a nose curved like a hawk's beak under close-set brown eyes. The women, on closer inspection, were adolescent girls, with close-set brown eyes over a less prominent version of the man's hawk-like nose.

"Which of you discovered the body?" he said, directing his query to all of them.

"I did," the tavern keeper said, "but only at the behest of Sergeant Inchcape, and only because I had the keys to open the door to Captain Sweeney's room. Otherwise, I would still be abed, which is where I belong." He stifled a yawn to emphasize his point.

"What do you do here?" Kyle said to the hawk-nosed man.

"I work in the kitchen," the man said. "My daughters help with the cooking."

"Where were you last night?" Kyle said.

"In the kitchen," the man said.

"All night?" Kyle said.

"I sleep there," the man said. "My daughters sleep there, too." He turned a hostile and forbidding countenance on the tavern keeper. "My presence keeps the Southrons from dallying with my girls."

"I have no control over those Southrons," the tavern keeper said, in a whining tone. "Ye should know that by now."

"Did you see or hear anything out of the ordinary last night?" Kyle said.

The man shook his head. "Neither did they," he said, before Kyle could make a similar inquiry of the girls. "They was with me the whole time." His close-set brown eyes held Kyle's gaze in an unwavering stare. "In the kitchen."

The man was lying, and Kyle knew it. Perhaps Sweeney tried to "dally" with one of the girls, and the man killed him in a fit of rage. He scrapped that theory, however, since anyone with a modicum of intelligence would have fled after committing such a crime, as fear often prompted the guilty to do. Although capable of violence, the man appeared to be the sensible sort who would take flight if necessary, and enough of a parent to bring his daughters with him.

The thought then crept into Kyle's mind that the man might have recognized Sweeney's murderer and was determined to shield him.

Or her.

Kyle's eyes strayed to the girls as possible suspects. The gullibility and innocence radiating from each of them caused him to reject the notion without even giving it another thought.

"You and your daughters are free to go," he said to the man. He watched them leave, resigning himself to look elsewhere for the murderer.

"What about me?" the tavern keeper said.

"Don't leave the premises," Kyle said. "I may need you later."

Voices coming from the direction of the gate brought his head around. He started across the courtyard, leaving the disgruntled tavern keeper muttering under his breath.

"Good morrow, Master John," Kyle said, drawing near to the older man to whom the English soldier admitted entry. "I'm glad you're here."

John returned his greeting. "Upton told me Sweeney is dead," he said, dismounting from his mule. His gray hair glistened with early morning dampness. Gray stubble bristled on his chin, unshaved apparently because of his haste to meet Kyle. "He also mentioned somebody got stabbed in the woods. His details were rather sketchy, so perhaps ye can fill me in."

Kyle told John about the attack on them during the night and their subsequent retreat back to the garrison.

John whistled low, shaking his head. "If they had succeeded in killing the French envoy," he said, "King Philip would no doubt place Scottish vessels under the same embargo he imposed on English ships. That would cripple our trade relations with Flanders. The only thing worse would be if Philip declared war on Scotland. We can ill afford to have both France and England fighting against us." He started, as though something just occurred to him. "Should I not attend to the envoy's wound without delay?"

"I looked in on him earlier," Kyle said. "He should be all right until you finish here. I won't keep you that long." With his back to the English soldier, he removed Count Jardine's belt from his pouch. He lifted the thin leather flap along the inner side to expose the folded pieces of vellum concealed along its length. "I want you to place this in a jar and hide it somewhere in your shop. Seal the cover with wax and sprinkle it with dust so it won't stand out from the other jars."

John took the belt, rolled it up, and shoved it to the bottom of his medicament pouch, burying it under containers of salve and rolls of bandages. "It appears to be documents of some kind," he said. "Have ye read them yet?"

"Nay," Kyle said. "When Count Jardine is well enough to travel, you must return the belt to him. Until then, let no one know you have it. Don't even tell me where you put it."

"As ye wish," John said. "What about Sweeney? Have ye any idea who killed him?"

"I have my suspicions," Kyle said. "But first, I'd like you to take a look at his body. I need your best estimate as to the time of death."

He led the way into the dark interior of the tavern and up the steep wooden steps against the back wall. At the top of the stairs, light from a tiny window on the landing dispelled the gloom in the long hallway ahead of him. With John trailing behind him, he approached the man standing guard at one of the seven rooms on the second floor. The door to the guarded room was closed, whereas the other doors along the hallway were open.

The guard was an English soldier, a big muscular man in his forties, with a flat broken nose in a brutish face and a drooping moustache that framed thin lips and a clean-shaven chin. He was completely bald, and when he turned toward Kyle and John advancing on him, light glistened on the oily surface of his skull-like head.

"Sergeant Inchcape," Kyle said. "Upton told me you'd be here."

"So you're the sheriff's deputy," Inchcape said. The words sounded like the rumble of thunder, so deep was his voice. Calculating eyes, dark and heavy-lidded, swept Kyle from tawny head to booted toe, taking his measure. He seemed to revel in the fact that he was brawnier and taller than the lawman standing before him.

Kyle took an instant dislike to Inchcape and saw his own sentiment reflected back to him. There was something predatory about the way the man watched him. The two of them eyed each other like a pair of dogs about to scrap over a single bone, hackles up, ready to go for the throat.

John looked from one to the other. "We're here to examine Captain Sweeney's body," he said.

"And to investigate his murder," Kyle said. "Tell me, Sergeant, why did you ask the tavern keeper to open Captain Sweeney's door earlier this morning?"

"Because it was locked," Inchcape said.

For a brief moment, Kyle wondered if Inchcape was trying to be witty. He dismissed the notion at once, for there was no trace of humor on the man's face. "Let me put it to you another way," he said. "Why did you want to get into his room?"

"Jack never answered when I called out to him," Inchcape said. "He came here often, but not too long ago, he had a little run-in with a jealous husband. After that, he liked me to stay close in case there was trouble. I was kind of weary last night, so I sat down outside the door just to rest my eyes. I must have fallen asleep, because the next thing I knew, it was morning."

"If you were sleeping," Kyle said, "he might have left without you knowing it."

"Not Jack," Inchcape said with conviction. "He always let me know when he was ready to leave. He never liked to spend the whole night here."

"So, you called out to him," Kyle said. "Then what did you do?"

"I knocked to see if he was, uh, busy," Inchcape said. "He never answered, so I called out to him again. He still didn't answer, and that's not like him. I roused the tavern keeper and got him to unlock the door." Color ebbed from his face. "That's when we found him."

"Did you or the tavern keeper touch anything?"

"We never even went in."

"If you didn't go in," Kyle said, "how can you be sure the murderer wasn't still in the room? The tavern keeper bragged that nobody could climb out of those windows."

"I didn't see anybody in there," Inchcape said, his tone defensive.

"Not if he was hiding behind the door," Kyle said, gritting his teeth. "I don't suppose you posted someone to watch the room while you went to fetch Upton?"

Inchcape shook his massive head, his expression like that of a scolded child.

"I didn't think so," Kyle said. He took a deep breath and plunged on. "Since you didn't check his condition, how did you know he was dead?"

"Oh, he was dead, all right," Inchcape said. He stepped aside to let them enter the room, favoring his left leg as he did so. "See for yourself."

The sight of Inchcape's limp made Kyle wonder whether the man might have been the assailant on whom he inflicted a flesh wound with his dirk last night. There was no use asking him how he came by his injury because he would only lie about it, as the guilty were prone to do.

Looking into Sweeney's murder was more important at that moment, so Kyle brushed past Inchcape to open the door and walk into the small room.

The metallic scent of blood tainted the air, as he expected. What he saw was totally unexpected. "God have mercy!" he cried, stopping so abruptly that John bumped into his back.

John leaned around Kyle's shoulder to peer into the room, only to draw in a sharp breath.

A stub of a candle burned listlessly in its holder on the bedside table until a sudden draft from the open door sent the flame dancing. Sallow highlights and deep shadows flickered across Sweeney's body sprawled on the bed, lending to it a macabre animation. The man lay on his stomach, dressed only in leggings, his head turned toward the entryway. His eyes were wide and staring, his lips parted as though in astonishment. The play of light and darkness across his once-handsome face gave the impression that his mouth was moving.

After recovering from the initial shock of seeing a dead man come to life, Kyle chided himself for overreacting to nothing more than an illusion caused by the wavering flame.

He let his gaze rove around the room. The furnishings consisted of a bed and a table on which the candle sat, with a pitcher and a bowl beside it. The window in the outer wall was tall enough to admit light, yet its limited width prohibited anyone but a child from crawling through it.

He noted the stippling of dried blood on the bedcovers around the body and on the wall above the bed. A black puddle stained the floor at the foot of the bed, with long smears in it that reached all the way to the doorway. There were dark streaks on the wood casing and on the door handle inside the room.

"That's strange," he said, frowning down at the dead man.

"What do ye see?" John said from the doorway.

"There's blood everywhere," Kyle said, "except on the body."

John entered the room, picking his way with care around the bloodstains on the floor to cross over to the table. He ran his finger over the last hour-marker scored into the thick base of the candle. "If this was new when he lit it," he said, "then he's been here for nearly seven hours."

"When did he die, do you think?" Kyle said.

John tested the rigidity of Sweeney's limbs. "I'd say four, maybe five hours ago," he said. He closed the sightless eyes with his thumb and forefinger.

"That would put the time of death shortly after midnight," Kyle said. "That's about when we got back to the garrison last night."

John made a cursory inspection of the body. "There are no marks anywhere on his back," he said. "Help me turn him."

Kyle went around the far side of the bed and put his hands on the cold flesh of Sweeney's arm. It was then he spotted the purple bruise on the upper right shoulder. "Well, well," he said to himself. Macalister suspected Sweeney of leading the raid on Ogilvy's homestead, and here was proof, which he put there with his own battle axe.

He and John grappled with rolling over the body, its rigid legs extended and its stiff arms raised as though to ward off calamity. The bedcover came up with it, glued to bare skin with dried blood.

John peeled back the encrusted fabric, exposing a thin gash on the left side of Sweeney's chest. "The blade slid between the ribs and pierced his heart," he said. "Blood from a wound like that can spurt out with great force."

"That would account for the mess up there," Kyle said, glancing at the dried blood spattered on the wall. He came around the bed to look over John's shoulder.

"See that?" John said, indicating the slashed skin under

Sweeney's chin. "A wound like that bleeds profusely. Yet, there's very little blood here, which means it was done postmortem." He beckoned for Kyle to lean closer. "Do ye see that old scarring on his neck?" He pointed to the thin white stripes in the mutilated flesh. "Somebody tried to slit his throat some time ago, but he managed to survive it."

"I reckon that's how he earned the name 'Lucky Jack,' " Kyle said. He looked for scratches, especially those made by fingernails, on Sweeney's arms and upper body, but the skin was without blemish, except for the angry red stab wound on his chest.

He was about to move away from the bed when he saw something on the floor between the table and the wall. He dragged aside the table and retrieved a linen shirt stained with blood. Wrapped within its folds was a solid object that, when he shook it out, clattered to the floor. It was a dagger, with polished gems studding the hilt and a long thin blade caked with dried blood.

He showed the dagger to John. "Could this be what killed him?"

John matched the width of the blade against the length of the fatal wound in Sweeney's chest. "Either it," he said, "or one just like it."

Kyle called Inchcape into the room. "Have you ever seen this dagger before?" he said holding it out for the man's inspection.

Inchcape reached for the dagger. "It belongs to Jack," he said.

Kyle stayed Inchcape's hand. "This may be the murder weapon," he said. "As such, I must turn it over to Sir Percy. He can then send it on to Captain Sweeney's family."

"Fair enough," Inchcape said. "Jack's wife will want to keep it for their son."

"There's nothing more for me to do here," John said. "I

should go on to the garrison now to take a look at the—"

"You do that," Kyle said, cutting him off. He practically shoved John from the room. "Thanks for your help. I'll join you later."

John, who was no fool, apparently understood without being told the need for discretion where the French envoy was concerned. "I'll see ye there, then," he said, before hurrying out of the room.

Inchcape remained just inside the doorway. His only reaction to the odd exchange between Kyle and John was to lift a dark eyebrow. If he was at all curious, he kept it to himself. "Any idea who did it?" he said, glancing over at the dead man on the bed.

"Not at the moment," Kyle said. "Send for a wagon with an escort to take the body to St. John's."

After Inchcape limped away, Kyle gazed slowly around the room, his pale blue eyes intent on every detail. He thought it peculiar that Sweeney's belongings were nowhere in sight. If the man undressed there, then his gear must be somewhere nearby. On a hunch, he knelt down to look under the bed. He was rewarded with the discovery of a black leather jerkin, a worn leather belt with scabbard and sword attached, and an empty sheath of a size to fit the dagger he found earlier. He inspected each item before laying it on the bed beside the body. The only thing he learned was that Sweeney was remiss about the upkeep of his sword, the blade of which was pitted with rust.

He perused the long smears in the dried stain on the wood floor. It looked as if the murderer skidded in the blood as he came around the bed to get to the doorway. The dark smudges on the casing and the handle most likely came from the man's bloody hands as he attempted to open the door.

For a moment, he pondered how the murderer got out of the locked room. He toyed with the idea that the man might have, indeed, slipped away after Inchcape left the door unlocked and unguarded. He dismissed the thought because of the significant question it raised: if the door was locked from the inside, which meant Sweeney used the key to lock it, why didn't the murderer simply use that same key to get out of the room?

He peered into the pitcher on the table beside the bed, as if the answer might be found somewhere in its hollow depths. "Empty," he said.

That, too, was significant. Without water, the murderer could not wash off the blood. In order get to the street, he must go down the steps and through the tavern, which put him at risk of being seen with blood on his clothing.

He went over to the window, which was the only other feasible avenue of escape. He inspected the sill, inside and out. Under the lip outside, he found a shred of common homespun caught on a jagged splinter of wood. He extricated the threads and tucked them into his coin purse.

He stuck his head through the cramped opening of the window to consider the murderer's options. Above him, the eaves extended out too far to permit access to the roof. Below him was a twelve-foot drop to the ground. There was another window directly beneath his, with a casing around it that offered a two-inch toehold halfway down the face of the outer wall. It seemed improbable to go that way, but not necessarily impossible.

He looked down into the alley, but the early morning light was still too muted to clearly see the ground below. He left Sweeney's room, closing the door behind him. He descended the stairs and went out the back door of the tavern, intent on examining the alleyway for prints or other evidence left from the night before.

A tiny walled courtyard in the rear separated the wooden tavern from a stone structure housing the kitchen. The only way in or out was through the alley. Vendors and merchants unloaded food goods and other supplies in the courtyard for the cook, though they barely had room to turn their pony-carts around because of the clutter of old barrels, discarded boxes, and firewood stacked against the outer kitchen wall.

Smoke rose from the kitchen's wide chimney, and the scent of baking bread drifted in the air. He noted that anyone standing in the kitchen doorway, the cook for instance, could look straight into the alley, and at night, light from the windows on the tavern's ground floor would enable him to see along the entire length of it.

He caught a flicker of movement out of the corner of his eye as a heap of rags stirred inside a fallen barrel beside the kitchen wall. He dismissed it as a rat or some other scavenger looking for scraps of food, until the rags began to crawl from the barrel.

It turned out to be a beggar swaddled in tattered clothing, reeking of body odor and stale ale. The man climbed stiffly to his feet, which were shod with ill-fitting felt shoes. An empty sleeve, where his arm was missing, hung down from his shoulder. He appeared to be an old soldier, thin from want of regular meals. The gray streaks in his grizzled beard put him in his fifties.

Kyle stared at the beggar for a moment, uttering a silent prayer of thanksgiving that the scar on his face was the only reminder of his years as a mercenary. "Have you been here all night?" he said.

"Who wants to know?" the beggar said in a gravelly voice.

Kyle introduced himself. "There's been a murder in the tavern," he said. "Did you hear anything unusual last night?"

The beggar shrugged his shoulders, his expression vague, as though unsure of either the question or the answer.

"Never mind," Kyle said. He dug a silver penny from his purse and pressed the coin into the beggar's grubby hand. It wasn't much, but it was enough for the man to buy his bread with dignity, rather than to beg for it.

"God bless," the beggar said. He wandered toward the kitchen door, as if drawn by the smell of baking bread.

Kyle turned into the alley, from which came the stench of urine. It was a common practice for men to relieve themselves against the stone wall along the alleyway before going back into the tavern to drink more ale.

He walked down the alley until he stood directly beneath the window to Sweeney's room. The dirt should have been pitted from foot traffic and churned from the wheels of carts and the hooves of ponies. The ground was smooth as far as he could see in either direction, except for the imprint of his own boots coming from the kitchen courtyard.

Someone, it seemed, saw fit to sweep the alley clean. Rather than being discouraging, the knowledge buoyed his spirits. It meant he was on the right track. The murderer did, in fact, exit the tavern through the window. Otherwise, why take the time to wipe out the telltale signs of his presence there? In addition, he now knew something about the murderer he didn't know before: his physical description. Only a very thin man could fit through the cramped opening of the window.

He heard the sound of labored breathing behind him. He turned to find the tavern keeper hurrying toward him with a purposeful expression on his plump face. Over the tavern keeper's shoulder, he caught a fleeting glimpse of the cook retreating behind the kitchen door. He wondered how long the cook had been watching him, and whether it was to see what he found in his search of the alley.

"I've something to tell ye," the tavern keeper said, after pausing to catch his breath. "Something I remembered about last night."

CHAPTER 8

"There was a young man here last night who lost at gaming," the tavern keeper said. "A Ross retainer, I think. I remember him because of the fuss he made. He claimed he was cheated. Stormed out of the back room in a foul temper, he did. Before he left the tavern, he threatened to get even with them that cheated him. Those were his exact words."

"How much did he lose?" Kyle said.

"I don't know, but it must have been a lot from the way he carried on. There were others who heard him, too. His sister, for one."

"Where can I find her?"

"She'll be here this evening to serve the tables," the tavern keeper said. He fixed a withering stare upon Kyle. "I don't suppose that's going to happen now, though."

"Why not?"

"Because ye shut me down."

"I'm done here," Kyle said. "You can carry on as usual. I still need to talk to the girl, however. What is her name?"

The tavern keeper seemed barely able to contain his joy at being back in business so soon. "Maize," he said with a broad smile.

Kyle started to leave, but he turned back. "By the way," he said, "to whom did the young man direct his threat?"

The smile vanished from the tavern keeper's plump face. "Why, Captain Sweeney, of course."

Kyle walked up the alley to Harbour Street and went around to the front gates of the tavern. The English soldier stationed there let him in, at which time he instructed the man to let no one else enter until Inchcape came to take the body away.

He rode back to the garrison, and after stabling the gelding, he crossed the courtyard to the castle. He went up to Count Jardine's chamber, pausing outside the door to inquire of the English soldier posted there whether anyone tried to gain entry.

"Only John Logan," the soldier said. "He's still inside."

"Good," Kyle said. He entered the chamber just as John was tucking a roll of linen into his medicament pouch.

The count reclined on a raised bed, with his back propped against cushions. His maroon brocade dressing gown was open at the chest, showing the clean bandages swathing his injured shoulder. A charcoal brazier burned nearby, and blue velvet privacy drapes had been tied back against the bed posts on either side to let in the warmth.

With a nod of greeting to John, Kyle approached the count's bed. "How do you feel, *m'sire?*" he said.

"Better," the count said. "Much better." His face was still pale, but his voice was strong. "Master John gave me something for the pain."

"Rest now," John said, "for ye have lost a good deal of blood. I shall return on the morrow. In the meantime, take a little more of this poppy juice if ye cannot sleep." He set a stoppered phial on the small table beside the bed. He then took his leave and withdrew from the chamber.

"I posted a guard outside your door for your protection," Kyle said after John left.

"Not much point now, is there?" the count said, watching him closely.

"I've removed the item to a safer location," Kyle said, "if that is what concerns you. It will be returned to you at once, however, should you wish it so."

"Where is it?" the count said.

"In trusted hands," Kyle said, "where no one would ever think of looking for it. And to set your mind at ease, no one, including me, knows what it contains."

"I suppose I must be content with that," the count said with a sigh. "Forgive my undue concern. I have learned the wisdom of treading with care in the presence of friend and foe alike." A shiver prompted the count to fumble with the silken ties to close his dressing gown.

"If I may," Kyle said. At the count's nod of appreciation, he secured the ties and moved the brazier closer to the bed.

The count settled deeper into the cushions. "The young man Upton impressed me yesterday with his honesty," he said, "and I don't impress easily. Can you tell me something more of his character?"

"I've known him for less than a week," Kyle said. "Yet, I like what I've seen so far. He's a reliable, serious-minded fellow."

"Do you trust him?"

"I do," Kyle said, after a moment of thought.

"I want him to return to France with me as my aide. Do you think he will accept the position?"

"That is for him to say."

The count stifled a yawn. "I do hope he will at least consider it," he said. His eyelids drooped as the poppy juice began to take effect.

Kyle retrieved his own belt and put it on. He left the count's chamber, closing the door quietly behind him. He went out into the courtyard and crossed over to the sheriff's office, where he found Upton waiting for him out front.

"I just got back from seeing Brodie," Upton said. "His daughter claims he was in the house with her yesterday evening and all last night. She says he never left, or she would have heard him."

"Did you believe her?"

"No reason not to."

"How's Turnbull?"

"Grouchy as ever."

"I mean his injury."

"He's on the mend. How is Count Jardine?"

"So far, so good," Kyle said. "By the way, the count wants to take you to France to serve as his aide."

Although mildly surprised, Upton appeared pleased to hear it. "I'm grateful you told me, so I can give it some thought," he said. "I have family ties in England, but as a second son with no inheritance, I must make my own way in the world. The position as aide presents an opportunity for advancement in rank, which I will need to get ahead." He uttered something that sounded like a humorless laugh. "It is ironic that as an English soldier, I am obliged to fight against the French, yet I may end up as aide to a French envoy who opposes the English." An unaccustomed solemnity clouded his pleasant features. "Despite that, I am sorely tempted to accept the count's offer. Not that I particularly want to be an aide, mind you, but it will provide the means to escape from this place." He waved a hand at the garrison around him. "Never to return, to get as far from strife and conflict as I possibly can."

"I don't believe there is a country, far or near, free from either strife or conflict."

"Anywhere would be better than here," Upton said with feeling.

"If you do move on," Kyle said, "I shall miss you. There are few English like you, who treat us Scots with dignity and respect."

"There are more Englishmen like me than you think. They, too, disapprove of the abuses heaped upon your countrymen, but they, like me, lack the authority or the power to put a stop to it."

"I would settle for one such man just now, to stand in as sergeant when you leave. Can you recommend someone?"

"You'll have me packed before I'm ready to go," Upton said with a grin. "If I do depart, however, I would suggest Vinewood. He's a good man."

Kyle made a mental note to take Vinewood along on his next outing to see if he agreed with Upton's assessment.

Later that same evening, Kyle rode back to the Bull and Bear. He handed the reins to a waiting groom before crossing the small courtyard to enter the tavern. He ducked under the low-hanging lintel and stood erect in the stifling warmth inside. The murmur of voices within sounded like the hum of bees. The smell of roasted chicken reminded him that he was hungry.

Oil lanterns hung from the rafters on long chains, filling the air with a smoky haze and casting a mellow light upon chewed bones and dirty straw strewn about the planked floor. The wooden stairs on the back wall led up to the second floor.

A dozen or so trestle tables were situated about the room in no particular order. Most of those seated there were English soldiers, who nursed cups of brew or hunched over their supper. A black-haired young woman was serving ale to a group of rowdy soldiers, one of whom was a handsome young man with seductive dark eyes who put an arm around her waist and refused to let her go.

Kyle made his way over to her through the maze of tables. "I'd like a word with you, mistress," he said.

The young woman turned her face to him. She was no beauty, but her youthful complexion was fresh and smooth. Her tight bodice accentuated her full breasts, and the soft fabric of her dress showed every curve of her shapely body. Smudges of weariness under her soft brown eyes made her look older than her sixteen years, and the direct gaze that rested on Kyle held no illusions as to her lot in life. She slipped from the handsome young soldier's grasp and stepped out of his reach.

The handsome young soldier accepted her evasive maneuver with good humor and laughed with his fellows. "Next time, Maize, you won't get away so easy," he said to her with a gleam of mischief in his dark eyes.

Maize flashed a parting smile at him before leading Kyle over to an empty table in a quiet corner.

He sat down, gesturing for her to sit on the wooden bench across from him.

She perched on the edge of the bench, studying his features. "I know ye," she said. "Ye are the new deputy." Her eyes lingered on the faded scar that ran from temple to jaw on his face. "I can only stay for a minute. This is the busiest time of day."

"Tell me about your brother," Kyle said. "The one who was here last night."

A shadow of fear crossed her face so fleetingly, he wondered if he imagined it.

"What do ye want to know?" she said evenly.

"What is his name?"

"It is Hew."

"Is he still in the employ of Aiden Ross?"

"I believe so."

"A witness claims Hew went into the back room to game with the English. How long did he stay back there?"

"An hour," she said. "Maybe two."

"Did you see him come out?"

"I didn't need to see him. I heard him, like everybody else."

"Did you hear him threaten the English for cheating him?"

"I don't recall," she said, rising abruptly. "I must go now. They're calling for me." She leaned close to add, "Hew might

161

get unruly and loud when he's drunk, but he's no murderer. It wasn't him what killed that Southron."

Kyle watched her walk away, aware that he knew no more now than when he first entered the tavern. Although she believed her brother was innocent, he would find out on the morrow what Hew had to say for himself and whether the young man was worthy of his sister's loyalty to him.

He caught the tavern keeper's eye and beckoned him over to his table.

"So," the tavern keeper said as he approached. "What did Maize have to say about her brother?"

"Bring me stew," Kyle said, evading the question with as much skill as Maize when she earlier slipped from the handsome soldier's grasp.

"It was her brother who did it, was it not?" the tavern keeper said, a smug expression on his plump face. "I knew it."

Kyle fixed a bland stare on the heavyset man. "I'll take a mug of ale, too," he said.

"As ye wish, Master Deputy," the tavern keeper said. He bustled away, as though bursting with the gossip he was about to spread.

While waiting for his supper to arrive, Kyle let his gaze rove about the room. The older soldiers seemed to prefer the company of others like themselves, who ate and chatted quietly together. The younger soldiers were a more boisterous lot who drank heavily and laughed heartily.

A particularly raucous group of young soldiers at a table nearby launched into a bawdy drinking song. At the end of each chorus, they clanked their pewter cups together, sloshing the contents and roaring with good-natured drunken laughter.

Before long, Maize brought to Kyle's table a cup of ale and a hollowed-out loaf of stale bread filled with thick chicken stew. After paying her for his food, he started in on it. It smelled better than it tasted, but it was hot and he was hungry.

As Maize walked away, the handsome young soldier caught her around the waist and pulled her onto his knee. He and those at the table with him joined in the singing. This time, she stayed put, as though transfixed by the angelic tenor of his voice, which soared above the earthbound, and sometimes off-key, baritones around him.

Kyle finished eating just as another soldier tried to wrestle Maize from the handsome young soldier's grasp. The ensuing tussle rapidly escalated into a brawl, with onlookers jostling each other and throwing punches at anyone within reach.

A pair of scuffling soldiers tumbled onto Kyle's table, squashing the remains of his meal beneath them. He heaved them onto the floor and got to his feet. Rather than attempting to break up the fracas, he started toward the door. It would soon end anyway, when the participants grew either too weary or too thirsty to continue brawling.

A burly soldier with a red face barred his way, balling a meaty fist to take a swing at him. Kyle blocked the punch and landed a solid blow to the man's stomach, causing him to fold over and crumple to the floor, his hands clutched to his fleshy belly.

Kyle pushed his way across the room, thrusting aside all who crossed his path. He almost made it to the door when someone crowded him from behind. He would have ignored it, except for the slight tug he felt on the sheath at his side. He turned in time to see the handsome young soldier directly behind him, grappling with an older man who clutched a familiar-looking dirk in his calloused hand.

The young soldier clasped the wrist of the older man's knife hand and wrenched his other arm up his back. "Drop it," he said, applying pressure to the twisted arm.

The older man complied, his yellow teeth gritted in pain. "I didn't mean no harm," he whined. He was leaner and taller than the young soldier holding him fast. The skin of his face was pitted from a childhood disease, and a prominent nose dominated his sharp features. His eyes were as black as obsidian and filled with malice.

The young soldier shoved the older man away and stooped to retrieve the dirk. "I believe this is yours," he said, handing it back to Kyle, who returned it to his sheath.

The older man cast a baleful glance at both Kyle and the handsome young soldier before he disappeared into the fray.

"Thanks," Kyle said. He went on through the tavern door, grateful to be outside. He filled his lungs with the cold night air as he crossed the courtyard to the stable.

At sunrise the next morning, the bells of St. John's rang in the hour of prime. The sky was clear and held the promise of a fine spring day to come.

Kyle mounted the steep wooden steps to the guard walk along the top of the garrison wall to seek out the officer of the watch. "How fares Turnbull since his injury?" he said, addressing the stout Englishman standing at his post.

The officer of the watch huddled in his wool cloak against the sharp wind blowing in from the firth. "Master John says he'll be fit for duty in a day or so," he said. "I look forward to when he's on his feet and out from under mine."

"At least he's on the mend," Kyle said. "I'm going to see Sir Aiden Ross this morning about one of his retainers, and I want Upton to come with me. I'd like to take Vinewood, too, if he's available."

"That won't be a problem. I'll send someone to tell them to saddle up and meet you at the sheriff's office."

"They are to bear light arms, without armor. Sir Ross is a mite twitchy about English troops invading his keep."

"But it will just be the two of them."

"Sir Ross is likely to take it amiss if he sees even a couple of fully armed soldiers tramping across his drawbridge. You don't want to be responsible for causing an incident, do you?"

"Of course not," the officer said with a worried frown. "I'll advise Upton and Vinewood to dress as you request."

Kyle gave the man a reassuring nod before he descended the steps. He crossed the courtyard to the stable, where he saddled the gelding. He went back to the sheriff's office, leaving the horse tied to the rail outside.

A quarter of an hour later, a knock on the door brought him to his feet. He opened the door to Upton, with the handsome young soldier from the tavern standing behind him, holding the reins of their horses in his hand.

Both young men were bareheaded, clad as though for a day's outing, in tan leather jerkins over off-white linen shirts and brown wool leggings. Each wore a sword under his short russet cloak.

"This is Vinewood," Upton said, jerking his thumb at his companion.

"We've met," Kyle said with a wry smile.

"So he told me," Upton said. "I understand Weems tried to stab you from behind last night."

"Without success," Kyle said. "Thanks to Vinewood."

"He's not to be trusted, that one," Vinewood said. "If I was you, I wouldn't turn my back on him."

"I don't plan to," Kyle said, "now that I know who he is."

"It's a pleasant day for a ride," Upton said with a wide grin.

"That it is," Kyle said, glancing up at the streaks of bright gold across the eastern sky. "Let's away."

The three of them mounted their horses and rode from the garrison. They turned south to follow the coastal road past Alloway. Sandy beaches sloping gently into the sea soon gave way to rock formations, high cliffs, and pounding surf. Seagulls spiraled down from roosts on the crags, filling the air with piercing screams as they swooped and glided on the updrafts.

Kyle was thankful to be out in the open, with the wind in his face and the crash of breakers in his ears. Upton seemed especially pleased to be in attendance, as reflected by the contented smile on his face when he apparently thought no one was looking.

The Ross keep soon came into view, perched on the edge of a precipice, overlooking the churning waters of the Firth of Clyde below. High stone walls protected the inland sides, while the sea guarded its back. The single round tower, visible over the curtain walls, was smaller than that of most of the fortresses situated along the western coast, but it was equally imposing with its crenellated parapets and slotted windows. A narrow causeway led up to the wooden drawbridge spanning a deep gorge. The lowered portcullis barred access to the arched entryway.

The ring of hooves on stone alerted the gatekeeper, who hailed them from a watchtower on the wall above them. Kyle identified himself and those with him, after which the gatekeeper signaled for someone within the walls to raise the portcullis.

The heavy chain that hoisted the great iron barrier screeched and groaned until the winch ground to a halt. They passed under the iron teeth of the portcullis and rode through the stone entryway into the courtyard beyond, where a dozen men and women went about their daily duties. A stable, a store house, and other outbuildings lined the inside of the curtain wall, along with pens filled with pigs and cows. Chickens roamed freely, pecking and scratching the hard surface of the ground at will.

A young groom came out from the stable to take the reins of the horses as Kyle and the two English soldiers dismounted.

A comely young woman in her late teens with hair the color of honey came down the steps leading up to the tower. Light green ribbons dangled from her dark green linen dress, richly embroidered at the neck and around the cuffs. She started across the courtyard to greet Kyle, although her step faltered when she saw Upton and Vinewood standing behind him.

Kyle remembered seeing her with Joneta at the marketplace a couple of days ago. Her presence there at the keep jogged his memory as to why she had looked so familiar to him at the time. "Elspeth Ross," he said. "You're all grown up now, and just as pretty as can be."

She blushed, which only added to her childish beauty. "Ye flatter me, Master Kyle," she said. "I know ye came to see Father, so I'll take ye straight up to him." She hesitated, her eyes on Upton and Vinewood. "Perhaps they should remain here. Ye know how Father is."

"I do, indeed," Kyle said. He was well acquainted with Aiden Ross's opinion of the English, which obviously remained unchanged since he last spoke to the man six years earlier.

Elspeth's eyes seemed drawn to Upton. Her expression softened as her gaze clung to his face, intent on every detail. He returned her ardent look with naked longing for her.

Vinewood flashed a winsome smile her way, but she hardly spared him a second glance, despite his handsome features.

"Well, well," Kyle said to Vinewood in a low voice. "So that's the way the wind blows. No wonder he was so keen to come here. Does Sir Ross know of his daughter's amour with an Englishman?"

"I don't think so," Vinewood said. "Otherwise, he would bar Upton from entry."

"They need to be discreet," Kyle said, "or word will reach Sir Ross soon enough." He let out a sigh. Only one woman ever looked at him like that, and that was many years ago. He started toward the tower, shaking his head over the folly of youth, leaving the lovers together, oblivious to all but each other, she with her light green ribbons fluttering in the breeze, and he with a crooked grin on his face.

Before he reached the steps leading up to the tower, Elspeth tore herself away from Upton and hurried to catch up with him.

"Forgive my lapse in manners, Master Kyle," she said. "I don't know what came over me."

"No harm done," he said, with a twinge of regret. Without meaning to do so, she gave him a glimpse of what was missing from his life.

Together, they mounted the hewn steps. At the top, he opened the door to the tower and held it for her to pass through. "It's been a while since I've seen your father," he said. "Is he keeping well these days?"

"As well as can be expected," she said.

She led the way across the main hall and up a flight of steps in the curved stairwell. At the landing, she paused to knock on a sturdy oak door. When a muffled voice inside the chamber bade her to enter, she opened the door and stepped aside for Kyle to go in alone.

Sir Aiden Ross rose from one of a pair of high-backed chairs situated in front of a crackling blaze in a fireplace large enough to roast an ox. He was short and stocky, with graying hair and blunt features in a bearded face. He crossed the timber-plank floor of the tower room to greet his visitor. His stride was vigorous for a man of middle age, and he carried his head low in his powerful shoulders, giving the impression of a charging bull. The woolen tunic he wore was as unadorned as the circular stone walls around him.

"Come in, come in," he said in a forceful tone. "Warm yerself by the fire."

Kyle entered the chamber, which smelled of newly cut logs

and burning hardwood. A trestle table in the center with benches on either side held a decanter and goblets made of silver. Heavy beams overhead supported the floor of the chamber above. Narrow slits in the thick stone walls let in not only chilly air and morning light, but the incessant crash of frenzied waves against the base of the cliff far below.

Sir Ross poured wine from the decanter into two goblets and thrust into each a hot poker from the fireplace. He held out the goblets, letting his guest choose one and taking the other for himself. They settled themselves in the chairs before the fireplace and exchanged the customary civilities while they sipped their drink.

"Good wine, this," Kyle said, stretching out his legs to the fire to warm his booted feet. "French, I think."

"Aye," Sir Ross said. "Hard to come by in these parts, unless ye know a smuggler or two who will oblige."

Kyle cast an inquiring glance at his host. "Really?" he said.

Sir Ross shifted in his chair, as though he suddenly recalled that he sat in the company of a man of law. "Not that I would deal with smugglers or any of that lot," he said with fervor.

"Perish the thought," Kyle said. He took another sip of wine to hide a smile.

Sir Ross cleared his throat. "Glad we sorted that out," he said. "Now tell me, what brings ye out this way?"

"Murder, I'm afraid," Kyle said. "Captain Jack Sweeney of Ayr Garrison was found stabbed to death at the Bull and Bear Tavern early yesterday morning."

"What has that to do with me?"

"A retainer in your employ was heard to threaten Sweeney shortly before the murder took place. His name is Hew, and I have a few questions to put to him."

"I know the lad. He's a harmless pup. Otherwise, I would not let him drive Elspeth to town in the carriage whenever she wants to go. He drove her there the other day. I remember because she came back so late. She never usually stays out that late. That's the only reason I noticed."

"Is Hew here now?"

"He's around somewhere," Sir Ross said. "I'll send for him." He heaved himself to his feet and crossed the room to open the door. He bellowed for Elspeth, filling the stairwell with the echo of his booming voice.

A moment later, she appeared in the doorway. "Ye called, Father?" she said.

"Fetch Hew for me, will ye?" Sir Ross said. He closed the door and resumed his seat before the fire. "Nasty business, murder. Heard some unsavory things about Sweeney, though. I cannot say I'm sorry to hear he's dead. He and his men trampled a tenant of mine about a month gone. Hanged him on a tree in the woods, they did. Sir Percy heard of it, but he did nothing. The man ran, ye see, and Sweeney and his lot claimed they mistook him for the rebel they were chasing." He shook his head, a sad expression on his ruddy face. "Left a young wife and a newborn babe behind. A real shame."

"Sir Percy wants Sweeney's murderer brought to justice as soon as possible."

"Too bad," Sir Ross said without sympathy. He stared into the fire as he sipped his wine. "Such a pretty little thing, she was. I told her she could stay on here, but she took the babe and went to live with her in-laws." A knock on the door brought his head around. "Come in," he hollered over his shoulder. He got up to sit at the table and gestured for Kyle to join him there.

A freckled, coltish boy of seventeen, all knees and elbows in a sleeveless gray tunic, walked through the doorway. He stopped short when he saw Kyle seated at the table. His brown eyes shifted to Sir Ross. "Ye sent for me, Master Aiden?" he said in a respectful tone.

"The sheriff's deputy has some questions for ye," Sir Ross said.

The closed and wary expression on the young retainer's face did not perturb Kyle in the least. He often encountered such defensive behavior during official inquiries, even from those with nothing to hide. "Hew, is it?" he said.

"Aye," Hew said slowly, as though reluctant to admit to his name.

"You were seen at the Bull and Bear Tavern on Monday evening," Kyle said. "What was your business there?"

Fear stole across Hew's face, only to vanish in the blink of an eye. "Gaming," he said.

Kyle's eyelid twitched involuntarily at the mention of a pastime that had held him in its thrall years earlier. Although he steered clear of that particular vice nowadays, he understood the irresistible appeal it held for those who gave themselves over to it. "How much did you lose?" he said.

"Every penny in my purse," Hew said with vehemence. "And then some."

"Who extended credit to you?"

"A Southron by the name of Lucky Jack. They should call him 'Cheating Jack,' because that's what he does."

"A witness says you threatened Lucky Jack before you left the tavern."

"I might have done. He fiddled me out of all my money."

"All your money, and then some."

"Aye," Hew said. "He wanted me to square the debt by Sunday next, or else."

"Or else what?"

"He didn't say," Hew said, "but I've heard tales of what happens to those who cross him." He looked as though he was about to burst into tears. "There's no way I can come up with the money by then. I need more time."

"Are you aware," Kyle said, "that Lucky Jack was murdered shortly after you left the tavern?"

On hearing the news, Hew's mouth fell open in astonishment. His dubious gaze slid to Sir Ross, who nodded his head in confirmation. "Dead," he said with reverent awe, although he looked more relieved than worried.

Kyle lapsed into silence, his eyes on Hew, who was of a size to fit through the cramped tavern window. The young retainer was certainly strong enough to lower himself to the ground below without breaking a bone in the process. In spite of that, Maize's assessment of her brother seemed to be accurate after all, for Hew did not strike him as a murderer.

Hew fidgeted under Kyle's scrutiny, shifting from one foot to the other. Then suddenly, his eyes widened in horrified comprehension. Anxiety crowded out the relief on face. "Ye don't think I did it, do ye?" he said, visibly shaken.

"What time did you arrive back here on Monday night?" Kyle said.

Hew gnawed on his bottom lip. "Shortly after compline," he said. "I heard the bells ringing. There was time enough to rub down the horse and clean the tack before I sought my pallet for the night."

"Thank you, Hew," Kyle said. "You may go."

Hew hesitated for only an instant before scuttling away. He paused at the doorway to give Sir Ross a hasty salute, after which he vanished into the stairwell.

"What do ye think?" Sir Ross said.

"He didn't do it," Kyle said. "I shall speak to the gatekeeper on the way out to confirm the time of Hew's return on Monday night, but from what I gathered after speaking with him, he is not the one I seek."

"That's good to hear," Sir Ross said. "Hew's a decent sort,

even if he does have a lot to learn."

Kyle rolled the stem of the silver goblet between his thumb and forefinger, his brows drawn together. "Can you tell me," he said, lifting his gaze to his host, "anything about how my father died?"

Sir Ross spread his elbows out on the table. "I heard he was killed in the ambush at Loudoun Hill in 'ninety-two," he said. "The Southrons fell upon a band of rebels there in the pass and massacred every one of them. Left the bodies lying in the road to rot, they did. The incident stirred up such a furor against the officer who led the attack, the Castellan of Ayr transferred him to a garrison in some northern shire. That didn't do much good, because no one around here is likely to forget him or what he did."

Kyle leaned forward, his pale blue eyes intent on the older man. "What was his name?" he said in a controlled voice.

"Fenwick."

Kyle's blood ran cold at the mention of the officer's name, for the knowledge of it brought him a step closer to finding his father's murderer. It was a name he, too, would never forget, burned as it now was into his brain, as if with a red-hot branding iron. He already knew the answer to his next question, yet he felt compelled to ask it anyway. "Were the rebels betrayed, do you think?" he said.

"Of course, they were. Such a thing could not have taken place unless somebody informed the Southrons exactly when those rebels would be riding through that pass."

"I don't suppose you know where my father is buried."

Sir Ross shook his head. "I wish I could be more helpful," he said.

"You've been more than helpful," Kyle said. He drained the wine in his goblet and stood up. "I enjoyed our visit, Sir Ross, but I must no longer trespass upon your kind hospitality."

"Sorry ye came all the way out here for nothing," Sir Ross said, rising to his feet.

"Hew would not consider my finding him innocent as nothing," Kyle said.

"That's for sure," Sir Ross said, starting for the door. "Good luck in yer search for the murderer, though it doesn't seem fitting somehow to hang the man who rid the shire of a pestilent fellow like Sweeney."

"I share your opinion," Kyle said. "Unfortunately, it is my duty to hunt such felons, not to judge them."

Prior to his departure, Kyle sought out the gatekeeper. The man not only confirmed the time of Hew's return on Monday night, but he also swore that no one left the keep on his watch, which ended at sunrise on Tuesday morning.

Kyle hardly spoke a word to Upton or Vinewood during the ride back to the garrison, preoccupied as he was with Fenwick's part in his father's murder. The castellan prior to Sir Percy would have kept correspondence and other documentation concerning the incident at Loudoun Hill. He needed to get his hands on those records without arousing suspicion as to his motives for doing so.

The hollow clop of hooves on the wooden bridge leading into Ayr Garrison roused him from his reverie. As he rode into the courtyard, he spied Ewan and Gib, from the village of Harefoot Law, sitting cross-legged in front of the sheriff's office, with a small gray bundle on the ground between them.

When the two boys saw Kyle, they leaped to their feet and ran to meet him.

"We found it," Gib said, quivering with excitement.

Kyle reined in and dismounted. "What did you find?" he said, looking from one boy to the other.

"Megan's other shoe," Ewan said. He held out a small bundle of gray wool cloth tied round with a cord.

"Well done," Kyle said, taking it from the boy. As he hefted it in his hand, he heard the faint clunk of solid objects bumping together inside. "There's more than a shoe in here."

"Aye," Ewan said, with a sad expression on his face. "We found the bundle close to where we found the shoe. I saw no harm in opening it. When I found it were hers, I put the shoe inside so as not to lose it before we brought it to you."

"Can you tell me exactly where you found the shoe?" Kyle said.

"I can," Ewan said. "It were under the old holly that leans over the track. We passed by there on the way to see her grave in the wood the other day. Ye might remember the place, seeing as how the ground is high and dry along that stretch."

"I do recall ducking under a low-hanging branch that almost swept me from the saddle," Kyle said.

"That's the tree," Ewan said. He then frowned, puzzled. "I don't know how we missed seeing the shoe earlier. It was right there in the middle of the track."

"Perhaps some critter dragged it out into the open," Kyle said. He dug into his coin purse for a couple of halfpennies and gave one to each boy. "Here you are. You've earned this. Now, off you go."

After the boys scampered away, no doubt headed for the marketplace to squander their money on sweets, Kyle tied the gelding to the rail in front of the sheriff's office and went inside. He laid the bundle on the table and loosened the cord. He unrolled the gray wool cloth, which turned out to be a garment like the one Megan wore on the day she was killed.

Besides the soft leather shoe, there were two other articles in the folds of the material: a wooden comb and a small oval mirror of polished metal. There was nothing fancy about the comb. It was a serviceable item carved by hand from hard wood. The mirror, though, was another matter. Its edges were filed smooth and buffed to a high gloss like its face. It was too costly for someone of little means like Megan to afford, so he surmised the mirror must have been a gift.

He gazed down at the meager collection of Megan's worldly possessions. Vanity was cause enough for a girl to carry a comb and a mirror around. On the other hand, the only reason she would take clothing with her was because she meant to leave home. Was Megan planning to run away with her lover since she was pregnant? Or did she meet her end at the hands of her lover because she was pregnant? Who was her lover, and more to the point, was he the father of her unborn child?

There was much to think about, but he found it difficult to reflect on such weighty matters on an empty stomach. After feeding and watering the gelding, he went over to the main hall for the midday meal. He later returned to the sheriff's office to sit on the bench in the front room, his back against the wall with his booted feet propped on a stool, to ponder the village girl's death and how the random pieces of that puzzle fit together.

CHAPTER 9

Kyle woke with a start as the bells of St. John's rang in the hour of vespers. Although he really meant to stay awake, he did need the rest. Now refreshed, he washed and dried his face before going out into the fading dusk. He mounted the gelding and headed for St. John's to attend the evening service.

The interior of the church was gloomy, illuminated only by beeswax candles around the altar. From his position at the rear, he could see most of those standing ahead of him. He recognized the baker with his hat in hands that were large and strong from years of kneading bread dough. The tinsmith, a stout balding man in his forties, was there, too. He noted with interest the devout woman, veiled and kneeling, who still prayed with such ardor.

John Logan was also present and seemed mindful of the devout woman as well, in that he cast a furtive glance in her direction every so often. His attentions did not go unnoticed, for the instant the service ended, the gargoyle woman, who was apparently the devout woman's constant companion, hustled her by the elbow through the doorway and out into the night.

Kyle stepped back to let those in attendance file past him as they headed for the double doors.

John paused on his way out to speak to Kyle in the vestibule. "Come back to the shop with me," he said. "I'd like yer opinion on my latest brew."

"Still experimenting, are you?" Kyle said.

The corners of John's green eyes crinkled in merriment. "But of course," he said with a smile. "I spoil a batch now and again, but most turn out quite well, if I do say so myself."

"Count me in, then," Kyle said.

The two of them left St. John's and walked over to the rail to mount up. They rode down darkened streets to Tradesmen's Row, guided only by the faint illumination that seeped through the chinks in closed shutters along the way.

When they arrived at John's shop, they found Macalister out front with Fergus on a lead rope and his gray horse tied to the rail. They exchanged a greeting with him as they dismounted.

"Go on in," John said, unlocking the front door. "I'll join the pair of ye after I put up the mule." He led the docile beast down the wide alleyway alongside the shop and disappeared around back.

Kyle tied the gelding to the rail beside the gray and followed Macalister and Fergus into the herb-scented darkness inside. A tiny glimmer of light came from a brazier standing in the corner.

Macalister fumbled around for a moment to locate a couple of candles. He brought them over to the brazier, where he blew on the banked coals to bring them to rosy life. He touched each wick in turn on the glowing embers to light it, after which he set the candles in clay holders on the table.

Kyle took one of the lighted candles with him to examine the jars and pots on the shelves against the side walls. When he was satisfied that no single container stood out from the rest, he joined Macalister already seated at the table with the dog lying on the floor at his feet.

Macalister cocked a curious eyebrow at his companion. "Looking for something in particular?" he said.

Kyle shrugged his shoulders, reluctant to divulge the reason for his examination.

Apparently used to intrigues that necessitated discretion,

Macalister tactfully changed the subject. "Have ye caught up with the fellow who stabbed Lucky Jack?" he said.

"Not yet, but I aim to do so soon," Kyle said with an optimism he did not feel.

"John told me about the village girl's murder. Any leads to go on?"

"I'm working on that, too. By the way, how sharp is your dog's nose?"

"Better than a sleuth hound's," Macalister said with pride. "Once Fergus picks up a scent, he sticks with it." He leaned over to scratch the dog behind the ears. "Do ye plan to go a-hunting?"

"I do, but not for the usual quarry."

At that moment, John walked through the curtain separating his sleeping chamber from the shop. He carried a clay jug in one hand and three mugs in the other. "This will get us started," he said, setting them on the table. He removed the cork from the jug and poured foaming amber liquid into each mug.

Kyle chose the mug closest to him and lifted it to his mouth. The effervescence tickled his upper lip. Though slightly bitter, the brew was pleasing to the palate. "Not bad," he said. He glanced over at Macalister, who nodded in agreement after taking a tentative sip.

Macalister gazed into the depths of his mug. "It's neither ale nor mead," he said, raising his eyes to John. "What is it?"

"It's called beer," John said, looking from one to the other to observe their reaction. "I got a list of the makings from Father Ian."

Kyle drained his mug and held it out for a refill. While John obliged, he told them about his recent acquisition of the murdered girl's belongings. "I want to take a look at where the boys found her things. Something around there might indicate what happened to her."

"The wounds on the back of her head suggested a struggle with someone," John said. "Perhaps she dropped the bundle when she fell."

"Maybe," Kyle said. "But the killer would have seen it and disposed of it at the same time he got rid of her body."

"Maybe it fell unnoticed into the brush," John said.

"That is what I need to ascertain for myself," Kyle said. He then related the gist of his visit to the Ross keep earlier in the day. "As it turned out, Maize's brother didn't kill Sweeney," he said.

"What will ye do now?" Macalister said.

"I plan to question Brodie further," Kyle said. "So far, he's the only one with a compelling motive for murder."

John and Macalister exchanged a meaningful glance.

Kyle's pale blue eyes flicked from one to the other. "Is there something I should know?" he said.

"Lucky Jack's been raiding the countryside for years," Macalister said. "He did it in broad daylight in the Southron king's name, and on the sly at night, which ye witnessed with yer own eyes. Besides that, he was responsible for so many floggings and hangings executed in his king's name, every soul in the shire had cause to hate the very sight of him."

"What's more," John said, "he dallied with any woman who let him and forced himself on some who did not, which left many an irate father besides Brodie out to get him."

"He also ran the gaming at the Bull and Bear," Macalister said. "He rarely played, but he did like to squeeze payment from those who reneged on their debts. I believe he was rather fond of hurting people."

"Ye can be sure there's many a victim," John said, "who can point the finger at Sweeney, but none so foolish as to make such an accusation in public."

"So," Kyle said. "Aiden Ross was right to call him a pestilent fellow."

"Indeed," Macalister said. "Neither Scot nor Southron will grieve his passing, apart from his own men, who profited from their association with him. I doubt if even Jack's wife sheds a tear over his demise."

"Perhaps the raiding will cease now that he's dead," John said in a hopeful tone.

"Surely the raids generated a hefty profit for everyone involved," Kyle said. "I would assume that Inchcape or Archer or Weems will carry on in Sweeney's place."

"Those oafs lack the wit to plot and plan such an undertaking," Macalister said. "I pray John is right. Folks hereabouts need a respite from those Southrons."

Kyle stared into his mug for a moment, his brow furrowed in thought. "I recall that Sweeney was stationed here when I last lived in the shire," he said, "though I'm not certain about his men. I wouldn't mind laying my hands on the billet list from six years ago."

"Why six years ago?" Macalister said before John could stop him.

"That was when raiders burned my holding," Kyle said, lifting his eyes. A cold hard glitter flashed in their pale blue depths. "That was when I lost all I held dear."

"Ah," Macalister said, enlightened.

"What ye seek can be found in the registry in Neyll's keeping," John said. "He would know where to find it. He's privy to everything that goes on in the shire."

"I noticed," Kyle said, remembering his last encounter with Sir Percy's clerk. "He knows too much about other people's business to suit me. I'll bide my time asking after those records, so as not to appear too eager to see them."

"Good thinking," John said. He emptied the last of the beer

into his own mug and rose to fetch another jug from the back.

On his return, John topped off all three mugs before resuming his seat at the table. "I don't know if ye are aware," he said to Kyle, "that Robert Wishart, Bishop of Glasgow, stands in opposition to Edward of England in support of our cause."

"I didn't know that," Kyle said. "So, the good bishop is an advocate of the rebels, is he?" He chuckled. "I should have guessed that was what Father Ian meant when he mentioned friends in high places." He added with good humor, "Let's have no talk of rebel activities within my hearing. As deputy, the less I know of such things, the better."

"It's the raiders I'd like to know more about," Macalister said. "For instance, where do they dispose of the booty?"

"I've often wondered that myself," Kyle said. "They must ship the goods out from a quay along the coast."

"Not from any place near here," Macalister said. "We would have heard about it by now. Too many in the shire have lost too much to keep that sort of thing quiet for long."

"What about Leith?" John said by way of suggestion. "The French king's embargo on Southron ships does not affect Scottish vessels at all. They come and go at will from the harbor there and can easily reach Flanders and beyond without hindrance. Who's to say how many of those shipmasters would take on questionable cargo if it profited them to do so?"

Kyle sat upright at the notion. "You might have something there," he said. "The raiders dare not use the port of Ayr due to the risk involved. Embarkation from any other harbor along the western coast would entail a lengthy voyage around the northern isles to get to Flanders." He contemplated the matter for a moment, swirling the amber liquid in his mug. "The only way to be sure is to take a look at some of those outgoing cargo manifests."

"That means going all the way to Leith," Macalister said, a

dubious expression on his bearded face. "It's a fortnight's trek there and back."

"I still think that's how they're doing it," Kyle said. "How else can they send goods out of the country with no one the wiser that the stuff was stolen?"

In celebration of resolving such a vexing problem, they toasted each other for the next couple of rounds.

The beer was stronger than Kyle expected. "There is something wrong with the floor," he said, gripping the edge of the table. His tongue felt thick in his mouth, and he had difficulty forming his words.

John cast a bleary gaze around his shop. "What's the matter with my floor?" he said.

"It's moving," Kyle said.

Macalister laughed as he gave Kyle a good-natured shove to keep him from sagging off the bench.

"Thanks," Kyle said, making an effort to focus his eyes on Macalister. "I met a woman, you know. A real beauty." He turned to John. "Don't you think she's beautiful?"

John shrugged his shoulders. "Never saw her," he said. He seemed to be having a problem with his lips, for he kept fingering them as though to make certain they were still there.

"I met her in the marketplace," Kyle said. "Twice." He heaved a deep sigh before lapsing into a brooding silence. "No use longing for her or anyone like her," he said after a moment. "It's just not for me."

"What's not for you?" Macalister said, holding his mug out to John for a refill.

"Marriage, of course," Kyle said. His chin sank to his chest. "I had a wife and a child, but I let them down when they needed me the most." He lifted his face to his companions, his handsome features etched with pain and grief. "My boy was only eight years old. I should have been there for him, but I wasn't."

"That accounts for why ye treated Ogilvy's grandson, Hob, so gently," Macalister said with compassion. His eyes then took on a distant look. "Eighteen months ago, I lost my mother, my father, and my sister at Berwick when Edward torched the entire city." He stared at some horrific inward vision, his dark brows locked in a frown. "Some of the burghers there wanted revenge against the Southrons for past grievances, and rightfully so, but they took out their anger on Southron merchants who did nothing to deserve it. Right there in Berwick's own harbor, the burghers murdered those merchants and burned their warehouses. Edward sent five of his ships to deal with the burghers, but the vessels foundered in the mouth of the Tweed. The burghers climbed onto them and killed or captured every one of the seamen aboard.

"Shortly after that, Edward marched to Berwick at the head of his army to contend with those burghers himself. They mocked him from behind the safety of their walls, baring their backsides to him and hurling insults. That was when Edward brought out the Warwolf, a war machine that battered down the city's walls in a matter of hours. The burghers tried to surrender, but Edward paid no heed to their pleas for mercy. For the next three days, thousands of men, women, and children in and about Berwick fell to the sword, butchered like cattle, until Edward saw fit to call a halt to the carnage. Before he departed, he set fire to everything that would burn."

The tale had a sobering effect on Kyle. "How did you escape?" he said, now surprisingly clear-headed.

"A few of us managed to skirt the Southron army and flee westward," Macalister said. "We ended up here, in Ayr, determined to start afresh." He laid a hand on Kyle's arm. "I shall never forget what the Southrons did to my family, nor will I fail to exact revenge whenever I can. However, time has done much to heal the sting of loss. The dead are gone, and I must let them rest in peace. Ye must do the same. Ye cannot let past tragedies erode yer soul, for who knows but that the morrow may bring the chance to set matters straight."

"He's right," John said to Kyle. "But then," he added ruefully, "there are times when those lost to us do not leave us in peace, like my Colina with the light brown hair."

"You have my sympathy, old friend," Kyle said. He assumed the woman about whom John spoke was deceased, although he had no idea how her death came to pass. He drained the contents of his mug and held it out for more beer.

Flames from a raging inferno pressed in upon Kyle. Red embers fell from timber beams burning overhead, singeing his hair, searing his skin through his linen shirt. Dense smoke stung his eyes. Tears blurred his vision. He inched along the earthen floor on his hands and knees in the scorching heat, filled with dread at what he would find ahead of him.

The persistent thud of a fist hammering on a wooden door woke him with a start in the cool darkness of the sheriff's office. He rolled from his pallet, his heart pounding in his chest. Although relieved it had only been a dream, he feared that the nightmares, which had not plagued him for three years now, were starting up again.

He padded on bare feet to the front room, his pace slow to keep his head from toppling from his shoulders. With a grimace, he opened the door to the hulking form of Inchcape standing outside in the murky pre-light of dawn. "Well?" he said, wincing at the sound of his own voice.

"There's been another murder," Inchcape said. There was none of the usual arrogance on his brutish face. He seemed genuinely afraid. "An English soldier."

Kyle's concern over his inability to recall leaving John's shop last night took second place to Inchcape's news. "Who is it?" he said, his interest piqued despite the throb in his temples.

"I don't know," Inchcape said. He nervously smoothed the drooping moustache that framed his thin lips and clean-shaven chin. "That lad just reported it," he added with a jerk of his thumb.

Kyle lifted his eyes to gaze beyond Inchcape's beefy shoulder.

John Logan sat astride his mule, his handsome face drawn and haggard, his eyes red-rimmed from lack of sleep.

A skinny eleven-year-old boy in an ill-fitting brown tunic perched on the mule's rump behind John. The boy's countenance reflected a general mistrust of foreigners, which was undoubtedly why he sought out John, rather than enter an English garrison on his own to fetch the sheriff's deputy.

"Good morrow," Kyle said to John. It crossed his mind that he probably looked as bad as the older man did, thanks to the quantity of beer they consumed last night. "What do you know of this matter?"

"Erskine here woke me," John said, "to tell me of a dead Southron he found earlier this morning. I thought ye should take a look at the body before somebody else happens upon it. He says it's in a shepherd's hut a mile or so to the southwest."

Kyle turned to Inchcape. "Tell Upton and Vinewood to hitch up a wagon," he said. "They'll need it to fetch the body."

Inchcape departed without argument to do as he was bidden.

Kyle went back inside to dress. He put his leather scale armor over his clothing, after which he set out for the stable to saddle the gelding.

In a short time, he and the English soldiers followed John and Erskine from the garrison. They turned south and headed down the coast. The only sound they heard was the low rumble of wagon wheels and the muffled clop of hooves on the dirt road.

The eastern sky grew brighter with each passing moment. A

cool breeze blew in from the Firth of Clyde, and the fresh air somewhat lessened the ache in Kyle's head.

Before they reached the village of Alloway, the boy urged them to turn inland. They continued across rolling grasslands until they came to a wooded area.

"Over there," Erskine said, pointing to a dark shape barely visible through a thicket of trees.

The shepherd's hut stood in the center of a shadowed hollow, the vertical timbers of its outer walls warped with age. A thin mist hovered close to the ground, glazing every stone and blade of grass with a silver sheen. The first rays of the sun would soon reach into the vale to dispel the morning chill and gild the small wooden structure with a brilliant gold to make it warm and inviting. Just now, though, the hut squatted in the gloom, its narrow door ajar. With no windows to let in the light, the dark interior looked more like a tomb than a dwelling.

A bay horse, saddled and bridled with hobbles on its forelegs, grazed a short distance away. The fine creature lifted its head and pricked its ears at their approach.

Kyle dismounted and tied the reins to a nail poking out from the weathered boards on the side of the hut. An inspection of the ground around the entryway showed nothing. If there had been any footprints earlier, they were gone now, obliterated by sheep tracks all over the place.

He opened the door to look inside. The morning light, although dim, was sufficient to show the gruesome sight in the center of the single room.

A man lay on his side, pinned to the earthen floor by a sharpened stake through his temple. Though his face was in shadow, the red slashes on his throat stood out against the pallor of his skin. A Norman helmet, bull hide armor, and a sword on a leather belt, all of which marked him as an English soldier, reposed on a bale of hay at his booted feet.

Despite the cool air outside, the interior of the hut was warm. The source of the heat was a small brazier standing in the corner.

John entered the hut and went down on one knee beside the body to test the rigidity of the limbs. "I'd say he's been dead for at least ten hours," he said. "I'm going to need more light to examine him." He climbed to his feet to rummage around the bottom of his medicament bag. After a moment, he extricated a tallow candle and a pair of flints.

Kyle took the candle from John's hand and crossed over to the brazier to blow on the coals. When the frilled gray lumps began to glow, he touched the wick to them.

Upton walked into the hut just as the candle flared to life. He stopped in his tracks, uttering a small sound deep in his throat, his eyes fixed on the dead man's face.

"You know him?" Kyle said as he passed the lighted candle to John.

"That's Archer from the garrison," Upton said quietly.

Kyle leaned down to get a better look. "So it is," he said with mild surprise. He did not like Archer, but he would never have wished such a fate on the man. "I wonder what he was doing out here."

John tipped the candle and dripped hot wax onto a wooden shelf attached to the back wall to make a secure seat for the base. The flickering yellow light gilded a pair of pottery cups at the far end of the shelf.

Kyle inspected the cups, one of which was unused. The other held an ounce of brew, which he gave a tentative sniff before he handed the cup to John. "Does that mead smell peculiar to you?" he said.

John brought the cup to his nose. "It does," he said. He dipped his little finger into the amber liquid and touched the tip to his tongue. "Somebody used it to mask the taste of hemlock." He scowled into the cup for a moment.

"What's wrong?" Kyle said.

"This reminds me of my own preparation," John said. "I prescribe hemlock only for hopeless cases, and I warn them to use it with care. A single drop can ease the pain for a while, whereas two drops will ease the pain forever. I've given it to less than a handful of people over the last six months."

"I'll need a list of their names," Kyle said.

"Certainly," John said. He rolled up his sleeves and bent down to grasp the shaft of the wooden stake. He gave it a tug to extract it from Archer's temple, but the bone in which it was embedded held it fast. After two more unsuccessful attempts, he put his foot on the side of the dead man's head and yanked hard on the shaft. The stake slid free, bringing with it bits of pinkish-gray matter from inside the skull.

At that point, Upton, ashen-faced and bilious-looking, stumbled from the hut with his hand over his mouth.

John laid aside the sharpened piece of wood and knelt down beside the body to commence his examination.

Ten minutes later, John rose to his feet. "It was the hemlock that killed him," he said, wiping his hands on a linen rag.

"How can you tell?" Kyle said.

John indicated the raw gaping hole in the temple area where the wooden stake had been removed. "There is no bruising on the skin around the entry wound in his skull," he said. "In addition, there is no bleeding from the slashes on his throat."

"They are just like the ones on Sweeney's neck," Kyle said, musing over a recent memory. "Is there anything else? Anything that might indicate who did it?"

"Not that I can see," John said. "Other than the obvious damage, there are no marks of violence on him." He glanced over at Kyle, confounded. "I don't understand why anybody would cut the throat of a man who was already dead."

"Maybe he didn't know Archer was dead," Kyle said. "Then, there is the possibility it was done out of hatred or revenge. That's completely understandable in Archer's case, for he was a rather disagreeable fellow." He raised his eyes to the shelf with the cups on it. "That's curious."

"What is?" John said, following his gaze.

"There's no jug for the mead," Kyle said.

"Perhaps," John said, "the murderer didn't want anyone who came upon the body to drink the poisoned mead."

"A considerate murderer," Kyle said with a tight smile. "How ironic."

He went outside to look for Upton and Vinewood. He found them standing together, engaged in quiet conversation. "John is finished in there now," he said.

The two English soldiers went into the hut to remove the body. It took all four of them to wrestle the dead weight of Archer's body onto the wagon bed.

"You can take him on to St. John's for burial," Kyle said to Vinewood. To Upton, he said, "I want you to come with me. You can use Archer's horse."

CHAPTER 10

Vinewood drove the wagon out of the wooded hollow, bound for town.

Archer's body lay on the hard planks of the wagon bed. Since he was unmarried and childless, his horse and his gear would be sold to pay for his burial. The silver coins in his purse would be given to the prior at St. John's to buy food to distribute to the poor.

John rode beside the wagon as it bounced along the grassy track. He alone served as escort for the dead English soldier.

Erskine was long gone, having departed shortly after their arrival at the shepherd's hut. Kyle saw no reason for the boy to linger, being satisfied that his only involvement in Archer's murder was in finding the body, and nothing more.

With Upton on Archer's bay, Kyle headed inland, bound for Brodie's house. The sun in the east looked large and mellow through the morning haze.

In a short while, they rode into Brodie's front yard, scattering chickens before them. The house was made of logs, with pitch clogging the chinks between the fitted timbers. A fat sow roamed freely with a litter of piglets trailing behind her. The ploughed land behind the dwelling was rife with beans, peas, and other edible crops.

Kyle dismounted and tied the gelding to a fence post. "Go around the back in case Brodie tries to flee," he said. He walked up to the front of the house and knocked on the door.

A black dog sunning itself in a bare patch of dirt raised its head to peer at him. After a moment, it lost interest and went back to sleep.

Esa opened the door. On seeing Kyle, her plain face lit up. "Come in," she said. She wiped her hands on the off-white apron tied around the waist of her gray tunic and stepped aside to let him enter.

Kyle walked ahead of her into the kitchen, where she went back to kneading a mound of raw dough on a wooden table under the window.

"Is your father at home?" he said, watching her capable hands massage loose flour on the surface of the table into the sticky mass.

"Aye," she said. "He's in the garden out back."

"Where was he last night?"

"Ye can ask him that yerself."

"I'm asking you."

"He were here in the house all night," she said. "The same as me." She punched the dough with more force than was necessary. "Does that answer yer question?"

"Maybe," he said.

"Ye don't believe me?" she said, her brown eyes flashing.

"You do realize," he said, "that in vouching for your father, as you did for the night of Sweeney's murder, you also vouch for your own whereabouts."

"Do ye think I killed Lucky Jack, then?"

"Not really," he said. "I think you are capable of doing so, but I don't think you did it."

His response seemed to please her, but he was unsure whether it was because of his confidence in her innocence or because he thought she was capable of murder.

She paused at her labors, her fingers sunk to the knuckles in the soft brownish dough. "Life was simpler before ye Southrons came to this country," she said.

"You mistake me for English," he said. "I am a Scotsman to the bone, born and bred in this very shire."

Her eyes searched his face for the truth of his claim. "Why then do ye stand up for the Southrons?" she said. "Their pompous judges sit in their fancy courts and presume to speak for God. The old folk sought justice the old way. That should be good enough for ye."

"The kinsman of a wronged party still has the right to act as blood avenger," he said, "but only within the confines of the law. He can challenge the guilty man to fair combat before witnesses, but if he goes out alone and strikes the man down, though the man be guilty, the kinsman places himself outside the law, and thus subjects himself to punishment under the law." He paused before adding: "Whether the law is English or Scots, as sheriff's deputy, I am sworn to uphold it."

She made no comment as she separated the kneaded dough into three equal portions and shaped them into loaves. She then placed a damp cloth over the raw dough to allow it to rise.

She rolled up her sleeves and proceeded to wash the flour from her hands in a bowl on the side board. "Something must have occurred to bring ye out this way," she said. "Was another Southron murdered in his bed?"

He marveled at the accuracy of her guess. "As a matter of fact," he began, but he fell silent when he noticed the distinctive pattern of the scratches on the inside of her right forearm. The marks were faint, long healed but still discernible. He leveled a pale blue gaze at her. "Did you kill your sister?" he said quietly.

She dried her hands on her apron, her eyes averted. "As good as," she said. "She told me Lucky Jack promised to marry her, and she planned to run off with him that very night. I tried to reason with her, but the silly girl was determined to leave. It was then she told me she was carrying his child. I grabbed hold of her to shake some sense into her, but she clawed at me with those sharp fingernails of hers. I shoved her away in anger. God forgive me for what I told her next. I said if she went away with him, she deserved whatever happened to her, for his kind would turn her out into the streets as soon as he grew tired of her."

She raised her head to look at him, her plain face set in stony grief. "If I thought that was the last time I would ever see her alive," she said, "I would have chained her to the fence outside and left her screaming abuses at me for doing so."

"I'm sorry," he said. He knew she was telling the truth, and at that moment, he felt it unnecessary to add to her distress by mentioning that Sweeney already had a wife.

He exited the house by the rear door, leaving her standing at the wash basin, staring inwardly at her own demons, oblivious to his departure.

Outside, Upton sat on a chunk of wood in the shade of a beech tree, his back against the smooth trunk. He watched with half-closed eyes as Brodie used a hoe to chop at the weeds growing in the furrows of the garden plot.

On seeing Kyle, Upton got to his feet. "I don't think Master Brodie even once looked my way," he said.

"It wouldn't matter if he did," Kyle said. "His daughter claims he was here last night, and that's that." He led the way around to the front of the house where the horses were tied.

The two of them set out for where Ewan and Gib had found Megan's belongings. The place was not difficult to find, since there was only one trail that was safe to follow through the mire.

Kyle dismounted when they reached the holly tree that leaned over the pathway. He poked around the immediate vicinity, but he found nothing more telling than the paw marks of smallish creatures in the soft mud between the stones. The tall grass on either side of the narrow trail showed promise, though, for it was deep enough to conceal Megan's bundle if she had dropped it before she was accosted.

When he finished his inspection of the area, he and Upton started back to the garrison. Around them, the birds chipped and flitted from branch to branch. Butterflies drifted languidly in the radiance of the afternoon sun.

They were still a good way from Harefoot Law when something hissed past Kyle's ear. He reacted instantly, leaning over the gelding's neck to provide less of a target, while driving his heels into its belly.

Upton followed Kyle's lead without question, urging Archer's bay to take flight.

A hundred or so yards down the track, Kyle reined in to look over his shoulder. "Someone loosed an arrow at me back there," he said in response to the curiosity on Upton's face.

"Are you sure you were the intended target?" Upton said. "I'm the one who's English."

For a long moment, they listened for sounds of pursuit, but all they heard were the cawing of crows in the distance and the incessant chattering of a squirrel high in the treetops.

"Whoever he was, he's gone now," Kyle said. He nudged the gelding forward, his expression thoughtful for the remainder of the trek back to Ayr.

As they rode into the outskirts of town, an ominous gray thunderhead rolled in from over the Firth of Clyde. The dazzling sun vanished behind a veil of leaden clouds. A soft breeze coiled about them, carrying with it the foul odor of the tannery.

Kyle sent Upton on to the garrison. He turned into the blacksmith's yard, only to be greeted by Fergus barking and straining at the end of a chain. He dismounted and was tying the reins to the rail just as Macalister came out from under the porch of his shop.

Macalister signaled to Fergus with his hand. The barking

ceased abruptly as the dog obeyed his silent command. "What can I do for ye?" he said by way of salutation. He ran an expert eye over the iron shoes on the gelding's hooves. "No trouble, I hope."

"Not at all," Kyle said. "I need your help, you and that dog of yours. Can you spare me a couple of hours?"

"When?"

"Right now."

"I reckon so," Macalister said. He glanced back at the empty porch. "Trade has been a mite slow today."

"You'll need to keep the dog on a lead where we're going."

"And where is that?"

"Harefoot Law."

"It's a little late in the day to go a-visiting."

"Not for what I have in mind," Kyle said.

"Can ye tell me what this is about?"

Kyle related the gist of his plan to him.

"It's risky," Macalister said, "but it may work. Give me a minute to saddle up."

It was late afternoon by the time they drew within half a mile of Harefoot Law. The hour seemed later, though, because of the heavy clouds darkening the sky.

Kyle slowed the gelding to a walk on the rutted track, which snaked through the trees.

Macalister eased back on the reins for the gray mare to keep pace alongside the gelding.

Fergus trotted behind the horses on a lead rope, sniffing the air and looking this way and that, apparently enjoying the outing.

"There's something I've been meaning to ask you," Kyle said. "How did you come to be at Ogilvy's on the night of the raid?"

"That wasn't by chance," Macalister said. "I had to sleep out there every night for a week before the raiders finally struck."

"Those scoundrels usually just reave stock," Kyle said. "What did Ogilvy do for them to burn him out?"

"He had a run-in with Sweeney's lads at the market after he sold a good bit of wool earlier in the day. They knew his purse was full, but he refused to pay when they tried to extort money from him. They let him off with a warning, but Guthrie, who was there with him, was not so fortunate. They beat him so badly that he took to his bed for a full week. Otherwise, he would have been out there with us that night."

"Ogilvy is still at risk, then," Kyle said. "The English will want to make an example of him to discourage others from standing up to them."

"Ye are right about that," Macalister said. "Guthrie's on his feet now, so he can help if there's trouble."

They reached the ford across the River Doon and splashed through shallow water to the village on the other side. They rode between the weathered timber houses to the stone chapel at the end of the dirt lane.

The door to the chapel was propped open. Father Ian was in the doorway sweeping the flagstone floor with a straw broom. When the old priest saw Kyle and Macalister out front, he hastened down the steps to meet them, his lined face beaming with delight. "Come in, the both of ye," he said. "Ye must be weary from yer journey."

Kyle politely declined the invitation. He remained astride the gelding, while Macalister climbed down from his mount with the dog's lead rope in his hand.

A frown clouded the old priest's countenance as his eyes settled on Fergus sitting on its haunches behind the horses, panting rhythmically. "Ye can come inside," he said to Macalister, "but that great beast stays where he is." He looked from

Kyle to the dog and back again. "Are ye on a hunt?"

"In a manner of speaking," Kyle said. He introduced Macalister to the old priest, after which he explained the reason for their visit.

"I don't like it at all," Father Ian said. "Someone's bound to get hurt."

"Someone already got hurt," Kyle said. "I need for you to assemble the villagers as they come in from the field. Keep them here until I return. I won't be long."

"Where are ye going?" Father Ian said.

"To fetch Brodie and his daughter," Kyle said. "I especially want them here this evening. Can I count on you to do as I ask?"

"Oh, aye," the old priest said in mock annoyance. "Go along with ye, so ye can get back before they start whining about missing their supper on a deputy's whim."

Kyle spurred the gelding into a canter. He swiftly covered the distance to Brodie's holding, only to find Esa home by herself. She told him that her father went to work in the field shortly after his visit there with Upton earlier in the day.

On hearing what Kyle intended to do, she readily complied with his request to retrieve a certain article from the bottom of the cupboard. She climbed up onto the gelding behind him with the item tucked under her arm.

They hurried back to the village, taking a short cut at Esa's suggestion. They rode into the chapel yard to find the villagers clustered in groups of twos and threes, apparently speculating among themselves as to why the deputy wanted to see them.

Kyle halted the gelding and helped Esa to the ground. He slid from the saddle and draped the reins over the rail. Before he escorted her inside, he paused to confer briefly with Macalister.

Father Ian was in the chapel, humming to himself as he

trimmed the smoking wick of the tallow candle beside the altar. When Kyle and Esa came through the doorway, he hurried over to them. To his surprise, Esa pressed a folded garment of gray homespun wool into his veined hands.

"I will ask you to bring this outside in a few minutes," Kyle said.

"I hope ye know what ye are doing," Father Ian said, placing the bundle behind the altar. He offered a short prayer for a successful outcome, after which he accompanied them outside to commence the proceedings.

Dusk was closing in around the village, brought on early by dark clouds scudding across the gray sky. A cool wind sprang up unexpectedly, snatching at long skirts and rustling leaves in trees and bushes.

Kyle stood on the chapel steps, tall and imposing in his leather scale armor. His dark red cloak billowed in the wind as he raised his hands for silence. He waited while the buzz of conversation slowly trailed away.

He scanned the faces of the villagers. Brodie stood among them, with Esa beside him. Ewan and Gib were there, too, their blue eyes wide with excitement. He noted with grim satisfaction the presence of Tullick, Alex, and Will, all three of whom lurked on the fringe of the small crowd.

Brodie's shaggy brown pony, Reggie, stood beyond those gathered, tied to a tree at the edge of the woods beside a pair of mules dozing with bowed heads. The pony, however, appeared bright of eye and quite alert.

A hush fell over the villagers as Kyle began to speak. "If you will keep your places for the next few minutes," he said in a loud voice, "you will soon be free to go home." He turned to Father Ian beside him. "Will you get the item that is in your possession?"

The old priest disappeared into the chapel and emerged a

moment later carrying Esa's bundle in both hands. With a dramatic flourish, he passed it on to Kyle in full sight of everyone present.

Kyle shook out the folds and held up for all to see a gray wool tunic that had been cut open from neckline to hem. "This is what Megan wore on the day she was murdered," he said, his voice raised. "The killer's scent still lingers on the dead girl's dress." He beckoned for Macalister to come forward from where he waited with the dog in the shadow of the trees.

On cue, Macalister walked through the midst of the villagers with the huge Alaunt padding along at his side on a lead rope. The close proximity of strangers seemed to annoy the dog, as evidenced by the curling lip and the low growl of warning rumbling deep within its chest.

The sight of bared teeth in the dog's massive jaws set off a round of animated protests from the villagers, who expressed fear for their own safety and that of their families.

Macalister brought the dog to the chapel steps.

Kyle held out the tunic for Fergus to smell. "No harm will come to those innocent of Megan's blood," he said in a forceful tone that sliced through the rising babble of voices. "Stand fast and let the dog do its job."

Macalister kept a firm grip on the lead rope as Fergus, with ears pricked and nose to the turf, started to prowl among the villagers. The knowledge that only the guilty were at risk kept most of them from cringing and shrinking away when the dog paused to sniff at their boots or nuzzle the hem of their garment.

Some of the women grew rather anxious when the great beast approached their children, but they relaxed as soon as it snuffled its way along the ground to the next pair of feet.

The premature dusk slowly faded into twilight. In the waning light, Kyle kept an eye on Brodie, who showed a keen interest in each man's reaction to the dog's assessment of them. As the number of those left to check dwindled, he noticed that Brodie's focus shifted to Tullick, who stood among the remaining few.

Some of the villagers, hungry after laboring in the field all day, started to complain that they wanted to go home. Kyle was about to dismiss them when he caught the look of desperation on Tullick's face as Fergus advanced on him.

Brodie evidently saw it, too, for he slipped around behind Tullick to forestall the possibility of escape on one of the mules a couple of yards away.

Kyle plunged from the chapel steps toward Tullick. The villagers turned to see where he was going, inadvertently getting in his way.

Tullick swung around, poised for flight, only to come face to face with Brodie, who blocked his path.

A dull flush stained Tullick's bearded features, for by his attempt to flee, he had owned to his murderous act against Megan.

Brodie's frowning brow and tightly drawn lips made it clear that he now knew the truth of it.

Tullick panicked. He pulled the dagger from the sheath at his side and cut the air with it, as though to intimidate Brodie into stepping aside.

Brodie stood his ground, his eyes more dangerous than the blade in Tullick's hand. "Don't be a fool, lad," he said, with thinly veiled menace in his voice.

Tullick lashed out with the dagger, intent on stabbing Brodie to get him out of the way.

Brodie leaped back like a scalded cat, colliding by chance with his own pony standing alongside the mules.

Reggie, as ill-tempered and unpredictable as ever, butted Brodie with its head. The forceful, unexpected blow from behind sent the older man stumbling to his knees.

Tullick grasped Brodie's forearm with one hand and twisted

it up his back. He held the blade to the older man's neck with his other hand.

Kyle, now on the scene, drew his sword and leveled it at Tullick's chest. "Stand down," he commanded.

Tullick hauled Brodie to his feet to use the older man's body as a shield. "Stay back," he said, his voice shrill with alarm. "Stay back or he dies."

To prove he meant it, he jabbed the tip of his dagger deeper into Brodie's straining throat, causing a trickle of blood to leak from the puncture wound. He took a step backwards, dragging his reluctant hostage with him.

"Why did ye murder her?" Brodie said, choking out the words due to the awkward angle of his neck.

"She were a whore," Tullick said, his mouth twisted in anguish. "I only plowed where others went before me." He forced his hostage back another pace. "I didn't mean to kill her. I just wanted to punish her for spreading her legs for that Southron."

A shocked silence fell over the villagers. Even Alex and Will stared at Tullick in disbelief. Although repelled by what they heard, they all nonetheless edged closer so as not to miss a word.

"Throw down, and let him go," Kyle said. "I'll see that you get a fair hearing."

"Fair or not," Tullick said, "it's the gallows for me now."

A streak of lightning forked across the sky. The momentary flash showed the apprehension on Tullick's face, whereas Brodie appeared to have aged ten years in as many minutes.

Tullick flinched at the loud clap of thunder that followed. He pulled Brodie, unwilling and struggling, back to where the mules were tied.

Now that his freedom was imminent, Tullick blazed into renewed confidence. Unfortunately, he forgot about Reggie.

CHAPTER 11

The shaggy brown pony struck with the speed of a viper. Its gaping jaws reached for Tullick's arm, but instead of sinking into flesh, the long yellow teeth clamped down on the baggy sleeve of his loose-fitting tunic.

The assault from the rear took Tullick by surprise. He spun about to confront his adversary, hauling Brodie around with him. He was clearly relieved to see that it was only Reggie, yet when he tried to reclaim his sleeve, the obstinate pony retained an unrelenting grip on the fabric.

That momentary diversion nearly cost Tullick his life, for Kyle lunged at him with his drawn sword. The young man whirled in time to thrust Brodie between himself and the sharp point of the blade.

Kyle pulled back before he pierced Brodie by mistake. He braced his booted feet, ready to spring forward should another opportunity present itself.

Tullick again attempted to jerk his sleeve from Reggie's teeth, but the stubborn pony hung on with galling tenacity. His frantic gaze swept the half-circle of grim faces watching him narrowly, waiting to see what he would do. The deepening twilight washed them all into shades of gray, making the chapel beyond shadowy and indistinct.

Tullick stole a glance at the nearest mule, so close he could reach out and touch its velvety nose. Before he could ride away, he must cut the tether binding the mule to the tree. If he took his dagger from Brodie's straining throat for even an instant to sever the rope, the man would turn on him, or else the vigilant deputy would strike him down.

Evidently aware of the hopelessness of his situation, Tullick made a reckless bid for freedom. He gave Brodie a hard shove from behind. Then with a mighty wrench, he liberated his sleeve from the pony's clenched teeth, not the least concerned that he left half of it behind.

Brodie staggered into Kyle, who lowered his sword to catch the older man as he fell. The villagers, with Esa among them, converged upon them, crowding around to render assistance.

In the confusion, hardly anyone noticed the solitary figure slip into the dusky gloom between the trees, only to vanish in the soft darkness of the forest.

The villagers milled about, chattering excitedly to one another. The waning moon, ringed with a dull halo of light, at last came out from behind slow-moving gray clouds to shed a silvery luminescence upon the chapel yard and those in it.

Kyle let his gaze rove over the villagers in search of Tullick, whom he did not expect to find. Brodie, whom he did expect to see, was nowhere to be found.

Both mules were there, as was the pony, which suggested Tullick fled on foot. Any hope of catching him depended on the chase to commence at once. Because of the prevalence of bogs in the vicinity, only a fool would blunder about the woods after dark without a light.

"I will need as many torches as you can muster to track Tullick down," he said to a couple of men beside him.

"One torch is all ye need," the first man said, "and that be for yerself."

"Aye," the second man said with a nod. "I know of none who would venture out into the mire at night, even with a torch."

He understood their trepidation, for the bogs were unforgiving and fed as hungrily on the careless as well as the ignorant. He was about to turn away when he noticed Brodie's pony wagging its head from side to side, like a dog, with the scrap of cloth still in its mouth. Perhaps there was another way to overtake the felon.

He plucked several handfuls of clover from the verge before going over to where Reggie stood with the mules. He held the sweet green grass just out of the pony's reach.

The wily creature extended its neck to sniff at the clover. It curled back its thick lips, as though presenting the limp rag clenched between its long teeth in exchange for the fragrant offering.

Kyle tossed the clover to the ground under Reggie's nose. As anticipated, the pony relinquished one prize for the other, more desirable, one.

On retrieving the fabric, part of which was moist with the pony's saliva, he went to look for Macalister, whom he found sitting on the chapel steps with the dog beside him. "Do you think Fergus can track Tullick with this bit of his sleeve?" he said.

"It's worth a try," Macalister said.

Esa, who had been following Kyle, walked over to join him. She brought with her a woman whom she identified as her father's sister and whom she introduced as Mistress Brodie.

"Do ye plan to set the dog on Tullick?" Esa said to Kyle with a worried frown.

"I do," Kyle said. "While the trail is fresh."

Esa wrung her hands, which seemed out of character for her, for she was normally calm and imperturbable. "I beg of ye," she said. "Do not loose the dog."

"Why not?" Kyle said. "Tullick must be caught, lest he get clean away."

Esa exchanged a dubious glance with Mistress Brodie. "My

father's scent is on Tullick," she said, "and Tullick's scent is on my father. I fear the dog might confuse one with the other."

Kyle gave her a sharp look. "Why should that matter?" he said. "Where is your father, by the way?"

She lifted her shoulders in a small shrug. "He went after Tullick," she said simply.

Kyle muttered an oath under his breath. Brodie's interference ruined any chance that Fergus might run Tullick to earth that night. Even if they set out at first light the next morning with the dog on a leash, Tullick would have had eight hours in which to escape.

Mistress Brodie drew her shawl about her narrow shoulders against the rising wind. "It don't seem fitting," she said, her weathered face implacable, "for the Southrons to punish Tullick for what he done to Megan. She were my brother's daughter, and as her father, he should go after the guilty bugger."

"It appears he already has," Kyle said dryly.

"Don't ye worry none," Mistress Brodie said. "Tullick won't get far. If them bogs don't get him, then my brother will."

"What if the bogs get your brother first?" Kyle said.

"They won't," Mistress Brodie said with certainty. "God will see that justice is done."

A flash of lightning lit up the sky, as though to confirm the truth of her words. The subsequent crash of thunder brought on a shower of large raindrops, which soon turned into a downpour that sent everyone scrambling for cover. Kyle and those with him, including the dog, took shelter inside the chapel.

Kyle fingered the remnant of sleeve, useless now that the driving rain obliterated the trail of Tullick's scent. He tucked it into his pouch, reluctant to discard it in case another occasion arose for him to use it.

"You're right about one thing, Mistress Brodie," he said with a sigh of resignation. "It's in God's hands now."

The rain finally let up as Kyle and Macalister entered the outskirts of town. They rode slowly along the muddy lane, mindful of the treacherous footing. Fergus trotted behind them, seemingly content to tag along at the end of the lead rope.

A strong wind from the firth began to dissipate the cloud cover, revealing myriads of stars in the night sky. The air was cool and damp, and water lay in glassy pools in the wheel ruts, reflecting light from the moon.

They reined in at the blacksmith shop, where Macalister climbed down from the saddle.

Kyle was about to continue on to the garrison when he glimpsed Macalister's ferocious scowl. "Is something vexing you?" he said.

"Do ye not find it shameful," Macalister said, his tone indignant, "that no one saw fit to wash the poor girl's dress after she was killed in it?"

Kyle pushed back the sodden hood of his dark red cloak. "It was washed," he said. "It would have been mended, too, except for a lack of time for Esa to do it. Now that Megan is gone, she must see to all the household chores by herself."

"If the dress was clean," Macalister said, "how then could Fergus pick up the dead girl's scent on it?"

"He couldn't," Kyle said. "I made that up as a ruse to draw out the murderer. I had my suspicions about those three young bucks from the village, but I needed to force the hand of the guilty one. If I was mistaken, no harm would come to them because of it. As it turned out, it was Tullick's fear of exposure that gave him away. It's not what I knew that mattered, you see. It was what he thought I knew."

"Well, I'll be buggered," Macalister said, grinning.

Kyle thanked Macalister for his help before taking his leave. He headed into town, but before going on to the garrison, he stopped at the Bull and Bear on Harbour Street for a bite to eat.

He chose a table in the corner. While waiting to be served, he let his gaze wander over the tavern's patrons. English soldiers occupied most of the tables. The young men were as boisterous as ever, while the older ones drank and talked quietly.

Maize approached Kyle's table, her expression more watchful than wary. "What can I get ye, Master Deputy?" she said.

"Something to eat and ale to wash it down," Kyle said. "I spoke to Hew yesterday. You were right about him."

His words seemed to comfort her, for she spared him a smile before she left to fetch his supper.

A few minutes later, she returned with a mug of ale and mutton stew on a trencher of stale bread. He gave her a halfpenny for the food and started in on it.

The mutton was tough, the stew thin, and the ale watered, but he consumed it all with the gusto of a hungry man. While he ate, an old soldier whom he recognized from the garrison walked into the tavern.

The man's weathered features were as ordinary as his nondescript clothing, and he sat at a table in the far corner, as though to observe those coming and going without being seen himself.

Kyle finished his meal and left the tavern. As he rode down Harbour Street toward the garrison, he had the uncomfortable feeling of being watched. Frequent glances over his shoulder revealed nothing, apart from the odd burgher or two hurrying along the rain-slick cobbles in the moonlight.

Once inside the walls of the garrison, he went on to the stable to feed and water the gelding. Only when he entered the sheriff's office to turn in for the night did the prickling sensation at the nape of his neck subside.

When he awoke the next morning, he removed a piece of parchment from a shelf in the rear chamber, along with a quill pen and ink. He went into the front room to sit at the table to write out an account of John's findings on Archer's death while the facts were fresh in his mind. Upon completion of his report, he would bring it to Sir Percy later in the day, after he broke his fast at the marketplace. It was much easier, he decided, to deal with the mercurial moods of the Castellan of Ayr on a full stomach.

The bells of St. John's rang in the midmorning hour of terce as he walked through the garrison gates and on to the marketplace. The weather was fair and sunny. White clouds overhead drifted in the chilly breeze coming from the firth.

The market grounds always bustled with folks buying or selling, or merely strolling around to gaze at luxury items too costly to purchase. Thieves and cut-purses worked the crowds, purposely bumping into well-dressed merchants or burghers to make away with their coin purses, if they could.

He glanced at the faces of those around him, looking for one in particular that would quicken the beat of his heart. Instead of the lovely Joneta clad in black, he glimpsed a bewhiskered stub of a man ambling through the rows of colorful stalls with a small boy beside him. Both man and boy were looking at everything around them, their eyes bright with interest.

He intercepted them at the cooper's booth. "Master Ogilvy, how goes it?" he said, falling into step beside the old man.

Ogilvy appeared surprised to receive such a cordial greeting, especially from the Deputy Sheriff of Ayrshire. "Fine, fine," he said, as though unsure of what was wanted of him.

"I see Hob remembered to wear his mantle on this cool morn," Kyle said. The garment he had given to the boy on the night of the raid had been trimmed to fit his diminutive body, yet left long enough to allow for later growth.

Kyle's friendly manner set Ogilvy at ease. "Aye," he said with a gap-toothed grin. "The lad never takes it off. He even sleeps in it."

Kyle bestowed a wink and one of his rare smiles upon Hob, who beamed at receiving such attention.

For the next few minutes, the boy practiced winking to get the hang of it, first with his right eye, then with the left.

"How go the repairs to your cottage?" Kyle said.

Ogilvy spat through the gap in his front teeth and hitched up his belt. "All done but the whitewash," he said with pride. He nudged Kyle's ribs with a sharp elbow, releasing a whiff of stale sweat from under his sinewy arm. "I want it finished before my bride sees it."

Kyle felt a tawny eyebrow arch upward in amazement. "Your bride?" he said. "Did you recently marry?"

"Nay," Ogilvy said, "but I aim to soon. Her name is Lizzy Hamilton. Things have not been easy for her lately. The Southrons put her out of her house. Her daughter took her in, so she's presently living with a pack of grandchildren underfoot." His coarse features softened for a brief moment. "I always fancied her, and I think she fancies me. I want to take her as wife, but I just never got up the courage before now to offer for her hand."

Kyle wondered whether the old man's bride-to-be was the same woman who had uttered that dire pronouncement against him and his companions barely a week ago. "I wish both of you the best," he said with sincerity. He bore no ill will to anyone, including the second-sighted Mistress Hamilton, who spoke the truth whether it pleased him to hear it or not.

For the next hour, he wandered around the marketplace with the old man and the boy, pausing here to watch a juggler or stopping there to buy sweet cakes from the baker's pushcart for all of them to eat. On impulse, he purchased an inexpensive toy horse from the woodcarver for Hob. The look of earnest gratitude he received from the boy for that simple act placed a suffocating pressure around his heart.

The sun was nearing its zenith when he glimpsed Upton striding purposefully across the market grounds toward him. The young man's grave countenance gave him the impression that he was not being sought for social reasons. With genuine regret, for he was enjoying himself for the first time in years, he took his leave of the old man and the boy, and went to meet his sergeant.

"Sir Percy requires an audience with you without delay," Upton said on drawing close.

"I don't suppose you know what he wants," Kyle said.

Upton shook his head. "If I did," he said, "I would tell you."

The two of them headed back to the garrison together. Kyle stopped at the sheriff's office to pick up his report on Archer's murder before going on to the castle by himself to call upon Sir Percy. He mounted the wooden stairs and walked down the long hall to the last doorway.

Neyll looked up from making an entry on an open parchment scroll as Kyle walked into the anteroom.

"Is Sir Percy available?" Kyle said.

"Wait here," he said, his tone curt but civil. "I'll see if he will meet with ye." He rolled up the scroll and returned it to its place on one of the shelves behind his desk. Only then did he leave the anteroom to enter the chamber beyond.

Kyle didn't bother to mention that Sir Percy sent for him. He was glad for a moment alone to glance through the stored rolls of parchment. The task was daunting, for there were so many. It would take hours to comb through them, so he resigned himself to invoking Neyll's assistance to locate the ones he wanted to examine.

Neyll reappeared and caught Kyle standing behind his desk, eyeing the scrolls on the shelves with interest. "Sir Percy will see ye now," he said. The civility of his voice was at odds with the frown of disapproval on his face. Although the records were public, he obviously considered that he alone was privy to them.

Kyle walked into Sir Percy's office.

Sir Percy waved him into a chair in front of his desk. "Master Shaw," he said without preamble. "Have you apprehended the rebels who are killing off my soldiers one by one?"

"The matter is still under investigation," Kyle said, taking a seat. He knew the futility of denying rebel involvement, for it appeared that Sir Percy had already made up his mind to lay the blame at their feet. He handed over his report on Archer.

Sir Percy perused the document for a long moment. When he looked up, he stared long and hard at Kyle, as though trying to make up his mind about something. "I find it coincidental," he said at length, "that these murders commenced shortly after you came to this garrison."

Kyle sat upright in the chair. "Is that an accusation?" he said, his voice deceptively mild.

Sir Percy got up from the desk and walked over to the unshuttered window to gaze down into the sunlit courtyard below. "I suppose not," he said with a sigh. "It's just that I am at my wit's end these days, what with rebel activity on the rise all over this godforsaken country." He swung around to face Kyle. "You can imagine my distress when a report reached me that you, a deputy in the service of the king, were seen consorting with suspected rebels. I must warn you that you are flirting with treason."

"Is not bending the king's law to suit one's greed also flirting with treason?" Kyle said.

"What are you implying?"

"It is common knowledge that the clerks here in the shire

collect double the taxes due, but turn in only the single tax."

"If that is true, they shall not escape punishment," Sir Percy said with righteous anger.

"What about the English justiciars, appointed by royal decree, who willingly accept a share of the excess taxes collected? Will they, too, be punished for taking money extorted from families struggling to get by?"

Color burned high on Sir Percy's cheeks. "You forget your place, deputy," he said.

"I think not," Kyle said. "I understand Edward of England is touchy about his treasure trove and frowns upon any who profit at his expense. What conclusion will your king draw when he discovers that this perfidy is going on under the very nose of the Castellan of Ayr and Warden of Galloway?"

"Are you insinuating that I partook in that wrongful conduct?" Sir Percy said coldly.

Kyle hoisted deprecating shoulders. "You must admit that it doesn't look good for you," he said.

"How dare you even suggest that I would condone such a scheme?" Sir Percy said. "It is treason to steal from the king," he added, his voice harsh with indignation.

"Exactly."

Sir Percy made an effort to regain his composure. "Because you are newly appointed here," he said with obvious restraint, "I shall overlook your rash words. May I remind you that the only reason I let Sheriff Crawford send for you was because he assured me that you would maintain civil order in the shire. Since your arrival, however, you have done nothing to prevent your countrymen from harassing English soldiers on patrol. That, Master Shaw, is not my idea of keeping these rustics in check."

"For years," Kyle said, "English soldiers have burned and pillaged Scottish homesteads throughout the land. It is the English who goad Scottish folk into defending themselves."

"A rebel raid on an English supply wagon is not an act of defense," Sir Percy countered.

For a long moment, they glared at each other in strained silence.

Sir Percy was the first to avert his eyes. He went over to his chair and sat down in it. He reached for a quill pen in the holder beside the inkwell, as though seeking an occupation for his hands.

"Let us set aside our differences and begin anew, shall we?" he said, lifting his gaze to Kyle. "I am, indeed, answerable to my king for the goings-on under my nose. Hence, I would appreciate being informed of any and all illegal activities, whether suspected or confirmed, from this day forward."

Kyle got to his feet and took his leave. He walked from the chamber, uncertain whether Sir Percy's abrupt change of tack came from a desire to help or from fear of exposure. He stopped in the anteroom and waited for Neyll to complete an entry on a sheet of parchment before he spoke. "Where can I find the names of the soldiers billeted here during the first English occupation ten years ago?" he said.

Neyll returned his quill pen to the holder and folded his hands in such a way as to show off the ornate ring on his middle finger. "Why do ye want them?" he said, his manner that of an inquisitor to a heretic.

"The names, if you please," Kyle said, insistent.

Neyll frowned, as though he was about to refuse, when Sir Percy summoned him. He got up from his stool, and as he rounded the corner of his desk, his eyes flicked involuntarily to the second shelf from the bottom, as though to assure himself that the scroll in question was still there.

Kyle waited until Neyll left the anteroom to start in on that particular shelf. After unrolling several scrolls to ascertain the contents, he found the one he wanted. The names were written in neat columns, with the dates of arrival and departure or death beside them. Sweeney was on the list, not as captain, but as an ordinary soldier. Farther down, he found Inchcape and Weems allocated as men-at-arms.

Near the end of the list, he came across Fenwick's name, the sight of which caused his scalp to prickle with apprehension. The man was designated as an English knight in charge of a company of troops.

A further search through the scrolls led to one that listed the soldiers from five years ago. A glance at the names showed Fenwick, Sweeney, Inchcape, and Weems still posted at Ayr Garrison at that time. The date of departure beside Fenwick's name coincided with what Sir Aiden Ross had told him.

He continued to sort through the scrolls until he came across the current list of soldiers stationed at the garrison. Fenwick's name was not on it, as expected, but Archer's was, with a notation beside it setting out the date of his death.

He was returning the scrolls to their proper places when he noticed the tax rolls on the third shelf. The year was inscribed on the outside of each scroll, which made it easy to sort through them. He opened the one for the prior year, which contained the names of those taxed and the extent of their taxable property. It occurred to him that it would be useful if he had a list of the raided homesteads to compare with the tax roll to see if there was any correlation between them.

He hunted around for the current year's tax roll, but he was unable to find it. He found, instead, bunches of letters, bound with cord, stored on the top shelf. He opened a few of them to see what they contained. Most were correspondence by Sir Nicholas de Segrave, Sir Percy's predecessor as Castellan of Ayr, ordering provisions, cataloging inventories of supplies and weaponry, and addressing petty complaints among the soldiery.

He followed the trail of dates to the year 1292, where he came across a letter that chilled his flesh to the bone. It was a report by Fenwick to Segrave, in which Fenwick stated that it was James Shaw who planned the ambush of the Scottish rebels at Loudoun Hill. Fenwick claimed that James Shaw fought valiantly before the rebels hacked his body to pieces, and that his mangled remains were buried there at the site. The report concluded with Fenwick's commendation of Sweeney, Inchcape, and Weems, among others, for their valor in effectively and efficiently dispatching the entire band of rebels.

He stared at the letter, hardly daring to breathe. He read the words again, gripping the parchment so hard that it shook in his hand. Surely, none of it was true. Yet there was no way to disprove it, except by digging deeper to uncover more facts relating to the incident.

He folded the letter and put it back on the shelf with the others just as Neyll walked into the anteroom. He assumed from the expression on the clerk's face that every letter on the top shelf would be inspected that very day to locate the one that might have been of interest to the Scots deputy.

He was about to leave when it crossed his mind that Neyll would know the whereabouts of the current tax roll. He knew the man would balk if asked directly, so he tried a ploy he hoped would work.

"A lot of hard work went into compiling those records," he said, tilting his head toward the wall of shelved scrolls. "It cannot be easy to keep up with tax collections, correspondence, and the like. Sir Percy is lucky to have such a conscientious clerk like you."

Neyll preened under the adulation. "Aye, he is," he said. "He appreciates the long hours I put in on them at home, too."

Kyle headed down the hallway, satisfied that he now knew the location of the current tax roll. The only question was how soon it would be completed and brought to Sir Percy's office.

On leaving the garrison, Kyle rode up Harbour Street, headed for Tradesmen's Row. He barely noticed the burghers going about their business in the bright noonday sun, preoccupied as he was with the contents of Fenwick's report.

Even if he discovered Fenwick's whereabouts and confronted him, it was unlikely the man would make himself out to be a liar by denying the truth of his own report. Neither could he expect cooperation from Inchcape or Weems, not only because they were English and he was Scots, but because by admitting what really took place at Loudoun Hill, they would implicate themselves.

He reined in at the apothecary shop, dismounted, and tied the gelding to the rail out front. He went inside, where the rich scent of herbs and spices hung in the air.

John Logan sat at the table, occupied with sorting a small heap of green sprigs into separate piles. He looked up to see Kyle, who was scowling and clenching his jaw, coming toward him. "Trouble?" he said with concern.

"Worse," Kyle said. He then told him about Fenwick's report.

John whistled in astonishment. "That's news to me," he said.

"I don't think it is news as much as it is fabrication," Kyle said. "I aim to prove it's a lie." The scowl reappeared on his chiseled features. "I'm just not sure how to go about it."

John sat in sympathetic silence, while Kyle pondered the thorny problem of exonerating his father.

After a moment, John dug in his pouch and produced a small square of parchment. "These are the names ye wanted," he said. "They are the ones who purchased hemlock in the last few months." He handed the list to Kyle. "I prescribe it with care, for it is a dangerous potion, intended only for those without hope of recovery, to make their remaining days tolerable."

Kyle glanced at the parchment, noting with sadness the first of the four names written on the list.

CHAPTER 12

"Sheriff Crawford?" Kyle said.

"Aye," John said with a nod. "It's only a matter of time for him."

"Does he know it?"

"If he didn't before, I'm sure he does by now."

Kyle heaved a sigh. His own problems seemed insignificant compared to the prospect of a slow agonizing death, yet that did not negate their importance to him.

"While I was rummaging through the garrison records," he said, "I came across last year's tax roll. What do you think of comparing that to the homesteads that were raided?"

"For what purpose?" John said.

"It may show why they were targeted."

John seemed convinced that the idea was a good one. "I can prepare a list for ye," he said, "but I'll need time to compile the information."

"I can wait," Kyle said. He tapped the piece of parchment. "In the meantime, perhaps you can tell me where I can find these folks, with the exception of the sheriff, of course."

He followed the directions that John gave to him to locate the second person on the hemlock list and ended up on a crooked street in the poorer section of town. He knocked at half a dozen doors before someone remembered the old man who lived in a tiny hovel behind one of the weathered houses farther along the way.

After some trouble from a big black dog that insisted on barring his path, he went down the alley, found the hovel, and called upon the old man in it. The door was propped open to let in the light, and the old man was too ill to get up from his straw pallet on the dirt floor. The sunken eyes and the state of emaciation were enough to convince him that the old man posed no threat to anyone.

He stayed for a few minutes to chat, and the old man seemed to appreciate the company. In the course of their conversation, the old man mentioned that his daughter stayed there to look after him. Kyle gave the old man a couple of groats before departing. Once outside, he took in a grateful breath of fresh air after the smell of the hovel.

He headed for the more prosperous part of Newton, in search of the third person on the list. He found the house that John told him to look for: an imposing two-story dwelling with a coat of whitewash that made it appear bigger than it really was. The first level was built of hewn stones, with a wooden upper portion studded with long narrow windows at intervals under the eaves. He entered the gates set in the high stone wall around the property and rode past the store house, the stable, and the kitchen. On crossing the manicured lawn to the house, he dismounted to knock on the front door.

A stout middle-aged woman who resembled a gargoyle answered the door. "What do ye want?" she said, fixing a baleful gaze upon him. Her voice was flat, with no inflection at all.

"I've come to see Mistress MacKay," Kyle said.

"What do ye want with her?"

"I'd like to speak to her."

"Why do ye want to speak to her?"

"Look here," he said, keeping a firm grip on his patience,

which was about to snap like a taut thread. "Just tell me if Mistress MacKay is in, all right?"

The gargoyle woman apparently saw that she would get no information from this man. "She's in," she said grudgingly. "Who shall I say is calling?"

"Kyle Shaw, Deputy Sheriff of Ayrshire."

The gargoyle woman blinked at him, as though trying to decide whether to believe him. She must have made up her mind, for she stepped aside to let him in.

"Wait here," she said. She left him standing just inside the door. She disappeared down a hallway, only to reappear a moment later.

"Walk this way," she said in her monotonous voice. She led him into a chamber with two women in it. She then stationed herself near enough to hear every word spoken.

One of the women was quite elderly. She was seated by the lighted fireplace, with a blanket tucked around her knees. The fingers of her veined hands plucked nervously at the soft fabric on her lap, tirelessly pleating and unpleating it. She did not even turn her head at Kyle's entrance.

He recognized the other woman as the one who prayed so devoutly at St. John's.

She set her embroidery aside and rose to greet him. "I am Mistress MacKay's daughter," she said. Her voice was pleasant, and from what he could see of her features, for she kept her face turned slightly from him, she was quite attractive. Her light brown hair was pulled back from her temples and bound in a tight bun at her neck.

"Mother is not well enough to receive company," she said. "I will stand in for her, if I may." She folded her hands at the slender waist of her russet velvet gown and waited for him to speak.

Instead of replying, he stared at her for several heartbeats, trying to discern why she looked so familiar to him, aside from the fact that he had seen her twice before.

She mistook his reticence as a silent reproach, for she quickly added, "Ye may wish to speak to my brother, Neyll, rather than to me."

"Ah," Kyle said. "You are Neyll's sister. That explains your resemblance to him." He showed her the piece of parchment with Mistress MacKay's name on it. "Your mother takes hemlock for the pain, does she not?"

"Aye," she said. "She is bound to the house, so I must get it for her from John Logan." She uttered his name with warmth, almost like a prayer, and her whole face beamed with joy at the sound of it.

The gargoyle woman caught the look on the younger woman's face and took a warning step toward her. "Ye know how yer brother feels about that man, Mistress Colina," she said in her flat voice.

Kyle wondered in passing if she was the Colina to whom John referred as his lost love. It was then he noticed the day-old bruise on her cheek, with a scabbed scratch across the center of the yellowed blotch of skin. The affected area was small, but unsightly, which explained why she tried to keep her face somewhat averted. It might have come from a fall, but more than likely, in his opinion, it came from a backhanded blow by someone wearing an ornate ring. His pale blue eyes flicked immediately to the gargoyle woman's fingers. Those plump digits, though, were devoid of jewelry.

Exposure of her injury to a complete stranger seemed to trouble Colina for some reason other than vanity. She appeared to shrink into herself, like a hunted animal trying to make itself less visible to a predator. Her gaze kept straying to the gargoyle woman with something akin to fear.

"John can prepare a mustard plaster for that bruise," Kyle

said to Colina, while keeping the gargoyle woman in his line of vision. "It will heal faster that way."

Colina pasted a smile on her lips and made a valiant attempt to keep it there. "I must have bumped into something," she said, putting a hand to her cheek. "It will be gone in a day or two, so there is no need to bother John about it."

He looked around the chamber, noting the tapestry hangings, the carved furniture, the abundance of beeswax candles, and other costly furnishings. "This is a very nice house," he said.

Colina seized the opportunity to steer the conversation away from herself. "Father built it for Mother when they married," she said with pride. "Neyll shall inherit everything when she passes away." She glanced at the old woman with real affection.

"It must be costly to keep up such a property," Kyle said.

"Neyll can stretch a silver penny farther than anyone else I know," Colina said.

"That's quite a feat these days," he said. He turned his gaze to the gargoyle woman. "What with keeping servants and grooms and the price of feed for all those horses."

Colina walked over to the window and stood with her back to him. "Berta is not a servant," she said. "She is the housekeeper and my companion. She accompanies me whenever I go out, for there are too many English about for a lady to walk the streets alone in safety."

She spoke in such a way that he got the impression the words were not her own, but someone else's, which she'd memorized.

He reflected on Berta's rough handling of her when he last saw the two of them at St. John's. At that time, the gargoyle woman acted more like a warden than a companion. Perhaps she was paid to keep Colina from escaping from her own home, or maybe even from broadcasting Neyll's business, whatever that was now that it was evident he needed a constant flow of funds to maintain his lifestyle. Colina did not seem to be the kind of woman who would do either, especially considering her mother's condition.

He wanted a private word with Colina before he left, but Berta hovered too near. His eye fell on the half-finished embroidery that lay on her chair, abandoned at his arrival. He picked up the cloth stretched across the small wooden frame and went over to stand beside her at the window, where the light was better.

He traced the stem of a flower with the tip of his finger. "The skillfulness of your stitch work is evident in this piece," he said aloud. "Mistress Colina," he hissed in an undertone for her ears only. "This year's tax roll is somewhere in this house. I must see it."

She seemed unruffled at his furtive manner or his peculiar request. "Why do ye want it?" she whispered.

He held up the embroidery, as though to admire it. "The information on it," he murmured, "may help us put a stop to illegal activities in the shire."

"Is my brother involved?" she said in a low voice.

"I don't know," he mumbled.

"I won't betray him," she said softly.

"I admire your loyalty," he muttered, "but lives may be at stake."

"Come back later," she whispered. "Just after dark."

He assumed that was when she would give the tax roll to him. "I'll do that," he murmured with relief. He handed the embroidery back to her. "Thank you," he said out loud, "for taking the time to receive me. However, duty calls, and I must go. Good morrow to you."

Kyle knocked on the door of the fourth and last person on John's list. The houses along the winding lane huddled together, separated by a network of alleyways that ran in every direction. Weeds grew in ragged clumps between the uneven stones of the cobbled paving and sprouted from wooden shingles on the rooftops. Grubby children playing in the street paused to stare at him.

After a moment, the door creaked open a cautious inch and a watery blue eye in a bed of wrinkles peered out at him through the crack. "State yer business or be off with ye," an old woman said in a brusque tone. She spoke with the pronounced burr and rolling tongue of the northern clans.

"John Logan gave me your name," he said, showing her the list. The bold black letters on the small square of parchment looked important, even if she could not read a word of it.

"Master John sent ye?" she said. She opened the door a bit wider to reveal a black-clad shoulder and a creased face that looked pale and wan, with a sickly undertone of yellow. Wisps of white hair protruded from under the black cap on her head. "Why would he do that?"

Now that he saw her, he remembered her from the marketplace in the company of Joneta earlier in the week.

"To check on your health, mistress," he said. It was true in the sense that the purpose of his visit was to see if she suffered from an infirmity that warranted the extreme measure of taking hemlock. While he was there, of course, he would ascertain whether she had a reason to administer the powerful medicament to Archer.

Her candid gaze swept him from head to toe, taking in the beige linen shirt over dark brown leggings. His sword hung from the saddle on the tall reddish-brown warhorse behind him. He wore no armor and carried no weapon, other than a sheathed dirk attached to the leather belt around his waist. His head was bare, and he went without a cloak due to the warmth of the early afternoon sun on that fine spring day. She seemed satisfied that he meant no harm to her or her household.

"Ye are the deputy, are ye not?" she said, her eyes narrowed in recognition.

"Kyle Shaw, at your service," he said with a slight bow.

When he first arrived, the neighbors had opened their shutters to hear what was going on. By now, they were leaning halfway out of their windows and craning their necks to see what they could.

"Do you mind if I come in off the street?" he said.

She threw open the door and stepped aside to let him enter. "Wipe yer feet," she said, without rudeness or intent to offend. It was merely the customary reminder by a house-proud woman to an oblivious male not to track dirt onto her floor with his muddy boots.

He looped the gelding's reins over a rusted nail protruding from the weathered timbers on the front of the house. He then scraped the soles of his boots on the wooden threshold, ducked under the low lintel, and stood upright in a room of modest size. Considering the condition of the exterior of the dwelling, the interior was unexpectedly neat and clean, and smelled of freshly baked bread.

The old woman, the top of whose head barely reached the middle of his chest, shuffled over to a cushioned settle by an unshuttered window and sat down to resume the task of plying a needle to a small tear at the bottom of a gray cloak.

"I know yer face," she said, without looking up.

"Aye," he said. "From the marketplace."

"I took care of yer mother years ago," she said, raising her eyes. "Before she died."

"I don't remember that," he said. He was quite young when he lost his mother, which is why he was closer to his father, who raised him.

"Ye were barely knee-high to a puppy at the time," she said

with a cackle. "Look at the size of ye now. I knew ye for a Shaw the moment I laid eyes upon ye." She fastened a steady gaze on him. "Ye have the look of yer father about ye. He were as big as ye are, if not bigger, and as handsome, too." Her eyes took on a faraway, unfocused look. "He took it hard when she died. I don't know as I ever heard him laugh after that. She were a gentle woman who never spoke a cross word in all her days, God rest her."

Like father, like son, he reflected grimly, to grieve for a beloved mate long after death claimed her. It warmed his heart, though, to hear his mother spoken of with such fondness. "I never really got to know her," he said. "Father rarely mentioned her."

"That's because he missed her sorely," she said. "I moved away several years ago and lost touch with him. Is he keeping well?"

"He's dead," Kyle said, more harshly than he intended.

She didn't seem to notice. "I'm sorry to hear that," she said with sympathy. She tied off the thread and looked around for something sharp with which to cut it. "So, what did ye say brings ye here?"

He drew his dirk and handed it to her hilt first. "You bought a phial of hemlock from John Logan," he said. "He would not have sold it to you unless you needed it."

She took the dirk and cut the thread with the edge of the blade. "I'm a good age, as ye can see," she said as she passed the weapon back to him. "I get to hurting at times for no reason. A drop or two of Master John's tonic helps dull the pain." She held the garment up to the light to inspect her work. "I reckon this will do it. My eyes aren't what they used to be."

Kyle walked over to join her in examining the repaired spot. "It's as fair a mend as I've ever seen," he said. He was still leaning over the old woman's shoulder when he heard someone with a light tread come into the room.

"There ye are, Gram," a familiar voice said. "Oh, I see ye have company."

His heart thudded in his chest as he turned to greet Joneta. His welcoming smile faltered at the sight of an infant suckling at her breast. His earlier assumption that the baby belonged to Joneta's niece, Meg, was apparently erroneous.

Joneta drew the loose flaps of her unlaced tunic over the exposed portion of her rounded breast to cover it, not out of shame, but for the sake of propriety.

"I believe ye are already acquainted with my daughter-in-law," Gram said to Kyle. "She's come to stay with me for a spell, her and that new grandson of mine."

He felt more than a twinge of disappointment at discovering that Joneta was married. Of course, someone as lovely as she was would be, wouldn't she?

"Did you travel far to get here?" he said, only to make polite conversation.

"Not really," Joneta said.

"Where did you come from, then?" he said.

"Down the coast a ways," Joneta said.

It was the vagueness of her responses that aroused his interest. Was she being evasive on purpose, or was she in essence telling him that where she lived was none of his business? Before he could press her further, the baby started to cry, and she hastened from the room to tend to its needs.

"Did ye get what ye came for?" Gram said, watching him closely.

"I reckon I heard enough," he said with a wistful glance at the doorway through which Joneta had departed. He bade goodbye to the old woman, who appeared relieved to see him go. He went out the front door into the sunshine beyond.

He unhooked the gelding's reins from the rusted nail and

was about to climb into the saddle when a matronly woman at the house next door beckoned to him. He recalled seeing her at John's shop not that long ago.

He walked over to find out what she wanted, or more likely, what she wanted to tell him. In his experience, gossipy neighbors were always willing to impart what they knew of other people's business.

"Good morrow," he said to her. "Mistress Campbell, isn't it?"

"How clever of ye to remember," she said with a smile. She crooked a finger for him to draw nearer, which he did. "Did ye come about the flogging?"

"What flogging?" he said, baffled.

Her round face grew serious. "Did ye not know Drew was flogged?" she said.

"This is the first I've heard of it," he said. "When did it happen?"

"Monday afternoon. The Southrons dragged the boy out of the house."

"On what charge?"

"Deforcement was what they told him."

"Obstruction of justice?"

"Nay," she said. "Resisting arrest, because he refused go quietly with them. They had to knock him on the head to take him away." She clucked her tongue. "He came back with red stripes all over him, but it was little Meg I felt sorry for. I suspect that Southron had his way with her when she went to see him about freeing her husband."

"Who had his way with her?"

"Captain Sweeney, of course."

"Do you know that for a fact?"

"I saw that poor child's face whenever she came back," she said. "She looked terrible upset." She pursed her lips and frowned in disapproval. "I know it's an awful thing to say, but Drew was lucky to have such a pretty wife to plead for him. They only applied the lash to his back, instead of cutting off some fingers or a hand or even his ears."

Kyle pondered the likelihood of the young couple's involvement in the murder of the two English soldiers. If what Mistress Campbell told him was true, both had good cause to kill them. It puzzled him, though, why either Drew or Meg would slit their victims' throats after they were already dead. He waited in silence to hear what else she had to say.

She shook her head, her countenance sad. "That household has had more than its share of misfortune," she said. "Take that tragic business with Mistress Joneta. She might only be Meg's aunt by marriage, but she's still family."

"What happened to her?"

"She buried her husband not a month past, and her with a new baby."

"She's a widow, then?" he said with repressed joy. What he heard next lessened the shame he felt at his elation over the man's death.

"Aye," she said. "It seems he was involved in some way with the rebels, and the Southrons hanged him for it."

He noticed that she kept a close eye on him as she spoke, as though to see if he reacted in some particular fashion. Being the master of his face, he composed his countenance to reflect only that of polite interest.

"Later that same night," she said, "when Joneta heard how her husband died, she collapsed and gave birth on the spot. She's been mourning the loss of her man ever since."

She leaned close enough for him to detect the smell of wood smoke on her long gray gown. "Another of that same family was killed here in town a few years ago," she said, her tone confiding. "Raped and murdered, she was, or so the tale goes. The whole family moved up north shortly afterwards. I don't think the old woman ever got over it. I heard she swore to find the man who did it, if it was the last thing she ever did. Those highland folk are like that, ye know. They never let a wrong get by them."

He could not picture Gram, ancient and doddering as she was, enticing either Sweeney or Archer to a clandestine rendezvous in order to kill them. Neither could he see her making her escape from a second-floor tavern window, nor walking to and from the shepherd's hut in the middle of the night. Although what Mistress Campbell had related to him might contain a grain of truth, it was more than likely tittle-tattle. In light of that, he would make inquiries to get the facts.

He thanked her for the information before he rode away on the gelding, glad to be gone from the presence of a nosy woman who meddled in other people's lives to brighten her own dreary existence.

He waited until nightfall before returning to Colina's house. The waning moon barely shed enough light for him to find his way along the dark narrow streets. As he approached the stone wall surrounding the property, he kept an eye out for the porter. Yet when he rode through the open gates, no one stepped from the gatehouse to challenge him.

A cool breeze rustled the leaves of the trees flanking the lane that led into the property. On reaching the first outbuilding, he dismounted in the shadows and tied the gelding to a nearby shrub. He glanced around as he crossed the open lawn to the front of the house. Not a creature stirred, not even a dog.

When he raised his hand to knock, Colina, who must have been watching for him, suddenly opened the door.

Her unbound hair hung like a curtain over the shoulders of her loose dressing gown, giving him the impression she was preparing to retire for the night. The hall behind her was dark, and she put a finger to her lips to warn him to silence.

"What ye seek is in Neyll's room," she said. "His window looks out from the rear of the house over the porch." Without any further explanation, she shut the door in his face.

An oath of incredulity exploded from his lips. Did she expect him, a man of law, to break into the house to steal the tax roll from Neyll's room? He turned on his heel and started back across the lawn.

He was halfway to where the gelding was tied when he began to have second thoughts about leaving the document behind. Perhaps taking it was not such a bad idea after all. Otherwise, he might have to wait weeks or even months for its completion. If his luck held after he "borrowed" it, he might be able to copy the information he wanted and return the roll before it was missed.

He turned around and headed for the back of the house to ascertain the difficulty of the task that lay before him.

The rear of the dwelling emerged from the gloom like a huge white edifice. Neyll's window, among others, was shuttered and dark. There was an outcrop of roof directly below it, which made access possible, but not necessarily easy.

He glanced around to make sure he was alone before he shinnied up one of the porch columns. His boots found little purchase on the slick vertical post, and the noise he made heaving himself up onto the roof was enough draw the attention of every servant in the house. To his relief, no one came to investigate, since it would have been embarrassing for him to explain what he was doing on the roof.

He crept along the wooden shingles to the window in question. When he tried to open the shutters, he discovered they were locked from the inside. He drew his dirk to jimmy the latch, but paused at the sound of someone moving about the room.

He looked between the slats of one of the shutters and saw Neyll inside lighting a lamp. He watched as the man sat at a desk to make a series of entries on a document, which he assumed was the tax roll. There was nothing for him to do but wait until Neyll withdrew from the room, at which time he could force the latch without being heard.

He sat on the shingles with his back to the window and pulled his cloak around him against the cool night air. He leaned his head against the shutter to listen for any sound that would indicate Neyll was exiting the room.

An hour later, judging by the position of the rising moon, he heard the scrape of boots on a wood floor coming from within. He turned around to peer between the slats, only to observe Neyll admitting into the room a visitor, whom he recognized as the grim-faced marshal from the garrison. He put his ear against the shutter to eavesdrop on their conversation, thinking that was what Colina meant for him to do, since she must have known he would be unable to enter the premises because of Neyll's presence.

He strained to hear, but the two men spoke in low tones. After a short while, the thread of light coming through the slats went dim and the voices in the room ceased.

He waited for a long moment before putting his eye to the crack between the slats to make sure the room was empty.

It was not.

The two men lay in bed together, their clothing in a heap on the floor. Even in the subdued lighting, he could clearly see what they were doing.

CHAPTER 13

Kyle descended from the porch roof as quietly as he could manage, leaving Neyll and the rotund English marshal entwined in a passionate embrace. There were occasions during his service as a mercenary when sexual liaisons between males were spoken of in hushed tones. Yet in all those years, he never actually witnessed such an act with his own eyes.

He walked as quickly as he could in the faint moonlight to where the gelding stood behind the farthest outbuilding, with a vision burned into his brain of the two naked men groping each other's private parts. It would be a long time before he could look either man in the eye without conjuring up that unholy image.

As he rode back to the garrison, his thoughts turned to Colina, who, in his opinion, was no fool. She undoubtedly suspected that her brother's undue prosperity came from smuggling or some other semirespectable enterprise, which, perhaps in her mind, explained how he could run such a large property on a clerk's paltry wage.

She might truly believe that her brother's activities, although illegal, affected only prosperous merchants who likely indulged in similar illicit activities, and because of that, she declined to turn him over to the law. She obviously had no qualms, however, about exposing his sodomistic proclivities, which explained her fervent prayers at St. John's, no doubt sent heavenward on behalf of her brother's lost soul.

Rather than risk catching another glimpse of Neyll and the marshal *in flagrante delicto*, Kyle decided to make use of the prior year's tax roll, which was more readily accessible, to glean the information he needed.

On entering the garrison, he stabled the gelding before going into the sheriff's office to turn in for the night.

Kyle woke early on Saturday. He put his leather scale armor on over his clothes before he stepped outside. The morning was clear and radiant, without a cloud in sight to mar the azure sky. He walked across the empty courtyard to the main hall, where English soldiers, armed and ready for a day's work, hunched over their food and chatted among themselves.

He spotted Upton on the far side of the hall sharing a table with Turnbull and Vinewood. He took a barley flatbread from the community wicker basket and poured ale from a pottery jug into a cracked clay mug before going over to join them.

"Good morrow," he said as he settled on the bench across from the three of them. "Turnbull, you are looking better than the last time I saw you. Are you now fit for duty?"

"As fit as can be," Turnbull said with a nod.

"I'm glad to hear it," Kyle said. He bit off a chunk of leathery bread and gnawed on it for a moment. "There's something I'd like for you to do," he said to Upton. "Today, if possible."

Upton pushed aside his empty mug and propped his elbows on the table. "I'm at your service," he said.

"I want you to ride out to Harefoot Law," Kyle said, "to make inquiries as to Tullick's whereabouts." He related the events leading up to Tullick's escape.

"Might he be the one who shot the arrow at us in the woods the other day?" Upton said.

Kyle took a sip from his mug. "I can't say for sure," he said. "However, he had good reason to want to keep us from snooping around where Megan was killed."

"What makes you think the villagers will even talk to an English soldier?" Upton said.

"They now know that Tullick murdered Megan," Kyle said. "They want him punished for it, so they might be more willing to cooperate with you. Take Turnbull and Vinewood along in case you do run across him."

Upton exchanged a glance and a nod with Vinewood and Turnbull. "We'll ride out there this morning," he said.

"I would take care of it myself, but I'm planning to head in the other direction," Kyle said.

"Where are you bound?" Upton said.

"For the port of Leith," Kyle said.

"I didn't think the count was well enough to travel," Upton said.

"He isn't," Kyle said. "I'm going on my own."

"While you're up there," Upton said, "you might want to take a look at the cargo manifests of outgoing vessels. I suspect you'll find some interesting items listed on them."

"I see you've given the matter some thought," Kyle said.

"It's the only logical port to use to ship stolen goods out of the country," Upton said.

Kyle frowned, aware that once again he had underestimated the young man. Just because Upton was English did not mean that he approved of his own countrymen's harsh treatment of the Scottish folk in general, or that he endorsed the raids or the raiders in particular.

"Tell no one where I am going, especially Sir Percy," he said. "If he hears of it, he may send you to fetch me back before I can finish my business."

He ate the rest of his bread and washed it down with a swig of lukewarm ale. "I'll see you in a fortnight, God willing," he said, swinging his legs over the bench.

Before he left the main hall, he picked up a couple of loaves and a chunk of cheese to take with him on his journey. He crossed the courtyard to the sheriff's office, where he wrapped the food in a cloth and tucked it, along with a change of clothes, into his saddle roll. He filled a skin bottle with water from the well, after which he went to the stable to saddle the gelding.

He secured his saddle roll behind the cantle and rode from the garrison. On the way out of town, he passed by John's shop to talk to him about Colina. The front door was locked, and the mule and the battered leather saddle in the back were gone, so he continued on his way.

The northeast road stretched out before him like a white thread through the open expanse of green fields and rolling grasslands. Trees were sparse and grew well back from the roadway. There were few houses along the way, and even fewer villages.

Kyle rode without haste, enjoying the warm sunshine and the cooling breeze. Not a single cloud marred the blue sky above him. If the weather held, the journey to Leith should take no more than four days. He stuck to the main road, passing dog carts, ox-drawn wagons, and travelers on foot along the way.

He made good time, and by the end of the first day, he reckoned he was somewhere between Kilmarnock and Kingswell. That meant he had covered at least twenty miles of his journey. Shortly before sunset, he spied a cluster of houses in the distance and turned off the road to seek shelter for the night.

As he approached the village, several men came out to meet him. On learning that he was a countryman of theirs, they ushered him into the largest house among them and sent their wives and daughters to bring food for him to eat. One brought rabbit stew, another brought a roasted goose, and still another brought boiled turnips and greens.

They crowded around him while he ate, eager for news from the southern part of the shire. They plied him with questions well into the night, until he pleaded fatigue. His host then showed him to a pallet laid for him beside the hearth to keep him warm throughout the cold night.

Early the next morning, the villagers sent him on his way with a hearty breakfast under his belt and a blessing ringing in his ears because of the silver coins he left behind on his host's kitchen table.

He rode throughout the day, stopping only to stretch his legs or water the gelding at the nearest stream. By midday, the sun retreated behind the gathering clouds. The rising wind snatched at his dark red cloak and ruffled his hair.

It was late afternoon by the time he entered the outer reaches of Glasgow. Gray clouds hung low over the city, trapping the odor of guttered streets and the smell of the River Clyde. Weathered houses along the way shouldered one another, with only the width of an alley between them. Both rich and poor hurried about their business in the streets, leery of strangers, keeping to themselves.

There were a handful of inns along the road that appeared to be the main artery into the heart of the city. He chose the busiest tavern at which to stop for something to eat, for that was where the food would likely be the most palatable. While he was being served, he asked the tavern keeper where he could find Robert Wishart, Bishop of Glasgow.

The tavern keeper's friendly chatter wavered away into silence. He shrugged his pudgy shoulders and walked away without another word.

Kyle finished his meal and left the tavern, unsure whether the tavern keeper's reluctance to divulge the whereabouts of the bishop stemmed from loyalty or fear. He was about to mount the gelding when he noticed a shabby beggar with a bandaged knee beside the road. He walked over to where the man sat in the dust and dropped half a penny into the upturned palm.

"Where can I find Bishop Wishart?" Kyle said.

"In the High Kirk, of course," the beggar said.

"Where is that?" Kyle said, being unfamiliar with the city.

The beggar glanced down at the halfpenny and looked back up at Kyle. He waited expectantly with his hand extended.

Kyle dug another half a penny from his purse and suspended it over the beggar's palm. "Where is the High Kirk?" he said.

"Just north of High Street," the beggar said.

Kyle made a motion to return the money to his purse.

"That way," the beggar said with alacrity, pointing northeast with a begrimed finger.

"Thanks," Kyle said, depositing the halfpenny in the man's hand.

A flash of lightning and a clap of thunder preceded the light rain that fell from the gloomy sky. He mounted the gelding and drew the hood of his cloak over his head. After negotiating a series of streets and alleyways, he rode through a stone archway, which opened into a large cobbled square before an imposing cathedral.

Situated on the far side of the open square, the High Church of Glasgow was an imposing structure of prodigious proportions, fashioned from brownish-gray blocks of hewn stone. A single conical bell tower at the center soared high into the air above the pointed arcades and the slender traceried windows that embellished the exterior.

He climbed down from the saddle and stood for a moment admiring the symmetry of the cathedral, which was as grand as any he had seen in France. When the bells in the tower rang out, calling the faithful to Sunday evening service, he tied the gelding to the rail out front and followed the stream of people going in through the huge double doors. He joined them in the central aisle to wait for High Mass to commence.

In a short while, the tinkling of a tiny bell summoned forth a priest in ceremonial robes who led a procession of tonsured monks out from behind the central altar.

The monks gathered in the choir section, and the priest went over to stand before the high altar. He conducted the service in Latin in a masculine singsong voice, while those in the choir chanted a response to his every utterance in the same language.

Kyle knelt with the congregation and responded to the litany in Latin, as they did. His attention, though, was taken with the impressive interior of the cathedral. Far above the marble floor, enormous bare beams vanished into the shadowy recesses of the vaulted ceiling. Three parallel aisles ran the length of the vast building, separated by magnificent arched colonnades, which supported the lofty roof. Behind the ornate high altar was the shrine to St. Kentigern, whose body reposed in the crypt below.

The priest sang the benediction and blessed the congregation, after which he led the monks from the chancel. Those in attendance began to shuffle toward the huge doors.

Kyle walked out into the fading dusk with the others. The earlier drizzle had stopped, leaving behind barely enough water to fill the cracks between the cobblestones in the open square.

"Doesn't Bishop Wishart usually conduct High Mass?" he said to the man beside him.

"He does," the man said. "Perhaps he's away. If ye want to know for sure, ye can apply to the convent round back."

It was completely dark by the time Kyle found the bishop's house within the walled grounds behind the cathedral. The young monk who received him was gracious and friendly, yet careful to let nothing slip as to the missing prelate's whereabouts or the date of his subsequent return.

Kyle told the monk that he would stop by again in a week or so. Prior to his own departure, he asked where he might find decent lodgings for the night. The young monk, who evidently knew his way around that part of the city, directed him to a reputable inn not that far away.

He rode from the cathedral grounds and turned to the left, as instructed. The stars were visible after the rain, yet the night was dark, for there was no moon in the sky, nor would there be for another week or ten days. It was more difficult than he thought to follow the monk's simple directions without moonlight to guide him through the maze of pitch-black streets.

He gave the gelding its head to find its way along the dark winding lanes and arched passageways ahead. He kept his hand on the hilt of his sword in case he encountered a villain waiting in the shadows for an unsuspecting traveler. To his relief, he made it to the recommended establishment without incident, after which he passed a quiet night.

He rose early on Monday morning and went out into a thick mist carpeting the ground. The white miasma swirling about his ankles hid from view the litter and garbage strewn about the damp streets and concealed the straggle of weeds sprouting from between cracked and broken cobbles. He set out along the eastern road with the sun in his eyes, content to leave the squalor of the big city behind him.

He rode all that day and most of the next, arriving at Edinburgh late on Tuesday afternoon. Instead of pressing on to Leith, he stopped at an inn to get a good night's sleep. He wanted to start out rested and refreshed in the morning.

Early on Wednesday, he rode the short distance to the port of Leith. On finding a place on the shore with an unobstructed view of the harbor, he slid from the saddle and tied the gelding to a piece of driftwood.

He hunkered down on his heels to gaze out over the vast expanse of the Firth of Forth. The restless sea shimmered with reflected light from the rising sun, and the continual breeze from the firth carried with it the salty smell of the water. He watched six tiny specks on the horizon morph into ships that grew larger and more defined as they approached land on the incoming tide.

The harbor at Leith, like that of Ayr, bustled with merchants and traders coming and going at all hours of the day and night. They drove their wagons onto the dock to load or unload their trade goods. They cluttered the piers with wooden crates, barrels, and kegs, along with sacks of grain, wheels of wax-coated cheese, and crocks of oil. There were rats everywhere, crouching in the shadows or furtively scuffling among the foodstuff.

Fenced enclosures on either side of the central pier held cattle, swine, sheep, and goats ready for export.

Kyle waited for all six ships to dock at the harbor. While each vessel's crew set about furling the sails and making ready to empty the hold, he headed for the central pier to intercept the seamen debarking from the largest merchant ship moored there.

"Where can I find the ship's master," he said to a man with a felt skullcap and a black wool mantle fastened at the neck with a silver pin.

The man in the skullcap pointed to a fellow several yards behind him. "That's him yonder," he said.

The ship's master strode up the wooden pier as if he owned it. He was a robust man on the downhill side of forty, with a barrel chest and a bushy ginger beard. His round head was set low in his thick shoulders, which made him look as though he had no neck at all. His wiry hair, which was as red as his beard, was clubbed back and tamed with a leather thong.

Kyle fell in step beside the ship's master and matched the man's brisk pace. "Kyle Shaw, Deputy to the Sheriff of Ayrshire, at your service," he said.

"John Gunn, Master of the *Ave Maria*," he said in a gruff voice with a Scottish burr. His candid blue eyes surveyed Kyle from head to toe. "Ye be a mite far from home, laddie. I trow ye didn't come all this way for naught. What is it ye want?"

"I'd like to take a look at your cargo manifest," Kyle said. "That is, if you don't mind."

Gunn stopped abruptly. He turned his head to scowl at Kyle from under lowered red brows. "What if I do mind?" he said.

"I'd like to see it anyway," Kyle said. "Shall we?" he added, with a sweep of his hand to indicate the way back to the *Ave Maria*.

Gunn gave a single bark of laughter. "Ye are a cheeky bugger," he said. He swung about and started back down the pier. "I shall oblige ye only to show I have nothing to hide."

When they reached the ship, Kyle followed Gunn across the gangplank and onto the deck, where the first mate was bellowing at the crew to off-load the cargo.

"Come along," Gunn said. He led the way to his own private quarters, where he produced a roll of parchment from the pigeonholed hutch at the back of his desk.

Kyle perused the list of items purchased and sold during the *Ave Maria*'s latest voyage. He did his best to decipher the scribbled words, but he gave up after a moment. "Who wrote this?" he said.

"The chirurgeon," Gunn said. "He also serves as the purser. It were him ye spoke to on the pier."

"I can't read his scrawl," Kyle said.

"Neither can I," Gunn said dryly.

"I trust he's better at curing the sick."

"Not really."

"I'll need him to translate this for me," Kyle said.

"He won't be back for a couple of days," Gunn said. "When he does return, ye must wait until he sobers up."

Kyle handed the parchment roll back to Gunn. "Perhaps you can tell me what I need to know," he said. "Have you ever had dealings with a big brute of a fellow with a shaved head, a flat nose, and a thin moustache, or a tall skinny hatchet-faced fellow with black eyes and pitted skin? They're both rather ugly, even for Englishmen."

"Aye," Gunn said with a chuckle. "I've taken their trade. And why should I not? They pay well enough and give me no trouble. I have not seen them for a while, though. I expect one or the other of them will come by fairly soon to collect what's due and owing to them."

"Do you transport livestock for them?"

"I do," Gunn said. "And silver plate or whatever else they bring. We always settle up whenever they come with another load. I've had dealings with them for years."

"What about the embargo?" Kyle said.

"What about it?" Gunn said. "Any ship flying the Scottish flag may trade out of this port and any other on Scottish soil, even with the ban in place. As I recall, business even picked up a bit after it went into effect. I have expenses to meet, so it is not my practice to question where merchandise comes from, especially if it turns a profit." His weathered face grew serious. "Besides," he added smugly, "I'm immune, no matter what I transport."

"How so?" Kyle said.

Gunn loosened the ties at the neck of his shirt and exposed a mat of wiry ginger curls. A gold chain hung around his thick neck, with a gold key dangling from it. He lifted the chain over his head and used the key to unlock a small carved chest taken from a storage locker against the side wall. He dug through an assortment of precious stones to extract a folded letter from the bottom of the chest.

Kyle took the letter from Gunn's hand and opened it. The date inscribed at the top showed it was written on the Fifth Day of April in the Year of Our Lord, 1297. The foot of the letter bore the signature and the seal of Philip IV, King of France. He scanned the contents, which stated that the bearer was free from recrimination for the import and export of any and all commodities during the embargo imposed by the King of France.

"How did you come by this?" he said.

"About a month past, I put my mark on a document in front of two witnesses," Gunn said. "I did it of my own free will, mind ye, without payment or promise of payment. The man who brought the document to me claimed that was very important. He said if I was ever questioned about it, that I should mention it. He exchanged the document with my mark upon it for this letter. He told me the letter will protect me from any trouble the document might cause."

"Who witnessed it?"

"Trustworthy men, chosen from my own crew."

"Their names?"

"Evan Macfie, Ship's Chirurgeon and Purser, and Bruce Sinclair, First Mate of the *Ave Maria*."

"What did the man who gave you this letter look like?" Kyle said.

"He were dark, like a foreigner," Gunn said. "His fancy clothing and the harness of his fine horse bespoke of wealth and importance." He went on to relate what he remembered of the man's physical appearance.

The description left no doubt in Kyle's mind that the man who gave the Master of the *Ave Maria* the letter of immunity was none other than Count Aymar de Jardine.

CHAPTER 14

Kyle sought out the masters of the other five ships in the harbor, and by the end of the day, he learned that each ship's master possessed a letter similar to that of Master Gunn. It was a short leap mentally to conclude that the documents concealed in Count Jardine's belt were the very ones on which Gunn and the other shipmasters had placed their marks.

Although unaware of the actual wording of those documents, Kyle surmised it had something to do with England's unlawful trade with Flanders. King Edward, wily fox that he was, was not one to sit idly by while the embargo, imposed by his hated French rival Philip, crippled England's economy and drained the royal treasury. The embargo went into effect several years earlier, when King Philip suspended all trade with England and Ireland to punish King Edward for offenses committed by English seamen against French seamen on French soil.

The King of France waived those restrictions with regard to its ally, Scotland, thus permitting only Scottish ships to trade in Flanders and France. All other merchant ships caught running the blockade suffered the confiscation of their vessel as well as their cargo as the penalty for violating the embargo.

Kyle could only assume that Inchcape or Weems saw Count Jardine when he was in Leith around the beginning of April. If Gunn told them about his letter of immunity, which seemed likely, they would almost certainly conclude that the count met with the other shipmasters for the same purpose.

The motive behind the recent attempt on the count's life was now clear, as was the count's undue concern that his belt should not fall into English hands. Those documents were still being sought, however, and they posed a serious risk for anyone who had them, which at present was John Logan. For John's sake, another place of concealment must be found for the belt until the count was fit to travel.

The pitched slate roofs of Glasgow came into view over the rise, a jarring change from the pristine landscape of verdant hills and grassy dales. The day was drawing to a close, and the western sky blazed with streaks of pink and gold and red. Mellow light from the setting sun spread a golden patina over the city's closely set houses and gilded the cathedral's tapered stone tower, which jutted skyward like a pagan obelisk.

Weary from his travels, Kyle sought out the lodgings where he had stayed during his earlier stopover in the city.

After an uninterrupted night's sleep, he awoke late the next morning. He broke his fast at the inn's tavern before riding to the cobbled square fronting the High Church of Glasgow to attend mass on Sunday morning.

A mitered priest in flowing scarlet robes made his entrance with an entourage of monks. Throughout the ritualistic celebration of the Holy Eucharist, his rich baritone dominated every voice in the choir chanting the litany and singing praises to God.

Kyle hoped the priest was the elusive bishop with whom he desired an audience. He did not want to linger in the city for days in order to speak to the man, though in his heart, he knew he would. There were questions to be asked, and the bishop had the answers, or so he believed.

At the conclusion of the service, he rode around to the bishop's house on the grounds behind the cathedral and knocked on the door.

The same young monk as before opened the door, but this time, he was admitted to the premises and asked to wait in the small chamber into which he was ushered.

Unlike the showy display of wealth in the cathedral, the décor of the bishop's receiving chamber was plain, the furnishings simple, without decoration or ornamentation to fill the empty spaces along the plastered walls. The only adornment was a crudely carved wooden crucifix that hung over a *prie-dieu* in the far corner. The kneeler of the wooden prayer stand was unpadded, which would surely cause its user a measure of discomfort while communing with God.

Kyle was examining the crucifix when the door behind him opened. The light quick step of someone advancing on him brought his head around.

The man who entered the chamber looked more like a soldier than a priest, with a tanned complexion and weather-beaten features that spoke of much time spent out of doors. The only indications of his religious calling were the tiny red cap covering his tonsure and the long red robe on his tall erect body. The silver hair and deep lines on the rugged face put him somewhere in his fifties.

"Bishop Wishart?" Kyle said tentatively, unsure of the identity of this vigorous creature.

"Aye, my son," the bishop said in the rich baritone that earlier reverberated throughout the cathedral during High Mass. He extended a calloused hand on which the delicate gold signet ring looked out of place.

Kyle went down on one knee to kiss the ring. When he stood up, he gazed into clear gray eyes on a level with his own. "Your Excellency," he said. "There is much I wish to say. Yet I don't know where to begin."

"I've looked forward to meeting ye for some time now," the

bishop said. "Please be seated, that we may talk." He settled on a hard-backed chair at a wooden table and indicated for Kyle to sit across from him.

"What do ye know about yer father?" he said.

The question caught Kyle off guard. He blinked, an unconscious reaction to stall for time to think, much like suspects did during his own interrogations of them. He nearly laughed out loud at getting caught at his own game. He schooled his face and his voice to reveal nothing. "He's dead," he said. "That's all I know for sure."

"I thought ye might have heard conflicting tales of his loyalty to the Scottish Crown," the bishop said.

"I have," Kyle said. "I trust you can tell me the truth of it."

"Many were the times I wanted to write to ye about yer father," the bishop said. "I dared not, for fear of putting others in peril." He got up from his chair and began to prowl the chamber like a caged beast. He clasped his hands behind his back, his head bowed, as if in prayer. The repressed anger on his face, though, was hardly prayerful.

"Ever since King Alexander the Third's untimely death eleven years ago," the bishop said, "Edward of England has sought control over the Scottish throne. In his insatiable lust for power, he now seeks to gain dominion over the Kirk by replacing us, the Scottish clergy, with English priests. He will never succeed in either as long as I have a breath left in my body." He paused, his gaze on Kyle. "Only a handful of men stand between King Edward and his total domination of Scotland. I am one such man. James Shaw was another, before they killed him."

"Before who killed him?" Kyle said, half-rising from his chair.

The bishop put a placating hand on Kyle's shoulder before resuming his seat at the table. "There is much ye don't know about yer father," he said. "It is true that he allied himself with the English, but only to gather information on King Edward's communications with English garrisons across Scotland. Since James was expected to reciprocate, he and I together determined which reports on rebel movements were harmless enough to give to the English to retain his credibility in their eyes.

"Sir Nicholas de Segrave served as Castellan of Ayr and Warden of Galloway prior to Sir Percy. About five years ago, James sent a message to me advising that Segrave had found him out. He was able to maintain his subterfuge, though, because Segrave could not accuse him of treason without implicating himself. If King Edward were to learn that James lent support to the Scottish rebels all those years under Segrave's command, it would look as though Segrave knew about it and had been a willing party to it. That would cost Segrave not only his post, but his head as well.

"About a month after I received that message from James, Captain Fenwick waylaid a band of Scottish rebels in the pass at Loudoun Hill. His men slaughtered every one of the rebels and left their corpses lying in the road as a warning to others. Unfortunately, James was killed in the fray. By the time I heard of the incident, all of the bodies had been removed, likely taken by kinfolk who gave them a proper burial." He looked Kyle in the eye. "I don't know who took yer father's body."

"Is it possible he was buried at Loudoun Hill?" Kyle said.

"What makes ye say that?" the bishop said.

"While I was looking through the garrison archives," Kyle said, "I came across Fenwick's report on the ambush. In it, he claimed the rebels hacked my father to death and that his mangled remains were buried there in the pass. He also claimed that my father was the one who instigated the ambush."

"Fenwick is an ambitious man," the bishop said with a heavy sigh. "Ambitious men tend to stretch the truth to suit themselves until it resembles the truth no longer."

"In other words, he's a liar," Kyle said. "From what you've

told me of my father and how he purposely misled those around him, I would say he was a liar, too."

"Ye are mistaken about yer father," the bishop said.

"I hope so," Kyle said, "because the man I remember, the man who raised me, taught me about honor and loyalty and trustworthiness. That man would never skulk around dark alleys to indulge in schemes and intrigues."

The bishop stood up and walked over to the *prie-dieu*. He opened the drawer at the top of the upright stand and removed a bronze medallion from it.

"Every day," he said, closing his hand around the medallion, "our countrymen are beaten, maimed, or hanged without cause or provocation. Women are abused. Children are left to starve. Homes are burned. Property is confiscated. Ormesby, the man responsible for this brutality, does so with the English king's blessing. Ormesby has chosen to set up his headquarters at Scone: the ancient symbol of our unity, the most sacred site in the heart of Scotland, the place where Scottish kings of old were crowned. His presence there is an affront to the Scottish people and a desecration to all we hold dear."

The bishop returned to his seat and laid the medallion on the table. "According to the Holy Scriptures," he said, "there is a time and a season for everything under the sun. A time to kill and a time to heal, a time to love and a time to hate."

His gray eyes lit with an inner fire. "It is now the time," he said, "for all of us with Scottish blood in our veins to take a stand against men like Ormesby and against those who rush to do his bidding. The English have already stripped us of our king, our heritage, and our dignity. They will soon strip us of our land and our lives. It is now the season, so saith the prophet Joel, to beat our plowshares into swords and our pruning hooks into spears."

He drew in a deep, calming breath and let it out slowly. "Yer father did his part for the Crown of Scotland," he said. "It cost him his life, as it will one day cost mine. Knowing the fate that awaits me does not stop me from doing what must be done." He put his forefinger on the medallion and pushed it toward Kyle. "If the time ever comes when ye think ye can fit into yer father's shoes to carry on his work, return this to me. I'll know what to do."

Kyle gazed down at the medallion. The image on it was that of St. Columba, the protector and advocate of the Scottish people, who during his lifetime served as a trusted advisor to the rulers of Scotland and went on diplomatic missions for them. He slid the medallion back across the table to the bishop. "I shall resign my post as deputy before I indulge in perfidy and deception for any cause," he said.

"Yer resignation would bode ill for those who look to ye for protection," the bishop said. "Ye alone are the bulwark standing between the Scottish folk and the English." He leaned forward to rest his elbows on the table. "Ye are yer father's son, Kyle, and God willing, ye will soon take up where he left off. Until that time, Quentin shall continue to look after my interests at Ayr Garrison and report to me whenever there is news."

"Is Quentin that old English soldier with a flair for making himself practically invisible?"

"I can't say," the bishop said with a shrug of his shoulders. "We've never met. We exchange messages by way of a mutual acquaintance."

"A black friar, I suppose, who comes and goes without being noticed?"

"So, ye did notice," the bishop said. "Well done."

"I keep my eyes and ears open," Kyle said. "Speaking of Quentin, has he ever mentioned anything to you, through your mutual acquaintance, of course, concerning Sir Percy's clerk?"

"Why him in particular?"

"Neyll is in a position to see all and hear all," Kyle said, "and he's a mite too friendly with the English marshal to suit me."

"That seems to be Quentin's favorite subject of late. He is of the opinion that Neyll is responsible for the raids on homesteads in Ayrshire."

"Neyll is up to something," Kyle said, "but I don't think he would go that far. I think Sir Percy is behind them. Unlike Neyll, Sir Percy is free to act without hindrance, answerable only to his king. He has the manpower at his disposal and the authority to enforce his orders. He has ready access to the tax rolls, from which he could obtain pertinent information to direct Sweeney and his men to the best pickings among the homesteads in the shire."

"I knew enough about Captain Sweeney when he was alive to believe him capable of that," the bishop said.

"I am certain of it," Kyle said. He recounted the discovery of the bruise on the upper right shoulder of Sweeney's body. "It was still purple, so it was relatively new, and it was in the same location as the blow I inflicted a day or so earlier upon a raider of comparable height and weight."

"Do ye think being a raider led to his murder?" the bishop said.

"I don't know," Kyle said. "I do know that folks hated Sweeney for his harsh treatment of them, and somebody made him pay for it." He leaned back in the chair and folded his arms across his chest. "I am sure there is a link between the tax rolls and the raided properties, and that a comparison between the two will show why certain homesteads were chosen, while others were passed over." He went on to relate how his recent efforts to procure the current tax roll ended abruptly with a glimpse of a sexual tryst between Neyll and the English marshal from Ayr Garrison.

The bishop sat up straight, his interest evident on his lined face. "Were they actually engaged in—?" he began. He left the question unfinished, but a raised gray eyebrow spoke volumes.

"Aye," Kyle said, with a slight inclination of his head. "It was a sight I won't ever forget."

"If word of that ever got out," the bishop said, "the consequences to them would be devastating. The Kirk would excommunicate them, and King Edward, who can barely tolerate the sight of his own son because of the young man's similar inclinations, would condemn them without mercy to burn at the stake." He stroked his clean-shaven chin in thought. "Would ye be willing to commit what ye saw to writing? Not the lurid details, naturally. Just the fact that it did occur and that ye were witness to it."

"What purpose would that serve?" Kyle said.

"Leverage, my son," the bishop said. "It has been my experience that the threat of exposure is more effective than actually revealing such information."

"It seems like a despicable thing to do."

"No more so than robbing folks of their means of living or burning them out of their homes. And the knowledge that this document is in my possession will surely encourage the English marshal to be more discerning in his choice of those upon whom he metes out punishment."

"I see your point," Kyle said. "I will do as you ask, under one condition. Neyll's sister must be kept out of it. I don't care what happens to Neyll or his lover, but I don't want Colina to pay for her brother's sins."

"Whatever action, if any, is taken against the sodomites," the bishop said, "ye have my word that Colina will be excluded from it."

"In that event, I agree to make a formal statement," Kyle said.

The bishop got up from the table to pull the bell cord on the wall beside the *prie-dieu*.

The young monk who earlier ushered Kyle into the chamber appeared at the door. He listened to the bishop's instructions, after which he withdrew, only to reappear a moment later armed with a quill pen, an inkwell, a stick of red sealing wax, and a sheet of vellum. He joined them at the table, and with the quill pen inked and ready, he waited for the dictation to begin.

Kyle collaborated with the bishop on the proper wording of his declaration of fact, and when it was composed to his satisfaction, he read over the document before he signed it.

The bishop inscribed his name and title under Kyle's signature. He dribbled hot wax onto the bottom of the vellum sheet and pressed his signet ring into the red blob. "My seal should belay any doubt as to the truth of yer statement," he said.

Kyle got up from the table and took his leave of the bishop, who accompanied him to the front door. As he stepped out into the sunshine, he felt a cold metal disc being pressed into his palm.

"In case ye have a change of heart," the bishop said. He retreated behind the door and closed it softly.

Kyle stood alone on the top step, peering down at the bronze medallion in his hand. Although he was tempted to toss it away, he tucked it into the pouch at his side. There would be time enough on the long journey to Ayr to ponder Bishop Wishart's words and to reaffirm his disapproval of his father's duplicity.

He walked over to where he had left the gelding grazing on a patch of grass within the convent walls. The sunlight was bright and glaring after the semidarkness inside. White puffs of cloud drifted slowly across the blue sky. He rode from the cathedral grounds in search of the main road that would take him south. On the way, he came across a busy market square beside the full flow of the River Clyde. He dismounted there and led the gelding through the maze of multicolored stalls and booths. Glasgow's marketplace was larger than that of Ayr, and so was the crowd on that warm Sunday afternoon.

He paused at a stall with a display of weaponry of various kinds and sizes. He chose an axe smaller than his own and hefted it in his hand to feel its balance. The merchant in attendance hovered at his elbow, anxious to point out other, more expensive pieces.

"This is the one I want," Kyle said. "How much?"

After the usual haggling, they settled on a price.

Kyle paid the man and secured the axe in his saddle roll. He moved on down the row until he came to a clothier with bolts of fabric and a selection of silky ribbons. He purchased two lengths of ribbon, one green and one gold, and he had the vendor wrap them in a bit of cloth to keep them clean. He slipped the tiny parcel into his coin purse and moved on.

The smell of roasted mutton drew him over to the food sellers. He bought a meat pie to eat while he wandered around the marketplace. There was much to see, and he spent the entire afternoon taking in the sights and sounds.

As the shadows lengthened, vendors began shutting down their stalls and packing up their goods. Since it was too late in the day to head out on the road, he sought shelter for the night at an inn overlooking the River Clyde.

He paid extra to have a room to himself. By the light of the single candle allotted to him, he carved three letters with his dirk into the handle of the small axe. Satisfied with his efforts, he snuffed the candle and sprawled out on a pallet stuffed with pine straw. After a good night's sleep, he would start out early on Monday morning.

It was late on Tuesday afternoon by the time he reached the stretch of road that took him past Ogilvy's homestead. He turned the gelding's head into the tree-lined lane and followed it around to the old man's cottage.

He rode into the open yard just as Ogilvy and his grandson, Hob, were coming up from the creek. Each of them carried a pail of water to dump into the trough just inside the sheep pen.

"Grandpa, look!" Hob cried, pointing. "It's Master Kyle."

The boy's shouts caused the wooly creatures to scurry to the far side of the enclosure.

Ogilvy rested his wooden pail on the rim of the trough, while Kyle rode around the pen to meet him.

He climbed stiffly down from the saddle and ruffled Hob's hair by way of greeting, pleased that the boy was wearing the wool mantle he had given to him. "How goes it?" he said to the old man.

"Tolerable," Ogilvy said. He held up his pail for the gelding to drink from it. "Ye look a mite weary."

"I've been on the road for close to two weeks," Kyle said.

"Pleasure?" Ogilvy said, more from curiosity than the need to pry.

"Business," Kyle said.

"Care for a bite to eat?" Ogilvy said.

"Nay, thanks," Kyle said. "I could use something to wash the dust from my throat, though."

"Fetch the jug," Ogilvy said to Hob, who hastened to do as he was bidden.

Kyle's gaze took in the fresh coat of whitewash on the cottage and the new thatch on the roof. "I see you've been busy," he said.

"I have," Ogilvy said with a gap-toothed grin. "Nearly finished, too." He set the empty pail on the ground, after which he stroked the gelding's reddish-brown nose.

Kyle reached up to loosen the ties on his saddle roll. He was extricating the small axe he had purchased in Glasgow, when

Hob returned with a brown pottery jug and a couple of mugs. "This is for you," he said, handing the weapon to the boy in exchange for the jug and the mugs.

The old man relieved Kyle of the jug and poured ale into the mugs, one of which he took for himself.

"Your axe looks just like mine," Kyle said, indicating the formidable battle axe hanging from the leather loop on his saddle.

A smile as wide and bright as a summer day lit Hob's face. He turned the axe over in his hands and saw the grooves carved into the shaft. He rubbed his thumb over them, unsure of what they meant.

"That's your name, H-O-B," Kyle said, touching each letter in turn. "Your grandpa can show you how to keep the blade sharp."

"Ye can play with the axe later," Ogilvy said to Hob. "Get along with hauling water now. That trough won't fill itself."

Hob stuck the handle of the axe through his rope belt before he picked up his pail and emptied it into the trough. He headed down the slope to the creek, holding the pail in one hand and the axe head with the other, as though to assure himself it was really there.

"I expect he's going to sleep with that thing, too, from now on," Ogilvy said with a shake of his head.

Kyle chuckled, delighted that his gift was so well received. He cast a glance toward the cottage. "Before I go," he said, "I want to pay my respects to your lady wife. Is she inside?"

"Nay," Ogilvy said. He upended his pail and lowered his skinny haunches onto the flat surface. "Mistress Hamilton accepted my offer, but we are not yet wed." He took a sip of the ale from his mug. "The date is set for a week hence."

"Is it, now?" Kyle said.

Ogilvy nodded. "We're both getting on a bit," he said. "We want to share what time we have left."

Kyle drained the contents of his mug and wiped his mouth with the back of his hand. He, of all people, knew how short life could be and how fleeting its moments of joy. Those two were such a mismatched pair: the scruffy old man who smelled like sheep and the arthritic old woman who might be a witch. Yet they shared a willingness to grasp at happiness before it was too late for them. He would do well to heed their example.

The sun hung like a dull red ball on the horizon. The whole expanse of the western sky slowly turned as pink as a maiden's blush. The weeds in the yard shivered in the cool breeze starting to blow in from the east.

"I wish you and Mistress Hamilton the best," Kyle said. He gathered up the reins to mount the gelding. "I must press on if I expect to reach the garrison by nightfall."

Hob came running across the yard to intercept Kyle before he left. "Can I go with ye?" he said, his expression earnest and imploring. "Just for a visit?"

Kyle hesitated, mentally weighing the possibility of keeping the boy with him for a day or two against the practicality of doing so. He decided it was not a good idea, for his duties as a lawman laid him open to dangers to which he did not want the boy exposed.

"There are too many English roving about," Kyle said. "You'll be safer out here. Besides, your grandpa will need your help to prepare for the wedding."

Hob seemed disappointed, but he accepted Kyle's explanation without complaint. "Was this yer son's before he died?" he said, indicating the small axe hanging on his rope belt.

Kyle shot a caustic glance at the old man, who at that moment appeared to take an inordinate interest in the contents of his mug. "Nay," he said to the boy. "I bought it for you. That's why I put your name on it." He laid the reins on the gelding's neck to turn its head toward the tree-lined lane. "I tell you what

I'll do," he added. "The next time I come out this way, I shall stop by to see you."

"Ye will?" Hob said.

"I will," Kyle said. "That's a promise."

After breakfast on Wednesday morning, a group of English soldiers ambled from the main hall, in no hurry to begin their daily tasks. Some trudged away to relieve their comrades on the guard walk around the inside of the garrison wall, while others went to sharpen their weapons or to practice with them to improve their skill.

Kyle followed the soldiers outside. With the salty smell of the Firth of Clyde in the air and the rising sun in his eyes, he headed for the sheriff's office. The week-old porridge he had just consumed sat heavily on his stomach. He was halfway across the courtyard when he heard someone call out his name. He turned to see John Logan hurrying to catch up with him.

"How was yer trip?" John said, falling in step beside him.

"Tediously long," Kyle said. "Although I must admit it was enlightening." He glanced over at his companion. "I stopped by your shop to see you before I left. I wanted to tell you I met with Colina."

John's handsome face seemed to brighten at the mention of her name. "How is she?" he said.

"Quite taken with you, if I am not mistaken."

"As I am with her."

"What is it, then, that keeps you apart?"

"It's complicated," John said, his countenance grave. "Her brother wants her to marry someone with connections, no doubt for his own advancement. He has forbidden her to form an attachment with me." He filled his lungs with cool morning air and let it out in a long hiss. "We meet only when she visits my shop for her mother's potions and such. Berta is ever at her side, so we hardly exchange a word on those occasions."

"That must be hard for both of you."

"It is, but I must bear it for her sake. Her brother can be cruel, and I don't want her to suffer at his hands because of me."

On reaching the sheriff's office, Kyle unlatched the door and propped it open to let in the light.

John followed him inside. He slipped the leather strap of his medicament bag over his head and set it on the bench under the window.

Kyle went into the rear chamber. When he returned a moment later with a jug of ale and two cups, John was already seated at the table. He settled on the stool opposite and filled both cups to the brim.

John picked up the nearest cup and sipped at the amber brew.

Kyle drank his ale in one go without even tasting it to wash the sour tang of porridge from his mouth. No one had died yet from the garrison cook's concoctions, but in his opinion, it was only a matter of time before someone did. He looked up to catch the frown clouding the older man's features. "Has the ale gone off, too?" he said, setting down his cup.

"Not at all," John said, still frowning.

"What is it, then?"

"It's Count Jardine."

"Has his wound turned septic?"

"Worse."

Kyle sat up straight. "Is he dead?" he said, bracing himself for bad news.

"Nay," John said. "He's up and about, and feeling quite fit, as a matter of fact." He leaned closer and lowered his voice. "I think another attempt has been made on his life."

"You don't sound very sure of it," Kyle said.

"There's no way to prove it, ye see," John said. "I have only

Count Jardine's word that someone tried to poison him."

"Oh, is that all?" Kyle said with relief.

"The outcome could have been serious," John said with dismay.

"That would depend on how much porridge he ate," Kyle said. The dubious expression on John's face prompted him to add, "Have you tried it lately?"

John shook his head. "I don't take meals at the garrison," he said.

"If you did, I would recommend that you steer clear of the porridge. It's hard to tell if it's gone off until after you've eaten it."

"It can't be the porridge," John said. "The count never eats it." He wrapped both hands around his cup and peered into its liquid depths. "He says the incident occurred about a week ago. The orderly brought his supper up to his chamber, as usual. When he started in on the stew, he thought it tasted peculiar. He ate no more of it, but the little he did consume was enough to make him sick. He now comes down to the main hall for his meals. He won't eat anything but what he takes from the pot shared with the soldiers."

"Was the orderly questioned?"

"Upton talked to him," John said. "The orderly says he took the tray up to the count and left it there, and that's all he knows."

"Do you believe him?"

"There is no reason to doubt him," John said, "given the number of people who had access to the tray before he carried it up." He opened his medicament bag and removed a rolled piece of vellum, which he handed to Kyle. "Here is the list ye asked for. It's the best that Macalister and I could recall of the homesteads raided and the date of each raid."

Kyle perused the information on the scroll. "This is just what I need," he said after a long moment. "Thanks."

"Ye say the trip to Leith was enlightening," John said. "How so?"

Kyle recounted his conversation with John Gunn, Master of the *Ave Maria,* concerning King Philip's offer of immunity from prosecution for the duration of the embargo in exchange for a signed statement. "The other shipmasters in port stated basically the same thing," he said.

"Did any of them reveal the contents of the document they signed?" John said.

Kyle shook his head. "Since every one of them was guilty of transporting English goods across the French blockade under the Scottish flag, I can only assume they admitted that in writing in return for King Philip's protection."

"I cannot imagine that King Edward would be foolish enough to violate the embargo so flagrantly," John said. "Doing so would make him liable to Philip for exorbitant penalties and the possible forfeiture of his French lands. That loss of revenue would strain England's fragile economy to the point of bankruptcy."

"That's why Count Jardine's life is still at risk," Kyle said. "If such news were to reach Philip, Edward would be made to pay dearly. Edward might not personally bribe Scottish shippers to carry English merchandise, but he surely knows about it, which would suggest his approval of it. That alone gives Philip grounds to take punitive action against him. And speaking of risks," he added, "I should not have involved you in the count's intrigues."

"Are ye referring to the belt?" John said.

Kyle nodded. "I shall look for another place to hide it," he said.

"Leave it be for the time being," John said. "Nobody knows it's there. Besides, the count will be gone in a week or two, and there's an end to our worries."

"As you wish," Kyle said. "In the meantime, watch your back."

"I always do," John said with a humorless smile. He stood up to retrieve his medicament bag from the bench. "The morning is wearing on. I must get back to the shop."

"Before you go, I have a question for you," Kyle said. "Do you remember anything about the rape and murder of a Scots girl here in town five or six years ago?"

"It sounds familiar," John said, "but I don't recollect the details. Sorry I can't tell ye more." He took a step toward the doorway just as Upton burst into the sheriff's office, red-faced and breathless from running.

"I just came from Sir Percy's office," Upton said, between breaths. "He's going to arrest Count Jardine." His wide-eyed gaze shifted from one to the other. "For treason."

CHAPTER 15

Kyle stood so abruptly, he knocked over his stool. John dropped the medicament bag onto the bench under the window, evidently changing his mind about departing. They both listened as the young man told his tale.

"Early this morning," Upton said, "I picked up a packet for Sir Percy from a merchant ship that arrived with the tide. I spied the royal seal of England on one of the letters, so I put that one on top. I delivered the packet to Neyll and called his attention to the letter with the royal seal on it. He immediately brought it in to Sir Percy. I hung about the anteroom in case I was needed to take a reply back to the merchant ship. Good thing I did. That's when I overheard Sir Percy instruct Neyll to write out a warrant, as ordered by King Edward himself, to arrest Count Jardine for treasonous acts committed against the Crown of England. I came directly here to tell you about it."

"What charges can Edward possible lay at Count Jardine's feet?" John said.

"As King of England," Kyle said, "Edward can do as he pleases to anyone whom he perceives as a threat to the monarchy." He stroked his chin, his brow puckered in thought. "If we intend to rescue the count, we must act quickly, for the arrest will surely take place this very day. Sir Percy would not be slow about ridding himself of the man who has caused him so much trouble."

"They will likely arrest him at noon," John said. "That is

when the count ventures forth from his chamber to dine in the main hall."

"I agree," Kyle said. "Sir Percy would like nothing better than to humiliate the Royal Envoy of France in front of the entire body of English troops by hauling him away in chains."

"Once they throw him into the dungeon," John said, "it won't be so easy to get him out."

"Then we must get to him before he is arrested," Kyle said.

"What do ye propose?" John said.

"I have something in mind," Kyle said. "However, Upton's participation is crucial for it to succeed." He laid a hand on the young man's shoulder. "What I am about to suggest will in all probability end your career as an English soldier. On the other hand, it may clear the way for a promising future."

"I'm due for a change," Upton said. "Let me hear what you have to say."

Kyle shared with them the details of a bold, yet simple plan.

A thoughtful expression crossed John's face, but he remained silent.

Upton licked his lips. It was a sign of nervousness, as though he appreciated the gravity of the situation and the part he must play in it. "Before I consent to this scheme," he said, "there is but one alteration I would make to it." He then told them what he had in mind.

Upton's disclosure brought a smile to Kyle's lips. "That won't be a problem," he said. "Off you go, but remember, midday will be upon us in less than two hours."

The three of them hastened from the sheriff's office to undertake the necessary preparation. John mounted his mule and set out at a jarring trot for the garrison gates, while Kyle and Upton headed for the stable.

★　★　★　★　★

Shortly before noon, Upton galloped through the garrison gates and into the empty courtyard. He halted in a swirl of churned earth before the main hall, inside of which were most of the soldiery at that time of day. He slid from the saddle and began swatting the dust from his linen shirt and the leggings beneath.

Kyle, who had been waiting for Upton's return, stepped out into the sunny courtyard. The air was still, without even the faintest cooling breeze from the firth. He gathered up the reins of the two saddled horses standing in front of the sheriff's office and led them across the courtyard. "Are you ready for this?" he said as he tied the bay and the roan to the rail beside Upton's mount.

Upton wiped the sweat from his upper lip with his sleeve. "As ready as I'll ever be, I suppose," he said.

They entered the main hall together. Upton went to the left, toward the side door nearest the kitchen through which the chief cook's helpers were wheeling a huge iron pot filled with hot stew.

Kyle turned in the other direction to stand in line behind the soldiers who were there waiting for the food to be served. Some moments later, to his surprise, John joined him in line. "I thought you didn't eat here," he said.

"I don't," John said. "Today is an exception."

"It is that," Kyle said. "Did you secure the saddle roll on the bay outside?"

"I did."

"I hope all goes as planned."

"It will," John said, looking rather pleased with himself.

Kyle chose a table from which he and John could see not only Sir Percy at the head table, but the front doorway as well, for that was where the soldiers would enter to make the arrest.

The midday meal was well underway by the time Count Jardine slowly descended the stairs from the upper floor of the main hall. He helped himself to stew from the community pot before walking over to the head table.

With a courteous nod to Sir Percy, the count seated himself at the far end of the head table. He had just finished eating when a couple of English soldiers, helmeted and armed with halberds, marched across the main hall to stand beside him.

The shorter of the two soldiers, whose face was half hidden under the nosepiece of his Norman helmet, handed his halberd to his companion. He removed a scroll from the leather pouch at his side, unrolled it, and held it up to read aloud from it.

"Hear ye, hear ye, Count Aymar de Jardine, Royal Envoy to Philip the Fourth, King of France," he said. "You are accused of perpetrating treasonous acts against the Crown of England. By order and command of His Royal Majesty, Edward of England, I hereby place you under arrest." He rolled up the scroll and stepped back to allow the count to rise from the bench. "You will now come with us."

The buzz of conversation around them died as those within earshot suspended all activity to stare openly.

Count Jardine remained in his seat, ignoring the curious glances directed his way. "May I see the warrant?" he said, holding out his hand.

The armed soldier hesitated for an instant before surrendering the document.

Count Jardine unrolled the parchment scroll. After a cursory glimpse, he rolled it up again. As he handed it back, he fixed a narrow and speculative look upon the soldier who took it.

The soldier tucked the scroll into his pouch, after which he retrieved his halberd from the other soldier. "You must come with us at once," he said to the count.

Count Jardine rose from the table without a word of protest. He brushed the bread crumbs from the forest green linen tunic, which he wore under a velvet mantle of the same rich color. The blood red ruby in the brooch at his neck glimmered and gleamed with each move he made.

A murmur swept through those looking on as the count set out for the entryway at a dignified pace, with an armed soldier on either side of him.

Kyle cast a fleeting glance at the head table. It gratified him to see Sir Percy smirking into his wine goblet, too smug and arrogant to notice that the soldiers escorting Count Jardine through the front door of the main hall were none other than Upton and Turnbull.

Upton walked out of the main hall into the blazing glare of the sun. His gaze swept the open courtyard for anyone who might pose a threat to their escape. Three soldiers across the way were drawing water from the well, but not one of them even looked in his direction. He started toward the saddled horses tied to the wooden rail twenty feet away, beckoning for Turnbull and Count Jardine to come with him.

They were halfway to the horses when Inchcape stepped into the courtyard from the barracks over a hundred feet away, at the head of a four-man squad of soldiers armed with halberds.

The sight of the halberdiers, undoubtedly the official squad sent to arrest Count Jardine, raised a prickle of sweat on Upton's brow that had nothing to do with the warmth of the midday sun. His first instinct was to run for the horses. He resisted the urge to panic, keeping his gait measured and steady until he reached the wooden rail.

Inchcape, who apparently recognized Count Jardine and guessed that something was amiss, drew his sword. "Halt!" he shouted. "Stand where you are." He set out toward them at a jog.

The halberdiers followed Inchcape at the same brisk pace,

their lance-like weapons leveled and ready to wield.

Upton and Turnbull discarded their halberds, which were too cumbersome and awkward to carry with them during their flight. Upton freed three sets of reins from the rail before he leaped onto the back of his horse. Turnbull swung into the saddle, as did Count Jardine. They turned their mounts and urged them into a frantic gallop, bound for the garrison gates.

"Shut the gates," Inchcape bellowed at the startled guards. "Shut the bloody gates." He cut across the open courtyard at an angle to intercept the escapees, moving with surprising speed for such a big man.

The watchman in the gate tower nocked an arrow and let it fly at Upton, who at that instant swerved his horse around Inchcape and the charging halberdiers to avoid being struck by their blades.

The arrow thudded into the ground, narrowly missing one of the halberdiers.

The three horsemen hurtled through the gateway to freedom. The thunder of hooves rang out as their mounts galloped across the wooden drawbridge beyond the raised portcullis, only seconds before the two burly guards managed to close the gates.

Inchcape hurled his sword to the ground in a fit of rage. "Open the gates, you idiots," he bellowed, shaking his meaty fist at the guards. "Open the bloody gates." He pounced on the nearest halberdier, who made the mistake of pausing too long to catch his breath. "Don't just stand there with your head up your arse," he snarled, his red face accentuating the blue veins throbbing at his temples. "Mount up and give chase."

Inchcape's shouts brought a number of soldiers out from the main hall into the courtyard in time to see the quick-stepping halberdiers headed for the stable. Most of them were seasoned soldiers who knew which situations required the use of a horse, so they hurried after the halberdiers to join them in the impending chase.

Kyle and John followed the crowd outside. They stood beside the entryway of the main hall to watch the goings-on in the courtyard.

"Count Jardine was moving rather slowly when he came down to eat," Kyle said. "I fear he may not hold up under a grueling pursuit."

"There will be no pursuit," John said. Kyle's raised eyebrow prompted him to explain. "After our conversation this morning, I went to my shop to fetch the belt. While I was there, I mixed a powder extracted from poppies with honey to make a sleeping draught. When I came back here, I put the belt in Count Jardine's saddle roll, as ye requested. After that, I ducked into the stable to a smear a bit of the dosed honey onto the lips of each of the forty-odd horses in there." He indulged in a wry smile, which caused a dimple to flash in his left cheek. "Those horses aren't going anywhere for at least two hours."

"My gelding, too?"

"Of course. Ye don't want yer mount to stand out from the others."

"Good thinking. It won't hurt him, will it?"

"Not at all."

Kyle glanced over at the older man. "From now on," he said dryly, "I shall be more careful to stay on your good side."

Upton slowed his mount to a trot as he, Turnbull, and Count Jardine drew abreast of St. John's Church. He did not want to draw undue attention by galloping up Harbour Street through pedestrian traffic.

He turned to the right at the first corner, only to turn right again at the next corner, which brought him to the road that followed the coastline to the south.

"This will throw them off our scent for a while," Upton said.

Turnbull gave the young man a piercing look. "I hope you know what you're doing, boy," he said.

"It's something I should have done a year ago," Upton said. He laid the reins on his mount's neck and turned to the left.

The three of them set out along the coastal road. They turned inland at Alloway and followed the River Doon to Harefoot Law. Before they reached the village, Upton and Turnbull disposed of their helmets and their bull hide armor somewhere in the woods off the beaten track. They rode into the chapel yard and halted in front of the chapel.

Father Ian appeared in the arched doorway and descended the steps to welcome them. "As soon as ye left here this morning," he said to Upton, "I sent a trusted fellow to fetch Mistress Elspeth. She should be here any time now."

Count Jardine placed both hands on the saddle bow and leaned back against the cantle, his gaze on Upton. "I have not yet thanked you," he said, "for removing me from Sir Percy's reach."

"Until you leave this country," Upton said, "you will remain within Sir Percy's reach."

"At the risk of sounding ungrateful," Count Jardine said, "I cannot return to my homeland without certain documents of vital importance to my king."

"Those documents are in your saddle roll," Upton said.

Count Jardine opened the saddle roll to find his belt inside. He checked the lining to make sure the documents hidden within were intact. He closed his eyes for a brief moment, as though overwhelmed with relief and exhaustion at the same time. "Words fail me," he said as he fastened the belt around his waist.

"Though you are a stranger to our shores, *m'sire le comte*," Upton said, "you are not without friends." He took a deep breath to steady his nerves, for the count's reply to the question he was about to pose would determine his future course. "About three weeks ago, you asked me to serve as your aide. Is that offer still open?"

"It is," the count said with a nod.

"Then I accept," Upton said, relieved now that a weight had been lifted from his mind.

"How does the lady for whom we are waiting figure into this?" Count Jardine said.

"You are a hunted fugitive," Upton said, "as am I at present for helping you escape. I propose a trade to balance the scales: your life and your freedom for a boon."

"What is it you want?" Count Jardine said with a slight frown.

"When you take me with you to France as your aide," Upton said, "I ask that you book passage for Mistress Elspeth and Turnbull, too."

Turnbull's head snapped around. "Now, hold on a moment," he said.

"What's the problem?" Upton said. "I want you to come to France with me."

"Don't be daft, boy," Turnbull said. "You have your whole life ahead of you, you and Mistress Elspeth. In France, you'll have a new life and a new occupation." He shook his head. "I'm too old, too cranky, and too set in my ways to start over in some foreign country."

"You will be hanged if you go back to Ayr Garrison," Upton said.

"I don't intend to go anywhere near that or any other garrison," Turnbull said. "I plan to head to the border to see your father. Before I left to play wet-nurse to you, he told me I would always be welcome if I ever wanted to go back there."

Whatever Upton was about to say was drowned out by the crunch of wheels from the one-horse open carriage that rolled into the chapel yard.

The young woman in the driver's seat waved to Upton with one hand and pulled back on the reins with the other to stop the horse. Sunlight glinted on the golden highlights of her honey-colored hair. Her brown dress was suitable for traveling, as were her sturdy leather boots.

The thirteen-year-old boy sharing the driver's seat with the young woman jumped to the ground and held out his hand to help her down.

She rewarded his gallantry with a luminous smile.

A blush suffused his youthful face all the way to the tips of his ears. His expression left no doubt that he was clearly smitten.

Upton slid from the saddle and went over to meet them. "I appreciate your bringing Mistress Elspeth here so quickly," he said to the boy. "Your name is Ewan, isn't it?"

Ewan nodded, grinning. He set about unhitching the horse from the carriage traces.

Upton took the young woman's hand and brought it to his lips. "Dearest Elspeth," he said, with a warm smile. "I've longed for this moment."

"I came as quickly as I could," Elspeth said. "I packed only a few things so that no one would notice I was going on a journey."

"I come to you with what I have on," Upton said, indicating his tan linen shirt and brown leggings. "We left in rather a hurry, you see." He clasped her hand between both of his own. "Are you sure about this? I don't wish to press you into doing something you will later regret."

She looked directly into his eyes. "I didn't come here because ye invited me," she said. "I came because I wanted to be with ye, of my own free will."

"My darling girl," Upton said, caressing her cheek with his fingertips.

By that time, Turnbull, who had climbed down from the saddle, walked over to join them. He greeted Elspeth in a cordial manner, touching his forehead with his knuckle as a sign of respect.

Count Jardine dismounted to accompany Father Ian to where the others were standing by the carriage.

After the introductions, the count gave Elspeth a courtly bow. "You are quite lovely, my dear," he said. He turned his gaze to Upton. "I now understand why you are determined to take her with you. You have my word that her passage will be secured."

"Thank you, *m'sire le comte*," Upton said. He exchanged a glance with Elspeth before he turned to the old priest. "Father Ian," he said, "we want to marry."

"That's wonderful, my children," the old priest said. "When do ye wish to do so?"

"Now, if you please," Upton said.

"But the banns," Father Ian said in dismay. "They must be announced three weeks ahead. And Sir Ross must be present to show his consent by giving his daughter away."

"We will be departing," Upton said, "within the hour to embark on a two-week journey to a country across the sea. I will see her bound to me by marriage before I do anything that would cast a shadow upon her good name. Will you bless our union, or must we look for some other priest who will?"

"This is most unusual," Father Ian said, wringing his hands. "I suppose the banns can be dispensed with." He glanced over at Elspeth. "But yer father," he added, with a disapproving shake of his head. "He will be sorely vexed when he hears that ye ran away with an Englishman."

"Then I shall make my peace with him," Elspeth said, "but at some future date, after the deed is done."

"Does not a man and a woman," Count Jardine said, intruding into the conversation, "simply pledge their troth before witnesses to bind themselves in matrimony?"

"The bride and groom must also jump the broomstick," Elspeth said.

"Even so," Father Ian said, "only a priest can bless their union in the eyes of God."

"If you wish to proceed," Count Jardine said to Upton, "I will stand as witness for you."

"I will, too," Turnbull said.

Ewan had been listening to their conversation while he saddled the carriage horse for Elspeth and tied her bundle behind the cantle. He gathered a handful of clover flowers from the verge before easing up beside her. "For the bride," he said, handing the tiny cluster to her. He blushed scarlet at the grateful smile that she bestowed upon him.

Father Ian turned and headed for the chapel doorway. He disappeared inside, reappearing a moment later with a straw broom in his hand. "If ye are determined to go through with this," he said, "then it must be done proper." He went down the steps to where they waited in the chapel yard.

Under a canopy of blue sky, with the birds in the trees singing in the background, Upton and Elspeth stood facing each other on that sunny afternoon in early May. In front of witnesses, they exchanged vows to love, to care for, and to be faithful to one another all the rest of their days together. Hand in hand, they jumped over the broomstick lying in the grass at their feet. Father Ian then raised his hands to pronounce a blessing upon them.

The newly wedded couple received with pleasure the pats on the back, the kisses on the cheek, and the congratulations of those in attendance.

Now that the ceremony was over, Turnbull started toward his horse.

Upton put out a hand to delay Turnbull's departure. "I shall miss you," he said, enfolding the older man in a bear hug. It was difficult to speak around the lump in his throat.

Turnbull extricated himself from the young man's embrace. "Take care of yourself, boy," he said gruffly, as though he had a lump in his throat as well. "And your lady, too."

"I'll write to you when we get settled," Upton said.

"I'd like that," Turnbull said as he mounted his horse. "So will your father." With a wave of farewell, he set out for the road that would take him south to Upton manor house across the English border, perhaps to resume his former post as a retainer to old Lord Upton.

Upton and Elspeth prepared to leave with Count Jardine, to travel to some isolated quay along the southern coast of the Firth of Forth, where a hired seagoing vessel would take the three of them on to France.

Chapter 16

Shortly after Upton, Turnbull, and Count Jardine rode from the garrison, Sir Percy bustled out of the main hall with a forbidding scowl on his face.

"It appears he heard the news," Kyle said, tilting his head toward the disgruntled Castellan of Ayr.

"I think it best if I depart," John said, "lest anyone get the notion I had a hand in it."

Kyle glanced around the open courtyard, where most of the soldiers had gathered in tight knots with their heads together. "Where's your mule?" he said.

"I left him tied to the rail at the kirk," John said. "I didn't want him laid low like the horses. It's too far to walk back to my shop."

"I'll let you know later what Sir Percy decides to do," Kyle said.

"I will be at the tavern tonight," John said, after which he headed for the garrison gates.

Kyle directed his attention to the matter at hand.

From Sir Percy's frowning countenance, it was apparent he doubted the reports carried to him by hitherto reliable men. With a visible tightening of his lips, he strode across the courtyard to see with his own eyes the strange malady that seemed to afflict every horse in the garrison stable.

Kyle followed along behind Sir Percy, as did the soldiers in the courtyard.

On entering the stable, Sir Percy walked down the entire length of the center aisle, pausing at each occupied stall to stare in disbelief at the collapsed creature within, on which the only sign of life was the rise and fall of its rounded belly.

At the end of the long aisle, Sir Percy paused in front of the last stall to gaze down at his own steed: a dappled gray lying on its side in the straw. He broke the protracted silence he had maintained during his inspection of the downed horses by rounding on the groom beside him. "What did you do to them?" he cried, grasping a fistful of the hapless man's shirt.

White-faced and trembling, the groom could only shrug his shoulders, his expression reflecting his perplexity as to why such ill luck should befall him alone. "I did nothing, my lord," he said. "They just lay down like that on their own."

"Every one of them?" Sir Percy said.

"Every one of them, my lord," the groom said, bobbing his head.

Sir Percy released his hold on the groom's clothing. "Then perhaps it is something you should have done," he said, as though unwilling to absolve the wretched man of responsibility where the care and keeping of horses, especially his own, was concerned.

The groom scratched his head as he peered into the gray's stall. "It's like someone placed a curse upon them," he said, mystified.

"A very timely curse for Count Jardine, if you ask me," Sir Percy said, his eyes narrowed in suspicion.

Inchcape pushed his way through those gathered to stand before Sir Percy. "Do you want me to commandeer horses here in town to pursue the fugitives?" he said.

"What's the use?" Sir Percy said. "By the time you round up a sufficient number of suitable mounts, Count Jardine will be halfway to France."

★　★　★　★　★

It was midafternoon before the horses in the garrison stable began to stagger to their hoofed feet. After being fed and watered by the especially attentive groom, the creatures appeared to revive completely, without any sign of relapse. The groom sent word of their miraculous recovery to Sir Percy, who paid another visit to the stable.

Since the horses had recuperated from their earlier debilitated state, Sir Percy at once dispatched a troop of soldiers into the countryside to search for Count Jardine. It was a perfunctory gesture, without expectation of actual success. He did it because he was answerable to his king for his actions, or in this case, his inactions, which would surely reflect laxity on his part if he did not at least make an effort to pursue a traitor to the Crown.

Kyle went to the stable to check on the gelding. To his relief, all was well, as John predicted it would be. He returned to the sheriff's office to write out a report on Count Jardine's escape. He would, of course, exclude certain incriminating details that resulted in the timely execution of that event.

He was seated at the table with the door open to let in the light, engrossed in composing the account, when he heard a knock on the doorjamb. He looked up to see a matronly woman in a long gray gown standing outside the sheriff's office. She carried a longish object wrapped in an oilskin in one hand, and a bunch of freshly cut flowers in the other hand.

"Mistress Campbell," he said, rising from the table. "What can I do for you?"

"Do ye mind if I sit for a moment?" she said. "I walked all the way over here."

"Certainly," he said, indicating for her to sit on the bench.

She settled on the hard wooden surface and laid the oilskin bundle down beside her. She held onto the flowers so as not to bruise the tender blossoms.

"Now," he said, resuming his seat at the table. "Tell me what brings you out this way."

"I would like for ye to take me to my daughter's farm," she said.

"I'm rather busy at the moment," he said. "Perhaps some other day."

"Please," she said. "There is something out there I must show ye."

He hesitated, not relishing the idea of being a captive audience to a gossipy woman, until he caught the grave expression on her face. "What is this about?" he said.

"Would ye humor me for a bit?" she said. "I promise ye, it is something ye will want to see for yerself."

With an effort to stifle his growing impatience, he returned the quill pen to the holder on the table and stood up. "Wait here while I fetch a wagon," he said.

He went over to the stable to strap the gelding into the traces of one of the wagons stored there. He drove the wagon to the sheriff's office and helped Mistress Campbell into the seat beside him. She held the flowers gingerly to keep them from being crushed.

On leaving the garrison, he drove past the marketplace, where he recognized Reggie the pony hitched to a cart. Brodie's daughter, Esa, was climbing down from the wooden seat. The sunlight brought out the reddish highlights in her thick brown hair, which was spread out over the shoulders of her brown tunic.

He stopped the wagon beside the pony cart. "Good morrow, Mistress Esa," he said. After introducing Mistress Campbell to her, he said: "How goes it with you?"

"Fine," Esa said with a smile. "Thank ye for asking."

"And your father?" he said tentatively, for he was unsure of the outcome after Brodie followed Tullick in the woods that rainy night not so long ago. "Is he well?"

"Quite well," she said.

"I'm relieved to hear it," he said.

"I shall tell him ye asked after him," she said.

"You do that," he said. "By the way, has anyone spotted Tullick lately?"

"About two weeks ago," she said with a nod of her head. "In a bog," she added with grim satisfaction. "From what I heard, he sank like a rock."

"Ah, well," he said. "That just goes to show the wisdom of letting God decide who is guilty and who is not." He took his leave of Esa and shook the reins for the gelding to walk on.

At Mistress Campbell's behest, he drove the wagon due east, headed for a location several miles outside of town. She talked the entire time, and since her conversation required no response, he tuned her out after the first few minutes. The warmth of the sun and the drone of her voice lulled him into a drowsy state for most of the trip, until her sudden exclamation startled him to full wakefulness.

"There it is!" she cried, clutching the flowers to her ample bosom. "Turn there." She pointed to a track on the right that crossed through a grassy meadow to the woods beyond.

He turned the wagon onto the track and followed it through the rising grass, which was rich with foxglove and bellflowers nodding in the soft breeze.

The track climbed gently toward the wooded area and came out on the far side, where she bade him to stop the wagon, which he did.

The track continued on through the plowed field ahead of them to a thatch-roofed stone cottage a short distance away.

"My daughter lives there," she said, indicating the cottage.

"Is that where we are bound?" he said.

"Nay," she said. "What I wish to show ye lies yonder." She

directed his attention to the left, where a gnarled yew tree grew at the edge of the woods, with several flattish stones jutting from the ground under its spreading branches.

He turned the wagon toward the yew tree. As he drove closer, he noticed that the jutting stones were grave markers laid out in a neat row, one beside the other.

He stopped the wagon and jumped down to help Mistress Campbell to the ground, taking care not to damage her flowers.

She walked over to the nearest stone marker and placed a portion of her flowers on that grave. "This is where yer father is buried," she said.

Her simple statement caught him off guard. He stared in astonishment at the marker, on which "J. Shaw 1292" had been chiseled into its rough surface. "Why did you not tell me this before now?" he said, unable to keep the reproach from his voice.

"I wasn't sure I could trust ye," she said, "until after I spoke to John Logan. He vouched for ye."

She moved to the second marker and placed another portion of her flowers upon that grave. "This is where my husband lies buried," she said.

He looked down at the marker with "Thom Drummond, 1247–1292" chiseled on it. "I'm sorry for your loss," he said, genuinely contrite at his earlier outburst. He wondered if it was a coincidence that her husband and his father died in the same year. Her next words not only resolved that mystery, but claimed his undivided attention.

"I went to fetch my husband's body from Loudoun Hill after the ambush," she began. "I was one of the last to get there because of the trouble I had in borrowing a wagon. A man there who knew my Thom helped me load his body onto the back of the wagon. There was one body left unclaimed, which I recognized as yer father. I heard ye were out of the country, so I knew ye were unable to come for him. I took his body away with me and buried him beside my dear husband here on my daughter's property." She raised apologetic eyes to him. "I didn't know where else to put him."

"You have rendered a great kindness to my father," he said, "and through him, to me."

"I was afraid ye would be angry," she said.

"Not at all," he said. "If anything, I am in your debt."

She seemed content with his reply. She set about dividing the rest of the flowers into three small bunches to place on the three other graves under the yew tree.

He went down on one knee beside his father's grave to brush the rotted leaves from the marker stone with his hand. "Tell me, mistress," he said. "Was my father's body badly damaged?"

"There was but one wound on him," she said, turning to face him. "And that was at the back of his head."

He climbed slowly to his feet, his eyes intent upon her. "Are you sure?" he said. "A report in the garrison archives stated otherwise."

"I saw the gash for myself when I washed him for burial," she said. "Someone struck him with a mighty blow from behind. He was surely taken unawares, for his axe was still in his belt and his sword still in its sheath."

"Fenwick lied in his report," he said, half to himself.

"Fenwick," she said. She spat on the ground at the mention of his name. "May the devil take him!"

"So, my father was, indeed, betrayed," he said, his lips drawn tight.

"Of course, he was betrayed," she said. "So were my Thom and the others who fell that day at Loudoun Hill. They walked right into the trap the Southrons set for them in that narrow pass."

"I reckon he never knew what hit him," he said, gazing down

at his father's grave. He pondered Bishop Wishart's words about how Segrave had discovered James Shaw's subterfuge. It followed that Segrave, in order to keep his head as well as his exalted position as Castellan of Ayr, would thereafter seek to dispose of Shaw. Such an opportunity obviously presented itself at Loudoun Hill. Fenwick, no doubt enticed by Segrave's promises of advancement and monetary gain, ordered his men to slay Shaw, whose untimely death Fenwick ascribed in his report as an unfortunate casualty during their encounter with the rebels.

"What will ye do now?" she said.

"I don't know," he said. "Are you ready to go back?"

"I think I'll stay with my daughter for a few days," she said. "I haven't seen my grandchildren in a while."

"What shall I do with the bundle you left in my office?"

"I brought that for ye," she said. "Yer father's axe and sword are in there. I knew ye would want them."

He helped her climb aboard the wagon seat, after which he drove to her daughter's cottage. "Thank you for what you did for my father," he said, as she debarked with his assistance. "I shall never forget it."

With the late afternoon sun in his eyes, Kyle drove the wagon back to the garrison. On the way, he pondered the question of who was ultimately responsible for his father's death. Was it the man who struck the blow? Was it the officer who ordered the blow struck? Was it the man who paid the officer to order the blow? Was one less guilty than the others, or were all three equally reprehensible?

The answer to that conundrum continued to elude him as he drove through garrison gates and headed for the stable to unhitch the gelding from the wagon traces. Upon entering the sheriff's office, the first thing he did was to open the longish parcel lying on the bench under the window.

Over the past five years, the oilskin had protected the items within. Yet it was evident from their condition that James Shaw took excellent care of his weapons. Scars from use marred the smooth hardwood handle of the axe, but the metal head showed no nicks or pits from rust. The sword was well-honed and razor-sharp, and the long narrow strip of leather binding the hilt ensured the user of a good grip. The large bronze ball at the end of the hilt served well to counterbalance the weight of the steel blade.

The sight of those weapons brought images of the past flooding into his consciousness. Any hope in his heart that his father might be still alive was now gone. James Shaw considered the world a dangerous place in which to live, and as such, he never went anywhere without that axe or that sword.

Kyle put the weapons back into the oilskin and wrapped them up. He would decide later what to do with them.

As the slanting rays of the setting sun reached into the sheriff's office, he sharpened the point of a quill pen and set about finishing his report on Count Jardine's fortuitous departure earlier that day.

On completing the account, he lifted his eyes to gaze outside. Hardly anyone moved about the courtyard, for the day's activities were beginning to wind down. He was thinking about getting something to eat when a lean man with a prominent nose and coal-black eyes appeared in the open doorway.

"What do you want, Weems?" he said. His lack of affability stemmed from the fact that, during a tavern fight several weeks ago, the man tried to stab him in the back with his own dirk.

"Sir Percy wants you to attend to him at once," Weems said.

Kyle rolled up the parchment, tightened his sword belt a notch, and slung his cloak around his shoulders. With the scroll in his hand, he stepped into the courtyard and started toward the main hall with Weems walking beside him. "Did you or Inchcape ever serve under Captain Fenwick?" he said, watching the man's reaction from the corner of his eye.

The pitted skin on the sharp-featured face turned white with tension. "I—I think, I mean, I know," Weems said with faltering speech, "that Inchcape, uh, served under him a while back. That was some time ago."

"What about you?" Kyle said, turning the full brunt of his gaze upon him.

The query seemed to affect the man's eyes, for he blinked repeatedly before replying.

"I'm not sure," Weems said after a moment. "It's been so long. I've been billeted here and there. It's hard to remember."

Kyle suspected that Weems not only served under Fenwick, but that he also participated in the Loudoun Hill massacre. The most compelling reason for his reluctance to own up to his association with Fenwick, especially to the son of a murdered man, was because of his complicity in that murder.

When they drew near to the main hall, Weems scurried away toward the barracks, while Kyle went inside and made his way to the second floor.

Neyll was absent from the anteroom, so Kyle knocked on the doorjamb leading into the office chamber beyond.

Sir Percy glanced up from the sheet of vellum spread out on the marble top of his desk. When he saw Kyle, a shadow of a scowl passed over his cherubic features. "Come," he said in a curt tone.

Kyle entered the chamber and presented Sir Percy with the scroll he had brought with him. "This is my report on Count Jardine's hasty exit from the garrison," he said.

"Hasty exit, my arse," Sir Percy said, taking the proffered document. He stood up, as though annoyed at having to look up at the Scots deputy towering over him. His lack of height apparently bothered him, and like some other men of modest stature, he had an enormous ego to compensate for it. "Let us call it what it was, Master Shaw. It was an escape, in which I suspect you had a hand."

"If that is so," Kyle said, "I wouldn't have stayed behind to face accusations. Besides, my own horse was stricken like the rest of them."

Sir Percy's skeptical expression made it plain he was still unconvinced. "Did you recognize either of the men who departed with Count Jardine?" he said, watching Kyle closely.

"It was difficult to make out their features under those helmets," Kyle said.

"When I find them out," Sir Percy said, pounding his palm with his fist, "and I will find them out, they will pay with their lives." He turned his wrath on Kyle. "I hold you responsible for Count Jardine's escape. As sheriff's deputy, you should have prevented it."

"As Castellan of Ayr Garrison," Kyle said, "you are accountable for the actions of the men under your command. It was your men who let Count Jardine ride through the gates to freedom."

A slow flush spread across Sir Percy's face, because he could not deny the truth of Kyle's words. "I understand that no trace was found of the man who murdered that village girl," he said, changing the subject abruptly. "How many more felons will you let slip through your grasp?"

"A reliable witness saw the murderer sink into a bog a fortnight ago," Kyle said. "That matter is now closed." He made a motion to leave the chamber. "Is there anything else?"

"Just a moment," Sir Percy said. He unrolled the scroll in his hand to scan its contents.

While Sir Percy was preoccupied with reading the report, Kyle's eyes fell by chance on the sheet of vellum spread out on the desk before him. Although it was the wrong way round, Fenwick's name jumped out at him, as did the date, which was that of ten days ago. Before he could decipher the body of the letter, he heard a strangled sound come from somewhere deep in Sir Percy's throat.

"This won't do at all," Sir Percy said, waving Kyle's report in the air. "You cannot say that Count Jardine simply rode out of the garrison in broad daylight. You make it sound as if no attempt at all was made to stop him." He flung the sheet of vellum onto his desk, inadvertently covering the Fenwick letter. "Oh, never mind. I'll see to the report myself."

Kyle took his leave with a stiff bow. He started to withdraw, but he turned back after a couple of steps. "By the bye," he said, "do you know the present whereabouts of Sir Nicholas de Segrave?"

"Buried somewhere in Leicestershire, the last I heard," Sir Percy said without looking up. "Why do you ask?"

"Just curious," Kyle said. He continued on to the anteroom, mentally ticking Segrave's name from the list of those with whom he had a score to settle. He went behind Neyll's desk to remove the prior year's tax roll from its place on the third shelf. He was stuffing the folded document into the pouch at his side when Neyll appeared in the doorway.

"What are ye doing back there?" Neyll demanded, his dark eyes narrowed in suspicion.

"Sir Percy wants to see you," Kyle said. He rounded the corner of the desk and brushed past Neyll on the way out, ignoring the blustering protests that echoed down the hallway behind him.

Shortly after sunset, Kyle rode the gelding from the garrison and turned onto Harbour Street. The failing light of dusk cast the houses along the River Ayr into shadowed relief against the muted orange of the skyline. He made his way to the Bull and Bear to keep his appointment with John Logan.

He entered the tavern, where a haze of smoke hung in the air from lighted oil lamps suspended on long chains from the rafters. His gaze swept the tables occupied by young English soldiers who were settling down for a night of gaming and perhaps a fight or two later to liven things up. He spotted John and Macalister seated at a table against the side wall and walked over to sit with them.

While they were waiting for Maize to bring their supper, Neyll entered the tavern and made his way to a nearby table. The surreptitious glances he cast their way made Kyle wonder if the clerk chose that location in the hope of seeing the missing tax roll come to light.

It was then that Kyle noticed the embroidered edges of Neyll's sleeves. The ivy pattern stitched in gold thread along the border reminded him of the description Father Ian gave of the altar cloth that was stolen, along with other items, from the chapel at Harefoot Law a month ago. He mentioned it to his companions, who listened to him with interest.

John looked over his shoulder at Neyll's sleeves. "That design," he said, "may be the product of his sister's excellent handiwork. She sews beautifully, ye know." He leaned toward Kyle to make himself heard over the raucous voices of the tavern's patrons. "Just before ye arrived, I was telling Macalister here about Count Jardine's successful flight from the garrison."

"Well done," Macalister said, glancing from one to the other. "Upton should get credit, too, I suppose, even though he is a Southron." A fierce smile stole briefly across his bearded face. "When King Edward hears of it, he will likely remove Sir Percy as castellan. That should take that pompous popinjay down a peg."

"What did Count Jardine see on the scroll," John said, "to make him trust Upton so readily?"

"The scroll was completely blank," Kyle said. "There was no time to write a word on it. Yet, that was the very thing, it seems, which convinced the count that Upton was there to aid him, not to arrest him."

"He's a clever man, Count Jardine is," John said.

"Speaking of clever," Macalister said, after which he related to John how Kyle used Fergus the dog to expose Tullick as Megan's murderer.

"Have ye caught Tullick yet?" John said.

"I didn't have to," Kyle said. "During his flight through the woods, the hapless fellow stepped into a bog."

"What about Sweeney and Archer?" John said. "Are ye any closer to solving the mystery of who killed them?"

"The mystery is why Archer was killed at all," Kyle said.

"Perhaps he saw who murdered Sweeney," John said. "He might have tried to extort payment for his silence, so the murderer killed him, too."

"You might be on to something," Kyle said. "The two of them died by different means, yet the slashes on their throats after death point to a single murderer."

At that moment, Maize arrived with their food on a tray. She set the trenchers on the table, along with three cups of ale. She collected the money for the meal from each of them before she walked away.

They all started in on the rabbit stew while it was hot.

"The use of hemlock," Kyle said between bites, "indicates that the murderer intended to kill Archer, for it had to be mixed with the mead ahead of time."

He paused to take a sip of ale. "If Archer meant to stop briefly at the hut," he continued, "he would have tied his horse outside the door. Instead, he hobbled the horse to let it forage for food, which meant he intended to linger there for a while, perhaps spend the night. That is what leads me to believe the murderer of both men could be a woman."

John choked on his ale and had to wipe his chin with his sleeve. "Surely, ye are mistaken," he said, aghast. "A woman could never do such a thing."

"Reason on this for a moment," Kyle said. "Only a woman could have got close enough to Sweeney to slip a dagger into his heart. Only a woman could have lured Archer to his death in the shepherd's hut. Only a woman would need to drug a man, since she does not possess the strength to overpower him." He fell silent to let his words sink in.

John frowned, evidently struggling with the concept of a woman committing murder. "Who do ye think would do something like that?" he said.

Kyle took another sip of ale and set the cup on the table. "There is Esa, Brodie's elder daughter," he said. "If she truly believed Sweeney murdered her sister, she would have dealt with him herself. I don't know about Archer, though, unless she suspected he, too, had been involved."

"I thought it was Tullick who killed Megan," John said.

"It was," Kyle said, "but Esa could have killed Sweeney and Archer prior to learning of Tullick's guilt."

He paused to consume the last of his rabbit stew, after which he cleaned the bits of food from the blade of his dirk. "We cannot overlook Fenella, who is Mistress Hamilton's daughter," he said, returning the dirk to the sheath at his side. "She had cause to hate Sweeney because of his ill treatment of her mother. Archer was there when her mother was evicted, so she might have settled the score with both of them."

"I admit that Fenella harbors resentment toward the Southrons," John said, "but I don't think she would do anything as rash as that."

"There is also Mistress Joneta," Kyle said. "She possesses a rare beauty which few men can resist. However, shortly before Sweeney and Archer were murdered, she was confined to a birthing bed. Her weakened condition would make it difficult, but not impossible, for her to deal with the pair of them.

"Then, there is little Meg, Joneta's niece by marriage and Gram's granddaughter. She is young and pretty enough to turn a man's head. According to Mistress Campbell, their next-door neighbor, Meg had reason to hate Archer for taking her husband away to be flogged or worse. She had more reason to hate Sweeney for his foul use of her when she went to plead for her husband later that same day."

As he spoke, something else Mistress Campbell had told him niggled at his memory. It seemed like an insignificant detail at the time she mentioned it, yet it now troubled him, like a tiny pebble in his boot.

"There is another reason the finger of guilt points to Meg," he said, giving voice to the troubling thought. "An aunt of hers, one whom she favored in both looks and temperament, was murdered here in town a few years ago. An English soldier was implicated, but there wasn't enough proof to charge him. Archer was stationed elsewhere at the time, so he had no part in it at all."

John shook his head, his lips compressed around a grimace. "It is hard to say whether guilt or praise should be imputed to this murderess whom ye seek," he said. "The loss of Sweeney and Archer is no loss at all, in my opinion."

"There are many who would agree with you," Kyle remarked dryly. "However, there is more to tell," he added, growing serious. "I saw a letter of recent date on Sir Percy's desk with Fenwick's name on it. There was no time to read it, but I am sure it was the same Fenwick involved with the rebel ambush in 'ninety-two."

He went on to relate how Fenwick's report from five years ago conflicted with Mistress Campbell's first-hand account of his father's fate. Fenwick claimed James Shaw engaged in mortal combat with the rebels at Loudoun Hill and that his mutilated corpse was of necessity buried somewhere in the pass. On the other hand, Mistress Campbell said she retrieved Shaw's body from the ambush site, at which time she found his weaponry sheathed and unused. Her examination of his body revealed damage only to the back of his skull consistent with the infliction of a single crushing blow from behind. Shortly after that, she oversaw the interment of his body on Campbell land and marked his grave for posterity.

"Mistress Campbell has nothing to gain by fabricating such a tale," he said. "The same cannot be said of Fenwick, who received commendation based on the events set out in his report. I choose to believe Mistress Campbell. My faith in her is not misplaced, for there are witnesses aplenty who can support her assertions."

John and Macalister exchanged a long and thoughtful look.

"If you know aught of this matter," Kyle said, gazing from John to Macalister and back again, "you must tell me of it."

"Mistress Campbell never divulged any of that me," John said to Kyle. His tone reflected ambivalence over whether to be offended or relieved at being excluded from that amorous lady's confidences. "She did approach me recently to inquire as to yer trustworthiness. I assured her that ye were a man of honor who was loyal to the Scottish throne."

Kyle acknowledged John's endorsement with a nod of appreciation. Without it, he might never have learned the truth about his father's death and burial.

John glanced around to make sure none of the tavern's patrons were close enough to overhear his next words. "As for Fenwick, it is known in certain quarters that he is soon to travel to Ayr Garrison on a mission for King Edward. There is much speculation as to the nature of that mission, but no one knows what it is for sure."

"Fenwick will never set foot on this side of Loudoun Hill," Macalister interposed, his chin thrust out in determination. "When he rides through the pass there, we shall be waiting for him, just like he waited for our countrymen in 'ninety-two."

The notion that Fenwick would soon get his comeuppance filled Kyle with an immense, albeit perverse, satisfaction. He downed the last of his ale, reflecting on the logistics of planning such a deadly reception. Knowledge of what day and at which hour Fenwick would be passing through Loudoun Hill was crucial for the success of such an undertaking, as would the co-operation of those set to execute the attack. Yet Fenwick himself had managed to pull off a similar feat when he waylaid that band of Scottish rebels without anyone the wiser, including James Shaw, until it was too late.

An abrupt movement at the table nearby brought Kyle's head around. Neyll was sitting bolt upright, dark eyes fixed on something that captured his interest. He followed the direction of the clerk's gaze to the tavern door, inside of which stood the corpulent English marshal, his round head swiveling from side to side as though looking for someone.

Neyll got to his feet and hastened over to greet the English marshal, who took him by the arm to hustle him out of the tavern.

With Neyll out of the way, possibly for the rest of the night, Kyle felt free to remove from the pouch at his side the parchment roll with the names of those taxed during the prior year and the amounts collected. He laid it out on the table and placed beside it the list John had given him of the raided homesteads, with the dates of the raids noted beside the owners' names. For the next few minutes, he and his companions perused the two lists.

"It appears the raids were not random, after all," John said. "Only those with assets worth taking were targeted."

"From the dates listed here, it looks like the raids took place after the taxes were collected," Kyle said. "That makes sense. Otherwise, the owners would have no means to pay what was due."

"Armed with this information," John said, "Sweeney could have planned those raids himself."

"Perhaps," Kyle said.

"But ye don't think he did," John said. It was more a statement than a question.

"I do not," Kyle said. "Sweeney was the kind of man who expected others to do the work while he took the credit of it."

"So, ye think someone supplied the information to him," John said.

"Aye," Kyle said.

"Sir Percy, maybe?" John said.

"I thought so at first," Kyle said. "However, he already owns vast land holdings in England and Scotland in return for his service to King Edward. It would be foolish for Sir Percy to risk all that to dabble in criminal activities prohibited even by English law."

"What about Inchcape?" John said. "I suspect he's in it up to his eyebrows."

"That fellow has more brawn than brains," Kyle said. "The subtle plotting and planning necessary to arrange a successful raid would be beyond him."

"Who, then?" John said.

"Who hungers for recognition, power, and money?" Kyle said. "Who is in a position to hear all, see all, and tell all, if he was so inclined? Who compiles the tax rolls year after year and knows who owns what and where they live? Who knows practically everything that goes on in the shire?"

"Neyll, of course," John said. "I wonder if Sir Percy suspects his own clerk's involvement in such goings-on."

"That's not as important as making such a charge against Neyll stick," Kyle said. "Any accusation brought against him will never hold up in court unless he can be held publicly accountable as to the source of his income. He maintains a large household, keeps a stable of fine horses, and wears expensive garments. Yet the clerk's wage he earns would barely support one such endeavor, let alone all three." He laid John's list on the tax roll and folded them up together. "There must be some way," he added as he stuffed the documents in his pouch, "to use Neyll's prosperity against him."

"And if not?" John said.

"Then there is another, more disagreeable, course available," Kyle said. He had in mind his own sworn statement recently given to Bishop Wishart attesting to Neyll's impious dalliance with the English marshal. That was to be implemented, however, as a last resort because of the damage it would surely cause to innocent parties, like Colina. He was grateful neither John nor Macalister questioned him further about the "more disagreeable course" on which he purposely failed to elaborate.

"I fear Colina may suffer collapse on learning of her brother's guilt," John said.

"She is made of sterner stuff than that," Kyle said. "Besides, when Neyll is brought to heel, he will likely be more amenable to letting her marry whom she pleases, namely you."

"I am not sure she still wants me after all this time," John said.

"She does," Kyle said with certainty, reflecting on Colina's joyful countenance at the mere mention of John's name.

A slow smile of pleasure spread across John's handsome face.

Kyle glanced over at Macalister to ask what he thought of

catching Neyll in his own web. At that moment, though, the burly blacksmith seemed preoccupied with watching a scruffy old soldier with one arm make his way to the tavern door through the clutter of tables.

When the one-armed soldier reached the doorway, he turned to look directly at Macalister, after which he stepped outside.

Macalister drained his cup and placed it on the table. "I must be off," he said, rising to his feet. He started for the tavern door without haste, but it was obvious he meant to follow the old soldier outside.

"What's going on?" Kyle said, tilting his head at their departing companion.

"Yer guess is as good as mine," John said with a shrug. He pushed away his empty cup and stood up. "I reckon I ought to go, too. I have a busy day tomorrow." Before withdrawing, he placed a hand on Kyle's shoulder. "Ye might want to be quick about returning that tax roll, lest Neyll notice its absence."

"He already noticed," Kyle said. "If I put it back now, he might alter it, in which case it will be of no use as evidence against him."

"Have a care, then," John said. "If Neyll sees ye as a threat, he may seek a way to harm ye."

"Rest assured," Kyle said. "I shall be on my guard."

Chapter 17

After John left the tavern, Kyle remained seated at the table against the side wall for a long while. He paid no attention to the raucous sounds around him. With his usual objective detachment, he mulled over the matters so recently discussed with his companions. Instead of answers, though, he came up with more questions. What was the best way to deal with Neyll? Would the murderer strike again? Who would be the next victim? Why did Edward of England order Fenwick's return to Ayrshire?

There was a brief scuffle among the young soldiers gaming at a table across the way. The comrades of each contender stepped in to break it up before the tavern keeper ejected the lot of them from the tavern.

Kyle hardly noticed the start or finish of the minor altercation, preoccupied as he was with more pressing concerns. Soon the smoke from the oil lamps began to sting his eyes. He scrubbed at them with his knuckles. It had been a long day, and he was weary. Perhaps after a night's sleep, he reasoned, the elusive answers would come to him. If not, he would be no worse off than he was now.

He slid from the bench and headed for the tavern door. He stepped into the cool darkness outside, drawing in a breath of fresh air after the stifling atmosphere inside. Thousands of pinpricks of starlight filled the night sky, and the newly risen moon floated like an enormous yellow ball above the rooftops to the east.

He called for the groom to bring the gelding out from the tavern stable, after which he rode from the courtyard and through the open gates. He was about to turn down Harbour Street toward the garrison when the dark form of a man stepped from the alleyway into the moonlight.

"A moment, Master Shaw," the man said. His face was in shadow, but his identity was discernible from the empty sleeve that hung from the shoulder of his garment.

Kyle held the reins taut to steady the gelding while he waited for the old soldier to speak.

"I bear a message from Macalister," the man said. "He says there will be trouble at Ogilvy's tonight."

"He mentioned nothing about that to me," Kyle said.

"He only just learned of it himself," the man said. "He says if ye want to help, ye must meet him there as soon as possible."

Kyle dug a silver penny from his pouch and tossed it to the old soldier, who snatched the coin deftly from the air with his hand.

"Bless ye," the man said. He touched his forehead with his knuckle, after which he sank back into the darkness of the alley.

Kyle nudged the gelding with his heels. As he rode down Harbour Street, he could not help but wonder why Macalister did not go back into the tavern to deliver the message himself. Was it a ruse, perhaps by Neyll, to send him on a fool's errand, or was it for real? Either way, he would rather go all the way out to Ogilvy's homestead to discover he had been duped than to leave the old man unprotected and at the mercy of raiders.

He hastened to the garrison. Once inside the sheriff's office, he removed his pouch and hid it in his sleeping chamber in case Neyll was indeed involved and had hired brigands to accost him on the road to retrieve the tax roll in his possession. He chided himself for overreacting, but he preferred to err on the side of caution where Ogilvy was concerned.

He donned his chain mail hauberk and fastened his leather scale armor over it. He put a padded arming cap under his bascinet, which was the type of helmet he preferred because, unlike a nasal helm, it had no nosepiece to obstruct his vision. He was about to leave the sheriff's office when he decided on a whim to take his father's axe with him, in addition to his own. He removed the weapon from the oilskin and went outside to tie it behind the saddle.

Before riding all the way to Ogilvy's, he decided to pass by the blacksmith's shop to see if Macalister was there. He found the shop deserted and Fergus the dog gone, so he turned the gelding's head to the north and set out at a lope, with only light from the moon to guide him. Along the way, he kept a sharp lookout for highwaymen. For most of the journey, though, he had the whole road to himself.

It took him an hour to reach his destination. Even before he turned off the main road, he saw the glow of a fire beyond the trees. Afraid he might be too late, he urged the gelding into a full gallop. As he hurtled down the lane that led to Ogilvy's homestead, something slammed into his chest and swept him from the saddle. He landed flat on his back on the beaten earth, the impact of which drove the breath from his lungs and stunned him clean out of his wits.

Pinpoints of light behind his eyelids exploded into a blinding radiance that was terrifying to behold. Like in a dream, the image of his cottage from six years ago took on shape and substance, its roof ablaze with flames leaping skyward. As in a nightmare, the screams of fear and pain coming from within his home chilled his blood and wrenched at the pit of his stomach.

Heedless of danger, he plunged inside through the front door. A blast of intense heat drove him back. He circled around to the rear of the house and kicked in the back door. Smoldering rafters flared to life at the influx of fresh air. Dense smoke billowed around him. Scorching heat singed his hair. He rushed in blindly, only to catch his foot on a yielding object in his path. He pitched headlong onto the earthen floor. Filled with dread at what he would find, he fumbled behind him until his hand grazed the object that tripped him. It was a body. His darling wife. He gathered a handful of her skirts to pull her outside. As he drew her body along, he encountered another, smaller body, the size of an eight-year-old boy. His beloved son. A desolate cry of anguish erupted from his throat. It was an inhuman sound mercifully drowned out by the roar of the raging inferno around him. If only he had not spent half the night out gambling. If only he had arrived sooner to foil the raiders. If only he had stayed at home in the first place to protect his family. But there was no time to castigate himself for what might have been. Falling embers from the blazing timbers overhead burned through his thin linen shirt, searing the skin beneath. Smoke stung his eyes. Tears of loss blurred his vision. He crawled back the way he came, dragging his sad burdens along with him to the doorway and out into the yard beyond. Only then did he pause to look behind him. What he saw was not just a house on fire, but his joy, his hopes, and his dreams going up in flames.

Something warm and soft gently nuzzled his cheek. Please, God! Please let it be his wife's caressing touch. He opened his eyes to find the gelding's thick lips an inch or so above his face. Beyond the creature's head, the stars in the night sky winked benignly down at him.

The urgency of his mission suddenly flooded back to him. He climbed to his feet, ignoring the throb in his temples and the ache in his heart from unrelenting memories, which had returned so vividly to his conscious mind.

The dull gleam of moonlight on a conical metal object in the dirt a yard away drew his eye. It was his helmet, dislodged no doubt when he hit the ground. He picked it up and settled it on his head. He put his booted foot into the stirrup and hauled his bruised body onto the saddle.

That was when he noticed the taut rope slung across his path, its ends tied to a tree on either side. It was apparently meant to throttle him as he hastened down the lane to Ogilvy's homestead. The deadly tactic would have worked but for his height in the saddle. Thanks to his stalwart Viking progenitors, he was taller than most men, and the rope meant to break his neck merely caught him across the upper chest. Although he took a tumble, he suffered minimal damage, the worst of which was the loss of valuable time.

The smell of smoke and the sound of angry shouts from the direction of Ogilvy's homestead prompted him to nudge the gelding into a canter. He leaned low on the horse's neck in case there was a second rope strung across his path. He reached the far end of the lane without mishap. On turning into the clearing, he came upon a scene that looked all too familiar to him.

Crackling flames engulfed Ogilvy's newly thatched roof. Buds of fire blossomed into dazzling blazons of red and gold, spitting glowing embers high into the night sky.

There were half a dozen horsemen in the open yard, their hooded forms no more than black silhouettes against the backdrop of the burning cottage, yet instantly distinguishable as raiders.

This time, there were a number of men on hand to repel the raiders. Although they were on foot, they wielded Lochaber axes or sharpened pitchforks with deadly intent, more than making up for the lack of a steed.

This time, Ogilvy's wooden barn was on fire and the fenced enclosure was empty. Stray sheep bustled about the open yard, bleating in fright and generally getting in the way.

The defenders, identifiable as such for being afoot, were likewise silhouetted against the flames. Macalister was easy to spot among them because of his height. Fergus the dog was there, too, bounding back and forth to nip at the heels of the raiders' horses. His point-eared shadow flitted along the ground like a horned demon cavorting in the firelight. Ogilvy stood near the trees at the edge of the open yard, waist-deep in sheep, holding a pitchfork in his hands.

Kyle withdrew the battle axe from the loop on his saddle. He was about to make his presence as a lawman known, for he did not want to be mistaken for a raider, when a hulking figure on a huge black steed broke away from the other raiders in the open yard.

That particular raider spurred his black warhorse into a gallop, his sword poised to strike, headed straight for Ogilvy, whose attention at that moment seemed taken with someone crouched in the shadow of the trees several yards away from him.

Kyle urged the gelding into a gallop. He shouted a warning to Ogilvy, but he was too far away to be heard. He watched in helpless dismay as the raider bore down on the unsuspecting old man.

The sudden stir of wooly creatures brought Ogilvy's head around, but it was too late for him to run.

Firelight flashed on naked steel as the raider's blade descended, striking Ogilvy squarely on the top of the skull. The old man's knees buckled, and down he went.

An undersized figure, immediately recognizable as Hob, darted out from the shadow of the trees beyond Ogilvy's body, brandishing a small axe and screeching like a banshee. To Kyle's horror, the boy ran straight for the raider who had struck down the old man.

The raider, by that time, had turned the black warhorse around and started back to where Ogilvy lay unmoving on the ground.

Hob swung the small axe with all his might at the chain mail skirting on the raider's thigh, which was as high as he could reach. Instead of a howl of pain, a rumble of laughter came from deep within the man's chest.

Before the boy could land another blow, the raider leaned down to grab his cloak from behind, hoisting him into the air and letting him dangle there choking, until he dropped the axe to claw with both hands at the tight fabric strangling his throat.

The raider then tossed the boy, kicking and sputtering with indignation, across his saddle bow like a sack of potatoes.

Kyle rapidly closed the distance between them, scattering sheep in every direction. Without warning, another raider cut across his path to head him off. He strained back on the reins, causing the gelding to shudder and balk and swerve at the last instant.

The intervening raider's sword stroke missed Kyle by a hair's breadth. Undeterred, the man wheeled his mount and struck out again with his sword.

Kyle parried the blow and countered with a downward chop at a vulnerable spot at the side of the raider's neck, above his armored shoulder and below the rim of the metal helmet under his hood.

The raider's cry of anguish ended in a choking gurgle as the axe blade cleaved through chain mail links, sinew, and bone.

The gelding snorted and pranced, its eyes rolling at the smell of fresh blood.

From the corner of his vision, Kyle glimpsed Macalister and another defender running toward him, undoubtedly to render assistance. He waved them away, positioning the gelding directly in front of the raider holding Hob, who was wriggling and squirming like a worm on a hook. From that angle, light from the blaze on the cottage roof illuminated the man's face, while casting his own features in shadow.

The gelding minced and sidestepped, its nostrils flared, its teeth clamping at the bit. "Let the boy go," Kyle said, keeping a steadying hand on the reins.

"Why should I?" the raider said in a deep baritone.

Kyle had already identified the man from the shape and size of him. The familiar sound of his voice merely confirmed it.

"Because, Sergeant Inchcape," he said, "only a craven coward would hide behind a child."

Inchcape pushed back the hood of his cloak, exposing the Norman helmet on his head. "Are you calling me a coward?" he said in a threatening tone.

"You are not only a coward," Kyle said, "but a liar, a thief, and a murderer, too."

Hob quit struggling to glance from Kyle to Inchcape and back again, ostensibly more interested in their conversation than in his own predicament.

"I should kill you for saying that," Inchcape said. "Filthy Scotchman," he added, his upper lip curled in contempt.

Kyle felt the heat of fury rising in his body. "You murdered my father," he said through clenched teeth. "I know how you did it, where you did it, and when you did it."

"Prove it," Inchcape sneered, evidently confident such a thing could not be done.

"I intend to do just that," Kyle said. "In the meantime, you are under arrest for the murder of James Shaw, whom you bludgeoned to death at Loudoun Hill five years ago."

Fear and desperation crossed Inchcape's face for only an instant before he regained his composure. "The man was a traitor," he said. "He deserved to die."

"You struck him down from behind," Kyle said. "A contemptible thing to do, even to a traitor, is it not?"

The two men glared at each other over the heads of their horses, oblivious to the clang of steel, the shouts of men, and the incessant bawl of sheep around them.

"Will you come along quietly?" Kyle said.

"I don't plan to come along at all," Inchcape said.

"Do you deny you are answerable to a court of law for your crime?" Kyle said.

"I answer only to my king," Inchcape said.

"You will answer to your Maker this very hour for murder," Kyle said. "As blood kin to James Shaw, I challenge you to trial by combat."

"To the death?" Inchcape said. He sounded hopeful.

"To the death," Kyle said grimly. His honor and that of his father required no less.

Inchcape let the boy slide to the ground, his eyes fixed on Kyle's face. He lifted his sword to hold it upright in front of him, after which he swept it out to the side in a mock salute. "Let us lay on, then, shall we?"

As soon as Hob scampered clear of the horses, Kyle and Inchcape began to circle one another, each looking for an opening to strike the first blow.

The others in the open yard, raiders and defenders alike, heard the challenge issued by the Scots lawman and the terms of acceptance by the Englishman. All of them paused in their fighting, as though in mutual accord, to witness the outcome of God's judgment upon the combatants.

The pop and crackle of the blaze on the cottage roof sounded loud in the hush that followed. Gray smoke from the charred rafters curled listlessly into the air. The tops of the trees, dark against the starlit sky, encircled the open yard like the walls of an arena.

Kyle tightened his grip on the handle of the battle axe. His rancor drained away, leaving in its place an icy calm. He learned long ago as a mercenary never to engage the enemy in the heat of anger. He closed in on Inchcape, prepared to fight for his life. No quarter was expected, and no quarter would be given.

Without appearing to do so, he took his opponent's measure. Even with God on his side, he was realistic enough to assess the chances of his own survival against such a foe.

Inchcape was a heavily muscled man who carried most of his weight in his upper body. His arms were of a length to give him the advantage of a long reach with a sword. Although a blow with the edge of such a weapon might cause massive damage that could maim or cripple a man within protective armor, the killing power of a sword lay in its tip, which, if driven in with sufficient force, could pierce even the chain mail links of a hauberk. A battle axe, on the other hand, was deadlier than a sword, for both the curved blade on one side and the tapered spike on the other could kill with a single well-placed blow.

Kyle watched Inchcape's every move. As he looked on, he noticed something he previously failed to discern. The man was holding his sword with his left hand. A memory flashed into his head of the night on which Count Jardine was wounded. The hooded man with whom he exchanged blows in the woods also held his sword with his left hand.

The left was called sinister because, as everybody knew, a left-handed man was the bastard spawn of Lucifer himself, whereas the right or dexter signified divine favor.

Kyle doubted the truth of the former. However, in Inchcape's case, he would make an exception. Neither did he give credence to the latter, for he had killed his share of right-handed men in battle. What he did believe was that Inchcape and the hooded man in the woods were one and the same.

There was no more time to think on the matter, for Inchcape set spurs to his horse's flanks.

As the black warhorse passed the gelding on the left, Inchcape leveled a sword stroke at Kyle's neck.

Steel clanged against steel as Kyle lifted his axe to deflect the blade. As the warhorse lumbered away, he followed through to land a blow on Inchcape's armored back. Though the angle was awkward, the curved axe blade left a deep gouge in the hardened bull hide.

Inchcape turned his mount and came back to deliver a hacking blow to the left side of Kyle's body.

Kyle blocked the stroke with the flat of his axe, twisting in the saddle to let the sword blade glance harmlessly off his leather scale armor. He countered with a mighty wallop to Inchcape's armored ribs, eliciting a grunt of pain from the man.

Inchcape retreated for several yards, only to bring the black warhorse around to charge again. This time, he swung his sword in a tight arc at Kyle's head.

Kyle parried the blow, retaliating with a downward chop aimed at Inchcape's neck.

Inchcape flinched away at the last instant, so that the tip of the axe blade merely hewed out a chunk of bull hide, instead of cleaving the flesh beneath. He then purposely wheeled his mount to collide with the gelding.

As the horses staggered to keep their footing, Inchcape reached out to seize the gelding's bridle.

The two horses spun as one, nose to neck, ears laid back and teeth bared at being forcibly thrust together.

With Kyle unable to move out of range, Inchcape lashed out with his sword.

Kyle presented the shaft of his axe to fend off the blade. Before he could reciprocate with a stroke of his own, Inchcape rained down upon him blow upon mighty blow. Each unrelenting stroke probed for an unguarded flaw. Each hit sought a weakness in his defense.

The clang of metal rang out as Kyle blocked and parried each hacking blow with his axe, summoning all the skill and dexterity he had acquired over the years. The gelding beneath him bucked and plunged in an effort to divest itself of Inchcape's restraining hold on its bridle.

Though Kyle was younger and more agile, Inchcape possessed the strength of an ox. The pounding blows began to take a toll on Kyle's right arm and shoulder. His stressed muscles screamed for relief. His fingers were cramped and nerveless from tightly gripping the handle of the axe.

Inchcape seemed to sense that his opponent was growing weary, for he leaned close to direct a particularly hard blow at Kyle's head.

Kyle bent to the side, his right arm raised to meet the blade with the shaft of his axe. The force of the blow shattered the hardwood. Flying splinters struck him about the face and neck. The descending sword slammed into his armored shoulder. He gritted his teeth in agony at the jarring impact, certain his right arm had been torn from its socket. Blackness closed in around the edges of his vision. The ground swam around him, and the roar in his ears deafened him. With a great effort, he wrenched himself back from the brink of the bottomless pit that yawned before him.

A fleeting glance at the injured limb assured him it was still there, though it now hung at his side, limp and useless, unresponsive to his command. He raised his head to look Inchcape in the eye, his body braced for what was sure to come next.

CHAPTER 18

Rather than delivering the killing blow, Inchcape placed the tip of his sword under Kyle's chin to lift his head an inch or two. The flush of triumph on his brutish features was unmistakable, even in the moonlight. His thin lips drew back in a cruel smile, as though to savor the sweet taste of victory.

In spite of cold steel pricking into the bare skin of his throat, hope burgeoned in Kyle's heart, not for clemency, but for the gift of those few precious seconds he desperately needed to untie the battle axe secured to the saddle roll behind him. The sheathed sword on his left was of no immediate use, for any attempt to draw it with his left hand would be slow and clumsy. Inchcape would surely strike him dead before the blade even cleared the scabbard. His only chance, then, lay in freeing his father's axe.

His fingers plucked frantically at the leather ties. So intent was his concentration, he barely heard the clank of steel on steel and the angry shouts start up again in the open yard. Evidently, both raiders and defenders saw fit to resume their fighting now that one of the two challengers had prevailed.

"I want to hear you beg for mercy, Scotchman," Inchcape said. "Like your rebel of a father did on his knees to me."

"So, you admit you murdered James Shaw," Kyle said, stalling for time to work on the last stubborn knot.

All of a sudden, the axe came loose in his hand. He grasped the handle firmly, scarcely able to contain his elation. He must wait for the right moment to strike, and then he must strike hard. The blow must count, for there may be no chance to strike again.

"I never said I didn't," Inchcape snapped. He tugged on the bridle to bring the gelding and its injured rider even closer. "I'll see you in hell!" he growled. Instead of a quick thrust to the throat, he swung back his arm with the confidence of a man about to dispatch a helpless foe.

"After you!" Kyle snarled. He swung the axe with all his might in a left-handed stroke, spike forward, at the right side of Inchcape's neck.

The gelding lurched at that moment to break the curbing grip on its bridle.

The unexpected motion threw off Kyle's aim so that the spike punctured the bull hide armor on Inchcape's upper right arm. Sharpened steel tore through the muscle and sinew beneath.

Inchcape howled in outrage and disbelief, his face twisted in anguish. The sword in his left hand swung wide of its mark. Even with the spike of the axe lodged in his upper arm, he somehow managed to hang onto the gelding's bridle with his right hand. Such a grievous wound would have incapacitated any ordinary man, but it only appeared to provoke him further. His countenance blazed anew with murderous rage.

Kyle saw his own death in Inchcape's eyes. His left hand flew to the hilt of his sword. As he drew it forth, the scrape of the emerging blade against the metal lip of the scabbard seemed to go on forever.

Inchcape flung back his arm to land the final stroke with his sword.

At that instant, an ear-splitting shriek rent the air. Hob burst into the open yard from the shadow of the trees to heave his axe at Inchcape's helmeted head. Moonlight glittered on polished steel as the small weapon cartwheeled through the air.

Inchcape took his eyes from Kyle for no more than a split second to glance in the boy's direction.

That was long enough for Kyle, in one swift graceless motion, to drive the point of his drawn sword into Inchcape's throat through the chain mail links of the hauberk.

Inchcape's sword faltered in mid-swing. His eyes flared in surprise. His mouth moved in soundless agony.

Kyle freed his blade from Inchcape's neck with a sharp jerk.

Blood streamed from the gash in Inchcape's throat to stain the breast of his armor. He toppled from the saddle like a felled tree, dead before he crashed to the ground.

Kyle gazed down at the body of his vanquished foe, reflecting on whether honor and justice had now been served. Why then did Inchcape's death, or more accurately, execution, leave him feeling empty and dissatisfied? Was it because what he really sought was revenge and because there was still a third man from whom an accounting was due? He would deal with Fenwick at some later date. At the moment, there was a raid underway and raiders with whom to contend.

When he glanced around him, he saw men on foot moving without hindrance about the open yard. The sight of the five riderless horses led him to conclude that all but one of the raiders had been slain. While he was looking on, the remaining raider made a bid for freedom by wheeling his mount to head for the lane, which would take him to the main road.

Macalister also saw the raider trying to escape. He shouted for Fergus to go after the man, who by that time was more than halfway to the tree-lined lane. The dog took off like a shot, its ears pricked and the hair bristling along the ridge of its backbone.

Kyle climbed down from the saddle next to Inchcape's body, taking care not to jar his injured limb. He wiped his sword on the dead man's cloak before returning the blade to his scabbard. He put his booted foot on the bloody shoulder piece to jerk his father's axe from the bull hide armor. After he slipped the handle through the loop on his saddle, he looked around for his own axe. On finding the broken pieces, he tucked the salvageable metal parts into his saddle roll.

He was searching for Hob's axe when Macalister walked over to stand beside him. "Did anybody get hurt?" he said, looking up briefly.

"A few cuts and bruises," Macalister said. "Nothing that won't mend."

Kyle continued the hunt, his eyes to the ground. "Too bad one of the raiders got away," he said.

A long keening howl came from the direction of the main road. Both men paused to listen to it.

"He didn't get far," Macalister said grimly. He bent down to retrieve something embedded in the dirt and held it out for Kyle to see. "Were ye looking for this?" he said.

"I was," Kyle said, taking the small axe from Macalister's hand. He wiped the mud from it and stuck the shaft under his belt.

Macalister stood facing Kyle in the moonlight, his blunt features in shadow. "For a while there, during that fight with Inchcape," he said, "I thought ye were a goner."

Kyle clapped Macalister on the shoulder with his good hand. "For a while there, I did, too," he said.

"I notice ye favor yer arm," Macalister said. "Is it broke?"

"I'm not sure," Kyle said.

Macalister probed the damaged shoulder with his fingers. "It feels sound," he said. "There's no blood, either. It might be out of joint."

"Do you know how to fix it?" Kyle said.

Macalister grasped Kyle's elbow with one hand and his upper shoulder with the other hand. He rotated the arm for a moment before giving it a forceful tug.

Kyle grunted at the sharp pain, but the persistent ache from the injury subsided almost immediately. He flexed his arm experimentally. "That's much better," he said with appreciation.

A second keening howl brought Macalister's head around. "I'd better check on Fergus," he said. He then set out for the lane.

Kyle noticed Hob's small form hunched over a man lying on the ground in the shadow of the trees. He gathered the reins and headed that way with the gelding in tow. As he drew near, he saw that the man was Ogilvy, who was either unconscious or dead. He went down on one knee beside the boy and slipped a comforting arm around his thin shoulders.

"Grandpa hasn't moved since he got hit on the head," Hob said. "Is he dead, do ye think?"

Kyle placed a hand on the old man's chest and felt the steady hammer of his heart. "Nay, he's not dead," he said. "But I would be but for your quick thinking." He pulled the small axe from his belt and handed it to the boy. "You were very brave to take on that raider by yourself. You saved my life."

Hob turned and buried his face in Kyle's chest. "I didn't want ye to die," he said, his voice muffled.

Kyle was at a loss for words. He folded the boy in his arms. After a moment, he grasped him by the shoulders to hold him at arm's length, noting the smudged marks of tears on his thin face. "Here, now," he said. "Let's have no more of that."

Hob rubbed the heels of his hands into his eyes. "Will Grandpa go to heaven, like yer son?" he said, blinking hard to clear his vision.

Kyle was sure the old man would come around, but he was unsure when that would be. "Don't you worry about your grandpa," he said. "He's too ornery to die."

Ogilvy opened one eye to fix a baleful stare on Kyle. "I heard that," he said. He tried to sit up on his own, but gave it up with a loud moan. "Oh! My head!" He pressed a hand on either side of his temples. In doing so, his felt cap slipped back to reveal the bascinet beneath.

"So that's how you managed to cheat death," Kyle said, his eyes on the dent in the metal helmet.

"Not for long, the way I feel," the old man growled. "Help me up."

Between the two of them, Kyle and Hob hauled the old man, grunting and groaning, to his feet. To keep him that way, they propped him against the trunk of the nearest tree.

By that time, the other defenders began to gather round. Some bore superficial wounds crusted with drying blood, while others appeared to be unscathed.

A young man, to whom Hob bore a fair resemblance, spoke up first. "I can help ye rebuild, uncle," he said to Ogilvy.

"Nay, Guthrie," the old man said. "I've had enough. After I wed Mistress Hamilton, I plan to take my lady wife and what's left of the flock further north. The Southrons will never find me up in those hills. Hob and his mother are coming with me. Ye are welcome to come, too."

While the old man was talking, Kyle let his gaze rove over the faces of the men gathered there. He was astonished to see the baker, the chandler, the tinsmith, and the silversmith from Ayr. They seemed like ordinary men in every respect, yet it was evident that each was willing to take extraordinary measures to protect his family and his home, as well as that of his neighbors. Bishop Wishart had encouraged him, Kyle, to do likewise, even going so far as to give him a medallion to return, should he decide to do so. A light touch on his arm interrupted the thread of his thoughts.

"Master Kyle," Guthrie said. "I speak for all of us here when I say we're grateful ye came when ye were needed."

The others nodded and murmured their agreement.

"Like yer father did in the old days," the baker said.

"My father?" Kyle said.

"Aye," Guthrie said. "He were always there to help whenever the raiders beset us. Neither me nor my sister, she's Hob's mother, would be alive today if it weren't for James Shaw."

Just then, Macalister walked up leading a dark horse with a body draped across its back. Fergus trailed along at his heels.

"I reckon Fergus must have tore out his throat," Ogilvy said, indicating the dead man.

Macalister shook his head. "There's not a mark on him," he said. "When I got there, he was lying on the ground with his neck broke."

Kyle bent closer to look at the face of the dead man slung over the saddle. "It's Weems," he said, straightening his back. Mistress Hamilton's dire pronouncement echoed in his mind, the words of which he recited aloud: " 'Three a violent end shall meet, the fourth shall cause his own defeat.' "

"What does that mean?" Macalister said.

"Mistress Hamilton was looking at me when she uttered those words," Kyle said, "but they were meant for Sweeney, Inchcape, Archer, and Weems, who had just departed from there that day. Sweeney, Inchcape, and Archer perished by violent means, whereas Weems broke his neck on his own rope. He strung it across the path to catch me, but in his panic to escape, he forgot it was there." He made a move to leave. "I'd better see to it before somebody else gets hurt."

"I already took it down," Macalister said, indicating the hemp rope coiled around the saddle bow.

"Good man," Kyle said. "It is rather a coincidence, is it not, that such a fate actually befell each of those men?"

A couple of the tradesmen shifted uncomfortably from one foot to the other, as though convinced the deaths were anything but coincidental.

"One of the other raiders might have put that rope there," Macalister said, unconvinced.

"I doubt it," Kyle said. "Only a sneak like Weems was capable of such an underhanded thing."

"It is just and fitting then," Macalister said, "that he got caught in his own trap."

Kyle scanned the faces of those around him. "I'm sure nobody has any objection," he said, "if I take those dead men back to the garrison with me. They are proof that English soldiers are involved in the raids."

"I'd lend ye a wagon," Ogilvy said, "but it went up in flames with the byre."

"I've got one ye could use," Guthrie said. "It's not in great shape, but it should hold together long enough to get ye back to town. I can take ye to where it is, if ye wish it."

Kyle mounted the gelding and held out his left hand to pull Guthrie up behind him. "I reckon it'll take me a while to fetch that wagon," he said to those gathered. "When I get back, I won't notice if any of that gear or all of those fine horses go missing. I just want the bodies."

He then turned the gelding to head across the field beyond the burned-out shell of Ogilvy's stone cottage.

It was well after midnight by the time Kyle drove Guthrie's wagon down Harbour Street and on to the garrison.

The gates were closed, as they should have been at that hour, and the guard on duty in the watchtower leaned over the edge of the parapet to look down at the wagon. "Who goes there?" he bellowed.

"Kyle Shaw, Deputy to the Sheriff of Ayrshire."

"Oh, it's you," the guard said. "You may enter."

"Send a man straightaway to awaken Sir Percy," Kyle called

out before the guard disappeared from view.

After a long moment, the wooden gates creaked apart wide enough for the wagon to pass through.

Light from the moon shone down into the empty courtyard as he drove the wagon over to the main hall and stopped out front. He was unhitching the gelding from the traces when Sir Percy stuck his head out of the window above him.

"It's the middle of the night," Sir Percy shouted. "What do you want?"

"You wanted proof," Kyle shouted up to him. "I've got it."

Sir Percy muttered an unintelligible expletive. "Oh, very well," he said. "I'll be right down." He withdrew his head from the window.

Five minutes later, Sir Percy strode through the door of the main hall in a loose-fitting nightgown, with slippers on his feet and a lighted candle in his hand. His hair, disheveled from slumber, stood erect on his head. "What is so important that it cannot wait until morning?" he said, his tone peevish at being roused from his bed. The soldier who woke him followed him out into the courtyard and waited silently behind him.

"See for yourself," Kyle said, with the sweep of his hand toward the wagon.

Sir Percy walked up to the rotted slats on the near side of the wagon, the candle held high to see into the back of it.

The wavering flame shed a soft yellow light on six scantily clad bodies laid across the wooden bed.

Sir Percy's countenance changed from annoyance to anger in a single blink. It was evident from the resolute set of his mouth that he recognized Inchcape and Weems among the dead men. "Who did this?" he demanded, raising his eyes to Kyle's face. "Surely it was Scots rebels," he added in response to his own query.

"Those men were killed not three hours ago in the act of

burning out a homestead a few miles north of Prestwick," Kyle said. "I was there to help stop them."

"Impossible," Sir Percy said, although without conviction.

"It was Neyll who planned that raid and likely all the others," Kyle said.

"Where is your proof?" Sir Percy said.

"In my office, written in Neyll's own hand," Kyle said. "He evidently had an arrangement to split the profits with the soldiers who actually carried out the raids. He must now answer for his part in them, as these dead men already have."

"What are you going to do?"

"I plan to arrest Neyll at first light. I shall then send a formal report to Edward of England charging Neyll with the wanton destruction of property, theft, exploitation, coercion, profiting from the sale of stolen goods, and the collection of illegal taxes, to name a few. I must warn you that your name will also be mentioned in connection with those and other charges."

"How dare you!"

"If you claim no involvement in the whole affair, you should have no problem exonerating yourself in the eyes of your king."

Sir Percy fumed silently for a moment, his brow furrowed in thought. "Make your arrest, then," he said at length. "Send your report to my lord the king. See where it will get you."

"The charges will stand under Scottish law."

"Scottish law no longer exists under the English occupation of Scotland," Sir Percy said. "Besides, who do you think sanctioned those raids in the first place?"

"Even King Edward wouldn't stoop that low," Kyle said.

"You would be surprised how low he has already stooped," Sir Percy said. "He considers Scotland and all those in it nothing but shite on his boot. If you dare to arrest Neyll, your head will end up on a spiked pole over the garrison gates, with your headless corpse left to rot beside it."

"If that's the kind of king you serve, you deserve each other," Kyle said in disgust.

He was glad Count Jardine got safely away and that Edward of England would get his comeuppance from the French king for violating the trade embargo, even though that was not punishment enough, considering the damage caused to lives and property thus far because of Edward's greed.

He put his foot in the stirrup and mounted the gelding. "I should mention," he said, "that Bishop Wishart has in his possession a document, which, if it ever fell into King Edward's hands, will raise a stench in this shire that you will never live down. And," he added, looking down at Sir Percy, "it has nothing to do with raids or raiders."

With a nudge of his heels to the gelding's belly, he set out at a lope for the garrison gates, brooding on how often truth conflicted with justice, and that the law at times promoted neither truth nor justice.

Sir Percy stared after Kyle from where he stood beside the wagonload of rapidly stiffening cadavers, oblivious to the hot candle wax dribbling down the back of his hand.

CHAPTER 19

Kyle rode slowly up Harbour Street. Beside him, lambent light from the moon flickered on the purling water of the River Ayr. Sleep for him was out of the question, for his mind churned with disquieting thoughts of Neyll, a shameless man without soul or conscience who profited at the expense of his own countrymen; of Edward of England, an unyielding and spiteful king; and of the Scottish people, a force with which King Edward must soon reckon.

He was now ready to follow in his father's footsteps as an advocate for the Scottish people, but he would do so in his own way and on his own terms, without spying or intrigues. As a deputy sheriff sworn to uphold the law, he would do his best to stay within the framework of the judicial system to thwart Neyll and men like him who preyed on the weak and the unprotected. That failing, however, he would not hesitate to employ other means to bring such villains to justice.

He made his way down winding streets, empty and silent except for the steady clop of the gelding's hooves on the cobblestones. He hardly noticed the shapeless houses crouched in deep shadow on either side of him. Only the angular rooftops were sharply defined against the starlit sky.

He stopped the gelding and dismounted before one house in particular. The moment he sat on the top step out front, a heavy weariness overwhelmed him. Every muscle in his body ached. He shed his helmet and the chain mail coif beneath, drawing in a grateful breath of cool night air. After removing the gauntlets from his hands, he propped his elbows on his knees and put his head on his crossed arms.

The click of a door latch woke him. He had no idea how long he slept. He lifted his head to look behind him.

A young woman stood in the open doorway. She wore a yellow shift, with a gray cloak draped over her shoulders. Her unbound hair framed the pale oval of her face and hung loose on her neck.

His fatigue melted away at the sight of her. "Good morrow, Mistress Joneta," he said.

She did not seem surprised to see him. "What brings ye here, Master Kyle?" she said.

"I couldn't sleep," he said, as if that explained his presence on her doorstep at that time of night.

"Neither could I," she said, as though she believed him.

"I don't know if you've heard yet," he said. "Elspeth is going to France with Sergeant Upton. I will take word to Sir Ross in a day or so to give them a fair head start. The news that his only daughter has married an Englishman will wound his pride, and he will feel impelled to go after them to bring her back."

She stepped outside and shut the door behind her. "I'm pleased to hear of their marriage," she said quietly. "They both deserve a chance to be happy." She sat down beside him, hugging her cloak about her slender body.

"Are you cold?" he said, his eyes on her profile.

She shook her head.

He drew in a deep breath and let it out in a heavy sigh. "There's something that's been bothering me for a while now," he said.

She glanced over at him, waiting in silence for him to go on.

"At first," he said, "I was sure it was Brodie who murdered Sweeney. Then, I saw Gram's reaction that day at the marketplace. She turned as white as Sweeney did when he saw Meg's hair in the sunlight. Then your neighbor told me that some years back, Gram's daughter died at the hands of an English soldier. I figured there might be a connection, so I asked around to find out more about it." He gave her a tight smile. "Folks rarely forget that sort of thing."

He stared into the middle distance to gather his thoughts, conscious of her gaze boring into him.

"The girl who was killed was Meg's aunt," he said, "Seeing as how the girl was kin, I thought perhaps it was Meg who lured Sweeney and Archer to their death. Then, it occurred to me that, although little Meg is pretty enough, she's too high strung to follow through with something like that. She would fall apart before the deed was done."

She lowered her gaze to stare at her hands clenched together in her lap.

"Not to be overlooked is Meg's husband, Drew, who is related to Gram by marriage," he said. "If called upon, he might avenge his wife's aunt. Even so, there are others with a prior claim as blood kin, like Gram herself. Now, she might be willing, but she's too old and too frail to leap from a second-floor tavern window. Neither could she run four miles to and from the shepherd's hut in the dead of night."

He looked at her, sick at heart for what he must say. "But you could," he said. "You are clever and resourceful, with beauty enough to charm even a cautious man into lowering his guard."

"Even if I could," she said, avoiding his eyes, "that does not mean I did."

"There is a witness that puts you on the scene," he said.

She turned her head slowly toward him, her eyes wide with dread. "Who?" she said, in a barely audible voice.

He removed a couple of short thick strands of gray homespun

thread from the bottom of his coin purse and laid them in his open palm.

She gazed down at the strands of thread. "I don't understand," she said, truly perplexed.

He reached for the hem of her gray cloak and matched the length of the threads with the mended tear just above the bottom edge.

She shut her eyes, her brow furrowed as though she were in great distress. Her fingers trembled visibly where they clutched the folds of her cloak.

"Why?" he said softly.

She opened her eyes to gaze at him. "Five years ago," she said, "Meg's aunt, my sister-in-law, was raped and murdered. The man who did it was a Southron from the garrison. He went free because no one came forward to accuse him. Gram swore to avenge her daughter, but we had no idea who the man was until that day at the market. We all saw Captain Sweeney's reaction to Meg, who could be a twin of her dead aunt."

She wrung her hands in her lap. "I had to get a look at Sweeney's neck to be sure it was him, for that was where my sister-in-law cut him while she fought him off. He overpowered her, raped her, stabbed her in the stomach, and left her to die in some back alley. A passerby helped her get home before she died, which is how we knew she had marked him thus," she said, passing a finger across her throat under her chin.

She bowed her head, as if from shame. "Later on, I went to the tavern to talk to him," she said. "I did not know Meg had gone to see him earlier that same day. I was afraid of him, but he spoke gently to me. I thought nothing of it when he suggested we go up to his room to talk privately. He acted like a gentleman." She shuddered as she added, "Until he shut the door. He came at me like a madman. He tore at my clothes. He tried to pin me to the bed. I drew his dagger and struck out at him to make him stop."

"And did he?" he said, watching her.

She nodded. "He just stood there with blood spewing from his chest. I ran to the door before I remembered I was covered with blood. I wiped my face and hands on his shirt. When I heard footsteps outside the door, I grabbed my cloak and climbed out the window for fear of being accused of killing him, which I did, but only to keep him from forcing himself on me."

"You left by the window," he said, "but not before you used the dagger to slit his throat, even though he was already dead."

She lifted her chin. "That was for my sister-in-law," she said. "To finish what she started before he killed her."

"Did anyone see you climb out of the window?" he said.

She made no effort to respond.

Her silence gave him the answer he sought. He surmised that the cook at the Bull and Bear must have been looking through the open kitchen door into the alley just as she was exiting the second-floor window. He may have even helped her down, knowing the kind of man Sweeney was and perhaps guessing what had occurred from her appearance. It was enough that she was a Scot, as the cook was, and his hatred of the English was sufficient to ensure his silence.

"Why was Archer killed, then?" he said. "He wasn't even billeted here when your sister-in-law was murdered."

"Archer was one of the Southrons who hanged my husband a month past," she said.

"Your husband knew the risks involved when he sided with the rebels," he said.

"My husband was no rebel," she said. "He was just in the wrong place at the wrong time. Earlier that night, raiders attacked a homestead, but the owner was ready and waiting for them. The raiders were repelled and had to flee for their lives.

Those same raiders came across my husband on his way to the shepherd's hut to check on a ewe about to drop its kid. The raiders were angry, and their blood was up. When they saw my husband, they chased after him. He ran, of course, as would anyone with four horsemen bearing down upon them. They trampled him with their horses and dragged him over to the nearest tree."

"How do you know any of that?" he said.

"There was a boy from Harefoot Law in the shepherd's hut that night," she said. "He saw what they did to my husband, that he wasn't even conscious when they hanged him. They wanted someone to blame, and my husband served their purpose because he was handy, not because he was guilty. The boy told Father Ian, who took the matter to Sir Percy, but nothing ever came of it."

He recalled that Father Ian mentioned such an incident several weeks ago. The subsequent break-in and theft of valuables from the chapel must have been retaliation by the raiders against the old priest for bringing charges against them.

"Your neighbor told me that the shock of hearing of your husband's death hastened the birth of your child."

She nodded her head.

"I am sorry," he said. "Such a blessed event should be a joyful occasion."

Her eyes glistened with unshed tears. "I cherish my son," she said. "He is all I have left of my husband."

"What about Archer?" he said.

"I didn't kill him, if that is what ye are asking," she said. "I would have done, but somebody got there before me. It was my right and duty to avenge my husband, even more so since Father Ian's appeal for justice to the Southron castellan failed. I was thinking on how to go about it, when I was asked to take a written note to Archer."

"When was that?" he said.

"The night before he died," she said. She made a halfhearted attempt to smile. "Do ye not deem it fitting that a shepherd killer should himself be killed in a shepherd's hut? I wish I had thought of that."

"Who gave you the note?"

She lifted one shoulder noncommittally, but said nothing.

"I know you are protecting someone close to you, someone you love," he said. "It's Gram, isn't it?"

The fear on her face, even in the darkness, gave her away.

"Let me tell you what I think happened," he said. "Gram knew Archer was there when her son was hanged. She could not read or write, but Drew could. After the flogging the English marshal gave him, he was in no shape to tackle Archer by himself. Yet, he had no objection to penning a note to him, especially when he learned its purpose.

"Gram gave you the note to pass along to Archer. She rightly suspected Archer could not read and would have to find someone who could. That would allow you the time to get away from him. The message was most likely an invitation to a tryst with you at the shepherd's hut, which would without doubt lure him there.

"When he went to the hut at the appointed hour, the mead laced with hemlock was there on the shelf. He would naturally take a drink to steady his nerves for an assignation with a beautiful woman like you. He was probably already dead when Gram went inside to do what she did. After that, she rode back to town on the horse she had borrowed from a neighbor to get there, with no one the wiser."

"I know nothing of that," Joneta said. "All I know is that there were four in the hanging party. There are still two who must answer for my husband's death. Only when all of them are dead will I be ready to ask God's forgiveness."

"You need forgiveness only to get what you don't deserve," he said. "You have no idea what it means to need forgiveness." He went on to relate how his gambling caused the death of his wife and his son, how he returned home on that awful night six years ago, only to discover that raiders had torched his house with his family inside. The burn scars on his chest and arms were a constant reminder of his negligence and his guilt. "It was the end of time for me," he said.

"When ye turn me over to the Southrons," she said, "I won't need forgiveness as much as mercy."

"You only need mercy to keep from getting what you deserve," he said. "You got something far more valuable than mercy. You got justice, and Sweeney and Archer felt the sharp edge of it." His eyes grew hard. "Inchcape did, too, by my own hand not four hours past. He murdered my father, but there was too little evidence to arrest him for it. His admission that he did the deed was enough for me. Weems was also there when my father was killed, but he broke his neck before I could deal with him."

"Inchcape and Weems are dead?" she said.

"They are," he said. He went on to tell her about Mistress Hamilton's pronouncement against the four English soldiers.

She stood up and wiped her hands on her shift, as though to cleanse them. "Inchcape and Weems were also there when my husband was hanged. Now that they are dead, I am ready to stand before the assize."

He let the threads in his hand fall to the ground. "If I had learned sooner," he said, "that Sweeney had been a party to my father's death, and perhaps even that of my wife and my son all those years ago, I would have killed him himself. You simply beat me to it. In a case like yours, however, the law allows for defense of self. That means although you did kill Sweeney, you did not murder him."

She looked down at him, her face clouded with doubt. "Will the Southrons see it that way?" she said.

"Probably not," he said. "But then, neither would an English judge hold Sweeney, Inchcape, or Weems accountable for my father's death. In fact, they might even receive a promotion for their part in it." He passed a palm over the stubble on his jaw. "I see no need to bring any of this before a court of law."

She sat abruptly, as though her knees gave out under her. "Are ye saying ye are not going to arrest me?" she said.

"That is what I'm saying," he said, with a nod of his head.

"What about Gram?" she said.

"Earlier tonight," he said, "I executed justice upon Inchcape, who was guilty in my own eyes. I cannot fault Gram for doing the same. In trial by combat, men use axes and swords, whereas women employ more subtle means."

"Like poison," she said.

He shrugged his shoulders. "In the end," he said, "justice prevails, no matter the weapon used to bring it about."

"So, ye aren't going to arrest Gram, either?" she said.

"I cannot do so without proof of her guilt," he said. "Mere conjecture on my part will never support a case against her. I am only a sheriff's deputy, not a judge. Gram must stand before her Maker to answer for her deeds, as I must when that time comes."

"But I heartily wished for Archer's death," she said, "and I rejoiced when it came to pass."

"If everyone who thought about harming their neighbor was arrested for it," he said, "there would not be dungeons enough to hold them all."

She studied his face for a moment. "Gram wants to go up north," she said at last. "She wants to spend some time with her family. She's unwell, ye know, more so than she lets on." She watched him closely as she added, "She asked me to go with her, to help her whenever she gets too weak to help herself."

Kyle felt an unexpected sense of loss and loneliness at the thought of her departure. "So, you're moving up north, are you?" he said.

"Only for as long as Gram needs me," she said. "I want to raise my son down here, in the house and on the land that belonged to my husband. I shall hold that property for him until he comes of age."

He lifted his eyes to gaze over the rooftops to the east. The whole expanse of sky on that side was beginning to lighten. Along the street, the houses that were earlier smothered by darkness slowly took on shape and substance with the dawning of the new day.

"When someone you love dies," he said, "part of your heart dies with them. But life goes on, and so must we. You must mourn the loss of your husband, just as I must put to rest the ghosts of my past. We must look forward, not back, for who knows what the future may hold."

He rose to his feet and was about to take his leave when he remembered a purchase he had made at the Glasgow market. He opened his coin purse and removed a tiny parcel from within. "Here is something to remember me by," he said, pressing it into her hand.

She opened the parcel to find a gold ribbon and a green ribbon rolled up together. She shook them out to admire the silky streamers gleaming in the muted light. "Even without these," she said, looking up at him, "I shall never forget ye."

He reached for her hand and brought it to his lips. As he kissed each of her fingers, his heart thudded violently against his ribs. Beads of sweat broke out on his brow, despite the chill in the early morning air. "I shall never forget you, either," he said, releasing her hand.

She got to her feet to catch both of his hands in hers. She

laid her cheek on them, causing her light auburn hair to cascade over his wrists. "I might be gone some months," she said, raising her head to gaze at him.

His turbulent heart moved up into his throat, choking him quietly. "I'll be here, waiting for you," he said, his spellbound stare fixed on her hazel eyes, which took on a greenish cast in the growing light of day.

They stood together for a long moment, moved but unmoving, their hands clasped, unwilling to part, until a woman in the house across the street opened her door to empty the slops from a chamber pot into the gutter.

Each let go of the other's hands with reluctance.

"The northward roads are unsafe these days," he said. "I would like to serve as your escort when Gram is ready to leave."

"I would like that," she said, clearly pleased at his offer.

"Till then," he said. He gathered up his gear and mounted the gelding. With a wave of his hand, he set out up the street. On reaching the corner, he turned in the saddle to look back. He was gratified to see her standing where he had left her, cradling the hand he had kissed, with the ribbons dangling from her fingers.

At that moment, he felt lighter of heart than he had in years. In fact, if asked, he would say that he was almost happy. Of course, that was not enough, but it was a start. It would do for now.

Chapter 20
Epilogue

May 15, 1297

Dusk was well on its way to becoming twilight as Kyle rode along Harbour Street, headed for the Bull and Bear. Sweet olive bushes along the River Ayr exuded a delicate scent that lingered in the air. Here and there, light shone through an unshuttered window as women set about preparing the evening meal for their families.

He wanted to have a chat with Neyll without being overheard, and there was no place more conducive to privacy than a public tavern. He turned into the courtyard and dismounted, handing the reins to the young groom who came out to meet him. He entered the tavern, which was hazy with smoke from oil lamps and filled with noisy chatter from soldiers eating and drinking and gaming. He spotted Neyll in a far corner in a dark blue cotte with matching leggings and walked over to his table.

"Do you mind if I sit here?" he said. Before Neyll could reply, he slid onto the bench across from him.

"I'm waiting for someone," Neyll said coldly.

"I don't mind at all," Kyle said. "In the meantime, perhaps you can help with something that's been troubling me."

Neyll inspected his manicured fingernails, pointedly ignoring the intrusion.

"It has to do with the marshal," Kyle said.

The statement commanded Neyll's attention, despite his effort to appear disinterested.

"I'm afraid he has come under scrutiny of late," Kyle said.

"Why?" Neyll said. "What has he done?"

"It's what he's doing that's the problem."

"And that is?"

"Engaging in conduct unbecoming an English officer in the king's army."

Neyll blinked. "What sort of conduct?" he said.

"He keeps the company of another man," Kyle said.

"So does every other soldier in the garrison," Neyll said with a shrug.

"There is more to it than that."

"How so?"

"Let me put it like this: if Edward of England were to discover what they do in bed together, he would order that the two of them be roasted alive."

Neyll's face took on a grayish cast. "Is the identity of the marshal's companion known?" he said in a voice a notch higher than before.

"That depends," Kyle said, regarding Neyll steadily. "How is your sister?" he said.

"My sister?" Neyll said, puzzled. "She's fine."

"She's in love with John Logan," Kyle said. "But you know that already." His stare impaled Neyll like a leveled lance. "I am sure you will do nothing to stand in her way if she wishes to marry him."

Color burned high on Neyll's cheeks. Then, a flash of enlightenment flickered across his angry countenance, and the blood drained from his face. His brows drew together in the set whiteness of his features, his dark eyes now bright with understanding. He appeared to consider Kyle's words in frowning silence for a moment, until he said with cold deliberation: "I would not think of denying Colina her heart's desire."

"There is also the matter of Colina's dowry," Kyle said.

The muscles tightened along Neyll's jaw. "Of course, she shall have a dowry," he said.

"And a generous annual endowment for her to spend as she pleases," Kyle said.

"That, too," Neyll said, glowering at Kyle.

"I shall expect you to keep your word," Kyle said. "Otherwise," he added, his tone potent with threat, "you may find it difficult to write without a thumb."

Neyll licked his lips, as though his mouth suddenly went dry. "And the other matter?" he said.

"Forgotten," Kyle said, rising from the bench. "Unless I have cause to call it to mind."

Neyll drew in a ragged breath and let it out slowly.

"A word of advice," Kyle said before he departed. "The only way two people can keep a secret is if one of them is dead."

Neyll left the tavern and hurried home to shut himself in his room. He sat in frowning silence at his desk, staring sightlessly into space as he gnawed on every one of his manicured nails.

July 1, 1297

Kyle was drinking the last of his breakfast ale when a soldier burst through the door of the main hall and hastened over to the head table.

"Begging your pardon, Sir Percy," the soldier said, his manner anxious and fretful. "There is something on the wall you must see."

"What now?" Sir Percy said. He threw down the crust of bread in his hand and rose with an exasperated sigh. He set out at a smart pace behind the soldier who had carried the message to him.

Curiosity brought Kyle to his feet. He went after them, as did the soldiers at the tables around him, to find out what would warrant the interruption of Sir Percy's morning meal.

He crossed the courtyard and was walking under the raised portcullis when he saw the townsfolk gathered outside the garrison gates. Everyone there was looking up at the outer wall.

Sir Percy stood apart from the crowd, his upturned face as red as a beet, his fists clenched at his sides.

Kyle followed the direction of Sir Percy's gaze to a severed head skewered on a pike, the long handle of which was lodged in a crack between the massive stones. Bloody sockets where the eyes had been pecked out looked bright red against the pasty white skin of the fleshy face, which bore no resemblance to anyone he knew. "Who is that?" he said, genuinely stumped.

"That, Master Shaw," Sir Percy ground out between his teeth, "is Sir Fenwick, lately in the service of Edward of England. I want to know who put his head up there."

Kyle received the news about Fenwick with a straight face, but beneath his sober exterior, he was thrilled that the last man involved in his father's murder was dead, even if he had no hand in bringing it about.

"Well?" Sir Percy demanded.

"How should I know?" Kyle said. "I've been away for the past four weeks."

"A likely tale," Sir Percy said, his disbelief evident in his voice.

"You may confirm my tale," Kyle said, emphasizing the word Sir Percy had used, "with certain men from this garrison who accompanied me to and from Aberdeen."

The purpose of the journey was to escort Joneta, her baby, and Gram safely to that city on the eastern coast, where Gram's family lived. As they traveled together, it seemed to him that the summer sun was brighter and the birdsong sweeter, because Joneta was there to share it with him. On departing from her, he felt as if his heart was being drawn out of him. All the way back to the garrison, his mind spun with thoughts of returning to Aberdeen, just to see her face once again. She made it clear that she cared for him, but he knew she must first grieve for her dead husband before she could let him fully into her heart. He was willing to give her all the time she needed, for to him, she was worth the wait.

"Oh," Sir Percy conceded with reluctance. "Well, then, take him down."

"Would not my time be better spent hunting for the rest of him?" Kyle said.

"Perhaps you are right," Sir Percy said. "The prior will need it to give him a decent burial."

Kyle went to look for Vinewood and another man to drive a couple of wagons. If asked how he knew where to search for Fenwick's body, he would say that he merely retraced the most likely route Fenwick would have taken to reach Ayr Garrison.

July 2, 1297

Kyle returned to the garrison with Fenwick's remains and that of his entire troop piled onto the beds of the two wagons. The carcasses of the slain horses were left where they had fallen in the narrow pass at Loudoun Hill.

ABOUT THE AUTHOR

E. R. Dillon was born in New Orleans and still lives in Louisiana, although she now resides on the north shore of Lake Pontchartrain. Her acquaintance with certain aspects of the law comes from working for civil and criminal attorneys for many years. As a medieval history buff and a fan of mysteries, she likes to incorporate both elements into her stories. Her current work in progress is another novel in her historical mystery series set in thirteenth-century Scotland featuring Deputy Sheriff Kyle Shaw.